NORTH CAROLINA
STATE BOARD OF COMMUNITY COLLEGES
LIBRARIES
WAKE TECHNICAL COMMUNITY COLLEGE

WITHDRAWN

Modern American Fiction

MODERN AMERICAN FICTION

Form and Function

Edited by

Thomas Daniel Young

Louisiana State University Press
Baton Rouge and London

Copyright © 1989 by Louisiana State University Press
All rights reserved
Manufactured in the United States of America
96 95 94 93 92 91 90 89   5 4 3 2 1

Designer: Patricia Douglas Crowder
Typeface: Linotron 202 Trump
Typesetter: The Composing Room of Michigan
Printer: Thomson-Shore, Inc.
Binder: John Dekker & Sons

LIBRARY OF CONGRESS CATALOGING-IN-PUBLICATION DATA

Modern American fiction: form and function / edited by Thomas Daniel Young.
    p. cm.
    Includes index.
    Contents: Complicit manoeuvres: the form of The wings of the dove/Douglas Paschall—The red badge of courage: form and function/John Conder—The affirmative conclusion of The sun also rises/Donald A. Daiker—The great Gatsby as well wrought urn/A. E. Elmore—The triumph of secularism: Theodore Dreiser's An American tragedy/Joseph K. Davis—Faulkner and the symbolist novel/Carol M. Andrews—Once more to the mirror: Glasgow's technique in The sheltered life and reader-response criticism/Julius Rowan Raper—The power of filiation in All the king's men/James H. Justus—Richard Wright in a moment of truth/Blyden Jackson—The harmonies of Losing battles/Peggy Whitman Prenshaw—Flannery O'Connor's Wise blood: forms of entrapment/Martha E. Cook—The moviegoer: the dilemma of Walker Percy's scholastic existentialism/Kieran Quinlan—Beyond existentialism, or, The American novel at the end of the road/Mark Winchell.
    ISBN 0-8071-1435-9 (alk. paper)
    1. American fiction—20th century—History and criticism.
I. Young, Thomas Daniel, 1919–
PS379.M54 1989
813'.5'09—dc19   88-15510
                                                                                    CIP

Excerpts from *Wise Blood* by Flannery O'Connor. Copyright © 1949, 1952, 1962 by Flannery O'Connor. Reprinted by permission of Farrar, Straus and Giroux, Inc.

The paper in this book meets the guidelines for permanence and durability of the Committee on Production Guidelines for Book Longevity of the Council on Library Resources. ∞

Contents

Thomas Daniel Young / 1
Introduction

Douglas Paschall / 13
Complicit Manoeuvres: The Form of *The Wings of the Dove*

John Conder / 28
The Red Badge of Courage: Form and Function

Donald A. Daiker / 39
The Affirmative Conclusion of *The Sun Also Rises*

A. E. Elmore / 57
The Great Gatsby as Well Wrought Urn

Joseph K. Davis / 93
The Triumph of Secularism: Theodore Dreiser's *An American Tragedy*

Carol M. Andrews / 118
Faulkner and the Symbolist Novel

Julius Rowan Raper / 136
Once More to the Mirror: Glasgow's Technique in *The Sheltered Life* and Reader-Response Criticism

James H. Justus / 156
The Power of Filiation in *All the King's Men*

Blyden Jackson / 170
Richard Wright in a Moment of Truth

Peggy Whitman Prenshaw / 184
The Harmonies of *Losing Battles*

Martha E. Cook / 198
Flannery O'Connor's *Wise Blood:* Forms of Entrapment

Kieran Quinlan / 213
The Moviegoer: The Dilemma of Walker Percy's Scholastic Existentialism

Mark Winchell / 225
Beyond Existentialism; or, The American Novel at the End of the Road

Contributors / 237

Index / 241

Modern American Fiction

THOMAS DANIEL YOUNG

Introduction

Since Henry James, readers and critics have become more interested in "the means by which an author makes his vision known." In *The Art of the Novel* James insists that the author should exert every effort possible to make dramatic all the summaries of the details necessary to present the narrative he is relating. In order to make the author less visible, in an attempt "to purge the authorial voice" as much as possible, he created a *ficelle* who could assist him in presenting his story dramatically. His aim, he writes in *The Art of the Novel,* was to make the author invisible. In Joyce's words, to place him "above, beyond, behind his handiwork, unconsciously paring his fingernails." It has been said that James's high regard for *The Awkward Age* (1899), surely not one of his most satisfying works to most critics, is based on the fact that in it he came closest to concealing the presence of the author.

At the conclusion of his book *The Craft of Fiction* (1921), Percy Lubbock gives his view of what he thought was James's conception of the ideal novel toward which he was striving: "The narrative . . . which must represent the story-teller's ordered and arranged experience, and which must accordingly be of the nature of a picture, is to be strengthened, is to raise to a power approaching that of drama, where the intervention of the story-teller is no longer felt."[1]

---

1. Percy Lubbock, *The Craft of Fiction* (New York, 1957), 122.

Anyone familiar with James's career knows that he became more and more interested in exploring what Lubbock calls the "scenic art" and less interested in narrating in his own voice. He came to employ a "center of consciousness," a point of view that would reveal the relation of the author to the story. The author should intrude as little as possible into his story, because by doing so he was likely to destroy "the illusion of reality" he was attempting to create. (Even Joseph Conrad apparently was not too much concerned with "the illusion of reality," since no audience could have listened to Marlow's telling the whole of *Lord Jim* in one sitting.) James believed, Lubbock points out, that the scenes of a story should become "visibly peopled with characters of the tale." The story should present in a series of scenic views all that's necessary to understand it; nothing should be imported into the story by summary or any other kind of authorial intervention.

Even if the teller of the tale, the point of view, is the author, it is better "to see him while his mind is actually at work." The reader should be placed at an angle of vision so that he receives not an account of an action but is allowed to observe an action while it is occurring. In other words most modern novelists, following James, think the action of a novel should be *shown*; most traditional novelists, even those most highly respected, thought the story should be *told*.

Some readers, according to Wayne Booth, proclaim *Tom Jones* half-novel, half-essay, because not only does Fielding not try to conceal that he is telling his story, he deliberately calls attention to the fact. Often he steps out of the story and speaks directly to the reader summarizing facts, suggesting interruptions and reader reaction. Time after time he forsakes his role of narrating a fictional action and destroys any illusion of reality he might have established by speaking directly to the reader, as in this passage: "We are now, Reader, arrived at the last Stage of our long Journey. As we have, therefore, travelled together through so many Pages, let us behave to one another like Fellow Travellers in a Stage Coach, who have spent several Days in the Company of each other; and who, notwithstanding any Bickerings or little Animosities which have occurred on the Road, generally made up at last, and mount for the last Time, into their Vehicle with Cheerfulness and Good Humour." And on another occasion: "And now, my friends, I take this opportunity (as I shall have no other) of heartily wishing thee well. If I have been an

Introduction

entertaining companion to thee, I promise thee it is what I desired."[2] Obviously Fielding has no relationship to the action of the novel he is relating; therefore he not only destroys any illusion of reality he may have created, but he also removes the reader from the conflict of the story he is relating by making no attempt to establish any connection between author and plot. Despite the ironic relationship he may have created with his readers, he is definitely obstructing the development of his plot, because he is not a part of the complication. He cannot be, because he has no role in the story; he is merely emphasizing that he is the teller of the tale. It is not only, as Ford Madox Ford has written, that the novelists from Fielding to Meredith do not care "whether you believe in their characters or not," but they do not seem much concerned that you take their stories seriously.

Another of the world's great novels, *War and Peace*, has such a loose, unstructured form that it is, Lubbock believes, "wasteful of its subject." Like Fielding, Tolstoy tells his story, giving his readers the facts, not revealed by the action, that they need to know. Often he interrupts the action to suggest the significance of certain events or to explain the reasons his characters have reached specific decisions. Although the book is lucid in individual parts, Lubbock complains that it is inconclusive. After having read it, one wonders what the book is about. The story covers "a succession of phases in the lives of certain generations." There are dozens of families and hundreds of characters passing through several generations. They seem to "suggest birth and growth and death and birth again," the continuity of life, that which has been and will be, youth and age, "the ebb and flow of life." This panoramic view of life seems to be Tolstoy's theme. On occasion, however, it seems to shift alignments, and as the title indicates, his narrative seems to be about war and peace, the impact of East against West in the Napoleonic clashes. But if Tolstoy is attempting to write two novels at once, he gives no signs of being aware of it. Finally one must admit that despite the impressive groups of characters and the overwhelming attraction of certain individuals, the novel is sprawling and unstructured. There seems very little if any connection among the several stories being told.[3]

2. Henry Fielding, *Tom Jones* (New York, 1973), 706–707.
3. Lubbock, *The Craft of Fiction*, 26, 4, 64.

When one begins reading *Madame Bovary*—to take another example of a well-known novel—he is confused because there seems to be little relationship between the point of view, the angle of narration, and the material being presented. Sometimes Flaubert seems to be relating what he, as author, has observed, and sometimes he seems to be giving the experiences or thoughts of his characters.[4] If the story is to be shown to us, we must know our relationship to the action and the actors. Is what we are observing occurring for the reason we think it is? Soon we understand that we must use the eyes of Emma; we share her experiences and her feelings about what she has experienced. Flaubert's intentions are to *show* us a vain and foolish woman and let us share her motives for choosing as she does, her values, her minor gains, and her major losses.

With *Madame Bovary*, then, we see the beginnings of modern fiction, a narrative that strives to offer a "picture of life." As readers we must first *realize* the novel and then "using our taste . . . judge whether it is true, vivid,—like life in fact. . . . Form, design, composition, are to be sought in a novel, as in any other work of art; a novel is better for possessing them." If a novel is to be a true record of human experience, and certainly it should be, it must be an "ordered and arranged account of experience," and it must be "of the nature of a picture." To *realize* it, a reader must first *see* it. The writer of fiction must approach as closely as he can the art of drama.[5]

If in older books, Wayne Booth argues, one searched for "meaning" and "theme," the contemporary reader is much more likely to be concerned with what the work "communicates" or "symbolizes." He attempts to find the "moral" and "emotional" content of every character and every separate action in the book. The modern novel, when compared with its counterpart in the eighteenth and nineteenth centuries, seems much more immoral, Booth states. Some even insist that love of a certain kind—a sort that contains a large measure of what was once called lust—can save humankind from the destructive forces of civilization.[6] The modern reader is less likely to be repelled by this theme than he is by an author's attempts to persuade him how he is to react to it. The reader feels as if he is being preached to. The problem is not so much that the subject matter is objectionable. It is that the reader is convinced that

4. *Ibid.*, 127.
5. *Ibid.*, 9, 122.
6. Wayne Booth, *The Rhetoric of Fiction* (Chicago, 1961), 73, 79.

the author is trying to dictate how he should react to it. As Lubbock has insisted, the modern reader expects the novelist to recapitulate human experience, not to make some comment about it.

Modern readers of fiction are less likely than those of a hundred or two hundred years ago to demand from their reading excitement from "action" or "plot"; neither do they demand emotional involvement or moral guidance. They are more likely to get their pleasure from "aesthetic" or "intellectual" qualities or from "contemplation of the artist's skills."[7] The reader should be prepared to furnish, James says, intelligence, discrimination, and analytical interest.

The essays that follow intend to give the reader an overview of the fiction created in America between about 1890 and 1970—its quality (as good as that produced anywhere else in the world), its technical dexterity, and its intention, stated or implied.

The first essay, Douglas Paschall's, on James's *The Wings of the Dove*, explores James's principle that a novel's subject should demonstrate its structure. Although the narrative presents the story of a doomed girl, it focuses on the persons around her, upon the cruel plot of a passive young man and a power-driven and grasping young woman as they attempt to use the stricken girl's misfortune for their personal gain. James tells his story indirectly. Although Milly is mortally ill, she is receptive, full of life. Although she is facing certain death, she lives life fully and apparently is never aware of the plot against her, for James never intrudes into her consciousness. Nevertheless, it is her story, for although she has little to do in the novel, she has to *be*, for it is on what she *is* that the story turns. As Paschall points out, the novel is indeed a paradox: "Though contrived . . . to encourage . . . interpretation," it manages at the same time almost to forestall a satisfactory reading. At the same time, the novel is surely worthy of an "intelligent, conscientious and perceptive reader's care . . . strictly on account of its essential intelligibility."

In his reading of Crane's *The Red Badge of Courage*, John Conder is concerned with naturalism, freedom to act, determinism, and Crane's extension of what is commonly meant by *persona*. Freedom, Conder believes, is permitted in "The Open Boat" only "because the society in

7. Ibid., 120.

which the experiences occur is so simple and uncomplicated." Many critics have been misled because they have refused to recognize this fact. The case is quite different in *The Red Badge* because Fleming is not intended to represent the common, average soldier in the Civil War, as many critics have suggested; instead he is a "case study, a psychological type." The narration, which is third-person limited, presents the conditions that give rise to Henry Fleming's thoughts, emotions, and actions. The narration presents Henry as if he were strictly a creature of nature—a rabbit or a chicken—and it is obvious that the narrator (the implied author) is a "behavioral scientist." All of the characters in *The Red Badge* act in the only way they can—how they act is determined by the conditions under which they act. The primary result of such a presentation—that is, of characters whose actions are completely determined—is irony, both structural and dramatic. Henry Fleming runs like a scared rabbit because that's exactly what he is; the irony is that this ignominious act allows him to receive a wound that will allow him to return to his unit with honor.

In "The Affirmative Conclusion of *The Sun Also Rises*," Donald A. Daiker argues that Hemingway's novel is not merely "a chronicle of a lost generation" or an "expression of nihilism" and that it is certainly not a "representation of motion that goes no place." Instead Daiker demonstrates that Book I is concerned with pressure but not grace; Book II, with grace but not pressure; Book III, again, with pressure but not grace; and Book IV, with grace under pressure. The developing action in this novel, so often cited for its experimental quality, follows a very traditional pattern. In Book IV there is a climax that definitely solves the narrative's basic conflict. Because of the experiences in which Jake is involved, he becomes a true Hemingway hero: he learns to act with consummate grace under extreme pressure.

Wayne Booth compliments Fitzgerald's use of a point of view, because Nick Carraway, Gatsby's next-door neighbor, can tell the story effectively and dramatically.[8] One reason Fitzgerald is able to get so much action into such a brief space is that Nick has information that the reader needs in order to realize the significance of each event as it occurs, and he gives us this information on the second page of the book.

---

8. *Ibid.*, 176.

Introduction

When I came back from the East last autumn I felt that I wanted to be in uniform and at a sort of moral attention forever; I wanted no more riotous excursions with privileged glimpses into the human heart. Only Gatsby, the man who gives his name to the book, was exempt from my reaction—Gatsby, who represented everything for which I have an unaffected scorn. If personality is an unbroken series of successful gestures, then there was something gorgeous about him, some heightened sensitivity to the promises of life.... No—Gatsby turned out all right at the end, it was what preyed on Gatsby, what foul dust floated in the wake of his dreams that temporarily closed out my interest in the abortive sorrows and short-winded elation of men.[9]

A. E. Elmore, however, is interested in other techniques and methods that allowed Maxwell Perkins to believe that this fifty-thousand-word novel includes everything it needs, despite its brevity. "To explain to [booksellers]," he wrote Fitzgerald, "that the way of writing which you have chosen and which is bound to come more and more into practice is one where a vast amount is said by implication, and that therefore the book is as full as it would have been if written to much greater length by another method, is utterly futile."[10]

Elmore's essay begins with this letter by Perkins, but he illustrates that Fitzgerald's method in *Gatsby* was more than "implying more and saying less." Fitzgerald altered our expectations of the novel by including all necessary details in short compass while maintaining "unity of tone and texture." His method is often impressionistic. We receive a lasting impression of Tom Buchanan from two or three sentences of dialogue; we know of the spiritless inertia of the characters from a brief description of an abandoned dentist's sign and the environment around it; we learn something essential about our characters when the climactic action occurs in an anonymous hotel room; we are able to put Gatsby's parties into perspective by the "old sports," the uncut books in his library, the "long distance" calls and the "blue" cocktail music. In fact, as Elmore points out, Fitzgerald uses few images except visual ones. Sounds, tastes, feelings, and smells are not important in Gatsby's world.

In "The Triumph of Secularism: Theodore Dreiser's *An American Tragedy*," Joseph K. Davis argues convincingly that the uncontrolled materialism of American society adversely affects its citizens. Although

---

9. F. Scott Fitzgerald, *The Great Gatsby* (New York, 1973), 2.
10. John Kuehl and Jackson Bryer (eds.), *Dear Scott/Dear Max: The Fitzgerald-Perkins Correspondence* (New York, 1971), 100–101.

the form of the novel, as has been pointed out more than once, shows the undeniable influence of naturalism, its basic thematic concerns are those of Thoreau and the Nashville Agrarians. Dreiser wants his characters, Davis writes, "to bear witness to the complex of ugly destructive forces that he himself had come to identify with modern America, specifically those forces generated by religious fundamentalism and the pursuit of money and pleasure." Although it would be difficult to demonstrate that any character in the book is a tragic hero—all of them are the victims of social, economic, and environmental forces beyond their control—it is obvious that American civilization has come to tragedy. This conviction is suggested by almost every detail in the novel. It is apparent, too, that Dreiser's major emphasis is on *American*. It is interesting to go beyond the structural differences between *An American Tragedy, The Great Gatsby*, and *The Sun Also Rises*—all published within a period of a year or a little more—to note the similarities of their basic thematic concerns.

One of the most successful experimenters with the American novel, surely, was William Faulkner. In *Light in August*, one of his best novels, he employs a point of view that is supposed to represent the attitude of the town of Jefferson, yet he does not hesitate to give us in his own voice details about his heroine, Lena Grove, that the reader needs in order to understand her character. These details could be known only by the author. "After she got to be a big girl," the narrator tells us, Lena would "ask her father to stop the wagon at the edge of town and she would not tell her father why she wanted to walk in instead of riding. He thought that it was because of the smooth streets, the sidewalks. But it was because she believed that the people who saw her . . . would believe that she lived in town, too." Only an omniscient narrator could read Lena's mind on this and several other occasions in the novel. (The narrator tells us of her feeling, for example, as she climbs out the window of her brother's house to go in search for the father of her child.) In *The Sound and the Fury*, with a minimum of narrative in the present—a young black boy's search for a lost golf ball so that he can sell it to get money to buy a ticket to the traveling show that is playing in town that evening—Faulkner manages to reveal to us the consciousness of a thirty-three-year-old idiot with the mind of a three-year old. In the same novel we discover the reason for a young Harvard student's suicide from a series of seemingly unrelated events that occur on the day of his death.

Introduction

Carol Andrews' interest, however, is to allow us to understand the source of much of this experimentation. Although the influence of the French Symbolist poets on Faulkner's poetry has been studied several times, no one has looked as closely as Andrews does at the influence of this group on one of Faulkner's major novels. All the suggested beginnings of the novel, and Faulkner has given several, draw upon an absence, as Andrews points out: the grandmother's death, Benjy's lack of reason, and Caddy's loss of innocence. Although Caddy appears in person only fleetingly in the novel, Faulkner returns "repeatedly to the image of Caddy." But, Faulkner insists, she "was still too beautiful and too moving to reduce her to telling what was going on." The most alive of the children, she is, paradoxically, "transformed by her absence, transfixed from reality to a dream." She becomes, finally, an image of the kind of knowledge that cannot be communicated: the precise state of the dead Damuddy. As André Bleikasten expressed it, Damuddy is a "symbolic reminder, perhaps, of the mythic mediating function of woman through whom, for man, passes all knowledge." Caddy's absence, then—its influence on the three brothers—serves in Faulkner's novel as major symbols do in Symbolist poetry—to convey that kind of knowledge that words cannot quite carry.

As Julius Rowan Raper reminds us, since the publication of M. H. Abrams' *The Mirror and The Lamp* in 1953 "critics have grown used to thinking of the literary work as standing in an intermediate position between three elements: the universe, the artist, and the audience." Glasgow's *The Sheltered Life* (1932) unifies these three elements because it "resembles a pyramid composed of three mirrors with one face toward the universe of its characters, another toward the author, and the third turned toward the reader." The nineteenth-century realists had their characters react to each other and to the setting in which they found themselves as they believed real people did. They used and were used; they saw other people as antagonists to be met and dealt with, as potential brides or husbands, as competitors in the struggle for existence. But in Glasgow's novel, characters use other characters to see images of themselves. General Archibald sees in Jenny a repetition of his own revolt against tradition. His daughter represents his suppressed desires. And a similar use is made of other characters by others in the novel.

Raper argues that "to the creative reader . . . fiction possesses [the] power to reveal the reader's self as in a mirror." The text creates an image in the reader's imagination that constitutes the meaning of the text. Raper's technique includes a close reading, therefore, in the manner of the New Critics, but he also borrows important elements from the reader-response critics, although he differs from the latter group in certain important respects. His reading of the novel, however, suggests ways by which the approaches of the two groups may be combined.

James H. Justus presents convincing evidence of the influence of Spencer and Shakespeare on Warren's *All The King's Men* (1946). It is commonly known that *All The King's Men* first appeared as a drama, *Proud Flesh*, the story of the rise and fall of a southern demagogue who became strong because of the weakness of others. The drama became a novel with Jack Burden its protagonist. Willie Stark assumed the role of a "catalyst in the slow but clarifying spiritual progress of Jack Burden." Although the question of power and its influence upon the one who possesses it was surely suggested by Huey P. Long, the Kingfish's image was fleshed out by that of Mussolini, not to mention "the extrapolation in political actuality of what he [Warren] had been reading in Shakespeare, Spenser, William James, Machiavelli, Dante, and Burckhardt." From these sources Warren learned that a natural leader not only abhors the "vacuum of power," but he also "absorbs the accrued weaknesses" of the others around him, their needs, their vacancies.

But there is not only the public drama of the conversion of "Cousin Willie with the Christmas Tie" into "the Boss," there is the private drama of the development of Jack Burden. The novel's real power lies in Warren's demonstrating the relationship—and it is a complex one indeed—between the private drama and the public drama.

Blyden Jackson, arguing that Richard Wright should be associated with the state of Mississippi, demonstrates the importance of his early life in the development of his artistic imagination. As Jackson points out, a knowledge of "Big Boy Leaves Home" is essential if one is to read intelligently either *Black Boy* or *Native Son*. The story is, in Jackson's words, "a moment of truth," an account of Big Boy's loss of innocence. The story does not explicate the Negro's will; it is, instead, "the psychology and the anthropology of American racism."

In Jack Renfro of *Losing Battles*, Eudora Welty has given us a new kind of modern hero. Unlike Jake Barnes, Jay Gatsby, and Jack Burden, he accepts life on its own terms. His "affirmation of life," as Peggy Whitman Prenshaw points out, "is one of the surest and deepest . . . we have in American literature, especially in modern fiction." The joy of the novel, as Seymour Gross wrote when it appeared, "is that it allows you to feel what it would be like *really* to believe in life."

When the novel appeared in 1970, the first book-length narrative Welty had written in fifteen years, it was almost universally acclaimed, a reaction far different from that received by Katherine Anne Porter's long-awaited *Ship of Fools*. *Losing Battles* is unlike any other novel written in this century. "It is rich with pleasure and laughter"—unlike *Gatsby*, *All The King's Men*, and *An American Tragedy*—and its seemingly unstructured, slow-moving development seems a throwback to the nineteenth century. In most modern novels the family's sense of peace, security, and happiness can be read as the result of its inability to face reality and accept the desperateness of its situation. But such is not the case in *Losing Battles*. An effaced narrator, used by many modern writers of the short story, is employed by Welty to allow the family members to talk or listen without interruption.

The tension in the novel is the result of the difference between the spoken and written word, between the sound of voices and the silence. At the same time that Welty dramatizes this conflict, she shows how the opposites complement each other. Family and teacher, love and separateness "form the central structure of Welty's psychic landscape."

Wise Blood (1952), Martha E. Cook argues, is "an artistic creation of considerable sophistication . . . tightly unified by patterns of images, by parallel events, by doubling of characters, all of which function together to develop a convincing theme." If one reads carefully, he can follow a series of deftly scattered clues that re-create Hazel Motes's experiences from disbelief to faith. Some readers are misled by O'Connor's ambiguity. The pattern of the novel is circular. Hazel keeps returning to the place where he began, but on each journey he has learned something. He is gradually closing in on his objective—peace, home, security—but the means by which he finds what he is seeking are seldom predictable. He learns to see (to understand) by becoming blind. With him seeing is believing: by destroying himself, following the Christian paradox, he finds himself and the ultimate freedom that faith offers. His way is not an easy way, and O'Connor's novel is not easy reading. By expertly using what some critics call a gothic grotesquerie, however, she allows the reader to know that which he can learn in almost no other way: how one can conceive of metaphysical reality.

In his essay on *The Moviegoer* (1960), one of the two novels that go beyond the period of "high modernism," Kieran Quinlan explores Percy's attempt simultaneously to hold two definitely contradictory views—existentialism and Christianity. One "of the two or three most philosophical novelists writing in America today," as Quinlan describes Percy, the novelist presents the conflict of his best-known work in existential terms and attempts to solve it by Christian dogma. But, Quinlan argues, Percy's *form* does not perform the *function* he intends. It is a "wonderful narrative"; however, it fails to "prove the truth of Percy's religious convictions."

The End of the Road and its companion piece, *The Floating Opera*, as Mark Winchell points out, take us beyond existentialism into nihilism, a long way indeed beyond Hemingway's highly subjective private code. Although it has sometimes been called a "novel of ideas," *The End of the Road* is actually, Winchell believes, a satire of the novel of ideas. Just a little too exactly, perhaps, Jake Horner and Joe Morgan represent two opposing points of view, but they both illustrate the same truth: there is no truth. Judged by purely pragmatic standards, the doctor is no closer to the truth than Jake or Joe is. He does not cure Jake; perhaps his only effect upon him is to make a fairly commonplace young man into a destructive demon. He tries to live out the role of doctor he is playing and allows Rennie Morgan to die. If man has lost the traditional religious values he once possessed, perhaps Barth is right. Maybe we are at the end of the road. There is no light at the end of the tunnel.

DOUGLAS PASCHALL

Complicit Manoeuvres: The Form of *The Wings of the Dove*

As a number of eloquent readers have attested, *The Wings of the Dove* is not a novel easy to characterize nor to convey quickly a sense of having grasped entire. The reasons for this fact go beyond its mere length and the notoriously idiosyncratic opacities and convolutions of James's late style, for neither *The Ambassadors* nor *The Golden Bowl* presents the reader with difficulties in this kind or degree. Virginia Woolf, writing to Lady Ottoline Morrell, confirms this impression unforgettably: "I actually read through *The Wings of the Dove* last summer, and thought it such an amazing acrbatic feat, partly of his, partly of mine, that I now look upon myself and Henry James as partners in merit. I made it all out. But I felt very ill for some time afterwards."[1]

Thus it is tempting to agree with Nicola Bradbury, who argues that "unlike *The Ambassadors*, *The Wings of the Dove* has no guiding rule of technique dominating every expressive element"; or with Kenneth Graham, that this "remarkably concrete and worldly book . . . resists any blatantly thematic interpretation"; or with Tony Inglis, that the "distinctive interest" in James's late novels in general "lies in the number and variety of the modes in which they offer meaning.[2] But to

---

1. Nigel Nicolson and Joanne Trautman (eds.), *The Letters of Virginia Woolf* (4 vols., New York, 1975–78), II, 543.
2. Nicola Bradbury, *Henry James: The Later Novels* (New York, 1979), 121; Kenneth Graham, *Henry James: The Dream of Fulfillment* (New York, 1975), 163; Tony Inglis, "Reading Late James," in Gabriel Josipovici (ed.), *The Modern English Novel: The Reader, the Writer, and the Work* (London, 1976), 77.

accept such judgments entails confronting a troubling paradox: that a novel so contrived throughout its closely-woven and extended narrative, literally moment by moment, to provoke, compel, encourage, and indulge the processes of interpretation should, at the same time, so deflect, subvert, qualify, and forestall the achievement of an interpretative calm.

Not that such a paradox is likely, nowadays, to trouble the sophisticated reader. We are increasingly inured to accounts of novels that employ conventions and tactics that normally assist interpretation for the purpose, instead, of demonstrating how interpretation can only be balked, deferred, or controverted. In our terror of subjecting a novel to a premature "foreclosure" of meaning, we have at another extreme assumed that its potentially infinite plurality of meanings would automatically proscribe recuperation of meaning—at least of any meaning pervasive or patent enough to justify "interpretation."

In what follows it will become clear that I believe such a radical *aporia* is unnecessary (that is, it can and should be hurdled or evaded) and unnecessarily constricting. I proceed on the basis of a simple assumption, or surmise: that *The Wings of the Dove* sufficiently embodies Henry James's experienced, conscientious, and prodigiously intelligent effort to write a novel responsive to and worthy of his readers' care and, moreover, a novel responsive to and worthy of such readers' care quite strictly on account of its essential intelligibility.

By no means discounting the "problematics" of reading for intelligibility, I find nonetheless that in directing my attentions to a work of fiction—in holding it in my memory, in keeping it stable enough for reflection—some means of recuperating its disparate details and my own developing experience is virtually necessary. Obviously, no single mode of recuperation, especially for an intricate and subtle book such as *The Wings of the Dove,* can ever suffice, not even for one's own experience; such means can be adopted only provisionally, correctibly, dispensably.

For the purposes of the sort of critical recuperation I describe, then, I am persuaded, putting it bluntly for the moment, that the notion of "complicit manoeuvre" helps to account for the complex literary form and functions of James's novel. And perhaps more to the point, this notion not only helps to clarify the book's moral complexities but also to emphasize why it ought to be valued by generations of readers to come.

In its fundamental sense, to be *complicit* is to join with another person as an accomplice, especially in deliberate wrongdoing, as certainly the manoeuvres of Kate and Densher in respect to Milly ultimately are. Earlier, of course, Kate and Densher are complicit in their vaguely directed alliance to outflank Mrs. Lowder, who, persistently determined to use Kate to promote her own social ambitions, is directly complicit both with Susan Stringham and Lord Mark, and powerfully if also unspokenly complicit with Lionel Croy and Marian Condrip toward the same end. But *complicity* may likewise refer to more fugitive, shifting, even unacknowledged agreements—to a whole range of accommodations, acquiescences, and compromises such as James's characters in this novel typically make or fall into.

The term *manoeuvre* principally denotes military tactics or actions, hence any planned, especially cunningly planned, action by means of which to gain advantage over another party. *Manoeuvring* need not always be done aggressively, of course, but may occur defensively, passively, as a countermove precisely to outmanoeuvre anyone attempting (to use the novel's own language) to "work" or "handle" or "deal with" you. Thus Milly may be said to adopt the "manoeuvre" of using her physical frailty, especially as its cause remains unspecified and its consequences entirely speculative, as a weapon of considerable power in gaining, and pressing, her own advantage.[3] Even in the novel's culminating events, Milly's bequest of her fortune to Densher—in one view certainly an act of mercy, forgiveness, magnanimity, charity—may also be seen as yet another "manoeuvre" in an intricate game, a manoeuvre, what is more, that enables her to exert, despite her absence from the closing scenes in death, by far her most powerful advantage yet over the destinies of her two antagonists.

Even without a detailed catalog of instances in the novel, it should be readily enough granted that all of its major characters are intent on manoeuvres, taken in complicity with others, that may work to their

---

3. Bradbury, *Henry James*, 100, argues that "Milly's perceptiveness, tact, and strength will adopt weakness as a policy."

own advantage—or, as with Sir Luke Strett, to the perceived advantage of someone else. If, for instance, Lionel Croy and Marian Condrip are entirely willing to manoeuvre in complicity with Aunt Maud for the sake of their own financial self-interest, then, at another extreme, Susan Stringham is just as eager to be complicit with Mrs. Lowder in order to further Milly's amatory interests in Merton Densher.

Moreover, the very notion of "complicit manoeuvre" should remind us that no individual plan of action, no single deed, can effect a consequence except through its relation to the persons and deeds of other people, whether as accomplices or antagonists; for even antagonists require a degree of mutual complicity, if only in that (say) duelists have to agree to meet within range of each other's weapons, boxers within the same small ring. The hard and perhaps distasteful truth is that *duplicity*, let us say of the sort Kate and Densher practice on Milly, can never be effective without at least some degree of *complicity*—some cooperation, either willing or coerced, on the part of the person being duped.

Such duplicity may be achieved by means of outright deception (*e.g.*, Iago patently lies to Othello), or it may be achieved or at least furthered by less blatant means (*e.g.*, Othello leaps to conclusions not strictly required by Iago's insinuations).[4] We would be right not to excuse either Kate or Densher simply because they have contrived never actually to *lie* to Milly: their evasions of the truth, their willingness to exploit mistaken interpretations of their words and actions, are quite as blameable as lies. On the other hand, that such a deception could occur and be sustained without requiring outright deceit suggests very strongly that Milly is not, in the fullest sense, innocent of complicity in it. And so, I believe, James is at some pains to establish. At the "whole center of the work, the misplaced pivot" of it (to borrow James's own reference to it in the Preface), just toward the close of Book Five and of Volume I, it is Milly's swiftness, eagerness even, to be complicit with Kate and Mrs. Lowder in their interested characterization of her as a dove that provokes and accelerates the novel's crisis. Here, Milly's response goes beyond mere passive acquiescence or accommodation to a kind of willing cooperation, to taking on a role for herself more demanded by the motives and interests of others than by her own. That she also perceives the role as serving well her own interests is likewise to the point.

4. Inglis, "Reading Late James," in Josipovici (ed.), *The Modern English Novel*, 92.

Thus Milly's betrayal by her newfound friends is brought about not so much because she is "American" and "innocent" and a "dove" (though these things obtain) as because, under the pressure of mortality and her intense determination to defy it as fully and for as long as she can, she willingly assists the manoeuvres of those around her and suffers the more deeply and strenuously on account of it. Under different pressures and in different relations, and of course out of quite different human natures, the same may be said, as we shall see, of both Merton Densher and Kate Croy.

The pressures and relations that impinge in Kate's life we see first, and a striking instance of how these main characters feel themselves either forced or almost irresistibly invited to enter into the complicit manoeuvres of others occurs in the paradigmatic opening chapter. "She waited, Kate Croy, for her father to come in, but he kept her *unconscionably*"—with which surprising word the novelist makes a complicit manoeuvre of his own, compelling the reader to hover uncertainly between hearing in the exaggerated moralism of the adverb (but then, is it truly exaggerated?) the judgment of Kate herself, or that instead of a closely observant, almost intrusive narrator; but requiring, either way, the reader's intimate and involved complicity if such dense, subtle, moment-by-moment "registrations" of experience are to be taken in.

Kate, while waiting, seems to have resources of independence and determined will, but in various ways her language reveals the extent to which she is cornered and will, at the last, have little choice but to "comply." Not yet "chalk-marked for the auction" (whether among her father's shabby things or Aunt Maud's rich heavy ones), she protests that the "broken sentence" of her father's and her family's "failure of fortune and of honour," "if she was the last word, *would* end with a sort of meaning." Kate even loses herself momentarily in the thought "of the way she might still pull things round had she been a man," but despite loving her name, the more on account of its "bleeding wound," she concludes, "But what could a penniless girl do with it but let it go?"

Thus hemmed in not only by her familial circumstances but by her simply being a woman, Kate, having attempted a manoeuvre in complicity with her father so as to escape from Aunt Maud's ruthless "conditions," departs Chirk Street with a keener sense than ever of being "worked," of being the sacrificial, even cannibalized, victim of the strangulating complicity of father and aunt, each intent on gains by means of her: "The moral . . . was that the more you gave yourself the less of you was left. There were always people to snatch at you, and it would never occur to *them* that they were eating you up. They did that without tasting."[5]

Even so, the reader is in no doubt at the beinning of Chapter 2 that Kate comprehends a crucially important aspect of her dilemma: "It wouldn't be the first time she had seen herself obliged to accept with smothered irony other people's interpretation of her conduct. She often ended up by giving in to them—it seemed really the way to live—the version that met their convenience" (29). That such is emphatically not "the way to live" Kate glimpses clearly enough in Chelsea. Though it is "through Kate that Aunt Maud should be worked," with Kate "to burn her ships, in short, so that Marian could profit," Marian's version of her is one that Kate struggles to obstruct and resist. But in wishing to evade the role that Marian would have her play, she nonetheless confronts all too vividly its apparent alternative—Marian's sisters-in-law, the unwed Miss Condrips, seen "as a warning for her own future . . . showing her what she herself might become at forty if she let things too recklessly go" (44). Finally, hardpressed by Marian, Kate succumbs so far as to deny "everything and every one," in its way a "relief," but the "prospect" of such "a clean sweep of the future . . . put on a bareness that already gave her something in common with the Miss Condrips" (45).

Later on, Kate's relieved confession to Milly of "her small success, up to the present hour, in contenting at the same time her father, her sister, her aunt and herself" leads Milly to divine that Kate hoards "some secret, some smothered trouble" not yet confessed (112). James's immense care to remind us of these complicities and the intricate connections among them emerges, for instance, in Book Eight, where Densher fears that in so contenting others he has left no will of his own: "There glowed for him in fact a kind of rage at what he wasn't having; an exasperation, a resentment, begotten truly by the very impatience of desire, in respect to his postponed and relegated, his so extremely manipulated state. It was beautifully done of her, but what was the real meaning of it unless that he was perpetually bent to her will?" And thus

---

5. Henry James, *The Wings of the Dove*, ed. Donald Crowley and Richard Hocks (New York, 1978), 39. Hereafter referred to by page numbers in the text.

"his question connected itself, even while he stood, with his special smothered soreness, his sense almost of shame" (280–81).

Merton Densher, who for most of the novel conspicuously lacks Kate's powers of self-definition, self-assertion, and sheer willpower, not surprisingly is even more ready than she to accept roles that others create for him. That he accommodates and, till near the end, lives up to Kate's preferred versions of him is clear, but it is no more than what the reader expects, given his passionate obsession with her. But James is careful to show us moments in which Densher embraces, far beyond any immediate necessity Kate herself pushes him to, the roles that others would prefer for him to play. An especially telling example occurs in Book Six, when he has accepted a late invitation to dinner at Lancaster Gate. I quote an unusually long passage in order to show how such a subtle complicity develops, shifts, and sustains itself to a conclusion.

He had thus had with [Mrs Lowder] several bewildering moments—bewildering by reason, fairly, of their tacit invitation to him to be supernaturally simple. This was exactly, goodness knew, what he wanted to be; but he had never had it so largely and free—so supernaturally simply, for that matter—imputed to him as of easy achievement. It was a particular in which Aunt Maud appeared to offer herself as an example, appeared to say quite agreeably, "What I want of you, don't you see? is to be just exactly as *I* am." . . . He would have liked as well to ask her how feasible she supposed it for a poor young man to resemble her at any point; *but he had after all soon enough perceived that he was doing as she wished* by letting his wonder show just a little as silly. He was conscious moreover of a small strange dread of the results of discussion with her—strange, truly, because it was her good nature, not her asperity, that he feared. Asperity might have made him angry—in which there was always a comfort; good nature, in his conditions, had a tendency to make him ashamed—which Aunt Maud indeed, wonderfully, liking him for himself, quite struck him as having guessed. To spare him therefore she also avoided discussion; she kept him down by refusing to quarrel with him. This was what she now proposed to him to enjoy, and *his secret discomfort was his sense that on the whole it was what would best suit him.* Being kept down was a bore, but his great dread, verily, was of being ashamed, which was a thing distinct; and it mattered but little that he was ashamed of that too.

It was of the essence of his position that in such a house as this the tables could always be turned on him. "What do you offer, what do you offer?"—the place, however muffled in convenience and decorum, constantly hummed for him with that thick irony. . . . The humiliation of this impotence was precisely what Aunt Maud sought to mitigate for him by keeping him down; and as her effort to that end had doubtless never yet been so visible he had probably never felt so definitely placed in the world. . . . He didn't believe in it [her dream of visiting America], but he pretended to; this helped her as well as anything else to treat him as harmless and blameless. (203–204, italics added)

The echoes of Kate's dilemma can easily be heard in Densher's own (compare "thick irony" here with "smothered irony," and "however muffled in convenience and decorum" with "the version that met their convenience"; similarly with their fear of being shamed, their sense of being "kept down" through Aunt Maud's shrewd indulgence). Densher comes closest here to being (as others have remarked) the prototype of the young man in Eliot's "Portrait of a Lady" or of Prufrock—intensely conscious of his own impotence, his wish not to risk dissension or a quarrel, his tendency to be ashamed and yet also ashamed of being ashamed, and with all that still preferring to play a role scripted for him by his antagonist, enabling him securely to go on being treated as "harmless and blameless," than to carve out boldly a mode of action truer to his inner life.

Such a self-defensive manoeuvre, here in moment-by-moment complicity with the superior will of Mrs. Lowder, is typical of Densher. A consistent habit of such manoeuvres is what, under the urgent drive of Kate's will, drags him along in complicity with her burgeoning plan until he is past the point of no return. An early instance occurs near the close of their first scene together (59–60); a late one during their tense scene in front of St. Mark's that ends with their arranged assignation in his rooms (308–12).

Densher's easing into complicity with Milly during the stay in Venice follows a similar pattern, except that in these encounters, Milly's "conscious compliance," her "doing very much what he wanted, even though without her quite seeing why," if anything runs slightly ahead of his own:

She might have been conceived as doing—that is of being—what he liked in order perhaps to judge only where it would take them. They really as it went on *saw* each other at the game; she knowing he tried to keep her in tune with his conception, and he knowing she thus knew it. Add that he again knew she knew, and yet that nothing was spoiled by it, and we get a fair impression of the line they found most completely workable. The strangest fact of all for us must be that the success he himself thus promoted was precisely what figured to his gratitude as the something above and beyond him, above and beyond Kate, that made for daily decency. (323)

Complicit Manoeuvres

Though in no other scene in the closing books does James allow his narrator to comment so fully or explicitly on the characters' mutually reinforcing complicities—each of them knowingly self-conscious in their mirrored role-playing—much the same dynamic manifests itself elsewhere. Two other significant points emerge from this passage. First, the degree to which the narrator demands and expects the complicity of the reader is heavily emphasized. "We" are expected to have taken in the same "impression" as the narrator of the "line they found most workable," and even more insistently we "must" accept what he sees as "the strangest fact of all" in the matter. That the narrator has gradually assumed the reader's complicity is clear in any case by the frequent obtrusion of first-person plural pronouns in a variety of asides: "*our* young woman" and "*our* friends" and "the young lady in whom *we* are interested" and "after the colloquy *we* have reported" and the like. Such comfortably complicit asides are now and then pointed with extra emphasis, as when Densher is caught watching Kate playing roles in Aunt Maud's well-directed theater at Lancaster Gate: "Such impressions as *we* thus note for Densher come and go, it must be granted, in very much less time than notation demands; but *we* may none the less make the point that there was, still further, time among them for him to feel almost too scared to take part in the ovation" (italics added).

Second, in Milly's knowing adoption of a role with Densher, and in his self-reflexive awareness of her playing to please him, the reader may perceive at least a glimmer of why neither he nor Kate must lie to her outright. Milly and Densher, we may conclude, find this "line . . . most completely workable" because its very artificiality, its distance from the heartfelt center of their motives, better enables pursuit of their self-consoling fantasies than the grim and imminent truth. In at least this respect, Milly is not more innocent than Densher, though, given her situation, she is unquestionably a great deal less culpable.

In turning to Milly's case in particular, a close look at the last two chapters of Book Five will trace just how her complicit manoeuvring at that point ironically takes her not to a "perch" of relative safety but instead to the precipice over an abyss. A passage that echoes narrative analyses of both Kate and Densher, as looked at above, occurs in Chapter 6, where Milly becomes suddenly, intensely, aware that she moves "in a current determined, through her indifference, timidity, bravery, generosity—she scarce could say which—by others; that not she but the current acted, and that somebody else, always, was the keeper of the lock or the dam. Kate for example had but to open the flood-gate: the current moved in its mass—the current, as it had been, *of her doing as Kate wanted*" (166–67, italics added). Milly feels herself being "dealt with," but chooses to "surrender to the knowledge, for so it was, she felt, that she supplied her helpful force" (167). With Kate seeming to be in top form, Milly envies her, feeling herself as never having such a special time: "She was never at her best—unless it were exactly as now, in listening, watching, admiring, collapsing." Thus passive, fragile, vulnerable, she feels her distinctly "American mind" break down in the face of this "monster," sensed but not comprehended; in her surrender she responds as if to "a lesson . . . in the art of seeing things as they were," before which she can only "gape."

Then Kate, going much further in candor than even she can have deliberately meant to do, advises her: "We're of no use to you—it's decent to tell you. You'd be of use to us, but that's a different matter. My honest advice to you would be . . . to drop us while you can" (170). Here, the reader may decide, is an excellent chance for Milly to penetrate to and grasp the truth of Kate's advice, especially as she quickly senses the menace in this encounter. Discomfited, even frightened, Milly feels herself "alone with a creature who paced like a panther," and questions Kate: "Why do you say such things to me?" To which Kate replies with the fatefully determining answer, "Because you're a dove"—an attribution, an *"accolade,"* as Milly reads it, "sealed" by Kate's firm kiss, an "inspiration" she could instantly accept as "the right one" (171): "She met it on the instant as she would have met revealed truth; it lighted up the strange dusk in which she had lately walked. *That* was what was the matter with her. She was a dove. Oh, *wasn't* she?—it echoed within her as she became aware of the sound, outside, of the return of their friends." With Mrs. Lowder's confirmation, then, Milly comprehends "straightway the measure of the success she could have as a dove," though of course "she should have to be clear as to how a dove *would* act." And swiftly assuming her new role, she abandons her appointment with Sir Luke in favor of a spontaneous and edifying visit to the National Gallery (172–73).

James's mastery by "indirection" and by a careful layering of inset frames, gradually revealing to Milly that it is actually Densher present in the Gallery, and then that Kate, close at hand, is obviously his intimate companion and not there by chance, makes the whole of Chapter 7 fairly crackle with dramatic tension.[6] Milly, who has just managed to recover her sense of dissolving identity by the manoeuvre of becoming a "dove," now, in an even more treacherous current, knowing herself "handled and again . . . dealt with," hits on the "inspiration" of playing the dove in "her own native wood-note," now covering her mounting dismay and disillusionment with American spontaneity and "New York agitation."

This slightly altered role serves through most of the subsequent tense luncheon, until Milly perceives that, in response to her American "dove," Densher, "like everyone else," is being "simplifyingly 'kind' to her"—taking, not his own particular view of her, but simply "*the* view"—though she decides it is enough for the moment to hold his attention, "this, and her glassy lustre of attention to his pleasantness about the scenery in the Rockies" (181). Milly has "pushed down" for the time being her anxiety about what prognosis Sir Luke may have meanwhile delivered to Mrs. Stringham, but it powerfully wells up again, and "because she was divided" from this knowledge that she presumes Susie in her "feverish glitter" to possess, "by so thin a partition . . . she continued to cling to the Rockies" (182).

Milly's complicit manoeuvre of acting as if she is not only a "dove" but an "American" dove has—between her anxiety over what she may learn of her health and what she may learn of Densher and Kate—left her only the most precarious mountain crag on which to perch. Not, as in her more confident perch in the Alps in Book Three, with the "kingdoms of the earth" before her ("Was she choosing among them or did she want them all?"), but instead threatened now by the imminent deprivation of her chances both for life and for love.

James's care to enforce at the very end of Volume I our sense of Milly's peril—the image of her "cling[ing] to the Rockies" becoming sharply visual rather than a mere metaphor for her conversation—inescapably reminds us of the first glimpse of a possible difficulty concerning Densher and Kate in Book Four. Directly at Mrs. Lowder's behest, Susan has asked Milly not to speak of Densher to Kate. But proceeding from "a respect for the facts," Milly has pointedly inquired, "Is it because there's

---

6. Cf. Mary Ann Caws, *Reading Frames in Modern Fiction* (Princeton, 1985), for a brilliant analysis of James's "framing" in the novel.

anything between them?" And she further wonders whether Mrs. Lowder isn't afraid . . . of their—a—liking each other." Susan's response is not strictly an answer: "My dear child, we move in a labyrinth," to which Milly gaily assents, adding: "Don't tell me that . . . there are not abysses. I want abysses" (119–20).

By the end of Book Five, Milly has already suffered an epiphany of self-recognition in the Bronzino portrait, "dead, dead, dead," and she has absorbed, more movingly still, a prolonged moment of insight while alone in Regent's Park, in "the same box . . . the same grim breathing-space" with "hundreds of others," who, in the most extreme figuring, precisely like herself, "would live if they could." She has suddenly found Susan's "inscrutable impenetrable deferences," intended as courtly and protective, instead "Byzantine . . . scarce more inquisitive than if she had been a mosaic at Ravenna," in sum "a porcelain monument to the odd moral that consideration might, like cynicism, have abysses" (156–57). The "abysses" she has yearned for she will have, and more and more she will look into them alone.

As Milly's surmise in Book Four, Chapter 3 (noted above) suggests, she is not deficient in percipience or quick intelligence. Yet on at least two highly emphasized occasions, Milly is pointed directly toward a conclusion regarding Kate's relation with Densher that she declines to draw. The first occurs just after Milly has speculated about there being something between them, when Kate's sister Marian has bluntly told Milly of Densher's love for Kate and asked her to intervene to prevent a "dreadful" match. In discussing the incident with Susie, at the end of the chapter, Milly is forced to consider Kate: "I don't think . . . I don't think Mrs. Condrip imagines *she's* in love." And in a question that Milly cannot answer, though she deflects it, Mrs. Stringham says, "Then what's her fear?" Milly chooses to iterate her own preferred version.

"It wasn't of anything on Kate's own part she spoke."
"You mean she thinks her sister distinctly doesn't care for him?" . . .
"If she did care Mrs. Condrip would have told me." . . .
"But did you ask her?"
"Ah no!" . . . Milly, however, easily explained that she wouldn't have asked her for the world. (129)

The second occasion occurs late in Book Seven in Milly's interview with Lord Mark, during which she urges him strongly to ply his suit with Kate and he inquires what is the use of doing so:

"Well, Lord Mark, try. She *is* a great person. But don't be humble." She was almost gay.

It was this apparently, at least, that was too much for him. "But don't you really *know?*"

As a challenge, practically, to the commonest intelligence she could pretend to, it made her of course wish to be fair. "I 'know,' yes, that a particular person's very much in love with her."

"Then you must know by the same token that she's very much in love with a particular person."

"Ah I beg your pardon!"—and Milly quite flushed at having so crude a blunder imputed to her. "You're wholly mistaken."

"It's not true?"

"It's not true." (275–76)

In the ensuing altercation, Milly claims passionately that Kate "has given me her word for it." But we know this not to be the case, however much Kate may have permitted Milly to believe as she prefers to believe, and thus we see in this encounter the extremity to which Milly must go in order to screen herself from the truth. Kate has "dissimulated" her feelings for Densher, just as Milly has done, but Kate has seen clearly how Milly feels, and to say no more, Milly has been given ample opportunity to do likewise.[7]

It should be clear from the attention I have focused on the three main characters only that their various imaginative, psychic, social, and moral complicities by no means exhaust such instances in the novel. In the late books especially, most of what happens can be described as one or another type of "complicit manoeuvre," from Lord Mark's brief visit back to Venice and Mrs. Stringham's alliance with Densher (even after she knows the truth) to the more central incidents of Kate's sexual surrender to Densher and their tense, strained, intricate manoeuvring over the bequest at the very end.

At least one immediate advantage of "recuperating" an experience of *The Wings of the Dove* under this notion is that it disallows simplistic moralizings of it. In summary form the plot of the novel indeed resembles the sort of melodramatic claptrap to which James was attracted on the stage, especially in the French theater, in which a dark and scheming

---

7. F. O. Matthiessen writes, "For one quality of this 'dove' is that she is not so innocent as she looks," but he proceeds to draw very different conclusions from such a judgment. *Henry James: The Major Phase* (New York, 1944), 65ff.

villainess (Kate) employs a spineless stooge (Densher) to defraud a beautiful, noble, and passive victim (Milly). Moreover, it seems superficially as if the predictable melodramatic conclusion is preserved: the villainess is discovered and deprived of the spoils of her plot, the stooge is converted through his exposure to the long-suffering and saintly victim, and the sacrificial victim herself is transfigured and apotheosized in the magnanimous charity of her dying act. Were this an adequate account of the matter, *The Wings of the Dove* would be glowing proof of that famous bon mot, that James chews a great deal more than he bites off.

Nor is such a caricature of the novel's moral calculus conspicuously wide of the mark, even in the most recent criticism. For example, Mary Ann Caws quotes approvingly Leo Levy's analysis of *The Wings of the Dove* in his *Versions of Melodrama*, seeing it as an example of "mock tragedy, in which virtue escapes free and intact. . . . This explains, I think, the reader's uncomfortable reaction to the novel, where the good suffer and die, thereby saving others, where the very bad, like Kate, inevitably lose out in the long run, and where only to the in-betweens, like Densher, does any question as to a future good or bad fate apply."[8]

In the light of the recuperation I have undertaken here, I do not see how such an account of the novel's moral significance can possibly be sustained. *The Wings of the Dove*, in terms of its fictional form, shows us an intricate web of its characters' manoeuvrings and complicities, working sometimes in concert with, at others in futile opposition to, the "shabby realities" (as the novel has it) of Money and Death. Milly must not be thought wicked simply because she is rich. But simply because her wealth frees her into a heady atmosphere of moral ozone (at the same time dramatizing in Kate and Densher their suffocation for lack of it), it does not free her of the other reality. Nor is Kate wicked simply because she is penniless. Both of these immensely attractive women wish to have life, and to have it more abundantly. They both wish to have, as the novel tirelessly insists, "everything." Not surprisingly, they both fail. In James's finely drawn moral discriminations here, "goodness" is not absolute but relative: Milly is not required to be deceived any more than Kate is compelled to deceive her, and both are complicit in their manoeuvring against "shabby realities" and in their respective destinies. Even so, Milly's bequest, whether it be a radically forgiving

---

8. Caws, *Reading Frames in Modern Fiction*, 125.

act of charity or—in implicit acknowledgment of her own complicity—an act of penance and recompense, has utterly the appropriate effect: it establishes a definite and luminous still point against which all their previous failures can be clearly and permanently measured.

In taking pains not to exempt Milly Theale from the full complexity of the psychic, economic, societal, and emotional relations among the characters in her world, James dramatizes the inevitability for all of us of undertaking our manoeuvres in life in a welter of delusive and potentially destructive complicities and thus reveals in *The Wings of the Dove* something profoundly true about the human predicament.

JOHN CONDER

The Red Badge of Courage: Form and Function

The function of the form of *The Red Badge of Courage* remains an especially significant issue because some recent criticism ignores the compelling conclusions that follow from the novel's subject. Those conclusions affect our understanding not only of this novel but of two of the three other crucial works in the Crane canon as well. This criticism might be seen as a continuation of the second of the two stages that criticism of Crane has gone through in the past: an avowal that determinism is a central presence in his work and a denial that it is a central presence or a presence at all. ("The Open Boat" is an exception to Crane's determinism because the story treats a primitive society whose very simplicity permits the existence of freedom.)[1]

The basic materials of the novel are the same as those of "The Blue Hotel" and *Maggie*. They are the *conditions* that generate the thoughts, emotions, and actions of the characters. This emphasis on conditions governing character, as opposed to an emphasis on character as autonomous agent, emerges because the characters are not individuals. Certainly the youth Henry Fleming is not an individual. What little history we learn of him from the flashback hardly individualizes him. What Bergson would have called "lived time," the growth and development of

---

1. John Conder, *Naturalism in American Fiction: The Classic Phase* (Lexington, Ky., 1984), 1–2. On "The Open Boat," see pp. 22–30.

the inner life of a human being, is not a concern in *The Red Badge*, because Henry Fleming is not really a person.[2] He is in fact a case study, a psychological type—the complex type called adolescence—and the novel is about the psychological type called adolescence meeting the congeries of conditions called war.

If the history of Henry in the flashback does not point to him as an individual, it does point to him as a social type. Though his adolescence is of primary concern in the novel, he is also a farm boy, a hick, and thus a social type recalling the treatment of character as social type in *Maggie*. (The distinction between social and psychological type in *Maggie* is not a hard and fast one, of course, but is a matter of emphasis.) The understated treatment of Henry as a social type also forecasts the various social types who constitute the world of "The Blue Hotel"—an Easterner, a cowboy, a hotel keeper, a ne'er-do-well, a gambler, and a host of nameless people of the small town who represent the average person writ large: the community. In these shorter works as well as within the novel, conditions emerge as the dominant basic material precisely because the characters are not individuals, then, but types. And this emphasis on types permits us to see characters as governed rather than as autonomous agents, either because the line between the type and the environment producing it is impossible to draw or because character is treated idiosyncratically so that it acts as condition for behavior.

This view of character in general in Crane's world is reinforced by an understanding of the form of *The Red Badge*. By its form, I mean the nature of the narrator, the special arrangement of materials that produces irony, and the use of the device of a sharp shift in perspective to emphasize the function of the irony. The point of view is third-person limited, and the narrator presents the conditions giving rise to Henry's changing thoughts, emotions, and actions in such minute detail that the clear effect is to see the narrator studying the youth as though this youth were a rabbit or a chicken being put through a series of behavioral tests. The narrator, in other words, is detached, and his is the voice of the

---

2. In describing duration, Bergson called it "the form which the succession of our conscious states assumes when our ego lets itself *live.*" Henri Bergson, *Time and Free Will: An Essay on the Immediate Data of Consciousness,* trans. F. L. Pogson (London, 1910), 100.

behavioral scientist, the voice that says: "The youth cringed as if discovered at a crime."[3]

The character of that voice is best captured by a line used in "The Blue Hotel" to describe the Easterner: "The Easterner's mind, like a film, took lasting impressions of three men." It is the voice that opens "The Blue Hotel" with the words, "The Palace Hotel at Fort Romper was painted a light blue, a shade that is on the legs of a kind of heron." It is the voice in *Maggie* that says, "The girl, Maggie, blossomed in a mud puddle."[4] Such detachment does not deny that a human being is different from other creatures in nature, any more than it denies that there is a difference between a chicken and a heron or between a heron and a panther. So this fact should be kept in mind when objecting that there is a separation between two worlds, the human and the natural, in *The Red Badge*. The human world is viewed in the same way as the natural world in the novel, and the same narrative angle of vision prevails in these other works as well.

The second aspect of form, the internal arrangement of materials producing irony, in fact produces two types of irony. The first, dramatic irony, surfaces when a character, or what passes as a character, is thoroughly ignorant of facts or aspects of reality known to the audience or reader. Both the narrator and the reader are spectators of Henry Fleming's thoughts, feelings, and actions, and through Crane's adroit juxtaposition of details, they see dramatic irony everywhere—in Henry's failing to recognize that a creature pouncing on a fish, for example, does not support his recently adopted view that nature is "a woman with a deep aversion to tragedy" (46).

In *The Red Badge* Henry's failure of recognition is a function of an overwhelming emotional state, guilt, and therefore he is beyond judgment. Likewise, in *Maggie*, Pete, Jimmie, and Mrs. Johnson are beyond judgment for their ignorance of their behavior as a factor in Maggie's downfall. The reader who has finished Chapter 4 of the novella knows that these characters are types, that as types they are products of an

---

3. Stephen Crane, *The Red Badge of Courage*, ed. Fredson Bowers (Charlottesville, 1975), 45. Vol. II of *The Works of Stephen Crane*. Subsequent references to *The Red Badge* are to this edition and will appear in the text.

4. Stephen Crane, "The Blue Hotel," in Crane, *Tales of Adventure*, ed. Fredson Bowers (Charlottesville, 1970), 159, 155. Vol. V of *The Works of Stephen Crane*; Stephen Crane, *Maggie*, in Crane, *Bowery Tales*, ed. Fredson Bowers (Charlottesville, 1969), 24. Vol. I of *The Works of Stephen Crane*.

environment, and that these products are incapable of serious or prolonged introspection.

If dramatic irony does not imply moral censure but instead exposes ignorance, much the same can be said of the second kind of irony operative in Crane's world: situational irony, in which an event gives birth to an unexpected outcome. Several examples appear in *The Red Badge*, one of which is at the heart of the action: a deserting soldier gives a wound to a deserter (Henry) that permits Henry to return to his unit with honor. There are other such ironies. The tattered man's expression of concern leads not to Henry's social reinstatement but to his further flight and alienation. Henry's actual reinstatement in his unit leads to his feeling of superiority over Wilson. Henry's uncontrolled, blind fighting earns him the commendation of "wildcat" and leads to his regarding himself as a hero. The sun appears through the clouds as if to confirm Henry's view of benign nature. Like dramatic irony, this second kind exposes ignorance, though in this case the reader must be included among the ranks of the ignorant. Neither reader nor character can foresee the unexpected consequence of an act. Neither dramatic irony nor situational irony, therefore, implies moral censure. Each does imply the weakness of man's mental machinery, so this fact should take care of the view that irony is necessarily moral in its thrust.

In *The Red Badge of Courage* a spatial retreat to a distance appears in references to the sun, but a pronounced shift in perspective of a different kind also appears in the last chapter of the novel. I will reserve full discussion of that chapter till later because I wish to discuss its special change in perspective in tandem with another major point, the novel's determinism. Here I note that the novel's various references to the sun issue collectively in the meaning of the novel's dramatic irony in the most comprehensive way possible. The youth may be astonished "that nature had gone tranquilly on with her golden processes in the midst of so much devilment" (38) when he first sees the sun, and his astonishment may very well change to gratitude that the appearance of the sun, at the end of the Appleton manuscript, confirms his view of a friendly nature, a view appearing in both endings of the novel.[5] But the reader witnesses Henry's (and man's) relation to nature from the true perspec-

---

5. For a discussion of the endings, see the bibliographical essay in Conder, *Naturalism in American Fiction*, 213–15.

tive of the sun—that is, from the eye of nature's cosmic indifference, a sight that shows man's place in nature to be pretty much the one exposed by the spatial retreat to a distance found in "The Open Boat."

Critics who object to the view that *The Red Badge* is deterministic fail to see that the novel's form—in this case, the arrangement of those governing conditions that constitute the basic materials of the novel—functions to meet a definition of determinism because they never offer such a definition. I stress this fact because a failure to define determinism handicaps critics of the novel, whether they deny or affirm its determinism or whether they simply ignore the issue by assuming the existence of freedom. Bernard Berofsky has issued a warning to philosophers that should be issued to literary critics as well: "In discussions of human freedom it is not uncommon to omit a definition or clarification of the thesis of determinism, although reference to it may be made. This is quite serious if one considers . . . the fact that this thesis often plays a fundamental role in conceptions of human freedom."[6] I hasten therefore to offer this definition of determinism, one that in fact is not my own but that seems to me pertinent to discussions of literary naturalism: "Determinism is the general philosophical thesis which states that for everything that ever happens there are conditions such that, given them, nothing else could happen."[7]

Traditional novelists assumed human freedom within obvious limitations. Crane's distinctiveness as a novelist depends on his fashioning his work into a coherent vision that forces the reflective reader to question the authenticity of man's freedom. The novel's form forces the reader to see that it advances the definition of determinism I have just provided, and the same form makes the appearance of freedom an illusion.

Of the innumerable ways of classifying novels, one can divide them into two groups according to the kind of axis they possess. A nondeterministic novel usually has a moral axis. It rests on the assumption that at some point or other characters could have acted in a way different from the one they did under the *same* conditions, an assumption that permits moral judgment because it grants freedom to the individual.

---

6. Bernard Berofsky, "General Introduction: Determinism," in Berofsky (ed.), *Free Will and Determinism* (New York, 1966), 1.
7. Richard Taylor, "Determinism," in Paul Edwards (ed.), *Encyclopedia of Philosophy* (8 vols.; New York, 1967), II, 359.

Crane's novel has what one might call a would-have-been axis. It rests on the assumption that the youth *would* have behaved differently *if*—if conditions had been different. And its basic material, the conditions generating the youth's thoughts, emotions, and actions, suggests that given these conditions, he could not behave other than as he does behave, a fact that undermines the possibility of moral judgment because it denies man's freedom.

The first skirmish in which the youth participates can demonstrate what I mean about the novel's axis. It divides into two parts that the reader inevitably juxtaposes in his mind. In the first, the youth does not run from battle *because* conditions permit him to be sustained by his consciousness of "the subtle battle-brotherhood" (35). He would have run from battle *if* conditions had been different, if he had not been conscious of "the subtle battle-brotherhood." That fact seems the whole point of Crane's having the youth initially hold fast in the first part of this skirmish and then run in the second part. And in the second part, run he does. He would not have run *if* he had still been conscious of "the subtle battle-brotherhood." But conditions have changed, the youth now sees panic-stricken faces among the brotherhood, and he also sees some men who seem to be running from the brotherhood. Thus he becomes the pawn of that overwhelming fear that earlier had been subdued by his sense of "the subtle battle-brotherhood." These two battle scenes, with their contrasting outcomes, emphasize the dominance of conditions governing thought, emotion, and action throughout the novel. The youth's discovery that his regiment had in fact held fast while he ran then becomes the condition for his guilt and subsequent rationalizations—feelings and thoughts which he would not have been bombarded with *if* conditions had not changed to induce his uncontrollable panic.

This would-have-been axis continues throughout the novel and challenges recent readings that dismiss the issue of the novel's naturalism (or determinism) with a flat, unsupported denial that it belongs in that camp and offer an analysis that simply assumes the existence of freedom in *The Red Badge*. Since both Donald Pease and William Wasserstrom treat Henry's first blind, wild fighting in battle (Chapter 17) as an expression of rage, it will be useful to focus on their treatment of the way that rage develops in order to illustrate my point. Pease locates the beginning of the rage with Henry's aborted philippic, whereas Wasserstrom locates it later, after Henry's learning "the lesson of yesterday" about retribution.[8] Despite this disparity, the forms of their arguments show the same deficiency, and so they can be treated as types of the same argument.

Pease argues that Henry deliberately and freely manipulates his emotions—especially fear and shame—for two related reasons: first, to create an identity for himself based on a rereading of conventional war narratives, though with significant variations to accommodate his own experience; and second, to give coherence to the incoherent. The literal experience of battle, that is, is incoherent, but Henry replaces this incoherence with narratives that by their very nature as narrative possess coherence. Through a "personal act of choice" he develops "an ethos of fear as his basis for a unique personality." By becoming a " 'mental outcast,' " for example, he becomes the star of the show through his special way of handling his fear. The coherence that he gives his experience in this way, breaks down with Jim Conklin's death (and is symbolized by the sun imaged as a wafer). Thereafter, Henry essentially reacts "with rage against the inadequacy of all rationales," and his blind fighting is a part of his waging "war on the discourses" that he used earlier to give coherence to his experience.[9]

I cannot go into all the steps in Pease's complicated argument but quote enough to show that he endows Henry with a good deal of self-control. The fact that Pease largely ignores the narrative voice that renders Henry's thoughts and instead makes Henry appear to be creating his own narrative reinforces this impression of autonomy.[10]

William Wasserstrom also gives Henry a good deal of autonomy. Reading the book in the light of William James's theory of human behavior in extraordinary situations, he finds Henry's instincts suppressed by a genteel civilization symbolized by his mother, and he thinks Henry escapes such suppression when he discovers that "the lessons of yesterday had

---

8. See Donald Pease, "Fear, Rage, and the Mistrials of Representation in *The Red Badge of Courage*," in Eric J. Sundquist (ed.), *American Realism: New Essays* (Baltimore, 1982), 155–75. For his denial of Crane's naturalism and also for his analysis of the beginning of Henry's rage, see p. 169. See also William Wasserstrom, "Hydraulics and Heroics: William James, Stephen Crane," in Wasserstrom, *The Ironies of Progress: Henry Adams and the American Dream* (Carbondale, Ill., 1984), 77–99. For his rejection of Crane's naturalism, see p. 86; for his treatment of the beginning of Henry's rage, see p. 93.

9. Pease, "Fear, Rage, and the Mistrials of Representation," 162–63, 171, 173.

10. For Henry as creating his own narrative, see *Ibid.*, 160, 161, 162, 169. For other examples of emphasis on Henry's will see pp. 163, 165, 174.

been that retribution was a laggard and blind" and that "he could leave much to chance" (86). According to this argument, Henry comes to see through the ethics of an America that promised sure and swift retribution for sin, an America represented by the mother who said, "Don't think of anything 'cept what's right" (7). Seeing the fraud, Wasserstrom writes, Henry "plans to replace this muddle of morals with plain fury." Like Pease, but for a different reason, Wasserstrom gives Henry a good deal of control by seeing his enraged fighting as a response to a lesson in fraud autonomously absorbed by a now-educated Henry. Wasserstrom writes: "Yesterday when his world had buckled he'd 'imagined the universe to be against him.' Today he knows that the universe is neutral, that his sole adversary is 'the army of the foe,' an enemy against which he now feels a 'wild hate.'"[11]

Both arguments miss the novel's would-have-been axis, the compelling relation between condition and perception or condition and action. Although the novel traces a thorough network of causal conditions leading from Henry's initial fear to his blind fighting, the details that I choose here will be governed by my attempt to show that the arguments that I have just summed up are but variants of Marston LaFrance's treatment of his selection of events leading to Henry Fleming's fighting successfully in battle; that a refutation of LaFrance's treatment can show that determinism is a presence in this sequence of events, as it is throughout the major action of the novel; and that a proper understanding of this sequence of events shows that determinism comes to embrace the novel's controversial ending, which does not initially appear to be deterministic and which Pease treats within a context of will.[12]

Marston LaFrance called attention to a "carefully wrought sequence" of "silly illusions," which he says collapse and lead to what he calls Henry's "willed commitment" to fight after his return to his regiment.[13] He had in mind those illusions that make Henry seem so obnoxious when he confronts the "formerly loud soldier" and that are represented by the ironic statement: "He had performed his mistakes in the dark, so he was still a man" (86). Wasserstrom ignores these illusions, and Pease alludes to them in a context of Henry's anticipating and

---

11. Wasserstrom, "Hydraulics and Heroics," 93.
12. Marston LaFrance, *A Reading of Stephen Crane* (London, 1971), 112–17. For will in the ending, see Pease, "Fear, Rage and the Mistrials of Representation," 174.
13. LaFrance, *A Reading of Stephen Crane*, 116–17.

neutralizing judgment against himself.[14] But those illusions are germane here both because they lead to Henry's blind fighting and because Crane treats them in a way that makes conditions of primary importance here as elsewhere. Henry's obnoxiousness, his feeling of superiority to Wilson, it should be stressed, has its condition: his release from his intense fear of exposure as a deserter. Such relief manifests itself through an exaggerated sense of superiority, and that sense in turn acts as the condition for Henry's lesson about retribution, a lesson that is only partly true. If "the lesson of yesterday" was accurate in teaching that "he could leave much to chance," nonetheless chance does not always see to it that "retribution was a laggard and blind." But this illusion is of great importance as a link in the chain of causation leading to Henry's fighting. The illusion permits the youth to gain sufficient confidence, through a chain of psychological causes and effects, to fight the enemy, a chain that terminates in these words: "He had a wild hate for the relentless foe. Yesterday, when he had imagined the universe to be against him, he had hated it, little gods and big gods; to-day he hated the army of the foe with the same great hatred" (94). Crane thereby shows that he understood the meaning of the psychological phenomenon called *transference* even if he was not aware of the term. For he stresses the youth's unconscious transference of hatred from hatred for a nonhuman universe that threatened him because it would not support his rationalizations for having run, to hatred for a human enemy that now threatens him. The confidence generated by the youth's unwarranted feeling of superiority, though momentarily deflated by the sarcastic man, remains sufficiently strong in his psyche to permit him to redirect his hate.[15]

The careful reader thus can see that these illusions in fact are parts of a causal network permitting Henry to fight, and thus the view that they lead to Henry's "willed commitment" to fight is undermined. So, too, is the assumption of freedom and autonomy underlying treatments of Henry's perceptions and thoughts prior to his enraged fighting. Conditions create Henry's fear and shame, conditions permit his reinstatement into his unit, conditions create his illusions, conditions induce his

---

14. Pease, "Fear, Rage, and the Mistrials of Representation," 172–73.
15. For a fuller discussion of the sequence of events between Henry's meeting Wilson again after his return to camp and the period when he develops his hatred, see Conder, *Naturalism in American Fiction*, 58–61.

(partly false) education about the nature of retribution, conditions inspire Henry's hatred, his rage against the enemy, and conditions thus permit him to fight.

Were the adolescent to have that authentic freedom asserted or implied by all these treatments, one must find somewhere in the novel some evidence that conditions do not dictate, that under the same conditions, this adolescent could behave in a way different from the way he does. To accommodate free-will readings of the novel, in other words, one must find a free-will axis in the work, for its existence implies that a character could act differently under the same conditions.

The emphasis on conditions in the major action of the novel seems to me to undermine any free-will axis there, but there does seem to be one in the flashback and in the ending of the novel, both in the version by Henry Binder and in the one that I choose as aesthetically superior, the edition of Fredson Bowers.[16] In this discussion of form and function, my emphasis on the events leading to Henry's enraged fighting makes it pertinent that I discuss the ending rather than the flashback, which is also part of the causal chain of mental and physical events constituting the career of that psychological type named Henry Fleming.[17] In both versions of the ending, we find that Henry is released from "the condition" of the "animal blistered" in war and can now activate his hitherto idle "machines of reflection" to reflect on, among other things, his "sin," and the very word *sin* thus suggests the presence of a free-will axis, here a moral axis that presupposes freedom (133, 135). Of course the reader knows that when Henry committed his "sin," that sin had no moral status, because it was impelled by his overpowering fear of social censure. Yet that Henry thinks in terms like *sin* suggests that he has entered a realm in which he can act other than as he does *under the same conditions*. But in fact the chain of causation that seems clearly deterministic in the major part of the work is related to the ending. In the conclusion, the reflective reader sees that a release from battle becomes the "new condition" (133) that makes the youth feel "that the world was a world for him" (135), and nature now seems distinctly friendly, not indifferent. The reader becomes conscious of conditions existing off the battlefield as well as on, in other words, and he becomes

16. See note 5 above.
17. For a discussion of the flashback, see Conder, *Naturalism in American Fiction*, 53–56

aware that off the battlefield they breed illusions just as they do on it. The major part of the novel and the novel's ending thus share an emphasis on a causal link between condition and illusion, and this shared emphasis deprives the reader of any certainty that the youth has entered the world of could-have-been. The reader is certain only of the existence of a would-have-been axis. And that axis is perfectly consistent with, in fact is an expression of, the thesis of determinism, the thesis that states that "for everything that ever happens there are conditions such that, given them, nothing else could happen."[18]

But there is even more to the matter of this novel's form because of what I have tried to show earlier. If the form of *The Red Badge of Courage* undermines current assumptions about freedom in its pages, then the fact that *The Red Badge* is a paradigm of two of Crane's three other major works makes it clear that such assumptions cannot be made about those works either.

18. See note 7 above.

DONALD A. DAIKER

The Affirmative Conclusion of *The Sun Also Rises*

Until relatively recently *The Sun Also Rises* had usually been interpreted as a chronicle of a lost generation, as an expression of nihilism, or as a representation, in Philip Young's words, of "motion which goes no place."[1] Within the past quarter century, however, some critics—though still in the minority—have discerned in Hemingway's novel a pattern of development; they have argued that at the end of the story Jake Barnes and Brett Ashley are not back where they started, that Jake has gained in self-mastery and acquired at least a measure of control in his relationship with Brett.[2] Surprisingly, even those who assert that Jake is a developing character pay scant attention to the crucial Book Three.[3] Although Hemingway underscores its importance through its

---

Reprinted from the *McNeese Review*, XXI (1974–75), 3–21, with permission of the editor.

1. James T. Farrell, *The League of Frightened Philistines* (New York, 1945), 20–24; Philip Young, *Ernest Hemingway: A Reconsideration* (University Park, 1966), 86. In *Hemingway's Craft* (Carbondale, Ill., 1973), Sheldon Norman Grebstein virtually repeats Young's assessment: The book's "thematic movement is circular and at the end of the novel the protagonists are headed back to where they started" (37). Numerous essays support the views of Young and Grebstein, for example, Robert W. Cochran, "Circularity in *The Sun Also Rises*," *Modern Fiction Studies*, XIV (1968), 297–305; and Harold F. Mosher, Jr., "The Two Styles of Hemingway's *The Sun Also Rises*," *Fitzgerald/Hemingway Annual* (1971), 262–73.

2. The most cogent arguments are Earl Rovit, *Ernest Hemingway* (New York, 1963), 147–62, and Dewey Ganzel, "*Cabestro* and *Vaquilla*: The Symbolic Structure of *The Sun Also Rises*," *Sewanee Review*, LXXV (1968), 26–48.

3. For example, although Arthur Waldhorn argues in *A Reader's Guide to Ernest Hem-

positioning and its brevity (it consists of but one chapter), Book Three has usually been dismissed with brief mention of Jake's symbolic cleansing at San Sebastian and of his ironic statement that concludes the novel. A close reading of Book Three reveals, I believe, that *The Sun Also Rises* is basically an affirmative book. Hemingway's first serious novel affirms through the characterization of Jake Barnes that you can get your money's worth in life, that you can learn how to live in the world, and that you can "act with grace under pressure." By the end of the story, Jake's sun has risen, and there is no suggestion that it will set.

Book Three opens with images of washing and cleansing. The fiesta finally over, waiters "were sweeping the streets and sprinkling them with a hose." One waiter, carrying a "bucket of water and a cloth," began "to tear down the notices, pulling the paper off in strips and washing and rubbing away the paper that stuck to the stone."[4] Since in Pamplona Jake has defiled himself, betraying Montoya and his *afición* by acceding to Brett's request to help her sleep with Romero, his description reflects his own need for emotional cleansing and spiritual purification. Jake recognizes the truth of Cohn's calling him a pimp, making him feel worse at the end of Book Two than at any other point in the novel. "I feel like hell," he tells Bill Gorton, and he later adds, "I was drunker than I ever remembered having been" (232, 233). Because Jake, like Hemingway, defines immorality as "things that make you disgusted afterward," (153) Jake's pimping ranks as his most immoral act.[5] The closing of Book Two—"The three of us sat at the table and it seemed as though about six people were missing" (234)—indicates Jake's sense of loss and, in echoing a casualty report, reinforces earlier suggestions that the fiesta has been another war for Jake, wounding him emotionally, as World War I had injured him physically. Yet even at the nadir of self-revulsion, there are signs of a new awareness growing within Jake. In telling Mike Campbell, "I'm blind" (233), he not only acknowledges that he is drunk but,

---

ingway (New York, 1972) that Jake is an "exemplary hero," he characterizes Book Three as "a deliberately anticlimatic vignette of futility" (111). For Delbert E. Wylder, in *Hemingway's Heroes* (Albuquerque, 1969), Book Three is no more than an epilogue (38).

4. Ernest Hemingway, *The Sun Also Rises* (New York, 1926), 237. Subsequent references to the novel are to this edition and will appear in the text.

5. In *Death in the Afternoon* (New York, 1932), Hemingway writes, "I know only that what is moral is what you feel good after and what is immoral is what you feel bad after" (41).

more important, hints that he is beginning to realize the cost to himself and others in his failure to see clearly the nature of his relationship to Brett. When Jake says, "I looked strange to myself in the glass" (234), he vaguely recognizes himself for what he has been: a panderer at least partially responsible for Cohn's bloody beating of Romero, for Mike's increased drunkenness, and for his own self-contempt. It is precisely this "strange" self that Jake seeks to wipe out and that creates his need for washing and cleansing, for the waters of San Sebastian.

Cleaning up the mess, the novel implies, is not easy. For the waiters "washing and rubbing" were necessary to remove the paper that stuck to the stone. It is relatively simple for Jake to empty the liquor glasses when Brett leaves his Paris apartment, but the emotional mess—"I felt like hell again" (35)—remains. In order to recover fully from the "nightmare" (67) of his repeatedly frustrating meetings with Brett, Jake finally finds it necessary to leave Paris altogether, to journey to the idyllic Burguete countryside for a week of fishing, relaxation, and masculine camaraderie with Bill Gorton.

It might at first appear that Jake's leaving the "nightmares" (232) of Pamplona for the beaches of San Sebastian exactly parallels his earlier movement from Paris to Burguete. This is a crucial consideration, for if Jake's experience in San Sebastian merely duplicates that of Burguete, he becomes not the developing character I believe him to be but instead a static figure who travels in circles and gets nowhere. To be sure, Hemingway consciously links Burguete to San Sebastian, but he does so primarily to invite attention to more important contrasts. There is a qualitative difference between Jake's interlude at Burguete and his self-restoration at San Sebastian that is ultimately explained by the impact upon Jake of Pedro Romero's bullfighting. Although Romero does not appear in person in Book Three, Jake travels to San Sebastian and then to Madrid with the example of the bullfighter before him at all times. At Burguete, by contrast, Jake had for guidance only the admirable but finally irrelevant figure of Count Mippipopolous.

The Count is the only character of Book One who offers Jake a possible means to achieve his goal of learning how to live. The other lesser characters—Frances Clyne, Robert Prentiss, Harvey Stone, Georgette, Krum, and Woolsey—obviously have nothing to teach Jake, since their own lives are characterized by falseness, dissipation, or dullness. Of all the Paris crowd, only the Count gets his money's worth.[6] He explains to Jake that "it is because I have lived very much that now I can enjoy everything so well" (63). And Jake notices that the Count does enjoy many things: buying champagne, eating a good meal, smoking cigars that really draw, drinking wine, watching Brett dance, ordering Napoleon brandy. At one point Jake describes the Count as "beaming" and "very happy" (64), a sharp contrast with Jake himself, who has been "having a bad time" (57). Before leaving for Burguete, Jake thinks about money and is reminded of the Count: "I started wondering about where he was, and regretting I hadn't seen him since the night in Montmartre" (99). At Burguete Jake consciously emulates the Count in getting his money's worth. In preparation for the trip he buys a "pretty good rod cheap" (92). At the inn in Burguete Jake convinces the innkeeper to include wine in the price of room and board. "We did not lose money on the wine" (114), Jake later comments. The entire Burguete episode demonstrates that Jake has profited from the Count's example, for the bus trip with the Basques, trout fishing in the Irati River, joking with Bill Gorton, and friendship with Harris all give Jake his money's worth of enjoyment.

But finally the Count cannot serve as a meaningful tutor, because, unlike Jake, he is not under pressure. Although the Count offers Brett money to go away with him, he is not emotionally attached to her. He appears not to care when Brett and Jake leave the restaurant together, and Jake notices that Brett's place at the Count's table is quickly taken by three girls (67). Because the Count is "always in love" (63), he is not deeply involved with any one person, and the shallowness of his emotional relationships precludes his being subject to the kind of pressure that, because of his abiding love for Brett, Jake must bear. Thus, the Count provides Jake with a code of conduct that functions well only in situations where pressure is not present, only in places like Burguete, where there "was no word from Robert Cohn nor from Brett and Mike" (129). But even in Burguete Jake becomes angry when Bill asks about his relationship to Brett (127), a foreshadowing of his more serious loss of control in Pamplona. Since Jake cannot forever reside in the primitive

---

6. See Claire Sprague, "*The Sun Also Rises:* Its 'Clear Financial Basis,'" *American Quarterly*, XXI (1969), 259–66, for a gathering of the novel's many monetary references. Disappointingly, Sprague reaches few meaningful conclusions.

and isolated man's world of Burguete but must return to the conflicts and tensions of modern society, the Count's example proves irrelevant to Jake's predicament. Finally, the Count's actions are like those of the false bullfighter who works at a distance from the bull's horns: "Something that was beautiful done close to the bull was ridiculous if it were done a little way off" (174).

Romero, by contrast, is the true bullfighter; he is "a real one" (170). Unlike the Count, Romero in the bull ring functions gracefully under constant pressure, subject at every moment to goring and possible death. Romero provides Jake with the code of conduct to face and subdue his bull—Brett—and it is with Romero's example in mind that Jake travels to San Sebastian.

The first detail that suggests that Jake's experience in San Sebastian will significantly differ from that in Burguete is his traveling alone. Although he misses the companionship of Bill Gorton—when Bill's train leaves, Jake says, "the tracks were empty" (241), the objective correlative pointing up Jake's sense of loneliness—he emulates Romero in resolving to go on by himself. From the first, Romero's aloneness is emphasized. When Jake is introduced to Romero, he notices that Romero stood "altogether by himself, alone in the room" (169). And later, in the center of the bull ring, Romero performs "all alone" (227). Jake further follows Romero's example in deciding to return to Spain. France, like Burguete, has a "safe, suburban feeling" (242) because everything there has "such a clear financial basis" (243). By contrast "you could not tell about anything" (244) in Spain. Jake's movement to San Sebastian thus exposes him to greater dangers and risks, in part because of the complexity of Spain and in part because it was at San Sebastian that Cohn and Brett had slept together. In the metaphor of the bullfight, Jake is moving closer to the terrain of the bull: "As long as a bull-fighter stays in his own terrain he is comparatively safe. Each time he enters into the terrain of the bull he is in great danger" (222). By choosing to leave France for Spain, Jake evinces the bravery and courage that Romero displays in working always within the terrain of the bull. "Each time he [Romero] let the bull pass so close that the man and the bull and the cape . . . were all one sharply etched mass" (226).

Having felt "tragic sensations" (222) by witnessing Romero's performance in the bull ring, Jake takes little interest in the bicycle racers he encounters in San Sebastian.[7] In contrast to the dedicated Romero, the bike riders "did not take the race seriously except among themselves" (246). Whereas the duel between Romero and the bull involved life and death, "it did not make much difference who won" (246) the bicycle race. When Jake has coffee with the manager of one of the bicycle teams, he responds to the manager's overstatements—"The Tour de France was the greatest sporting event in the world" (247)—with ironic enthusiasm. Asked if he would like to be awakened the next morning to watch the start of the race, Jake replies that he will leave a call at the hotel desk. In fact, Jake purposely avoids watching the race begin, awaking fully three hours after the riders have left. After watching Romero give "the sensation of coming tragedy" (222), Jake reacts only with mild amusement to the triviality of a bike race in which the greatest danger seems to be "an attack of boils" (246).

At San Sebastian the activity described in greatest detail is Jake's swimming. It relates to Romero's bullfighting in that each is a ritual act that functions in part to cleanse and purify. His face and body smashed by Cohn's fists, Romero in the bull ring "was wiping all that out now. Each thing he did with this bull wiped that out a little cleaner" (228). Although Jake, too, wipes out the degrading experiences of Pamplona in the waters of San Sebastian, his task is quite different from Romero's. "The fight with Cohn had not touched his [Romero's] spirit" (228), but Jake has suffered both physical and spiritual defeat. He has been physically beaten by Cohn and spiritually defeated by his inability to resist Brett's appeal for help. Foolishly clinging to the unrealistic notion that he and Brett can somehow develop a meaningful and permanent relationship, Jake moves closer to the position of the romantic Robert Cohn, as suggested by his sleeping in Cohn's room and wearing Cohn's jacket (165). Just as Cohn is prepared "to do battle for his lady love" (184), Jake asks Brett, "What do you want me to do?" (190) and "Anything you want me to do?" (215). Aware of his vulnerability, Jake had accurately foreseen that given "the proper chance," he would "be as big an ass as Cohn" (188). If Cohn is an emotional adolescent throughout the novel—even during his last appearance he sports his Princeton polo shirt (201)—Jake also acts immaturely at Pamplona. His telling Cohn, "Don't call me

---

7. See Wylder, *Hemingway's Heroes*, 45–47, for a perceptive discussion of the significance of the bicycle race.

The Affirmative Conclusion of *The Sun Also Rises*

Jake," and his making Cohn take back the name "pimp" (201) represent the same kind of prep-school stuff for which he had earlier chided Cohn. In agreeing to shake hands with Cohn, as Romero would not, Jake tacitly acknowledges that he and Cohn are linked by their falsely romantic attitude toward Brett and by their lack of self-control.

Thus, when Jake goes to San Sebastian, he attempts not only to wipe out his degrading experiences in Pamplona but also to re-create his inner self. Because Jake expects eventually to be summoned by Brett (250), he consciously strives to build a stronger self, one capable of recognizing the self-destructive nature of his relationship to Brett, subduing his passion for her, and resisting her appeals whenever they threaten his manhood. Jake's swimming and diving symbolically represent his efforts toward self-renewal. During the first day at San Sebastian Jake swims out to the raft and tries several dives: "I dove deep once, swimming down to the bottom. I swam with my eyes open and it was green and dark. The raft made a dark shadow. I came out of water beside the raft, pulled up, dove once more, holding it for length, and then swam ashore" (245). In swimming to the bottom of the sea, Jake is figuratively probings depths of his inner self. There he clearly recognizes the darkness and confusion that has motivated his conduct. Although the "dark shadow" of Jake's past hovers over him, he will build upon it, use it as a learning experience, pull himself up by it to create a new self. In this sense Jake's diving deep suggests that his new self will have depth and a sound basis; his holding the second dive "for length" signifies that his new self will last and survive.

When on the next morning Jake sees "nurses in uniform" and a wounded soldier (248), forcefully reminding him of the conditions under which he met Brett (39), he is not emotionally upset. Yet just as Brett in the past has made it difficult for Jake to preserve his emotional equilibrium, so this recollection makes it more difficult for him to stay afloat while swimming. He encounters rough surf and rollers that force him "to dive sometimes." Although such swimming tires Jake, the water feels "buoyant and cold," making him feel "as though you could never sink" (248). Having gained in self-confidence, Jake thinks he "would like to swim across the bay" but is "afraid of the cramp" (249). The swim across the bay represents for Jake the ultimate test; symbolically, it anticipates his next direct encounter with Brett, which will take place in Madrid. Although Jake's fear of cramp indicates that the outcome of that encounter, as of a bullfight, is in doubt, his final dive and swim suggest a newly won sense of power, purpose, and self-control: "After a while I stood up, gripped with toes on the edge of the raft as it tipped with my weight, and dove cleanly and deeply, to come up through the lightening water, blew the salt water out of my head, and swam slowly and steadily in to shore" (249).

When Jake returns to his hotel, he is handed a telegram that had been forwarded from Paris: "COULD YOU COME HOTEL MONTANA MADRID AM RATHER IN TROUBLE BRETT." Moments later a postman with a "big moustache" looking "very military" delivers an identically worded telegram that had been forwarded from Pamplona. The military appearance of the postman who brings Brett's telegram suggests a link between Brett and the war. Each is able to wound Jake: the war injures Jake physically; Brett damages Jake emotionally. Moreover, each produces within Jake a loss of self-control, a "feeling of things coming that you could not prevent happening" (151). Jake's receiving two telegrams from Brett forcefully drives home the repetitive quality of their relationship. In Book One Brett had told Jake, "I've been so miserable" (24), implicitly asking him to relieve her misery. In Book Two she begged Jake to "stay by me and see me through this" (190). In Book Three, again "rather in trouble," Brett again solicits Jake's help. Although Jake had earlier sensed the circular, unprogressive nature of their relationship—"I had the feeling . . . of it all being something repeated, something I had been through and that now I *must* go through again" (67, italics added)—he had felt impotent to change it. Now he feels differently, and his refusal to tip the concierge for the second telegram as he had for the first (250) indicates his determination to break the patterns of repetition.

If Jake is angered by Brett's telegram—"That means San Sebastian all shot to hell" (250)—he nevertheless feels responsible for Brett because of his part in arranging her affair with Romero. Thus he wires Brett that he is coming, but his thoughts indicate that it will be a changed Jake who arrives in Madrid: "That seemed to handle it. That was it. Send a girl off with one man. Introduce her to another to go off with him. Now go and bring her back. And sign the wire with love. That was it all right" (250). For the first time in the novel Jake looks with brutal honesty at his relationship with Brett. Frankly admitting to himself that he has been the panderer in Brett's liaison with Romero, he also acknowledges that he has been in part the cause of Brett's going off with Cohn. He realizes that, in Cohn's case, the sense of frustration created within Brett by being with the man she loves but with whom she cannot live causes her to escape an impossible situation by running off with any convenient male. Jake realizes, then, that his relationship with Brett is mutually destructive. Its continuance encourages Brett's promiscuity by allowing her to rationalize her actions even as it condemns Jake to nights spent crying in his room and days filled with feelings of self-revulsion. In repeating "That was it," Jake not only makes clear that he recognizes the irony of a "love" that destroys its participants but also seems to suggest that "This is it," that this is the end.

Jake travels to Madrid to see Brett, then, for three reasons. First, he knows that "the bill always came" (153), that his having to extricate Brett from trouble in Madrid is one way in which he must pay for the pimping that caused it. Second, he realizes that physical release from Brett provides no solution to his problem; he had earlier told Cohn that "going to another country doesn't make any difference. I've tried all that. You can't get away from yourself by moving from one place to another" (11). Third, he follows Romero's example in subjecting himself to "the maximum of exposure" (174). Jake is fully exposed, of course, only when with Brett.

The image of the bullfight provides the framework for understanding the final encounter between Jake and Brett. The meeting with Brett gives "the sensation of coming tragedy" (222), for Jake risks his emotional life in Madrid as surely as the bullfighter risks his physical life in the bull ring. When Jake reveals that on the train to Madrid he "did not sleep much" (250), recalling his sleepless nights in Paris, his vulnerability is underscored. Arriving in Madrid, Jake says: "The Norte station in Madrid is the end of the line. All trains finish there. They don't go on anywhere" (251). Their symbolic significance established through repetition, these sentences hint that Madrid will be the end of the line for Jake. Whether Jake has merely reached a "dead end," as Robert W. Stallman contends, or whether he will effectively end his destructive relationship with Brett remains at this point problematic, further building the tension necessary to produce "tragic sensations" (222).[8] In its extreme heat Madrid resembles Paris and Pamplona, testing

---

8. Robert W. Stallman, *The Sun Also Rises*—But No Bells Ring," in Stallman, *The Houses That James Built and Other Literary Essays* (East Lansing, 1964), 184.

places where Jake has suffered emotional defeat because he has allowed Brett to dominate him. Moreover, the Hotel Montana, where Brett is staying, sounds remarkably like Pamplona's Hotel Montoya, the scene of Jake's most recent failure. All the elements necessary to create the impression of imminent tragedy are present.

But Hemingway subtly yet decisively shows through his masterful selection of details that Jake wins a final victory over Brett and over his old, ineffectual, romantic self. The principal technique Hemingway uses is juxtaposition: he carefully contrasts the present and past relationship of Jake and Brett in order to suggest that their roles are reversed, that Jake rather than Brett is fully in control of the situation. For example, in Paris Brett had come to Jake's apartment, whereas in Madrid Jake comes to Brett's room. Brett had earlier experienced difficulty getting by Jake's concierge (32), but now Jake finds that the hotel operator is reluctant to admit him to Brett's room. Whereas Brett had found Jake in bed when she visited his Paris apartment, now Jake finds Brett in bed. In Paris it was Jake who kissed Brett when they were alone together for the first time (25); in Madrid it is Brett who kisses Jake (252). Earlier it was Jake who refused to talk about painful subjects—"Let's shut up about it" (26), he tells Brett; now it is Brett who exclaims: "Don't let's ever talk about it. Please don't let's ever talk about it" (254). When Brett came to Jake's apartment, Jake "lay face down on the bed" because he "did not want to see her" (57); when Jake comes to Brett's hotel room in Madrid, it is Brett who "would not look up" (255). In Madrid Brett does the crying that Jake had done in Paris.

What accounts for the radically altered nature of their relationship is that Jake, not Brett, has changed. Brett's greeting to Jake—"Darling! I've had such a hell of a time" (252)—duplicates her earlier "Oh, darling, I've been so miserable" (24). Her lack of self-control in *Madrid*—"How can I help it? (256) she asks Jake—corresponds to her previously having told Jake: "I can't help it. I've never been able to help anything" (190). Rather than Brett, it is Jake who has changed and, thanks to the example of Pedro Romero and his self-renewal at San Sebastian, changed dramatically.

Jake's change is best understood in metaphorical terms as his transformation from a steer to a bullfighter in relation to Brett the bull. Brett figuratively represents the menacing and murderous force of the bull in Jake's life because she alone has the power to gore Jake, to reduce him to tears, to sap him of his self-control and self-respect. Appropriately, Brett is frequently compared to a fighting bull. When Brett first sees a bull, she exclaims, "Isn't it beautiful" (144), an adjective equally descriptive of Brett herself. When Bill Gorton first sees Brett, he exclaims, "Beautiful lady" (76). Mike Campbell, who refers to Brett as a "lovely piece" (82), asks, "Aren't the bulls lovely?" (146). If the bulls are noted for their "breeding" (146), so is Brett, for Cohn remarks on her "breeding" (39), and the Count comments that she has more "class" than anyone he knows (60). The unloading of the bulls is an "extraordinary business" (145), and Brett is an "extraordinary wench" (171). Aside from the verbal echoes, Brett is likened to a bull in that each becomes an object to dance around. During the San Fermin religious procession a group of dancers "formed a circle around Brett and started to dance" (160). After Romero kills his final bull, a group of boys made "a little circle around him. They were starting to dance around the bull" (230). Like the bull, Brett becomes dangerous only when detached from the herd. Jake explains that the bulls want to kill only "when they're alone, or only two or three of them together" (145). In the same way, Brett poses no major problem for Jake when they are part of a larger group. If Mike identifies with Brett as a bull when he asks, "Is Robert Cohn going to follow Brett around like a steer all the time?" (146), Jake hints that he, too, recognizes an affinity between Brett and the bull when he says, "I think he [Romero] loved the bulls, and I think he loved Brett" (224).

Through the first two books of *The Sun Also Rises* Jake, as well as Cohn, plays the role of steer to Brett's bull. In the unloading of the bulls, steers function "to receive them and keep them from fighting, and the bulls tear in at the steers and the steers run around like old maids trying to quiet them down" (137). The passage symbolically delineates Jake's relationship to Brett, for he, too, is kept busy trying to calm Brett when her desires are aroused. Just as the steers are unable to protect themselves because "they're trying to make friends" (137), so Jake, who "had been having Brett for a friend" (153), proves incapable of warding off her assaults. During the unloading, Jake points out that the bull has "a left and a right just like a boxer," and Brett sees the bull "shift from his left to his right horn" (144) when he gores a steer, knocking it down. Jake is later identified as a steer when Bill Gorton calls him "the human punching-bag" (207) following his emotional battering by Brett and his being knocked down by Cohn. As long as Jake metaphorically remains a steer, he will obviously be vulnerable to the thrusts of Brett the bull and his emotional life will be constantly threatened.

By watching Romero subdue the bull, Jake learns how to come to grips with Brett. Just as Romero "dominated the bull" (174), so Jake dominates Brett in Madrid. Jake's dominance is shown in a number of ways. He treats Brett almost as if she were a child, stroking her hair, putting his arms around her when she cries and shakes, and comforting her by saying "Dear Brett" (254). Whereas Jake's immaturity was stressed in Book Two, in Madrid it is Brett who is portrayed as childlike and Jake as the adult. Jake's dominance is further suggested when Brett echoes Jake's words. After Brett says that Romero really wanted to marry her Jake replies, "You ought to feel set up" (254). Moments later Brett follows Jake's lead in saying, "I feel rather good, you know. I feel rather set up" (254). Earlier it was Jake who had imitated Brett, who even in his thinking had gotten "into the habit of using English expressions" (154). Jake's dominance is also indicated by the emotional detachment that characterizes his attitude toward Brett throughout their final meeting. When Brett kisses Jake, he could feel her "trembling in [his] arms. She felt very small" (252). Even while embracing the woman he has loved, Jake retains control over himself, his thoughts, and his sensations. Like Romero's bullfighting, Jake's responses are "all so slow and so controlled" (226).

Jake has learned from Romero how to transform his relationship with Brett from "a spectacle with unexplained horrors" to "something that was going on with a definite end" (173). The end Jake has in mind is the emotional independence of each from the other. Jake's awareness of Brett's psychological dependence upon him is heightened when he finds her hotel room in Madrid "in that disorder produced only by those who have always had servants" (252). Unlike Jake, whose room at San Sebastian is neat and orderly, Brett is unable to clean up the mess that she has created. She sees Jake in part as a servant who can always be counted on to tidy up after her. Jake is concerned, therefore, with both freeing Brett from her dependence upon him and liberating himself from her. Like Romero in the bull ring, Jake acts as he does in Madrid "for himself . . . as well as for her" (224). But also like Romero, he does "not do it for her at any loss to himself" (225). As his approaching Brett's room symbolically suggests, Jake has finally come to "the end" of the "long, dark corridor" (252) that represents his past relationship with Brett.

The Affirmative Conclusion of *The Sun Also Rises*

After Jake and Brett leave the Hotel Montana for cocktails and lunch, Jake's words and acts continue to demonstrate his emotional independence of Brett. When Brett tells Jake to think about her having already been attending schools in Paris at the time Romero was born, Jake responds with humor and detachment: "Anything you want me to think about it?" (256). Moreover, Jake metaphorically separates himself from Brett through his statements and conduct. When Brett asserts that "deciding not to be a bitch" is "what we have instead of God," Jake challenges her use of the plural pronoun: "Some people have God. . . . Quite a lot" (257).[9] During lunch their emotional separation is further implied by Jake's eating "a very big meal" (257) while Brett, like the sick and defeated Belmonte, eats very little. For the first time in the novel Jake feels "fine" while he is with Brett. He is now able to integrate the lessons of Count Mippipopolous and Pedro Romero, getting his money's worth out of life's pleasures in a pressure-packed situation. Like the Count, he can now "enjoy everything so well" (64) because through experiences he has gotten to know the values. "I like to do a lot of things" (257), Jake twice tells Brett. Like Romero, he can dominate his bull; it is Jake rather than Brett who controls the action, selecting the restaurant where they dine and deciding to take a carriage ride through Madrid.

Jake's drinking a good deal of wine does not mean, as Brett believes, that he is trying to drown his frustrations in alcohol. In Pamplona Jake may have gotten drunk to "get over [his] damn depression" (233), but this is a changed Jake. He drinks, as he explains, because he finds it enjoyable. Metaphorically, Jake drinks heavily to drive home the utter necessity of complete emotional severance from Brett, which is yet to come. Through the use of juxtaposition—in Paris, Brett had told Jake that he was "slow on the up-take" (33), but in Madrid it is Jake who says, "You haven't drunk much" (258)—Hemingway again underlines the reversal in their relationship. As Brett and Jake are about to leave the restaurant, Jake says, "I'll finish this" (258), a remark meaningful on at least three levels. Jake's draining his glass first indicates that he will not leave a mess behind him that he or others must later clean up. Second, by finishing his drink Jake makes sure of getting his money's worth of wine, just as he is now getting his money's worth of enjoyment from life.

---

9. See Rovit, *Ernest Hemingway*, 156.

Finally, "I'll finish this" conveys Jake's intention of permanently ending his romantic relationship with Brett.

The final and crucial test that Jake must pass before his victory is assured begins when he and Brett emerge from the coolness of the restaurant into the "hot and bright" (258) streets of Madrid. Previously, Jake had always conducted himself well in the shaded and breezy settings of Bayonne, Burguete, and San Sebastian, but in the heat of Paris and Pamplona his self-control has been lost. This time, however, Jake is master of himself and the situation. In contrast to the first taxi ride in Paris, Jake does not ask Brett where she would like to drive but instead chooses their destination himself, again signaling a reversal from their earlier positions but, more important, signifying that Jake knows exactly the direction in which he must proceed if he is to "finish this."[10] As the taxi starts, Jake is relaxed and confident. He sits "comfortably" (258) even when Brett rests her body against his. He does not stare at Brett as he had during the first ride or as the steers had stared at the bull (143). In fact, the cab ride in Madrid more closely resembles Jake's fiacre ride with the prostitute Georgette than the earlier drive with Brett. When Jake had gotten into the fiacre with Georgette he had "settled back" until, as he relates, "She cuddled against me and I put my arm around her" (15). This sequence of events is duplicated in Madrid. Having "settled back" in the taxi, Jake explains that Brett "moved close to me" and "I put my arm around her" (258). The point is that Brett no more dominates Jake in the present than Georgette had in the past.

When the taxi turns onto the Gran Via (258), Jake and Brett are on the "great way," the symbolic highway of life. Their responses, therefore, will reveal with high accuracy their current attitude toward each other and to life: " 'Oh, Jake,' Brett said, 'we could have had such a damned good time together.' "

Brett's remark is obviously inspired by self-pity. Since her affair with Romero has turned out badly—although Brett claims she made Romero leave, her crying and trembling, together with her refusal to "look up" (254), indicate that, as in Pamplona, she "couldn't hold him" (210)—she seems to have no alternative but to go back to Mike who, she honestly

---

10. Although Waldhorn amd Grebstein see the two taxi rides as essentially repetitive, Grenberg is clearly correct in arguing that the two rides present a "compelling contrast." Waldhorn, *Reader's Guide to Hemingway*, 96; Grebstein, *Hemingway's Craft*, 30; Grenberg, "The Design of Heroism," 285.

admits, is her "sort of thing" (255). But Brett wishes it were otherwise, and her feeling sorry for herself prompts her remark, aimed as it is both to rationalize her own failings by blaming circumstances and to evoke from Jake the sympathy and compassion she feels entitled to.

Jake, by contrast, refuses to indulge in self-pity or to share her illusions: "Ahead was a mounted policeman in khaki directing traffic. He raised his baton. The car slowed suddenly pressing Brett against me. 'Yes,' I said. 'Isn't it pretty to think so?'" (259).

In the closing line of the novel Jake suggests, as Mark Spilka has noted, that it is foolish to believe, even had there been no war wound, that he and Brett could ever "have had such a damned good time together."[11] But although Spilka properly recognizes the military and phallic references in the "mounted policeman in khaki" and the "raised . . . baton," his conclusion that war and society have made true love impossible for those of Jake's generation oversimplifies the psychological subtleties of the situation. The reference to the khaki-clad policeman and his erect baton function primarily to create for Jake the circumstances under which he would be most likely to revert to his old self, to lose control and to allow Brett once again to dominate him. Jake passes the ultimate and severest test of his newly won manhood by resisting the temptation, as Brett could not, to blame the failure of their relationship upon the war or his sexual incapacity. Under maximum pressure, created physically and emotionally by Brett's "pressing . . . against" him, Jake delivers in his final words the coup de grâce that effectively and permanently destroys all possibilities for the continuation of a romantic liaison between them.

It is Romero's experience with Brett in Madrid that has rightly convinced Jake that under no circumstances could he and Brett have lived happily together. Brett's unwillingness to let her hair grow out for Romero—he wants to make her "more womanly" (254)—is significant of her more general incapacity to become a complete woman even for the man whose masculinity is beyond doubt. Moreover, Brett tells Jake that Romero wanted to marry her so she "couldn't go away from him," that he "wanted to make it sure [she] could never go away from him" (254). Apparently Brett has given Romero a reason to doubt her con-

---

11. Mark Spilka, "The Death of Love in *The Sun Also Rises*," in Charles Shapiro (ed.), *Twelve Original Essays on Great American Novels* (Detroit, 1969), 255.

stancy. Romero's reaction to Brett is important because in Jake's mind Romero represents the epitome of manhood, the kind of man Jake thinks he might have become had he not been injured in the war. Since Romero, surrogate for the wounded Jake, grows ashamed of Brett's lack of womanliness and fearful of her inconstancy, Jake properly concludes that even were he uninjured there could be no "damned good time together."

Jake's behavior throughout the Madrid sequence but especially during the taxi ride is equivalent to Romero's performance in the bull ring. No longer the defenseless steer, Jake metaphorically functions as the bullfighter in relation to Brett the bull. Jake triumphs over Brett because, like Romero, he held "his purity of line through the maximum exposure, while he dominated the bull by making him realize he was unattainable, while he prepared him for the killing" (174). Brett's "we could have had such a damned good time together" corresponds to the final charge of the bull; Jake can still be gored if he succumbs to her attempt to revive their romantic love. Jake does not immediately respond to Brett, because, like Romero, he is "being very careful," because he does "not want to make any mistakes" (192). When Brett's body presses against Jake, it parallels the moment in the bull ring when "for just an instant he [Romero] and the bull were one" (227). The raised baton of the policeman suggests the drawn sword of the bullfighter. What directly follows in both the bull ring and the taxi is the death blow. Jake's ironic "Isn't it pretty to think so?" is the equivalent of Romero's driving the sword between the shoulders of the bull. Jake administers the metaphorical sword to Brett for the same reason that Romero kills the bulls: "So they don't kill me" (193). Although Brett is Jake's "friend" (153), and the bulls are Romero's "best friend" (193), each must be killed—the one figuratively and the other literally—in order that the emotional life of Jake and physical life of Romero may be preserved. Early in the novel Jake had told Robert Cohn that "Nobody ever lives their life all the way except bullfighters" (10). In Book Three Jake metaphorically becomes a bullfighter, suggesting that he is now living his life "all the way up."

Jake's goal of learning how to live in the world is achieved without real loss to Brett. Although she is the metaphorical bull who must receive the thrust of "Isn't it pretty to think so?" Jake's final statement aims not to destroy Brett as a person but to annihilate the romantic illusion that, until recently, had made Jake an emotional cripple and that, arousing Brett's feelings of helplessness and self-pity, has permitted her psychologically to justify her promiscuity and irresponsibility. In dispelling the illusion, Jake gives Brett the opportunity for self-renewal that she herself has been unable to provide. Because her experience with Romero has "wiped out that damned Cohn" (254), Brett now has the chance, thanks to Jake, of beginning afresh. The point is that even in severing the romantic ties that had united them, Jake treats Brett with kindness and consideration. Remembering that Brett "can't go anywhere alone" (105), Jake arranges for "berths on the Sud Express" (255) so as not to leave her stranded in Madrid. Hemingway altered what had originally stood as the last line of the story—"It's nice as hell to think so"—apparently because the use of profanity would indicate, as elsewhere in print, Jake's anger.[12] Hemingway wanted to avoid any such suggestion not simply because anger would indicate Jake's lack of full self-control but also because it might imply vindictiveness, Jake's punishing Brett for having made him miserable in the past. Jake does treat Brett with irony but also with a deep sense of pity and concern.

Since manhood for Hemingway is measured not by sexual prowess but by one's ability to master his own life, Jake Barnes has demonstrated, despite his physical imcompleteness, that he is fully a man in every sense that matters to Hemingway. He has mastered his life by gaining the strength and self-control to end once and for all his destructive relationship with Brett. For Jake, there will be no more nights spent in tearful longing for what might have been. Having known all along that "the world was a good place to buy in" (153), Jake has now learned how to get his money's worth of life's pleasures and satisfactions. Most characters in *The Sun Also Rises*, of course, do not learn how to live. The bankruptcy of Mike Campbell and the foolish purchases of Bill Gorton are metaphors for their inability to get their money's worth.[13] Cohn and Brett, both of whom cry during the final scene in which they appear,

---

12. Carlos Baker, *Ernest Hemingway: A Life Story* (New York, 1969), 155.
13. In "Bill Gorton, the Preacher in *The Sun Also Rises*," *Modern Fiction Studies*, XVIII (1972–73), 517–27, Morton L. Ross contends that Bill is the voice of Hemingway's code, but he has little to say of Bill's conduct.

obviously have not yet learned how to enjoy living. But Jake has, and it is Jake—as narrator, protagonist, and center of vision—who carries the weight of the novel and whose emotional growth and mastery of life make its conclusion quietly but deeply affirmative.

A. E. ELMORE

The Great Gatsby as Well Wrought Urn

> And if no peece of Chronicle we prove,
> We'll build in sonnets pretty roomes;
> As well a well wrought urne becomes
> The greatest ashes, as halfe-acre tombes.
> —Donne, "The Canonization"

As he was finishing the first full draft of *The Great Gatsby* in late August of 1924, F. Scott Fitzgerald wrote to Maxwell Perkins, his editor at Scribner's: "I think my novel is about the best American novel ever written. It . . . runs only to about 50,000 words & I hope you won't shy at it."[1] *Gatsby* was remarkably short to qualify just then as "about the best American novel ever written." Consider the leading candidates written before its publication in 1925: *The Scarlet Letter*, *Moby-Dick*, *Huckleberry Finn*, *The Red Badge of Courage*, *Sister Carrie*, and *The Portrait of a Lady*. Except for the special case of *The Red Badge*, *Gatsby* is in length a mere sonnet or urn compared with these pieces of chronicle or half-acre tombs. The shortest of the remaining five, *The Scarlet Letter*, runs closer to 100,000 words than to fifty, and *Moby-Dick* and *Portrait* each run to well over 200,000.

Crane's novel is a special case because it seemed to fall outside the mainstream of American fiction as it flowed until 1925. H. G. Wells,

---

1. John Kuehl and Jackson Bryer (eds.), *Dear Scott/Dear Max: The Fitzgerald-Perkins Correspondence* (New York, 1971), 76.

who greatly admired *The Red Badge*, said on its appearance that it was "a new thing, in a new school." But for thirty-five years it was to seem like a one-room school without pupils, until Fitzgerald published a novel in the same dimensions and something of the same style. Perhaps the reason for its lack of lineage was best stated by the English editor and critic Edward Garnett: "And we agreed," he said of himself and his friend Joseph Conrad, both of whom had shared Wells's enthusiasm for *The Red Badge*, "that within its peculiar limited compass Crane's genius was unique."[2]

Unlike *The Red Badge*, however, *Gatsby* changed our expectations of the novel. That is one reason its place among the greatest of American novels now seems secure. The change affected readers, critics, and other writers. Perkins became the prophet of the new, concentrated novel and sometimes, by necessity, its advocate, as in editing the work of that most famous of all twentieth-century sprawlers, Thomas Wolfe. (Fitzgerald himself counseled Wolfe as late as 1937 to apply his "unmatchable" talent to "the novel of selected incidents.") Consoling Fitzgerald about the slow sales of *Gatsby*, Perkins said: "To attempt to explain to [booksellers] that the way of writing which you have chosen and which is bound to come more and more into practice is one where a vast amount is said by implication, and that therefore the book is as full as it would have been if written to much greater length by another method, is of course utterly futile."[3]

Although disappointed by sales, Fitzgerald knew that his impulses in *Gatsby* had been artistically right. Just after its publication he persuaded his new friend Hemingway, whom he had recruited for Scribner's, to cut the original opening sections from *The Sun Also Rises* and begin in the middle of things with the account of Robert Cohn. *The Sun Also Rises* is another undeniably great work that compensates for brevity with compression and resonant implication. Faulkner, who honored his debt to both these writers with direct, sometimes comic imitation in *The Sound and the Fury* (1929), is honored to this day for another novel from the same period that was to be his shortest ever, *As I Lay Dying* (1930). Even *The Sound and the Fury* can be seen as a masterful

---

2. Stephen Crane, *The Red Badge of Courage*, ed. Sculley Bradley (New York, 1962), 203,197.
3. Andrew Turnbull (ed.), *The Letters of F. Scott Fitzgerald* (New York, 1963), 552; Kuehl and Bryer (eds.), *Dear Scott/Dear Max*, 100–101.

interweaving of four stories, each of which comes close to qualifying as an independent short novel.

That the novel of compression was more than an experiment of the twenties is illustrated by Hemingway's last great novel, *The Old Man and the Sea*, published in 1952. Perhaps the greatest tribute to Fitzgerald's influence, however, has been the work of J. D. Salinger. Salinger's novels are typically short and wonderfully evocative, and he makes *Gatsby* a central document for his Glass brothers as well as Holden Caulfield.

But if the American novel became more compact and concentrated after 1925, at least in one of its lines of descent, what was the price and what the compensation? Obviously whatever generalizations one might make cannot account equally well for *all* shorter novels of consequence. Thus this essay concentrates on *Gatsby* and leaves it to the reader to make whatever applications are appropriate to other works.

Shortly after the publication of *Gatsby*, Fitzgerald reacted to Mencken's criticism "that the central story was trivial and a sort of anecdote" by saying that Mencken had "forgotten his admiration for Conrad and adjusted himself to the sprawling novel." Years later, reacting to someone else's very different kind of criticism of *Tender Is the Night*, Fitzgerald made another distinction of interest, even though at that time he was denigrating *Gatsby* to make a case for the newer novel: "*Gatsby* was shooting at something like *Henry Esmond* while this was shooting at something like *Vanity Fair*. The dramatic novel has canons quite different from the philosophical, now called psychological, novel. One is a kind of *tour de force* and the other a confession of faith. It would be like comparing a sonnet sequence with an epic."[4]

Even if Fitzgerald overstated the distinction, *Gatsby* does indeed have the lyrical intensity of a sonnet sequence. The descriptions of the Buchanans' estate, of the valley of ashes, of Gatsby's glowing gardens and his first lovemaking with Daisy, of Nick's Christmas trips home, and of the Dutch sailors' vision of the New World are like poems themselves, lyrics of a high order. Nor does the lyrical intensity decline very much between these peaks.

A sonnet sequence is typically a set of dramatic monologues, with the poet imagining the physical presence of his beloved as he speaks. The

---

4. Turnbull, *Letters of Fitzgerald*, 342, 363.

new-scale novel was typically written in the first person and in a tone of near intimacy, as if the writer spoke to a specifically imagined reader sharing the same fundamental assumptions. This could be equally true when there were multiple first-person narrators, as in *The Sound and the Fury* and *As I Lay Dying*. A similar effect could even be achieved from the third-person-limited point of view, as in *The Old Man and the Sea*. Although among novelists Conrad was the great source for the smaller-scale novel, and although no one writer precisely originated all of its possible effects, there was one work above all others that changed the size, shape, and tone of twentieth-century American fiction. It was not a novel but a poem: *The Waste Land*, published in 1922.

Before 1922 Eliot had already achieved startling and influential effects in the dramatic monologue with "The Love Song of J. Alfred Prufrock." That poem seemed far more intimate and confessional than, say, any of Browning's poems in the same form. Even if the "you and I" of the opening line refers in part to the divided consciousness and heart of Prufrock, it certainly also encompasses the reader, who immediately becomes a silent partner in the poem. There is a further suggestion that some other voice is present throughout, the voice that repeats, like a chorus, "In the room the women come and go / Talking of Michaelangelo." In *The Waste Land* there are many voices, but again a choral-like center associated with the blind seer, Tiresias. The point of all this is that Eliot was collapsing some of the distinctions between the lyrical mode on the one hand and the narrative and dramatic on the other, creating a form and a voice that seemed peculiarly modern. In *The Waste Land* he made the "personal" poetry of the lyric seem larger and more public than before, and "public" poetry—the heroic epic and tragedy—seem more intimate. For an age that wanted more than the mock-heroic but questioned if it could be truly heroic, he created the ironically heroic. In this sense his greatest poem often seems closer in spirit to the epics and tragedies it echoes—to *The Aeneid* and *The White Devil* than to *The Rape of the Lock* or *Hudibras*.

The Waste Land contains only 439 lines. Yet its very smallness became part of its effect. Like a star violently changing form, the poem pulled in all the light and matter that fell into its huge gravitational field, from *The Satyricon* and *The Divine Comedy* of its prefatory lines to the Upanishads of its closing, and compressed it all into an astonishingly small circumference. Yet its smallness is no bar to the consensus that this is perhaps the greatest, certainly the most influential work of our language in this century. Although edited to the point of truncation, to ashes-and-urn size, it retains a curious and compelling unity. As Edmund Wilson observed in the best essay ever written about it, in *Axel's Castle*, it echoes other writers to near saturation without sacrificing its own style. "Eliot and Pound have, in fact, founded a school of poetry which depends on literary quotation and reference to an unprecedented degree," wrote Wilson. "Yet Eliot manages to be most effective precisely—in 'The Waste Land'—where he might be expected to be least original—he succeeds in conveying his meaning, in communicating his emotion, in spite of all his learned or mysterious allusions, and whether we understand them or not."[5] Wilson might have added that in addition to the weight of strictly literary allusion, the poem stays afloat under some massive and intricate intellectual systems as well—Frazer's *Golden Bough*, for the most famous example—and indeed sails with a beguiling grace. Many of these generalizations apply with equal force to *The Great Gatsby* and help to account for the richness that is so disproportionate to its length. In fact, much of the cargo on the two ships is identical, including *The Golden Bough*.

Despite differences of temperament and political philosophy, Fitzgerald and Eliot greatly admired each other's work. Fitzgerald owned a first edition of *The Waste Land*, perhaps the very book from which he read a section in Eliot's presence during a dinner party in 1933 "to show how it should be done." In 1925 Fitzgerald had inscribed a copy of *Gatsby* with typical misspellings but untypical praise: "For T. S. Elliot / Greatest of Living Poets / from his entheusiastic worshipper," to which Eliot had replied that *Gatsby* "seems to me the first step that American fiction has taken since Henry James."[6] *Gatsby* was the first and best in a chain of American novels that bear unmistakable marks as conscious responses to *The Waste Land* and subtle variations on its powerful themes—Hemingway's *Sun Also Rises*, Faulkner's *Sound and the Fury* and *Sanctuary*, and Bellow's *Henderson the Rain King*, to cite only the most celebrated examples.

Like Eliot, Fitzgerald edited his work with a drastic pen. He wrote

---

5. Edmund Wilson, *Axel's Castle* (New York, 1931), 109, 111.
6. Arthur Mizener, *The Far Side of Paradise* (Boston, 1965), 249; Daniel G. Siegel, "T. S. Eliot's Copy of *Gatsby*," *Fitzgerald/Hemingway Annual* (1971), 291–92.

Perkins that he had discarded or made other use of much that he had written on the novel in the summer of 1923—in one case, eighteen thousand words that became the short story "Absolution." His cuttings and corrections in manuscript are considerable and extremely apt, as anyone knows who has examined Matthew Bruccoli's facsimile edition of the holograph manuscript. Nor did the editing end there. Fitzgerald wrote Perkins in 1924: "I can now make it perfect but the proof . . . will be one of the most expensive affairs since Madame Bovary." In his introduction to the 1934 Modern Library edition of *Gatsby*, Fitzgerald wrote, "What I cut out of it both physically and emotionally would make another novel!"[7]

All of this editing produced finally a surface so polished that it easily blinds the hit-and-run reader to the remarkable depth and compression beneath it. Take, for example, the *Jazz History of the World*, a musical composition played at the first of Gatsby's parties. It appears in the pencil-written holograph as over seven hundred words of highly romantic stuff: "one of the most surprising pieces of music I've ever heard in my life. It facinated me."[8] These seven hundred words dissolved in two stages of revision to a few sentences of deft satire—barely a hundred words—summed up by the new name Fitzgerald invented for its composer, formerly Leo Epstien, now Vladimir Tostoff (tossed off). In its revised form the passage has much the same ironical and resonant effect as Eliot's "Shakespeherian Rag," which is "so elegant / So intelligent," in *The Waste Land*. Yet the hasty reader may see nothing but an amusing detail by an unreflective observer.

Such editing sharpened what was clearly an early decision on Fitzgerald's part to follow the impressionistic example of the revered Conrad. Rereading the preface to *The Nigger of the "Narcissus"* at the very time he wrote *The Great Gatsby*, Fitzgerald took literary impresionism—with its emphasis on the incremental impressions of light falling upon the eye of a single limited observer fixed in time and place— toward its extreme limits. He eliminated almost all images of sound, touch, taste, and smell in favor of images of the eye and then restricted

---

7. Kuehl and Bryer (eds.), *Dear Scott/Dear Max*, 69, 88–89; F. Scott Fitzgerald, Introduction to the Modern Library edition of *The Great Gatsby* (New York, 1934), 4.

8. F. Scott Fitzgerald, *The Great Gatsby: A Facsimile of the Original Manuscript*, ed. Matthew J. Bruccoli (Washington, D.C., 1973), 54–56.

these almost entirely to visions of 1) motion and stillness, 2) light and darkness, and 3) the primary colors.

Thus, in the *Jazz History*, for example, Fitzgerald struck most of the images of sound—"a wierd, spinning sound," "a bell now and then that seemed to ring somewhere a great distance away," "a muted violin cello"—in favor of a dominating and utterly silent visual image: "The nature of Mr. Tostoff's composition eluded me, because just as it began my eyes fell on Gatsby standing alone on the marble steps and looking from one group to another with approving eyes."[9] As a result of editing like this, the whole novel, apart from its flashes of primary color, is remarkably like the silent movies it so often alludes to. Imagine an industrial slum area—a valley of ashes—where nothing is ever said to have a smell. Only about a half-dozen times is a character said to "touch" anything or anyone, and the word *taste* appears not once in any form. Of the nine appearances of *eat*, four are preceded by *wouldn't* or another negative verb. Even when reporting impressions of other senses, Fitzgerald often does so in visual images, as in "yellow cocktail music" (40) and the "pale gold odor" of a flower (92). This extreme selectivity helps to produce a focused, lyrical intensity in place of the great narrative and sensual sweep of a novel like *Moby-Dick*.

Given such focusing and editing, one comes to question even the apparent oversights. Why, for example, does Daisy say, "There's a bird on the lawn that I think must be a nightingale come over on the Cunard or White Star Line" (16)? Fitzgerald evokes the nightingale, we may presume, for the same reasons Eliot evokes it in *The Waste Land*—to suggest the doom of Philomela, changed to the tragic-voiced nightingale after her violation by King Tereus. Eliot's "Twit twit twit / Jug jug jug jug jug jug / So rudely forced. / Tereu"—merely "Jug Jug" in another line—is comically but distinctly echoed in *Gatsby*: "With fenders spread like wings we scattered light through half Astoria—only half, for as we twisted among the pillars of the elevated I heard the familiar 'jug jug-*spat!*' of a motorcycle" (68). It is after all Gatsby's unjust doom at the feet of the "pillars of the elevated"—the Buchanans and their order—that is the subject of the novel. There is also glamor in using an elegant

---

9. Fitzgerald, *The Great Gatsby: A Facsimile*, 54; F. Scott Fitzgerald, *The Great Gatsby* (New York, 1953), 50. Subsequent references to the final version of the novel are to this edition and will appear in the text.

shipping line to get the Old World nightingale to the New, but why *two* lines? One has only to recall the two great doomed ships of the Atlantic, the White Star's *Titanic,* which sank near the New World in 1912 with the loss of 1,503 victims—the richest and most famous of whom was John Jacob Astor, direct descendant of that John Jacob Astor for whom the Long Island village of Astoria was named—and the Cunard's *Lusitania,* which went down in 1915 off the coast of the Old at the cost of 1,198 lives and countless more, since it helped pull the United States into World War I.

The traditional view of Fitzgerald is that he was not smart or literate enough to write a book with anywhere near the allusive weight of *The Waste Land.* In a graceful and often perceptive biography, Arthur Mizener nonetheless chose to perpetuate this misconception, calling Fitzgerald a writer who was "never very conscious of his literary debts" and who "had almost no capacity for abstract ideas or arguments." Alfred Kazin had already prefaced a collection of critical essays on Fitzgerald with a similar view: "It was even a joke on the copybook traditions of the past that Scott Fitzgerald should be so good; he spelled badly, he read little, his faking and his snobbery were awful. . . . Fitzgerald did not leave a great body of work; his range was narrow and the highlights are obvious. There are not many hidden details in his work to uncover." But anyone who has read Fitzgerald's letters so rich in references to other writers of all ages; his critical or intellectual reviews and essays, of which he wrote so many that Hemingway chided him for running with the hares at the expense of hunting with the hounds; his reading list for Sheilah Graham, which she made famous in a couple of books of her own; and the impressive, often annotated personal library left to Princeton University after his death can deny the consciousness of literary allusion in *Gatsby* only by re-inventing Fitzgerald as a sort of Gatsby. "In fact," says Kazin, "he was Gatsby."[10]

In his own essay from the collection he edited, Kazin invented a Fitzgerald "whose actual intelligence was never equal to his talent" and whose "talent was colorful rather than deep."[11] What is left for us to imagine but an idiot savant, capable of seeing and painting wonderful

---

10. Mizener, *The Far Side of Paradise,* 184, 112; Alfred Kazin (ed.), *Scott Fitzgerald: The Man and His Works* (New York, 1967), 12, 17, 178.

11. Kazin (ed.), *Scott Fitzgerald,* 180, 176.

colors in words we can not even be sure he understands? But if by "actual intelligence" Kazin means the measurable kind, he is demonstrably wrong. Two previously unpublished interviews I had in 1973 with a retired career Army officer reveal that Fitzgerald had the highest IQ score among the three or four hundred college-educated officers of his regiment and either the first or second score among the officers of the entire division, which contained three regiments.

During World War I the army administered to all its soldiers the first intelligence tests ever conducted on a mass scale in this country. Colonel Ben Venable, who was then a young captain and who went on to make the army a career in preference to his earlier choice of medicine, served with Fitzgerald at three different camps. Newly arrived at Camp Sheridan, Venable met Zelda Sayre at the same "old log cabin country club" where Fitzgerald met her and remembered her saying, "Ben, get my ass away from this stove," meaning the old wood-burning pot-belly that overheated one end of the hall. He got to know her well, especially after he began to date one of her best friends, and liked her "very sharp wit." But he thought the difference between Fitzgerald's "brilliant education" and her very modest one was a factor from the first in their competition for the spotlight. After the Armistice, Venable happened to gain access to all the personnel records of the 9th Division—"more or less secret documents," as he called them. Checking out a rumor that his own IQ score may have been the highest in his regiment, he discovered that it was a good score all right—in the 140s, as he recalled—but that the top score belonged to Lieutenant Scott Fitzgerald of the 45th Infantry's machine-gun company. Venable recalled only one other officer in the entire division with a score higher than his own, a personal friend from the 46th Infantry, whose father was the Episcopal bishop of Kentucky. But Venable could not be sure whether his friend's score or Fitzgerald's was the higher. He made no effort to check the scores of the approximately fifteen thousand enlisted men in the division but agreed that the top officers' scores were probably the top scores overall. Venable "didn't particularly like" Fitzgerald, saw him only once after the war, read *This Side of Paradise* for the people he recognized but found *Gatsby* "lousy," and regretted sending Sheilah Graham a photograph many years later that she never returned. In fact, what impressed Venable more than Fitzgerald's intelligence was that he was an "excellent dancer" who taught Zelda how to shimmy: "But it was *the thing.* If I'd been able to do it, I'd have been out there doing it with her myself, I suppose."

What Kazin and those who have perpetuated the same myth actually react to in Fitzgerald's writing may be his unguarded openness to ideas and his passion for those he fully adopted. In Fitzgerald, as in his intellectual hero Spengler, there is a romantic, unbounded passion for *knowing* that seems indiscriminate to the cautious minds of most critics. Fitzgerald was as incautious in his relationships with ideas as with people. "To record," he wrote in his notebook, "one must be unwary."[12] But the appearance of unwariness sometimes translates to the wary as either the mark of the simpleminded or the mask of the hypocrite.

Gatsby is so freighted with literary allusion that no other argument for Fitzgerald's intelligence ought to be necessary. A short essay can only suggest the nearly quarter century of impassioned reading—unwary but far from unaware—that shines on every page of *Gatsby*, published in the twenty-ninth year of its author's life. Like Eliot, Fitzgerald would have agreed with the art critic Kenyon Cox on the "Classic Spirit" that "loves to steep itself in tradition," that "would have each new work connect itself in the mind of him who sees it with all the noble and lovely works of the past, bringing them to his memory and making their beauty and charm a part of the beauty and charm of the work before him."[13]

Fitzgerald's very title echoes a whole set of ideas and writers. Alexander Tamke has observed that "gat" suggests gangster's slang for "gun" from the pulp fiction of the early twenties. David Trask sees Jay Gatsby as suggestive of "Jesus, God's boy," a notion that seems less far-fetched in light of the ancient history of "gad" as a form of "god," of Fitzgerald's choice of the fictional Gad's Hill as the place George Wilson reaches at noon on his way to the "crucifixion" of Gatsby (Gad's Hill has an additional evocative power as the name of the country home where Dickens lived and died), and of Fitzgerald's explicit depiction of Gatsby as "a son of God—a phrase which, if it means anything, means just that" (99). Horst Kruse recalls Mark Twain's episode in *A Tramp Abroad* about a man who put in at Gadsby's, the principal hotel during Jackson's administration, and spent the last thirty-three years of his life refusing to give up on a bootless little claim against the government. This is the comic

---

12. Matthew Bruccoli (ed.), *The Notebooks of F. Scott Fitzgerald* (New York, 1978), 196.
13. Kenyon Cox, *The Classic Point of View* (New York, 1911), 3.

version of Fitzgerald's Gatsby, who puts up at his own "Hôtel de Ville" (5) and dies in his early thirties without ever quite collecting his little claim against Daisy Fay and the rich and powerful who had kept her from him. Paul Makurath finds an equally plausible source in *The Mill on the Floss*, where George Eliot "refers to a figure named 'Gadsby,' who evidently resides with the rest of the novel's characters in the community of St. Oggs and whose first cousin is said in the passage to be 'an Oxford man.'" Almost certainly Fitzgerald was also influenced by a name from Conrad that is similar to Jay Gatsby's original surname, Gatz—the Kurtz whom T. S. Eliot invokes at the beginning of "The Hollow Men" and whose bundle Marlow delivers to the dead man's fiancée with the words: "I had heard that her engagement with Kurtz had been disapproved by her people. He wasn't rich enough or something." The very name Kurtz suggests the fate that awaited him when he pursued a dream beyond all reason into the heart of darkness—"cursed."[14]

There is no reason to select any one of these as *the* source of the name Gatsby or to rule out any of them as *one* source among many. The very word *source* can be misleading, as if we pointed to a stand of trees as the "source" of a house because it provided the lumber, or to some other house because its floor plan provided an inspiration. Clearly a house is more its final and unique shape and "feel" than anything else. Yet if we keep this always in mind, why should either the builder's or the critic's awareness of plans or planks be inimical to the mystery and beauty of the forest at the beginning or the finished house of fiction at the end? One source for *Gatsby* that has apparently never been exposed to view in the critical literature is Kipling's "Story of the Gadsbys," a story in the form of a play that runs just over a hundred pages in the Doubleday edition of 1913. (Like his others, this book bears Kipling's printed signature in a circle that also contains a swastika—a very likely source, long before the Nazis' misappropriation of this ancient symbol, for Meyer Wolfsheim's Swastika Holding Company.)

---

14. Alexander Tamke, "The 'Gat' in Gatsby: Neglected Aspect of a Novel," *Modern Fiction Studies* XIV (1968–69), 443–45; David K. Trask, "A Note on Fitzgerald's *The Great Gatsby*," *University Review*, XXXIII (1967), 198; Horst H. Kruse, "'Gatsby' and 'Gadsby,'" *Modern Fiction Studies*, XV (1969–70), 539–41; Paul A. Makurath, "Another Source for Gatsby," *Fitzgerald/Hemingway Annual*; Joseph Conrad, *Heart of Darkness and the Secret Sharer* (New York, 1950), 155.

Kipling represents a special problem in any discussion of the function and value of allusion. When T. S. Eliot and Fitzgerald echo Dante or Shakespeare, there is a reasonable expectation that their imagined reader will immediately recognize and respond. As one descends the literary ladder, however, the expectation becomes less and less supportable. One moves away from allusion—that ancient, inescapable attribute of great literature from Virgil's echoing of Homer to Dante's echoing of Virgil to Eliot's echoing of all of them—and toward something likely to be known only by the specialized scholar, as when Fitzgerald echoes popular novelists of his own day like Compton Mackenzie or Michael Arlen. If Kipling's reputation had held up like that of Twain or sunk to the level of Arlen's, there would be no problem. But what are we to make of a writer who survives more because of what he has meant to other writers than to modern readers? It bears recalling that the most famous phrase in *The Red Badge of Courage*—"The red sun was pasted in the sky like a wafer"—derives in part, as Scott Osborn first pointed out from Crane's passionate reading of Kipling. Chapter 9 of *The Light That Failed* contains the following sentence: "The fog was driven apart for a moment, and the sun shone, a blood-red wafer, on the water."[15] Of course the phrase derives even more significantly from the inspired variation Crane put upon it in the context he shaped for it. Fitzgerald, trading in the same currency, transformed Kipling into riches of his own. But whether he is to be praised for alchemy or for the magical coin-changing called allusion can only be answered by the value of Kipling's portfolio over time.

In "The Story of the Gadsbys," Kipling first "set" each scene, then developed it by dialogue alone except for occasional stage directions. The first scene, like that of *Gatsby*, opens in the spring. The hero, like Fitzgerald's, is immediately presented in thoroughly mysterious and romantic terms.

Miss D. Who is this Captain Gadsby? I don't think I've met him.

Miss T. You *must* have. He belongs to the Harrar set. I've danced with him, but I've never talked to him. He's a big yellow man, just like a newly-hatched chicken, with an e-normous moustache. He walks like this (*imitates Cavalry*

---

15. See Scott C. Osborn, "The Red Wafer of Controversy: Kipling and Crane," *American Literature*, XXIII (1951), 362.

swagger), and he goes "Ha—Hmmm!" deep down in his throat when he can't think of anything to say. Mama likes him. I don't.[16]

Like Gadsby, Jay Gatsby is a man whose physical appearance suggests confidence and even "grace" (64) but who often finds "little to say" (64) apart from stutter sounds like "old sport." He is a man about whom opinions are divided from the start. Also like Gadsby, Jay Gatsby is presented from the first in the color of yellow. In the poem prefacing the novel, he is to wear the "gold hat." His station wagon "scampered like a brisk yellow bug to meet all trains" (39), and we learn later that his Rolls-Royce is of a similar color. At the party where the narrator meets Gatsby for the first time, "five crates of oranges and lemons" arrive (39), pastry pigs and turkeys are "bewitched to a dark gold" (40), "the orchestra is playing yellow cocktail music" (40), and two girls appear "in yellow" five different times (42, 43, 43, 47, 51). Another suggestion of yellow or gold, and of much more, is the "wafer of a moon" that illuminates Nick's view at evening's end of "the figure of the host, who stood on the porch, his hand up in a formal gesture of farewell" (56).

Gatsby continues to be associated with yellow or gold throughout his story. He sees a "yellow trolley" (153) racing his daycoach as the sun sinks "in benediction" (153) on his sentimental journey to Louisville after Daisy's wedding. At his West Egg reunion with her he wears a "gold-colored tie" (85), and she smooths her hair with a brush from his "toilet set of pure dull gold" (93). Later George B. Wilson, searching for the "yellow car" (161) that has killed his wife, exacts his vengeance upon Gatsby under "yellowing trees" (162). The hair brush is of particular interest in light of the scene in which Kipling's Gadsby gets married.

Scene.—A bachelor's bedroom—toilet-table arranged with unnatural neatness. . . . Enter delicately CAPTAIN MAFFLIM of GADSBY's regiment. . . . Performs violent fantasia with hair-brushes on chair-back.[17]

Sitting up in bed, Gadsby says to Mafflim: "Haven't slept a wink all night." Not only the neatness and the toilet table and the hair brush but also the sleepless night—like Gatsby's outside Daisy's window—recall Fitzgerald's title character.

16. Rudyard Kipling, *Soldiers Three: The Story of the Gadsbys in Black and White* (New York, 1895), 112–13.
17. Ibid., 149.

The parallels between Captain Pip Gadsby and Jay Gatsby are as striking as they are extensive. Gatsby, too, was "a captain before he went to the front" (150). Kipling's hero is a cavalry officer, and Fitzgerald's says, "I used to ride in the army" (104). Gadsby belongs to the Pink Hussars, and Gatsby's notorious pink suit forms an insistent symbol (122, 144, 154). At the end of Kipling's story, Gadsby's son drops and breaks Captain Mafflim's watch just before Gadsby decides it is "time" to give up his career for home and family.[18] Gatsby grabs a clock falling from the mantelpiece on the day of his reunion with the woman he "felt married to" (87, 149). "I think we all believed for a moment," says Nick, "that it had smashed in pieces on the floor" (88).

Images of bird and egg run through both works. Both "Pip" and "Jay" suggest birds. We have seen that Pip Gadsby is first described as a newly hatched chicken. The two girls who are speaking at the opening of Kipling's story wonder if the captain waxes his moustache, because one of them has been told that kissing a man who *doesn't* is "like eating an egg without salt." This motif is taken up again later when Gadsby kisses one of the girls, who tells her friend, "It's quite true—about—the—egg." Later Gadsby marries the "little goose."[19] The white world of East Egg and the yellow of West Egg owe more to Frazer's *Golden Bough* and to Shelley's Neoplatonism than to Kipling, but who knows the exact genesis of a powerful image? Certainly Fitzgerald's sky view of these "enormous eggs" in "the great wet barnyard of Long Island Sound," their "physical resemblance . . . a source of perpetual confusion to the gulls that fly overhead" (4–5), seems indebted to Kipling's scene or chapter called "The Garden of Eden," particularly when one recalls the proximity in both settings of a waste land:

Scene.—Thymy grass-plot at back of the Mahasu dâk-bungalow, overlooking little wooded valley. On the left, glimpse of the Dead Forest of Fagoo; on the right, Simla Hills. In background, line of the Snows. . . . Overhead the Fagoo eagles.[20]

But the most important resemblance is the central conflict within each man between a definition of self in terms of isolated splendor—some sort of greatness founded on achievement—and a definition in

18. *Ibid.*, 211.
19. *Ibid.*, 113, 123, 165.
20. *Ibid.*, 161.

terms of the love of a woman. Gadsby confides in Mafflim: "I'm an ungrateful ruffian to say this, but marriage—even as good a marriage as mine has been—hampers a man's work, it cripples his sword-arm, and oh, it plays Hell with his notions of duty!" Kipling himself underscores this notion with a poem that follows the play, the refrain of which goes: "Down to Gehenna or up to the Throne / He travels the fastest who travels alone."[21] In even more poetic terms, recalling the great image of the Platonic ladder, Fitzgerald's hero, who "sprang from his Platonic conception of himself" (99), faces the same choice: "Out of the corner of his eye Gatsby saw that the blocks of the sidewalks really formed a ladder and mounted to a secret place above the trees—he could climb to it, if he climbed alone, and once there he could suck on the pap of life, gulp down the incomparable milk of wonder. His heart beat faster and faster as Daisy's white face came up to his own. He knew that when he kissed this girl, and forever wed his unutterable visions to her perishable breath, his mind would never romp again like the mind of God."

Pip Gadsby makes the reluctant, even regrettable, but apparently "right" decision to leave the service and settle down to a domestic life back in England. In the scene above, which Fitzgerald relocated and revised (e.g., "secret place" for "roof garden") in galley, where he also cut away an acre of chaff (about Gatsby as a teenage songwriter) that had separated "Platonic conception" and "son of God" from "salmon-fisher," Jay Gatsby makes the wrong decision by stopping his climb up the ladder and settling for the physical woman rather than what she should represent.[22] Beatrice had inspired Dante not to worldly love but to spiritual. But Daisy inspired Gatsby not to the fulfillment of his great dreams of earned glory ("Study needed inventions," 174) but to the mere pursuit of herself. Fitzgerald was fascinated by the question of what would have happened to him if he had never met or won Zelda Sayre. Would he have become a wayfarer pursuing her or someone like her or, on the other hand, a more dedicated artist, as Hemingway always believed? Such a question is more than autobiographical because it implies the larger question of the relationship between art and romantic love.

There are stories of gods who lose their immortality by mating with

---

21. Ibid., 210, 212.
22. Fitzgerald, *The Great Gatsby: A Facsimile*, 273, 280–81.

mortals, and this is what happens to Gatsby. But his union with Daisy is also, and nonetheless, an "incarnation" (112). Both Kipling's and Fitzgerald's protagonists are associated throughout with the Adam of the Old Testament and the Adam of the New, Jesus Christ. Kipling's hero lives in what Kipling himself calls the Garden of Eden, over which the eagles from the nearby Dead Forest circle. Captain Gadsby's wife is very nearly driven from the Garden by the hand of sickness and death in a scene called "The Valley of the Shadow" and subtitled "Knowing Good and Evil." But the captain keeps an all-night vigil—"*The dawn breaks as G. stumbles into the garden*"—while "his sweetest little angel that ever came down from the sky" raves of bonfires in the street, whether thinking of hell or the midsummer fires of June back in England. The wife cries out, "O Judas! Judas! Judas!" Like Jesus in the garden keeping his own death watch before the Crucifixion, Gadsby, whom his wife has earlier called "my prophet" and "my Lord the King" and asked about the battle scar or "mark" on his arm, prevails over death with the help of the doctor, and the wife is restored. Three years later, at precisely the age of thirty-three and in a scene Kipling called "The Swelling of Jordan," Gadsby chooses to return from the hell of war and India to the promised land of England, with mother and child.[23]

Jay Gatsby lives like Adam in an "enormous garden" (39). The word *garden* is a refrain in descriptions of his West Egg estate, in which it makes twenty-four of its twenty-six appearances before changing at the moment of Gatsby's fall from "the old warm world" (162) to a "new world, material without being real," exposed by "raw . . . sunlight . . . upon the scarcely created grass" (162). Between manuscript and publication Fitzgerald even changed the name of Gatsby's study from "renaissance" to "Adam" (92), recalling Genesis far more powerfully than the eighteenth-century Adam brothers who developed a new style of architecture and decoration.[24] The death of Gatsby, the "son of God" (99), directly recalls Jesus' ascent up Golgotha, when Simon of Cyrene had to help with the heavy tree of death: "Gatsby shouldered the mattress and started for the pool. Once he stopped and shifted it a little, and the chauffeur asked him if he needed help, but he shook his head and in a moment disappeared among the yellowing trees" (161–62). Gatsby's

---

23. Kipling, *Story of the Gadsbys*, 188, 196, 153, 190, 168, 176, 200.
24. Fitzgerald, *The Great Gatsby: A Facsimile*, 135.

exact age is never given, but it is close to Gadsby's and Jesus' at their ends. Nick says of his first meeting with Gatsby, "I was looking at an elegant young roughneck, a year or two over thirty" (48). But as Owl Eyes says of Gatsby, Fitzgerald "knew when to stop" (46). In manuscript Fitzgerald first buried his son of God in "Calvary Cemetary."[25] However, just as he had declined to make Gatsby explicitly thirty-three, he penciled through this and wrote, "here at the house" (242). Instead of fixing Gatsby's death at precisely the time of the Crucifixion—the ninth hour, three o'clock in the afternoon—Fitzgerald says that Gatsby went to his pool at two o'clock (161), waiting to hear from Daisy. "No telephone message arrived, but the butler went without his sleep and waited for it until four o'clock—until long after there was any one to give it to if it came" (162). Gatsby's Christlike death by fire and water, "saving" the real killer, Daisy, helps to make sense of Nick's opening epitaph that "Gatsby turned out all right at the end" (2).

An example of chaff which Fitzgerald spun into gold in *Gatsby* is *The Green Hat*, a best-selling novel of 1924 by Michael Arlen. This is one of the more superficial sources for the "gold hat" of the poem on Fitzgerald's title page. Arlen, who was born Dikran Kouyoumdjian, the son of an Armenian merchant in London, was a self-created man who lived on the scale of the great Gatsby himself after *The Green Hat* made him immediately rich and famous. He dressed in expensive clothes and drove an oversized canary-yellow Rolls Royce and a speedboat, just like Gatsby—or the other way around. His heroine was based on the tempestous Nancy Cunard and was named Iris Storm. Her flower name, suggestive of the Egyptian fertility goddess, Isis, and her fertility symbol of a green hat both play on ideas that *The Golden Bough* and then *The Waste Land* had blown into the prevailing winds of the 1920s. D. H. Lawrence, who wrote Arlen into *Lady Chatterly's Lover* as Michaelis, advised Arlen on his manuscripts and was no stranger to such ideas. Iris is a rich, beautiful woman still hopelessly in love with her late husband, Boy Fenwick. Fenwick had fallen to his death on his wedding night, an apparent monklike suicide who became a legend, a "figure midst a babble of confused rumour and knowing silences," and thus another forerunner of the mysterious, idealistic Gatsby. Iris drives a car that is "like a huge yellow insect"; Gatsby's station wagon scampers "like a

---

25. Ibid., 242.

brisk yellow bug."[26] The narrator is a sensitive young writer who himself falls in love with Iris. Daisy at one point asks Nick, "Are you in love with me?" (86); she is only kidding, but Nick is sensitive to her romantic power over men and falls "half in love" (179) with her alter ego, Jordan. Iris kills herself by wrecking her yellow car at the end of the novel. Daisy kills Myrtle Wilson with Gatsby's yellow car and, consequently, Gatsby himself. Like George Gene Nathan, who despised the fashionable notion that this was a great and serious novel, and indeed like the sophisticated Arlen himself, Fitzgerald knew *The Green Hat* was "hurried and second rate."[27] But having joined in the laughter against his own *Beautiful and Damned*, Fitzgerald also knew how to value and hold onto whatever was good in a bad book.

Another example of chaff is a book of no redeeming value whatever except that Fitzgerald put it to good use. Scribner's had published Lothrop Stoddard's *The Rising Tide of Color Against White World Supremacy* the same year it published Fitzgerald's first novel. Lewis A. Turlish has demonstrated that this is the book that inspired Tom Buchanan's line: "Have you read 'The Rise of the Colored Empires' by this man Goddard?" (13).[28] Like Oswald Spengler in Germany, William Butler Yeats in Ireland, and half the other intellectuals in the Western world after World War I, Stoddard, an American with a Ph.D. from Harvard, believed the West was dying. But unlike Spengler and Yeats, Stoddard believed that death could be averted by eugenic measures. Fitzgerald deeply valued Spengler. "He and Marx are the only philosophers that still manage to make sense in this horrible mess," Fitzgerald wrote in the year before America entered World War II. "I mean make sense by themselves and not in the hands of their distorters."[29] The ideas of Stoddard, on the other hand, are treated with contempt by all of Fitzgerald's characters except "the sturdy straw-haired" (7)—and straw-headed—Tom. Nick Carraway, the narrator, says of Tom on Goddard-Stoddard: "Something was making him nibble at the edge of stale ideas" (25). Tom's "impassioned gibberish" on a later occasion is also straight out of Stoddard: "Nowadays people begin by sneering at family life and

---

26. Michael J. Arlen, *Exiles* (New York, 1970), 103, 71, 16.
27. Matthew Bruccoli, *Some Sort of Epic Grandeur* (New York, 1981), 294.
28. Lewis A. Turlish, "The Rising Tide of Color: A Note on the Historicism of *The Great Gatsby*," *American Literature*, XLIII (1971), 442–44.
29. Kuehl and Bryer (eds.), *Dear Scott/Dear Max*, 263.

The Great Gatsby as Well Wrought Urn

family institutions, and next they'll throw everything overboard and have intermarriage between black and white" (156). To know how horrible this will be, one need only read *The Rising Tide of Color:* "Crossings with the negro are uniformly fatal. Whites, Amerindians, or Asiatics—all are alike vanquished by the invincible prepotency of the more primitive, generalized, and lower negro blood."[30]

Stoddard apparently made two other contributions to the novel: an image and a phrase. "There is no immediate danger of the world being swamped by black blood. But there is a very imminent danger that the white stocks may be swamped by Asiatic blood." This "Yellow Peril" provides additional significance to Fitzgerald's choice of yellow as the primary color of Gatsby and his edenic world. To Nick, Gatsby is the god who suggests some hope of renewal in the waste land, like Frazer's corn gods. But to Tom he is the Yellow Peril to the old, white established world of East Egg. Speaking of the materialistic philosophy he thought nineteenth-century Western man had evolved as he lost his idealism, Stoddard lamented that "Civilized man had just entered a new material world."[31] As Nick imagines Gatsby's idealistic dream collapsing before his eyes in the moments before his death, we seem to hear Stoddard's phrase in the evocation of "a new world, material without being real" (162).

But for all these good literary reasons for calling his character Gatsby and for placing him in a gold or yellow world, why did Fitzgerald call him "The Great"? Fitzgerald worried at one point because he had neglected to make anything of this description in the novel, even ironically.[32] But it is clearly part of a critical pattern of images and symbols that begins with the title and the title-page poem.

> Then wear the gold hat, if that will move her,
> If you can bounce high, bounce for her, too,
> Till she cry, "Lover, gold-hatted, high-bouncing lover,
> I must have you!"

Fitzgerald himself wrote this poem, ascribing it to one of the characters in his first novel, *This Side of Paradise.* Why did he think the poem so

---

30. Lothrop Stoddard, *The Rising Tide of Color Against White World Supremacy* (New York, 1920), 301.
31. *Ibid.*, 301, 85, 213, 158.
32. Kuehl and Bryer (eds.), *Dear Scott/Dear Max,* 94.

important that he seriously considered naming the novel *Gold-Hatted Gatsby*, though only once does the title character wear a hat at all (105)?³³ The gold hat makes little sense unless one recalls the harvest rituals described by Frazer in *The Golden Bough*, Eliot's own chief source, in which a young man is selected to play the king or god of the harvest. Sometimes he is dressed in green (Green George), sometimes in gold. Sometimes he merely wears a headpiece of one of these colors or is selected because of the blond or red color of his own hair, resembling ripe grain or autumn leaves, like that perfectly preserved prehistoric body of a red-haired and ritualistically strangled young man pulled recently from a peat bog in England.

Often, says Frazer, the king was executed after serving his office of encouraging nature to fruition. However, the duration of his reign was sometimes extended, even to the point that he could rule so long as he retained his potency or vigor. The measure of his strength was his ability to fight off challengers, typically younger ones. If the king lost his potency or vigor, the land was believed to become desolate or waste until he could somehow regain it or be replaced by a more vigorous successor. To demonstrate the continuation of his physical strength and his power to influence nature, the king was expected at least on ceremonial occasions to perform acrobatic dances or other feats of strength and skill. For three hours without a break, says Frazer in one example, a king "engaged in a frenzied dance, crouching on his hams like a tailor, sweating like a pig, and bounding about with an agility which testified to the strength and elasticity of his divine legs." Or such performances might be expected of a contender for kingship. "Thus it appears that the right to marry a girl, and especially a princess, has often been conferred as a prize in an athletic contest," says Frazer, and he cites the legend that the Olympics were originally run for no less a prize than a kingdom. The contest "may sometimes have been a mortal combat rather than a race."³⁴ Gatsby is described as a young man "beating his way along the south shore of Lake Superior as a clam-digger and a salmon-fisher" with "brown, hardening body" (99); as a heroic, highly decorated soldier who "seemed to bear an enchanted life" (66); and as an "elegant young roughneck" (48) when Nick meets him in his early thirties, "with that re-

---

33. *Ibid.*, 81, 96.
34. Sir James G. Frazer, *The Golden Bough: A Study in Magic and Religion* (New York, 1922), 113, 181, 183.

sourcefulness of movement that is so peculiarly American—that comes . . . with the formless grace of our nervous, sporadic games" (64). His physical heroism is ironically recalled at the end of the novel when Nick says, "tomorrow we will run faster, stretch out our arms farther. . . . And one fine morning—" (182).

But in Frazer the king becomes more than athlete or warrior. There are at least two stages of development beyond the warrior-king: namely, the magician-king and the god-king.[35] It is precisely to these three offices that human beings have traditionally applied the epithet of "The Great." Alexander the Great is the archetype of the warrior-king. Even the working, unregal magician of our own day is fond of billing himself as "The Great," a title he must sometimes share with his brothers of the circus, the acrobats; the Great Houdini, at the height of his fame when *Gatsby* was published, qualified under both callings. Jeremiah summarizes a never-ending tradition in calling the highest king of all "The Great, the Mighty God" (Jeremiah 32:18). In H. G. Wells's *Outline of History*, a book Fitzgerald owned by a writer he treasured, there is a memorable account of Alexander's assumption of godliness on top of his kingliness: "The young master of the world, it is related, made a special journey to visit [the temple and oracle of Amman Ra]; he came into the sanctuary, and the image advanced out of the darkness at the back to meet him. There was an impressive exchange of salutations. . . . So it was that the priests of Egypt conquered their conqueror, and an Aryan monarch first became a god." A note on the same page may have contributed to Fitzgerald's insistence that, as applied to Gatsby, "son of God" is "a phrase which, if it means anything, means exactly that" (99): Wells declares that he is "totally unable to accept" the argument that Alexander was "deliberately and cynically acquiring divinity as a 'unifying idea'" or "master-stroke of policy."[36]

Gatsby as great magician, king, or god owes more, however, to *The Golden Bough* than to any other source. Illustrating the idea that early man "sees in a man-god or god-man only a higher degree of the same supernatural powers which he arrogates in perfect good faith to himself" and that thus it was easy for "the magician . . . to blossom out into a full-blown god and king in one," Frazer cites among many examples a

---

35. See *Ibid.*, 171–94.
36. H. G. Wells, *The Outline of History* (London, 1984), 152.

sect "attired in the most fantastic apparel": "In the thirteenth century there arose a sect called the Brethren and Sisters of the Free Spirit, who held that by long and assiduous contemplation any man might be united to the deity in an ineffable manner and become one with the source and parent of all things, and that he who had thus ascended to God and been absorbed in his beatific essence, actually formed part of the Godhead, was the Son of God in the same sense and manner with Christ himself."[37]

All of these associations are developed in the body of the novel. "High in a white palace the king's daughter, the golden girl" (120) replaces Gatsby's earlier dreams. She is Daisy Fay—like Morgan le Fay, literally "the fairy." To win her back, he must not only "bounce high" on some simple physical level, he must create his own castle and legend and commit himself to "the following of a grail" (149). With his "enchanted life" (66), he becomes, like all magician-kings in Frazer, the changer of weather—rainmaker and bringer of sunshine, most notably on the day of his reunion with Daisy. Images of witchcraft and magic abound in the novel, where "ghostly" is a favorite description. As for Gatsby's association with divinity, Fitzgerald could not be more explicit. No sooner does Fitzgerald call Gatsby a son of God, insisting on the literalness of the phrase, than he describes his career as clam digger and salmon fisher (99). Gatsby's whole world, from beginning to end, is associated with images of water, and he dies at last in his own swimming pool, a version of Eliot's and Jessie Weston's fisher king, which Weston sees as the underlying myth in the knightly romances like those about Arthur and the Grail. The apparent echoes of Weston in *Gatsby* are as striking as those of Frazer, though there is not space to trace them here. Doubters who cannot concede a murder without direct evidence, no matter how closely the bullet in the body matches the bullet in the smoking gun, will object that neither Frazer nor Weston appears in any of the usual sources for "proving" that Fitzgerald knew a particular author or book. But Eliot's insistence on the importance of these writers to *The Waste Land* would have provided a powerful motivation for Fitzgerald to read them with his characteristic passion.

The high-bouncing, gold-hatted lover recalls at least two other sources of consequence. One is the scene in *The Satyricon* in which a

---

37. Frazer, *Golden Bough*, 106, 117.

slave boy performs a tumbling act that ends in mock disaster as the boy falls on the host, Trimalchio himself. Instead of punishing the boy, Trimalchio puts on his head the cap of freedom. Like Gatsby, Trimalchio rose from humble beginnings to become a rich host famed for his extravagant parties. In freeing the boy, he reminds his guests of his own lowly origins as a slave. Fitzgerald's abiding preference for a title, though fortunately no one else agreed, was *Trimalchio* or *Trimalchio in West Egg*. The other source is Lewis Carroll's *Through the Looking Glass,* which Fitzgerald's Aunt Annabel had given him as he turned twelve and which was still in his personal library at his death. The apposite scene is where Alice, after watching the White Knight "tumbling off" his horse, has "bounded across" the Eighth Square of the giant chess board: "'Oh, how glad I am to get here! And what *is* this on my head?' . . . It was a golden crown."[38]

Fitzgerald's debt to Carroll may include the closing as well as the opening lines of *Gatsby:* "Gatsby believed in the green light, the orgiastic future that year by year recedes before us. It eluded us then, but that's no matter—tomorrow we will run faster, stretch out our arms farther. . . . And one fine morning—So we beat on, boats against the current, borne back ceaselessly into the past" (182). The *meaning* of this is from Spengler, who argued that every age repeats the patterns of the past, only in new forms. But the *image* strongly suggests Alice's unsuccessful rowing of the boat that appears by magic just before she meets Humpty Dumpty. She can reach the beautiful rushes only when she *stops* rowing, though even then there is "always a more lovely one that she couldn't reach." Nor do her problems end when the boat abruptly vanishes: "The egg seems to get further away the more I walk towards it," Alice laments, and whatever she seeks is always not there or just beyond her.[39]

As in Eliot, the vegetation symbols, like Gatsby's gold hat, are treated ironically, for the modern world has lost its touch with revivifying nature. Thus, gold and green are explicitly applied not to crops or trees but to things made by hand or machine. Gatsby's gold toilet set, his two yellow automobiles, the "hot green leather of the seat" (121) in one of

---

38. Kuehl and Bryer (eds.), *Dear Scott/Dear Max,* 81, 85, 96; Turnbull, *Letters of Fitzgerald,* 478.
39. Lewis Carroll, *Through the Looking Glass,* in *The Complete Works of Lewis Carroll* (New York, 1936), 205, 207.

them, Daisy's famous green dock light, and the green card she pretends to carry with her to Gatsby's party. Gatsby's edenic garden appears in blue but never in green—"blue gardens" (39), "blue leaves" (152), "blue lawn" (182). Only toward the very end of the novel does green or gold attach explicitly to nature herself: in the yellowing trees beneath which Gatsby dies and in Nick's lyrical reconstruction of the Dutch sailors' first view of the "fresh green breast" (182) of the New World. "And year by year, when the trees were deciduous," writes Frazer, "every Adonis would seem to bleed to death with the red leaves of autumn and to come to life again with the fresh green of spring."[40] Even in death at the end of *Gatsby*, there is the same promise of renewal one hears at the end of *The Waste Land*.

But to a far greater degree than Eliot, Fitzgerald filled *Gatsby* with specifically Christian symbols. To some extent he may still have been following Frazer, who had seen Christianity as another version of the same vegetative rituals, and Christ as one more manifestation of the Attis-Adonis-Osiris myth—of the god who dies and is reborn to save his land and people. However, Fitzgerald was also following the more conventional sources of the King James Bible and *Paradise Lost*. He was "deep in Milton" that summer of 1924 when he completed the first full draft of *Gatsby*.[41] Milton of course knew all about Attis, Adonis, Osiris, Isis, and their whole race, specifically associating them in Book I of *Paradise Lost* with the fallen angels. But the major allusions in *Gatsby* to the poem are to Satan's entry into the Garden of "vegetable Gold" and "fruit burnished with Golden Rind," first like a wolf (consider Wolfsheim's role as the devil to Gatsby's Faust), then like a cormorant perched at the top of the Tree of Life, and finally as the serpent leading Eve "Beyond a row of Myrtles"—Venus' sacred plant, which gives its name to Tom Buchanan's mistress. In looking for a serpent whose form he can assume, Satan determines to "glide obscure, and pry / In every Bush and Brake."[42] Like bird of prey or serpent, George Wilson appears in Gatsby's garden as "that ashen, fantastic figure gliding toward him through the amorphous trees" (162), bringing death and "holocaust"

---

40. Frazer, *Golden Bough*, 394.
41. Kuehl and Bryer (eds.), *Dear Scott/Dear Max*, 71.
42. John Milton, *Paradise Lost*, Book IV, lines 219, 249, 183–99, Book IX, lines 627, 159–60. The edition of Milton I used is *Complete Poems and Major Prose*, ed. Merrit Y. Hughes (New York, 1957).

(163). Before Hitler's atrocities, *holocaust* was a rare and exotic word. In his marked copy of *Gatsby*, Eliot underlined the word and wrote "oh oh."[43] Although literally a sacrifice that is completely consumed by fire, it never appears where one would most expect it, in the King James Bible. But it appears at the very end of *Samson Agonistes*, where the chorus makes sense of Samson's death:

> Like that self-begott'n bird
> In the *Arabian* woods embost,
> That no second knows nor third,
> And lay erewhile a Holocaust,
> From out her ashy womb now teem'd,
> Revives, reflourishes, then vigorous most
> When most unactive deem'd,
> And though her body die, her fame survives[44]

Clearly "holocaust" in both this passage and *Gatsby* has a powerful suggestion of meaningful sacrifice, as opposed to mindless massacre. The sacrifice leads to some kind of resurrection or renewal, reinforced in Milton by the symbol of the phoenix.

Nick Carraway's descent into the valley of ashes is directly reminiscent of Dante's: "The valley of ashes is bounded on one side by a small foul river, and, when the drawbridge is up to let barges through, the passengers on waiting trains can stare at the dismal scene for as long as half an hour" (23–24). One of Eliot's notes to *The Waste Land* cites this translation of an apposite line from *The Inferno*: "So long a train of people, / that I should never have believed / That death had undone so many." But Fitzgerald knew Dante directly, leaving at his death three different translations in his personal library. In the line Eliot quotes, Dante is about to cross Acheron on Charon's barge and enter "the dolorous Valley of the Abyss," "the blind world here below."[45] Fitzgerald's major image in his own valley of ashes is the absence of light or vision, most memorable in the blind eyes of Dr. T. J. Eckleburg but also in such phrases as "this shadow of a garage must be a blind" (25), "the thickish figure of a woman blocked out the light" (25), and the woman's dog "looking with blind eyes through the smoke" (37).

43. Siegel, "Eliot's Copy of *Gatsby*," 293.
44. John Milton, *Samson Agonistes*, lines 1699–1706, in Milton, *Complete Poems and Major Prose*.
45. *The Inferno of Dante Alighieri* (London, 1900), 37.

Goethe is an even more important influence than Dante or Milton. Nick meets the devil Wolfsheim in a "well-fanned Forty-second Street cellar" (69), where he "discovered his tiny eyes in the half-darkness" (70). "A succulent hash arrived," and he "began to eat with ferocious delicacy" (71)—the only account of eating in the entire novel except for Wolfsheim's own recollection of Gatsby's eating four dollars' worth of food at *their* first meeting in "Winebrenner's poolroom at Forty-third Street" (172). "His eyes, meanwhile," Nick continues, "roved very slowly all around the room" (71)—exactly like a feeding animal's. As we observed in Milton, the wolf is a traditional embodiment or symbol of the devil, and *heim* simply means "home" in German. Wolfsheim's cuff buttons, "oddly familiar pieces of ivory," turn out to be "human molars" (73), perfect trophies for the home of wolf or devil. But Wolfsheim throughout is more comic than sinister. It is the Faustian comic spirit of *Gatsby*, reinforced by the understated wit of Nick Carraway, that is so often missed by those who turn the novel into plays or films. The most recent motion picture, for example, was as somber and stilted as a bad documentary. The actual demon in *Gatsby* is Tom Buchanan, even though he is presented, initially and ironically, in a white and airy setting suggestive of traditional pictures of heaven. Wolfsheim, in short, has far more in common with Goethe's Mephistopheles than with the Archfiend of Dante or Milton.

What Fitzgerald presents in Winebrenner's poolroom is a version of the meeting of Faust and Mephistopheles in *Faust*, Part I, scenes 1–4. This starts in Faust's study, which Goethe calls a "Gothic chamber" and a "dungeon." Soon, in scene 5, Mephistopheles whisks his new charge off to Auerbach's cellar in Leipzig. (Auerbach itself is one of the approximately one hundred surnames cataloged in *Gatsby*.) There the playful devil turns wine into fire before riding the cask out the cellar door. Only after the holograph did Fitzgerald insert *Winebrenner's* for *Felbaums*.[46] The name *brenner* literally means "burner," but one of its applied meanings is "distiller," so that a *winebrenner* is a winemaker. Jesus himself was a winemaker at the wedding in Cana, turning water into wine as later, according to the faithful, he would turn wine into sacrificial blood in the mass. Thus in Winebrenner's poolroom, where Gatsby eats the four dollars' worth of food, there is an inevitable suggestion of the Lord's

---

46. Fitzgerald, *The Great Gatsby: A Facsimile*, 245.

Supper but with a hint, too, of a black mass. For just after the Leipzig cellar scene in Goethe, Faust drinks a flaming witch's potion that prepares him for the Walpurgisnacht. Also suggested by later images in *Gatsby* is the familiar temptation of Jesus—the implicit counterpoint to Faust's temptation. Luke writes, "And the devil, taking him up into a high mountain, showed unto him all the kingdoms of the world in a moment of time" (Luke 4:5). Wolfsheim says, "I got him to join up in the American Legion and he used to stand high there" (172). Luke's devil also tempts the "Son of God" to cast himself down from the pinnacle of the temple on the theory that God's angels "shall bear thee up" (Luke 4:9). Wolfsheim says, "I raised him up out of nothing" (172).

Wolfsheim also illustrates how brilliantly Fitzgerald could interweave literary sources with other kinds. Fitzgerald almost certainly took the name from his friend Mencken, who had remarked in *The American Language* how American Jews change names such as "Wolfsheimer to Wolf" and had then cited a *Smart Set* story in which an Abe Rosenheimer changes his name to Abraham Lincoln Rosenheim (compare Fitzgerald's Stonewall Jackson Abrams) on his way to *Rosen, Rose,* and finally *Ross*. But *Wolfsheim* is also one of a whole series of animal-vegetable-mineral names, as if Fitzgerald was invoking not only Mencken and *The Golden Bough* but some of his own lists of things that Sheilah Graham said he loved to compile. For example, Klipspringer and the Blackbucks are two kinds of African antelope. When Fitzgerald placed Tom and Daisy's wedding in the Muhlbach Hotel in Louisville, did he simply confuse a Kansas City hotel with the Seelbach in Louisville, as Matthew Bruccoli believes, or was he intentionally associating "Mr. Buchanan . . . the polo player" (106) with a muleback?[47] Certainly he created Beluga, the source of caviar, to swim with the Beckers, Fishguards, Snells, Hammerheads, and Whitebait. His Orchid, Duckweed, Palmetto, and Hornbeams join girls "with the melodious names of flowers" (63) at Gatsby's parties. His Bunsen, Voltaire, and Flink may owe their presence, at least in part, to the minerals bunsenite,

---

47. H. L. Mencken, *The American Language* (2nd ed.; New York, 1921), 335; Matthew J. Bruccoli, *Apparatus for F. Scott Fitzgerald's "The Great Gatsby"* (Columbia, S.C., 1974), 42. Even in Germany, where three of Mencken's four grandparents were born, *Wolfsheimer* apparently disappeared. In the 1982–83 West Berlin telephone directory, for example, one finds *Wolf, Wolff,* and *Wolfsheim* but no *Wolfsheimer*. A historian named Hans Wolffheim, born in 1904, appears in the 1972 *Who's Who in Germany* (Ottobrun, nr. Munich: 1972), Vol. M–Z, p. 1645.

voltaite, and flinkite. Thus, Fitzgerald's justly praised catalog of those who attended Gatsby's parties, like so much else in his novel, has no single source, literary or otherwise. It invokes the epic catalogs of *Paradise Lost* in the same breath as the comical guest lists of Dickens' *Our Mutual Friend* (as has been pointed out by A. E. Le Vot) and Thackeray's *Vanity Fair* (as shown by Robert Long, who has also written well on Conrad's enormous influence on Fitzgerald).[48]

Wolfsheim also owes his presence in part, like so many other characters in this novel, to a model from real life—Arnold Rothstein, who fixed the 1919 World Series and was gunned down on the streets of New York a few years later, apparently for failure to pay a gambling debt. His first biographer, Donald Henderson Clark, had known him personally, just as Fitzgerald had. Rothstein, wrote Clark, "went into gambling seriously by opening a small basement place in West Forty-fifth Street," only two or three blocks from the cellar where Nick meets Wolfsheim and the poolroom where Gatsby had met him earlier. "The Rothstein eyes were features above all others that those who met him recalled most faithfully," wrote Clark, "restless eyes glowing in the pale but very expressive face". But another striking feature was his teeth: "Until about fifteen years ago Rothstein was not noted, as he was later, for his beautiful, white, even teeth. In later years, somewhere about the time of the murder of Herman Rosenthal and the conviction and execution of the four gunmen and Lieut. Charlie Becker [all cited in *Gatsby*], Rothstein parted from his own teeth, and replaced them with a set that made many professional beauties—Rothstein preferred blondes for scenery—extremely jealous."[49] What magic it was for Fitzgerald to transform Rothstein's celebrated teeth into Wolfsheim's cuff-buttons as "finest specimens of human molars" (73)!

Wolfsheim moves in a setting that never seems entirely infernal. In imagery at least, the true inferno of the novel is the dim, gray valley of ashes whose inhabitants can never escape. In manuscript Fitzgerald said the valley of ashes "could have passed for the back alleyway of Hell," a description he cut later than "Calvary Cemetary" and presumably for

---

48. A. E. Le Vot, "*Our Mutual Friend* and *GG*," *Fitzgerald Newsletter*, No. 20 (Winter, 1963), unpaginated; Robert E. Long, "*Vanity Fair* and the Guest List in *GG*," *Fitzgerald Newsletter*, No. 38 (Summer, 1967), unpaginated.
49. Donald Henderson Clark, *In the Reign of Rothstein* (New York, 1929), 19.

the same reason of too much explicitness.[50] West Egg begins as Eden and ends as fallen earth. Its primary colors like yellow are from the broken, many-colored light of the prism or rainbow, which to Shelley and other Neoplatonists signified the merely created universe—the "dome of many-coloured glass" that "stains the white radiance of eternity" in *Adonais*. East Egg is the white radiance itself—the ironic heaven of the novel. Downtown New York, the haunt of Wolfsheim, is utterly chameleonlike, taking on the coloration of whatever character enters it. It is the purgatory of the piece—a place of "stifling" heat (126) and confrontation from which, however, escape is still possible.[51]

Although Dante, Milton, and Goethe are the great shapers of this traditional universe, Edith Wharton's Pulitzer Prize–winning novel of 1920, *The Age of Innocence,* had consistently figured the New World as heaven, particularly the rose-and-white "society" of New York City, and the Old World that Ellen Olenska has just escaped as "that hell"—a distinction that proves as ironic as those in *Gatsby*. The worst of the fallen angels in this ironic heaven, Beaufort, is a clear model for Tom Buchanan: his "purchase of a new string of race-horses" parallels Tom's coming east "in a fashion that rather took your breath away; for instance, he'd brought down a string of polo ponies from Lake Forest" (6). The "pearl necklace which he had presented to his wife upon his return was as magnificent as such expiatory offerings are apt to be" and recalls both Tom's wedding gift of "a string of pearls valued at three hundred and fifty thousand dollars" (70) and the "pearl necklace—or perhaps only a pair of cuff buttons" (181) that Nick imagines Tom is about to buy when he sees him for the last time. The Gatsby-like "innocence" of Wharton's title describes the love between Ellen and Newland Archer, who marries conventionally and later, an aging widower, keeps an innocent-to-the-end twilight vigil outside his old love's rooms in Versailles.[52]

The four settings of *Gatsby* are also figured, like the first four sections of *The Waste Land*, in the elements of earth, air, fire, and water—a bit of

---

50. Fitzgerald, *The Great Gatsby: A Facsimile*, 72.
51. The case for this cosmos of light and color is made more fully in A. E. Elmore, "Color and Cosmos in *The Great Gatsby*," *Sewanee Review*, LXXVIII (1970), 427–43.
52. Edith Wharton, *The Age of Innocence* (New York, 1920), 18, 32, 73, 78, 133, 217, 161, 209.

magic Faulkner also took from Eliot for his four parts of *The Sound and the Fury*. West Egg, like Eden with its river forming the headwaters of the four great rivers of the world, is a land of water. East Egg is all air and floating. The valley of ashes is made of the element of earth—ashes to ashes, dust to dust. The city is fire and heat. The abundance and consistency of the imagery and the changes that advance it in manuscript and galley proof argue that all of this was entirely conscious, at least after a certain point in the writing.

Like Goethe's, Fitzgerald's Christianity is merely cultural. Their true faith is Romantic. This is a shorthand term that simplifies and often distorts an enormous richness of thought and feeling that survives our current impulses to put it behind us like an embarrassing adolescence. Romanticism is probably no more dead or confined to one age than any other major expression of the human spirit. Fitzgerald, at any rate, knew no greater gods than Keats and Shelley. Nick Carraway's assertion that Gatsby turned out all right at the end is a Romantic epitaph. The hero is dead. He will not rise again in a conventional heaven. Yet he turns out all right at the end because, like Prometheus and Faust and all other great Romantic heroes, he is faithful to his vision to the end, never saying, "Hold! Enough!" This Romantic notion took on new meanings or at least new metaphors in a controversial book of this period by Oswald Spengler.

Fitzgerald himself pointed to the possible influence of Spengler on *Gatsby* when he wrote Perkins in 1940, "I read him the same summer I was writing 'The Great Gatsby' and I don't think I ever quite recovered from him."[53] But when R. W. Stallman took Fitzgerald at his word and argued for Spengler's influence on the novel, Robert Sklar said this was "ludicrous" and "could not have been." Stallman had "not checked Fitzgerald's memory against the fact that the first volume of *The Decline of the West* was not published in English until 1926, and that Fitzgerald was not a reader of German." The idiot savant returns, not to be trusted even to remember the most memorable summer of his life! But since an absolute negative like Sklar's requires for its proof nothing less than omniscience by the asserter within the category of the thing asserted—that is, Sklar must be able to identify and rule out *every* possible means by which Fitzgerald's statement could have been true—

---

53. Kuehl and Bryer (eds.), *Dear Scott/Dear Max*, 263.

it is he who is not to be trusted. Sklar himself acknowledged that Kenneth Burke had published a partial translation of *The Decline of the West* in the *Dial*, beginning in November, 1924, but Sklar dismissed it as "too late for *The Great Gatsby*."[54] Since Sklar's pronouncement in 1967, sources accessible to Fitzgerald at the time in question (1924) have been specifically identified. Barry Gross identified the first.

> That year's July number of the *Yale Review* contains an article by Henry de Man entitled "Germany's New Prophets"—an article which outlines Spengler's basic theories in detail, and *Yale Review* is precisely the type of magazine Fitzgerald would have read to keep abreast of current literary developments. It is perhaps significant that Fitzgerald, who was then living in Italy [France—Italy later in the year], asked Maxwell Perkins for a copy of Havelock Ellis's *The Dance of Life* [in a letter of August 25, 1924], a book reviewed in this same issue of the *Yale Review*. This fact, together with Fitzgerald's later claiming to have read Spengler at exactly the time the article appeared makes it probable that the article was his source of information. Did Fitzgerald deliberately give his novel Spenglerian overtones on the strength of an eighteen-page article? Those familiar with the brashness and literary pretentiousness of Fitzgerald's early work will find it conceivable that he did.[55]

Except for the silly editorial at the end, which treats Fitzgerald as if he had written a dissertation rather than a novel, this is thoroughly persuasive scholarship. In its support is the fact that Fitzgerald's description of West Egg as "a night scene by El Greco" (178), which was added between the holograph manuscript and the typescript he mailed to Perkins in November, appears directly indebted to de Man's article. Spengler refers to El Greco by name only for bringing "the grand art of cloud-symbolism to Spain," but in paraphrasing certain of Spengler's observations about Faustian cultural history, de Man seems to give El Greco a pivotal position by placing him at the end of a representative list: "Plastic art could no longer express the Occidental 'Kulturseele' after it had reached a certain stage, about the eighteenth century; then instrumental music became 'the' Occidental art, because its technique alone could carry the yearning for the infinite ... beyond the point which had been reached by Rembrandt, Giorgone, and El Greco."[56]

54. Robert Sklar, *F. Scott Fitzgerald: The Last Laocoön* (New York, 1967), 135, 356.
55. Barry Gross, "F. Scott Fitzgerald's 'The Great Gatsby' and Oswald Spengler's 'The Decline of the West,'" *Notes and Queries* (December, 1967), 467.
56. Fitzgerald, *The Great Gatsby: A Facsimile*, xxx; Oswald Spengler, *The Decline of the West*, trans. Charles Francis Atkinson (2 vols.; New York, 1926–28), I, 240; Henry de Man, "Germany's New Prophets," *Yale Review*, XIII (July, 1924), 679–80.

In his biography of Fitzgerald, Bruccoli cites another summary dating from 1924, written by W. K. Stewart. It appeared in the September issue of *Century* magazine. Like de Man's, Stewart's summary noted Spengler's account of the three most recent ages of the Western world—Apollinian, Magian, and Faustian—which is the heart of Spengler's theory and which Fitzgerald seems so clearly to echo in his *Gatsby* settings. Bruccoli also repeats Sklar's observation that the *Dial* published three installments of a translation by Kenneth Burke between November, 1924 and June, 1925, "after Fitzgerald had completed *The Great Gatsby.*" Bruccoli agrees with Sklar that "Fitzgerald could not have read *The Decline of the West* at this time [the summer of 1924] because it was not translated into English until 1926 and he did not read German." No one has done as much as Bruccoli to advance what we know of Fitzgerald's life and work, but here he overlooks three critical facts: 1) the July *Yale Review* article discovered by Gross, which was almost certainly the single most important source for Fitzgerald's early knowledge of Spengler; 2) the fact that during the very summer of 1924 Fitzgerald entertained as his guest on the Riviera the editor of the *Dial*, Gilbert Seldes, who surely would have known all about a translation his magazine had already accepted for publication—knowledge that could only have enriched the context in which Fitzgerald read de Man's *Yale Review* article; and 3) Bruccoli's own observations in the *Facsimile* that Fitzgerald did not send the first completed manuscript to Perkins until November, that in addition to major changes in galley, he was still wiring spot changes up to the very moment of publication on April 10, 1925, and that some of the most memorable passages and details appeared for the first time *after* the summer of 1924.[57]

Nor should it be forgotten that Spengler's ideas were very much in the intellectual winds blowing out of Europe after the publication of his first volume in Germany in 1918 and that Fitzgerald knew some of the best wind catchers in the world in Dean Christian Gauss of Princeton, Edmund Wilson, John Peale Bishop, Mencken, and Seldes. Nor were Spengler's ideas all new money. Yeats was already writing about thousand-year cycles of history before the publication of his *Vision* in 1925.

---

57. Bruccoli, *Epic Grandeur*, 207n; Kuehl and Bryer (eds.), *Dear Scott/Dear Max*, 76.

The impending doom of the modern Western world had been prophesied if not proven by Marx. The notion that human beings repeat ancient patterns of behavior in new forms that may disguise their true meaning and lineage was fundamental in Freud and Frazer. Certainly Spengler was not the first to see Faust as the great symbol of modern man, and his view of the ancient world was essentially, as he himself said, from his great hero Nietzsche, whom Fitzgerald had read and admired long before he discovered Spengler.

Spengler divided the last three thousand years of history into three equal units. Borrowing from Nietzsche, Spengler called the thousand-year age before Christ "Apollinian"—after the sun god Apollo. This age was characterized by the light of reason and order. Its appropriate art form was the statue, its "prime symbol," the body. The millennium after Christ formed the "Magian" age, when culture centered in Alexandria. During this age the systematic reasoning of the Greeks and Romans yielded to a faith in the power of magical religion, though Spengler regarded Magian culture as bolder than the Apollinian, which was "that of the small, the easy, the simple." The prime symbol of the Magian age is the "way": "For the Egyptian, the pyramid over the king's tomb is a *triangle*, a huge, powerfully expressive *plane* that, whatever be the direction from which one approaches, closes off the 'way' and commands the landscape." This "two-dimensional" world of vertical and horizontal, full of right angles, united for a thousand years the various religions, which expressed in their basilicas a shared "*Cavern*-feeling." "The light shines through the cavern and battles against the darkness." Succeeding the Magian age was the Faustian, from A.D. 1000 until its projected doom around the year 2000. Its prime symbol is "endless space." "The Faustian soul looks for an immortality to follow the bodily end, a sort of marriage with endless space." Its "time" is deep night: "On Olympus rests the eternal light of the transparent southern day, and Apollo's hour is high noon, when great Pan sleeps. But Valhalla is light-less, and even in the Eddas we can trace that deep midnight of Faust's study-broodings, the midnight that is caught by Rembrandt's etchings and absorbs Beethoven's tone colours." De Man accurately paraphrased Spengler's observation that "Faustian music becomes dominant among the Faustian arts." Modern man is supremely restless, "ever roaming in the infinite," and "infinite solitude is felt as the home of the Faustian soul." America, home of the restless and solitary, is but a late and hasty blossom of the dying Faustian age.[58]

The ease and precision with which this fits *Gatsby* argues for Fitzgerald's knowledge of Spengler, in whatsoever form he gained it. The world of East Egg is figured in white, which is to say the unbroken, unrefracted light of Apollo, the sun. Daisy, who "dressed in white, and had a little white roadster" (75) during her "white girlhood" (20) in Louisville, has a name that literally means, as Crim and Houston have noted, "day's eye"—the sun (115). What Nick records on his visit to her East Egg estate is its elegant, restrained architecture and the tableaux formed by its athletic, graceful bodies. Both of Nick's visits to East Egg begin in sunlight and emphasize it, especially in revision. "I always watch for the longest day in the year," says Daisy, "and then miss it" (12). Like Sunday and the noon of every day, the longest day of the year—the summer solstice around June 21—would have been sacred to Apollo.

The valley of ashes is not merely cavelike and dark but also disquietingly magical or supernatural. "The world of Magian mankind is filled with a fairy-tale feeling" writes Spengler. "Devils and evil spirits threaten man; angels and fairies protect him. . . . And over all this is poured the quivering cavern-light that the spectral darkness ever threatens to swallow up."[59] Fitzgerald's valley, "bounded on one side by a small foul river" (23–24) and on another by the motor road, is a "fantastic farm" where railroad cars on an "invisible track" give out a "ghastly creak" (23) before "the ash-gray men swarm up with leaden spades and stir up an impenetrable cloud" (23). A "dust-covered wreck of a Ford crouched in a dim corner" (25). Nick sees Myrtle Wilson "walking through her husband as if he were a ghost" (25). "That locality was always vaguely disquieting, even in the broad glare of afternoon" (124). The narrow, two-dimensional "way" is perfectly reflected in Nick's description of "walking along the road under Doctor Eckleburg's persistent stare" (24): "The only building in sight was a small block of yellow brick sitting on the edge of the waste land, a sort of compact Main Street ministering to it, and contiguous to absolutely nothing" (24).

---

58. Spengler, *Decline of the West*, I, 188, 204, 189, 209, II, 233, I, 189, 289, 187, 231, 198, 186.
59. *Ibid.*, II, 237.

"The Egyptian soul saw itself as moving down a narrow and inexorably-prescribed life-path," Spengler writes, "to come at the end before the judges of the dead."[60]

"I took her to the window"—with an effort he [Wilson] got up and walked to the rear window and leaned with his face pressed against it—and I said 'God knows what you've been doing, everything you've been doing. You may fool me, but you can't fool God!'"
Standing behind him, Michaelis saw with a shock that he was looking at the eyes of Doctor T. J. Eckleburg, which had just emerged, pale and enormous, from the dissolving night. (160)

Nick first sees Gatsby under "the silver pepper of the stars," out "to determine what share was his of our local heavens" (21), especially the local heaven in which Daisy's dock light is the brightest star. Again and again Gatsby and his West Egg world appear under moon and stars, even at the end in the "night scene by El Greco" (178) and Nick's night vision of the Dutch sailors (182). Gatsby's world is filled with "Faustian" music, whereas there is no mention of even a song in the valley of ashes or on lovely, silent East Egg. For all his superficial restraints, including the Oxford affectations, Gatsby's essential quality is his "resourcefulness of movement": "This quality was continually breaking through his punctilious manner in the shape of restlessness" (64). Like so many other critical descriptions, this one was not added until galley corrections.[61] Spengler said that every age has a spring, summer, and fall, which he called culture, and a winter, which he called civilization. The peak of our own age was the Renaissance, when Faustian man found perfect outlets for his restlessness and yearning, including the New World. Nick's backward look at the end of the novel is especially poignant because it focuses on the last time in Faustian history when life was fully equal to man's "capacity for wonder" (182). By the end of the eighteenth century—in other words, the time of Goethe's *Faust*—our age was sinking into its winter of mere civilization. If there is a consolation, it is that history abhors the straight line and loves the circle. Out of the holocaust of the last Faust's death, a new world will be reborn like the phoenix. We are "borne back ceaselessly into the past" (182), for the

---

60. *Ibid.*, I, 188.
61. Fitzgerald, *The Great Gatsby: A Facsimile*, 268.

present recapitulates the past, only in new forms, as the future will recapitulate the present.

Fitzgerald's very style is Faustian, in Spengler's own terms:

> There is a word, "Impressionism," which only came into general use in Manet's time (and then, originally, as a word of contempt like Baroque and Rococo) but very happily summarizes the special quality of the Faustian way of art. . . . Be the artist painter or musician, his art consists in creating with a few strokes or spots or tones an image of inexhaustible content, a microcosm meet for the eyes or ears of Faustian man. . . . Matter quivers and flows like a solution under the mysterious pressure of brush-stroke and broken colours and lights. . . . When German music was at its culmination, this art penetrated also into lyric poetry . . . and gave rise to a whole series of tiny masterpieces, from Goethe's "Urfaust" to Holderlin's last poems—passages of a few lines apiece, which have never yet been noticed, let alone collected, but include nevertheless whole worlds of experience and feeling.[62]

As Fitzgerald was planning the novel that was to become *The Great Gatsby*, he told Perkins, "I want to write something *new*—something extraordinary and beautiful and simple and intricately patterned."[63] We have only begun to see how consciously and with what craft Fitzgerald wrought the urn by which he will be remembered long after our age has taken whatever place awaits it in the cycles of time.

62. Spengler, *Decline of the West*, I, 285–86.
63. Mizener, *The Far Side of Paradise*, 184.

JOSEPH K. DAVIS

The Triumph of Secularism: Theodore Dreiser's *An American Tragedy*

In 1900, in his first novel, *Sister Carrie,* Theodore Dreiser shows the impact of the modern city upon the lives of his major characters. Twenty-five years later, in *An American Tragedy,* he broadens his theme to comprehend the influence upon individuals of all aspects of American civilization. *An American Tragedy* is emphatically Dreiser's critique of civilization in the United States.[1] Underscored in this critique is how contemporary American civilization distorts values, twists the patterns of individual growth, and nurtures in the unsuspecting person an excessive desire for things and pleasures. Dreiser's true interests in this 1925 novel, consequently, are less in the personal traits and actions of his two victims, Clyde Griffiths and Roberta Alden, than in their

---

1. The notable critics of Dreiser's fiction agree on this point. See, for example, the treatments of the novel by the following authors: Dorothy Dudley, *Forgotten Frontiers: Dreiser and the Land of the Free* (New York, 1932); Robert H. Elias, *Theodore Dreiser: Apostle of Nature* (New York, 1949); Philip L. Gerber, *Theodore Dreiser* (New York, 1965); Richard Lehan, *Theodore Dreiser: His World and His Novels* (Carbondale, 1969); Francis O. Matthiessen, *Theodore Dreiser* (New York, 1951); John J. McAleer, *Theodore Dreiser* (New York, 1968); Ellen Moers, *Two Dreisers: The Man and the Novelist as Revealed in His Two Most Important Works* (New York, 1966); Donald Pizer, *The Novels of Theodore Dreiser* (Minneapolis, 1976); W. A. Swanberg, *Dreiser* (New York, 1965); Charles Shapiro, *Theodore Dreiser: Our Bitter Patriot* (Carbondale, 1962); Robert Penn Warren, *Homage to Theodore Dreiser on the Centennial of His Birth* (New York, 1971); Karl Heinz Wirzberger, *Die Romane Theodore Dreisers* (Berlin, 1955).

typicality and helplessness before the powerful forces of American society, chief among which is its thorough secularization.[2]

That the outcome of the narrative is genuinely tragic for Roberta Alden and Clyde Griffiths may be debated; that, for Dreiser, American civilization had come to tragedy is absolutely certain. In particular, Dreiser wants his characters to bear witness to the complex of ugly, destructive forces that he himself had come to identify with modern America, specifically those forces generated by religious fundamentalism and the pursuit of money and pleasure. By 1925 Dreiser's own thinking had moved from a narrow focus on the individual in confrontation with a limited urban environment to a larger view of the network of influences and interactions between any typical individual and American civilization. The outcome of Dreiser's changing concerns is *An American Tragedy*, a major work that marks the culmination of his career as a novelist.

The line of development in Dreiser's fiction from 1900 until 1925 has critical impact upon his effort in *An American Tragedy*. In *Sister Carrie*, *Jennie Gerhardt*, and *The "Genius,"* Dreiser stresses the impact of the new commercial-industrial order upon the lives of his characters. He wishes to show, in particular, how typical people meet the difficulties and the challenges of their environment, specifically the modern secular city. In these initial novels Dreiser's characters exemplify his own experiences and views: they attest to the author's personal conviction that the individual is so situated in this world that he must constantly struggle for existence, even if his efforts are finally unsuccessful and tragic in outcome. The pivotal characteristic of this general theme is the implied quest for some unifying principle of life, even some transcendental force, that suggests a pattern and a meaning inherent in the scheme of things. Thus, the characters evidence a desire to move beyond the secular values of their culture because those values are unable to provide them with such a sense of life's meaning.

Dreiser's personal fascination with the plight of the modern individual led him, between 1911 and 1915, to write two novels toward what

---

2. The use throughout of *secular* and *secularization* follows the American theologian Harvey Cox. *Secular* (from the Latin *saeculum*) denotes "this present age," that which is entirely contemporary. *Secularization* denotes, in Cox's words, "the liberation of man from religious and metaphysical tutelage, the turning of his attention away from other worlds and toward this one." See Harvey Cox, *The Secular City* (Rev. ed.; New York, 1966), 1, 15.

he then projected as "A Trilogy of Desire." His central character, Francis Cowperwood, is the ultimate individualist, a tycoon of finance. Yet in working with the materials of the Cowperwood story, Dreiser came to see that a ruthless individualism not only violates the interests of the vast majority but also is inconsistent with what he himself then acknowledged as nature's system of harmony and balance. Dreiser still believed that strength and brute force were ever present in the affairs of men, yet he had come to recognize that Darwin's "survival of the fittest" and the so-called Nietzschean "will to power" express only secondary, not primary, laws of nature. At the end of *The Titan* (1914), Dreiser argues that rapacious, aggressive individualism constitutes an inadequate explanation of human existence, that "even giants are but pygmies" when one surveys life fully and completely.

In the decade between 1915 and 1925, Dreiser turned to exploring the American scene. He came to feel very strongly about what he regarded as the materialistic bias of the urban-industrial civilization then rapidly coming to dominate the United States. Through various public activities, he came to know and to admire such men as Max Eastman and John Reed, with whom he joined forces in denouncing privileged individuals, commercial-industrial trusts, and all similar instances of exploitation of the masses.[3] He also developed a keen interest in the work of Dr. Abraham Brill, prominent psychiatrist and the American translator of Sigmund Freud. Finally, and more significantly for the development of his personal views, Dreiser became attracted to the ideas of Jacques Loeb, whose mechanistic interpretation of human motivation and behavior influenced his thinking.[4] Yet above all, Dreiser determined that the promises of America, the ideals of personal freedom and universal equality, were largely illusions. In his view there was no genuine freedom, real equality, or sustained public morality. Dreiser increasingly professed to see around him outrageous instances of injustice, sham, and hypocrisy, with the average individual everywhere controlled and manipulated by the privileged few. Money was king, Dreiser concluded, and actual conditions for the average citizen were much worse than even he himself had heretofore imagined. In particu-

---

3. See Swanberg, *Dreiser*, 180–233.
4. See Moers, *Two Dreisers*, 240–70, and Pizer, *The Novels of Theodore Dreiser*, 206, 212–13.

lar, he believed that the possibilities for the healthy development of individuals were far less capable of realization than anyone might think. Thus, in his own investigations of the role society plays in the life of every individual, Dreiser arrived at several rather grim conclusions about American civilization.[5]

His principal conviction at this time was that a society devoted to manufacturing and trade runs contrary to the true needs of its citizens. In the volume of travel and reminiscences, *A Hoosier Holiday* (1916), Dreiser makes his position clear:

> This matter of manufacture and enormous industries is always a fascinating thing to me, and careening along this lake shore [Lake Erie] at breakneck speed, I could not help but marveling at it. It seems to point so clearly to a lordship in life, a hierarchy of powers, against which the common man is always struggling, but which he never quite overcomes, anywhere. The world is always palavering about the brotherhood of man and the freedom and independence of the individual; yet when you go through a city like Buffalo or Cleveland and see all its energy practically devoted to great factories and corporations and their interests, and when you see the common man, of whom there is so much talk as to his interests and superiority, living in cottages or long streets of flats without a vestige of charm or beauty, his labor fixed in price and his ideas circumscribed in part (else he would never be content with so meager and grimy a world), you can scarcely believe in the equality or even the brotherhood of man, however much you may believe in the sympathy or good intentions of some people.[6]

Then, in 1920, Dreiser published *Hey Rub-A-Dub-Dub*, a collection of essays and sketches growing directly out of his investigations of life in the United States. The basic tenet underlying these pieces is that American civilization has fallen hopelessly into an all-consuming drive for money: "Here in America, by reason of an idealistic Constitution which is largely a work of art and not a workable system, you see a nation dedicated to so-called intellectual and spiritual freedom, but actually devoted with an almost bee-like industry to the gathering and storing and articulation and organization and use of purely material things."[7]

---

5. Dreiser's conclusions about American civilization are really part of that larger, better-known disenchantment with Western civilization widely in evidence following World War I and perhaps typified by the volume edited by Harold Stearns and others, *Civilization in the United States* (New York, 1922).
6. Theodore Dreiser, *A Hoosier Holiday* (New York, 1916), 180.
7. Theodore Dreiser, *Hey Rub-A-Dub-Dub: A Book of the Mystery and Wonder and Terror of Life* (New York, 1920), 258.

Comparing American society with that of the trading Carthaginians and Phoenicians, Dreiser argues that the entire structure of a commercial-industrial civilization is designed for the privileged few at the expense of the mass of its citizens.

In a final, summary essay in *Hey Rub-A-Dub-Dub*, "Life, Art and America," Dreiser characteristically attempts to use his own life as an illustration of what he believes American society does to the average youth. He stresses that the typical individual in America emerges from a naive, optimistic youth to become at maturity quite disillusioned and anxious to imitate secular standards. For Dreiser the fundamental reality of life in the United States is best described in terms of its threatening, even its destructive, manipulation of the unsuspecting average citizen: "The darkest side of democracy, like that of autocracy, is that it permits the magnetic and the cunning and the unscrupulous among the powerful individuals to sway the vast masses of the mob, not so much to their own immediate destruction as to the curtailment of their natural privileges and the ideas which they should be allowed to entertain if they could think at all."[8] Such pointed descriptions of the powers of the urban-industrial order foreshadow the unequal contest between the contemporary American secular city and Dreiser's next fictional character, Clyde Griffiths.

By 1922 Dreiser's views about America were sufficiently clarified for him to begin work in earnest on a novel he had planned for some years. The shape of this projected work was determined by his growing conviction that the average citizen is by and large controlled by his social environment, and Dreiser wanted to construct a story that would set forth precisely how American life in all its various, diverse ways conditions and manipulates its typical members. Especially did he intend to show that the pursuit of money and a narrowly moralistic point of view—both so characteristic to him of the deepest patterns of American life and its essential secularism—are instrumental in destroying the person to whom democracy traditionally guarantees equality and justice. He chose as his principal subject an average individual of poor background and inferior opportunities. Such a person, Dreiser felt, is particularly susceptible to the compulsive forces of modern, urban-industrial society. In an interview in 1921 Dreiser declares his support of

---

8. *Ibid.*, 257.

such an individual: "I never can and never want to bring myself to the place where I can ignore the sensitive and seeking individual in his pitiful struggle with nature—with his enormous urges and his pathetic equipment."[9]

With that struggle as theme, Dreiser determined also that his fictional narrative would be taken from real life and that it would involve a crime of passion and violence. The nucleus of his novel, he believed, should be an actual story and, preferably, one that was well documented and something of a public drama. Yet the conscious purpose behind this plan was not simply his wish to construct a social diatribe but his deep conviction that crimes of passion and violence are perfectly in keeping with the inner contradictions of American society. Since his newspaper days Dreiser had been keenly interested in the sensational crimes frequently publicized in the press. He often, in fact, clipped out these stories and filed them away. To Dreiser these crimes were basically the same in their general pattern: behind each one were the forces of social pressures—in particular, social aspirations—and the deep yearning for wealth and power.[10]

When he turned to write what eventually became *An American Tragedy*, however, Dreiser had uppermost in his mind not simply the reconstruction of an actual crime but a fictionalized study of the underlying bases for the crime. As in his "Trilogy of Desire," he was intent upon the investigation of circumstances, of social environments, and above all else of character—not upon the presentation of facts of the construction of a true-to-life plot. Throughout this work, Dreiser intended to emphasize how his characters are victims of a social system that by bitter paradox creates them and yet denies them full access to its promises and benefits. Indeed, Dreiser's conceptualization and artistic rendition of characters as victims are similar to what such writers as Dostoevsky, Kafka, and Camus achieve in certain of their novels—namely, the por-

---

9. Dudley, *Forgotten Frontiers*, 407.
10. Dreiser's interest in crimes of violence and passion may be seen in a play he wrote in 1916, *The Hand of the Potter*, the theme and central character of which foreshadow Clyde Griffiths and his story. Isadore Berchansky, son of poor, ignorant New York immigrants, is a sickly youth with a perverted desire for young girls. After sexually attacking an eleven-year-old girl, he is tracked down, tried, and convicted. Dreiser's play argues, however, that Berchansky is not a criminal, but merely a very sick individual, and that society itself is to blame for his condition because of the awful urban slums that create him and the cruel laws that arrogate his punishment.

trayal of an innocent who is thoroughly defined, if not in effect created, by his intimate relationship with an assailant. In Dreiser's mind, the "assailant" is clearly the secularized civilization of modern America.

After examining many actual crimes, Dreiser settled upon the case of Chester Gillette, a young man who had drowned his sweetheart Grace Brown in Big Moose Lake, in the state of New York, in July, 1906. This particular case seemed perfect for Dreiser's artistic purposes. First, in even the obvious facts of the case the enormous tensions of love and social pressures were clearly evident, and these tensions were exactly the subjective and the objective ingredients Dreiser knew and understood best. Second, the crime had been an international public sensation because the defendant seemingly had no guilty feelings and displayed only cold indifference throughout the lengthy legal proceedings of 1906–1908. A final bonus for Dreiser lay in the fact that fully documented records of the crime and the trial were available in numerous public sources.

Yet the narrative that Dreiser at last produced differs in major ways from the actual Gillette-Brown case. Dreiser well understood that his work was an artistic rendition, not a factual reporting; he constructed an entire first section of the novel largely out of his imagination, giving here a thorough treatment of his hero's family background and early years. Like Dreiser's own, Clyde's formative years are highlighted by narrow religious pietism and conditions of abject poverty. Similarly, Dreiser so alters the drowning of his fictional Grace Brown that legal, perhaps even moral, guilt is almost impossible to prove. The criminal lawyer Clarence Darrow concluded after reading the novel that Clyde Griffiths could never have been convicted in real life on the basis of the evidence given.[11] Finally, Dreiser ends his narrative by means of a short epilogue in which he constructs for the reader a parallel to the opening scenes in Kansas City and the mission work of the Griffiths family. Now in San Francisco, with Esta's natural son Russell in the place of Clyde, the Griffiths are continuing their shabby street singing and preaching. The brief scene projects Dreiser's story into the future, both visually and morally, suggesting that as long as conditions such as those depicted in the novel are allowed to exist, there will be other Clydes and Robertas.

Dreiser completed *An American Tragedy* on November 25, 1925, in

---

11. Elias, *Theodore Dreiser*, 222.

time for publication late in December of the same year. Within a year of publication, the novel became a best seller. Book royalties were higher than on any previous Dreiser work. When the motion picture rights were sold, together with various schemes for editions and reprintings, Dreiser found himself financially comfortable for the first time since his days with the Butterick publications twenty years earlier.

An American Tragedy is not, of course, a tragedy in the classical sense of the term. Certainly the narrative does not purport to show the acts of a great man or his fall from a high place.[12] Dreiser originally planned to call his novel *Mirage,* a title suggesting that reality is not all that it appears to be and that life itself is finally impossible to comprehend. The word *American* and the term *tragedy* were later accepted for the particular meanings conveyed: *American* because it defines the action as particularly connected with the culture of the United States, and *tragedy* because it reveals, at least in Dreiser's mind, the far-reaching, cruel nature of the events and acts he wanted to present.

As a work of fiction, however, the story does have a center, and that center is Clyde Griffiths, who carries the burden of Dreiser's message. Dreiser divides his narrative into three books, each of which concentrates on a particular aspect of Clyde's story. Book One treats Clyde's background and early years; Book Two, his activities in Lycurgus, New York, terminating with his participation in the drowning of Roberta Alden; and Book Three, his trial and execution. If the reader occasionally loses sight of Clyde in the mass of details, analyses, and incidental descriptions, Dreiser never allows the narrative itself to deviate long from its theme: the conflict between Clyde and the social and moral forces by which he eventually is destroyed. All elements of the novel are clustered around this conflict. Noticeably absent from the narrative are Dreiser's characteristic authorial interpolations and digressive comments. He was determined that this piece, above all his other novels, would tell its own story.

In Book One, Dreiser establishes in full, clear dimensions the background and the early years of his protagonist, a history much like Drei-

---

12. From 1926 until the present, critics have debated Dreiser's use of the term *tragedy.* Good discussions may be found in Matthiessen, *Theodore Dreiser,* 207–209; Warren, *Homage to Theodore Dreiser,* 131–32; and Pizer, *The Novels of Theodore Dreiser,* 280–81.

ser's own. Certainly many of the circumstances of Clyde's early years were all too familiar to Dreiser.[13] Two of these common circumstances shape Clyde's childhood and pervert his natural development: the narrow religious pietism of his parents and the poverty their urban evangelism forces upon them. The opening chapters of *An American Tragedy*, in fact, depict with stark realism the shabby and degrading occupation of Asa Griffiths, characterized by Dreiser as "one of those poorly integrated and correlated organisms, the product of an environment and a religious theory, but with no guiding or mental insight of his own, yet sensitive and therefore highly emotional, and without any practical sense whatsoever."[14] Modeled on a man Dreiser had worked for in Chicago during the 1890s—and no doubt endowed with many of the traits Dreiser identified with his own father—Asa Griffiths operates the Bethel Independent Mission, a hopeless religious enterprise that offers "the Door of Hope" to countless men who are without food or shelter. His wife, who is portrayed with more sympathy by Dreiser, is devoted to her husband's evangelism. Both parents are ignorant, nearly illiterate, and engaged in a futile and unrealistic religious crusade. The effect of such religiosity upon their children is devastating, committing them to a grinding daily existence of poverty, ignorance, and social ostracism.

According to Dreiser, the religious doctrines advanced by Asa and his wife are divorced from reality and thus, especially when combined with the daily hardships the family must endure, have only an adverse influence upon the lives of their children. To the sensitive and observant Clyde, their twelve-year-old son, the religious creed of his parents is devoid of any viable or useful truth. So embittered is he against the conditions that his parents' religion brings upon them all, that when Hester, his sister, runs off with an actor "he could not see that her going was such a calamity, not from the *going* point of view, at any rate" (I, 23).

This religious pietism and accompanying narrow moralism of Clyde's parents, manifest in their every utterance and act, thwart and stunt the boy's development. Dreiser points out again and again how Clyde is alienated from his neighbors and even from youths his own age who live

---

13. See Elias, *Theodore Dreiser*, 222, and Warren, *Homage to Theodore Dreiser*, 102–12.
14. Theodore Dreiser, *An American Tragedy* (2 vols.; New York, 1926), I, 10. Subsequent references to the novel are to this edition and will appear in the text.

about him. Forced to participate in the daily singing and preaching conducted on the streets of Kansas City, Kansas, Clyde feels humiliated and dishonored before his peers. In great anger he thinks: "His life should not be like this. Other boys did not have to do as he did. He meditated now more determinedly than ever a rebellion by which he would rid himself of the need of going out in this way" (I, 8). Clyde thus rejects the parents as total failures whose religious zeal has forced him to live amid poverty and daily personal humiliations. He has, in his own eyes, been denied the companionship of other young people and the normal social pleasures enjoyed even by the poor. Clyde therefore comes to young manhood badly confused and disoriented, especially with regard to basic questions of right and wrong. Deeply insecure and all too aware of his own social inferiority, he rebels against his parents and their way of life. He sees how the majority live around him, and he wants to be like them. At one point he exclaims, "Oh, the fine clothes, the handsome homes, the watches, rings, pins that some boys sported; the dandies many youths of his years already were!" (I, 15). Clyde has learned at an early age to identify success and happiness in this world with the urban-secular way of life—in particular with exterior appearances and the power of money.

In young adulthood Clyde begins to interact with his urban environment, the world of Kansas City. Time and time again, in fact, Dreiser points out how Clyde's surroundings overpower and corrupt him. Sensitive to all that is around him in the city, Clyde recognizes that the conclusions he reached as a youth hold true, that a person's esteem and worth are associated with appearances—with clothes, houses, cars, women—and thus, in essence, with all that money can buy. The menial labor and inferior status of his first job in a drugstore only serve to intensify the bitterness that he feels toward his lot in this world. By chance, he gets a second job as bellboy in the city's most fashionable hotel, where he is daily brought into contact with the other side of life—a world of material opulence and fashion he scarcely dreamed existed. Dreiser emphasizes that this environment operates as a formative influence upon the youth: "And so, of all the influences which might have come to Clyde at this time, either as an aid or an injury to his development, perhaps the most dangerous for him, considering his temperament, was this same Green-Davidson [Hotel], than which no more ma-

The Triumph of Secularism

terially affected or gaudy a realm could have been found anywhere between the two great American mountain ranges" (I, 46).

Not only the luxury and splendor of the hotel but also the other bellboys greatly influence Clyde. Dreiser observes that Clyde "was now daily in contact with a type of youth who, because of his larger experience with the world and with the luxuries and vices of such a life as this, had already been inducted into certain forms of libertinism and vice even which up to this time were entirely foreign to Clyde's knowledge and set him agape with wonder and at first with even a timorous distaste" (I, 53). Quickly accepting the values of these young people, Clyde learns to drink, smoke, curse, steal, and run with slatternly women. "So starved had been Clyde's life up to this time," Dreiser writes, "and so eager was he for almost any form of pleasure, that from the first he listened with all too eager ears to any account of anything that spelled adventure or pleasure" (I, 53). At every turn Clyde finds occasions to curse his parents for depriving him of things that his companions have been given. He feels that he must now race throughout the remainder of his life in an attempt to make up for what his parents and early home environment have denied him.

Beautiful women play an important role in Clyde's newfound life. But when he is in the company of women, Clyde usually falters in his efforts to attract them. As he had in previous novels, Dreiser shows in *An American Tragedy* that a man's yearning for the feminine is a manifestation of his own deep insecurities and alienation. His evaluations of these women are usually faulty. When Clyde, for example, begins to pursue a girl named Hortense Briggs, Dreiser informs us that Clyde's so-called love for her is in reality only "conscious lust" (I, 101). In his infatuation he is blind to her vain, petty nature. He scrimps and saves to give her presents and to take her to places where she can impress other boys whom she wishes to attract, thus allowing her selfishly and viciously to manipulate him.

The outcome of this first romantic episode serves as the conclusion of Book One and foreshadows Clyde's role in the death of Roberta Alden in Book Two. Returning in an automobile from an excursion in the country, Clyde, Hortense, and four other young people hit a pedestrian. Since the car they are in has been secretly borrowed from the rich employer of the father of one of the boys, they cannot stop and accept their guilt.

Pursued by the police, the group are themselves the victims of an accident when their car overturns. Afraid of criminal charges and moralizing parents, Clyde runs away; thus he begins three years of wandering from job to job, after which he settles in Chicago. Dreiser emphasizes that Clyde's action is typical of his nature; he is simply unable to face any personal crisis. Blinded by fear, motivated by the instincts of a cornered animal, and prey to a malevolent environment, Clyde acts without thinking or even clarifying the nature of his dilemma.

Book One of *An American Tragedy* contains, then, not only the most important material for an understanding of Clyde Griffiths but also the most significant statements by Dreiser on his attitude toward his fictive hero. Yet critics often pass too lightly over specific criticisms Dreiser makes of Clyde. While revealing that Clyde is a victim of religious fundamentalism and an ugly environment, characterized by poverty and daily humiliations, Dreiser points out repeatedly that the youth is an especially *willing* victim. Early in the narrative Dreiser remarks that "Clyde was as vain and proud as he was poor" (I, 14). Because of good looks and a sensitive nature, he feels that he is better than most people. When he decides to get a job, for example, his parents suggest various honest types of labor, but he haughtily resents the implication that he is to resign himself to a life of menial employment. His expectations, which are based on personal dreams and not on actual possibilities, constitute for Dreiser the typical American illusion of "unlimited opportunities for all." Dreiser puts the matter this way: "For true to the standard of the American youth, or the general American attitude toward life, he felt himself above the type of labor which was purely manual" (I, 14). Dreiser also criticizes his hero for his contemptuous attitude toward his parents. Although scornful of Asa and his wife for their zealous pietism, Dreiser cannot accept Clyde's total rejection of his parents and his disavowal of all filial obligations. When Clyde spends forty dollars on whiskey and prostitutes, Dreiser offers the comment: "And his mother and sisters and brother at home with scarcely the means to make ends meet" (I, 66). Similarly, when Hester, now deserted by her lover, returns home to have her baby, Clyde must give money to help provide for her. Angered by this additional burden, he complains bitterly that this is "typical of all that seemed to occur in his family.... It made him a little sick and resentful" (I, 96). Dreiser never agrees with this attitude, and he shows that Clyde is partly to blame for his misfortunes.

Later in Book One, Dreiser points out that Clyde has no basis for his pretensions and inflated ambitions. Ill prepared for life, without training or education, Clyde possesses badly distorted tastes and values: his "ideas of luxury were in the main . . . extreme and mistaken and gauche—mere wanderings of a repressed and unsatisfied fancy, which as yet had had nothing but imaginings to feed it" (I, 33). At the beginning of Book Two, Dreiser comments: "For to say the truth, Clyde had a soul that was not destined to grow up. He lacked decidedly that mental clarity and inner directing application that in so many permits them to sort out from the facts and avenues of life the particular things that make for their direct advancement" (I, 174). Hence, Dreiser's portrait of Clyde contains a basic ambiguity—namely, presenting him as not only a helpless victim of his environment but also as a free individual who is partly to blame for his selfish and cowardly nature. Clyde's pathetic early years in Kansas City may have largely determined him, but he is nevertheless personally involved in his own nature—in particular, he is involved in his actions, and thus if he is not literally culpable for these actions, he is at least morally responsible for them and what they produce.

Book Two moves the story to Lycurgus, New York, which Dreiser presents as a microcosm of the social and psychological patterns of life in twentieth-century America. Although Dreiser depicts it as a small town, Lycurgus is thoroughly secular and urban.[15] In this second section Dreiser portrays Clyde as being hopelessly involved in the class struggle of the town and forced to contend against its ignorance, prejudice, snobbery, and class values. Again partly a victim of his environment, he is caught between two levels of existence—that of the workers and that of the socially and financially prominent. Dreiser reveals the loneliness, frustration, and demoralization that the opposition of these forces exerts on Clyde. The rigid class stratification in Lycurgus forces him to struggle to better himself in terms of the values and social codes accepted by the people of Lycurgus. Above and behind all standards in the town is the pervasive power of money; both as fact and as symbol,

---

15. Warren, *Homage to Theodore Dreiser*, 101.

money is the center of the culture of Lycurgus. It is Clyde's efforts to achieve success in terms of the values and codes of the town that lead to his destruction.

When Clyde Griffiths arrives in Lycurgus, he immediately sees that life is structured by visible symbols of status—homes, cars, parties, and the like. Brought to town by his rich uncle Samuel Griffiths, whom he accidentally has met in Chicago, Clyde is from the first an outsider. He has no place in any social group, and he cannot fit into the rigidly class-ordered life of the town. Because of his connections with the rich and powerful Griffiths, he is an object of suspicion and envy among the laboring class with whom he must live and work. Similarly, because of the reluctance of his rich benefactors to associate with him, he is denied entrance into the circle of the ruling elite of the town. In both groups he is an interloper, hopelessly caught between the two social forces.

Despite the fact that he is all but ignored by the Griffiths family, Clyde cannot bring himself to associate with his so-called inferiors: " 'What!' he exclaims to himself. 'Mix with people so far below him—a Griffiths—in the social scale here and at the cost of endangering his connections with that important family. Never! It was a great mistake' " (I, 218). Often he stands outside the Griffiths' mansion, to him "the symbol of that height to which by some turn of fate he might still hope to attain. For he had never quite been able to expel from his mind the thought that his future must in some way be identified with the grandeur that was here laid out before him" (I, 309). In the novel the house represents the security and social respectability for which Clyde so desperately yearns. With an impulse close to frenzy, he covets everything that wealth and position represent. Dreiser suggests that Clyde would eagerly sell his soul to the devil for a place in this opulent social order.

Yet such aspirations are never to be realized. Lonely and confused by his ambiguous position in the town, Clyde at last enters into an illicit relationship with Roberta Alden, a working girl in the department he supervises at the Griffiths factory. Recognizing all too well the immense dangers to which he is exposing himself by his union with Roberta, he nevertheless cannot resist, for as Dreiser comments: "His was a disposition easily and often intensely inflamed by the chemistry of sex and the formula of beauty. He could not easily withstand the appeal, let alone the call, of sex" (I, 244).

Dreiser characterizes Roberta Alden as not merely sweet and innocent but also clever and socially ambitious: "And so it was that Roberta, after encountering Clyde and sensing the superior world in which she imagined he moved, and being so taken with the charm of his personality, was seized with the very virus of ambition and unrest that afflicted him" (I, 256). Roberta is drawn to Clyde because she is possessed of the same hopes, because she dreams the same dreams of security and love, of position and happiness, that animate Clyde. Behind her willingness to give herself sexually to Clyde is the firm conviction that he will marry her, a hope that represents for her the pinnacle of happiness and worldly success.

When, however, Clyde is accidentally given a chance to impress the rich Sondra Finchley, he quickly loses interest in Roberta. Earlier at the Griffiths home, where he had first met Sondra, Clyde had identified her with all that he felt to be beautiful, feminine, and socially desirable. Dreiser points out that she is hardly an ideal, describing her, in fact, as "a seeking Aphrodite, eager to prove to any who are sufficiently attractive the destroying power of her charm" (I, 329). Her social status alone, however, is enough to recommend her to Clyde. Because he flatters her and expresses an idealized affection for her, Sondra permits Clyde to see her. Gradually there develops an unusually strong feeling between the two, and Clyde discovers that at last he has achieved his goal—admittance to the inner circle of Lycurgus society. In the initial stage of his relationship with Sondra, Clyde continues to see Roberta. But when he is eventually faced with a choice, his decision is obvious. Clyde's love can ultimately be focused only on an object that is a part of the society he desires. "For Clyde," explains Dreiser, "although he considered himself to be deeply in love with Roberta, was still not so deeply involved but that a naturally selfish and ambitious and seeking disposition would in this instance stand its ground and master any impulse" (I, 304).

Caught between the mounting demands of the now pregnant Roberta and the dazzling prospect of his hope to marry Sondra, Clyde loses the slight degree of self-possession he has heretofore shown. To him, complete success and great failure are separated only by a narrow margin; he must now take decisive action or all will be forever lost. Dreiser observes that "the mind of Clyde might well have been compared to a small and routed army in full flight before a major one" (II, 40). Thus, when he reads in a local newspaper how a young couple has been drowned in a nearby lake, Clyde sees that the death of Roberta is a possible answer to his dilemma. Dreiser emphasizes that the presence of such a thought in Clyde's mind is a great shock to the youth, and he tries constantly to clear his mind of all such dark schemes. He cannot do so, however, and his inner voice counsels him to action: "Paw—how cowardly—lacking in courage to win the thing that above all things you desire—beauty—wealth—position—the solution of your every material and spiritual desire. And with poverty, commonplace, hard and poor work as the alternative to all this" (II,51).

From this moment until Roberta Alden is drowned, Dreiser constructs his narrative so that Clyde never fully acknowledges to himself the murderous impulses in his heart. Dreiser cautions that "never once did he honestly, or to put it more accurately, forthrightly and courageously or coldly face the thought of committing so grim a crime" (II, 52). A final ominous warning from Roberta forces Clyde to act. He now resolves to murder Roberta. Taking her to a lake, he rents a boat and the two paddle to the middle of the lake. Even now. however, he cannot execute his plan. When she excitedly comes toward him, he carelessly pushes her, she stumbles, and the boat overturns. Despite her cries for help, Clyde swims to shore, leaving Roberta to drown. Even the most thoughtful reader may find in these circumstances cause to ponder just how guilty Clyde Griffiths finally is of the act of murder.[16]

Book Three presents an even more direct indictment of the society that has produced a Clyde. Here Dreiser stresses how petty politics, self-interest, and the moral laxness of the general system of government prevent a truthful inquiry into the guilt or innocence of Clyde. Fred Hiet, the county coroner, and Orville Mason, the district attorney, use the crime for their own political and economic advancement. A member of their coterie actually constructs false evidence in order to prove his own abilities as a detective. Jephson and Belknap, the attorneys hired by

---

16. Critics do not agree on the fact or the degree of Clyde's guilt or innocence. In *Theodore Dreiser*, for example, Lehan thinks that "Clyde is really innocent of murdering Roberta," since he strikes her unintentionally (168). In *Theodore Dreiser*, McAleer sees Clyde as not guilty legally of the specific crime of which he is convicted (144). Gerber, however, in *Theodore Dreiser*, points to "the idea of the distribution of guilt," which he feels Dreiser writes into the narrative (144–47). Warren, in *Homage to Theodore Dreiser*, first alluding to "shadowy complicities" in the world in which Clyde acts, stresses the theme of "ambiguity—of complicity and responsibility" as Dreiser's basic message, not the emphatic either-or literality of guilt or innocence (123–25).

Samuel Griffiths to defend Clyde, refuse to allow Clyde to tell the truth, since that truth would hardly win the case. Instead, they concoct a fictitious, highly sentimental yarn for Clyde to tell. At every stage of the complicated proceedings, histrionics, local and state politics, mass media, and the public mood are used and manipulated by both sides.

Against the immediate background of lies, distortions, and personal interests, Dreiser places the larger forces of the community and the nation itself. Merchants, politicians, clergymen, and newspapermen use the sensational aspects of the story for personal gain. While Clyde is being tried, magazine stories and pulp-book accounts of the case abound. The business world misses no chance to make money on the criminal proceedings. Even the opening day of the trial itself is depicted by Dreiser as a local event that conveyed "a sense of holiday or festival, with hundreds of farmers, woodmen, traders, entering [town] in Fords and Buicks—farmer wives and husbands—daughters and sons—even infants in arms" (II, 222). The whole affair smacks of travesty and circus. Outside the courtroom are the cries of the barkers: " 'Peanuts!' 'Hot dogs!' 'Get the story of Clyde Griffiths, with all the letters of Roberta Alden. Only twenty-five cents!' " (II, 222).

Blended with this materialism is an inflated, false sense by the community members of their own powers of judgment. Inside, the gentlemen of the jury gather to begin hearing testimony: "And with but one exception, all religious, if not moral, and all convinced of Clyde's guilt before ever they sat down, but still because of their almost unanimous conception of themselves as fair and open-minded men, and because they were so interested to sit as jurors in this exciting case, convinced that they could pass fairly and impartially on the facts presented to them" (II, 231). However, the public is incensed at the murder of a seemingly hapless, poor, and innocent girl. Despite their moral obligation to objectivity, the jurors simply must find Clyde guilty. When one juror refuses to vote against Clyde because he personally likes the defending attorneys, the others threaten him with commercial ruin.

Finally, Clyde is found guilty and sentenced to death in the electric chair. Clyde spends his final days in the state prison at Ossining, New York. He is absorbed by fumbling, pathetic attempts to discover the nature of his guilt and to seek the forgiveness of God. According to Dreiser, Clyde's mind has been too thoroughly confused by his past to be able at this point to achieve any inner sense of religious atonement.

"Tortured by the need of some mental if not material support in the face of his great danger, Clyde was now doing what every other human in related circumstances invariably does—seeking, and yet in the most indirect and involute and all but unconscious way, the presence or existence at least of some superhuman or supernatural personality or power that could and would aid him in some way—beginning to veer—however slightly or unconsciously as yet,—toward the personalization and humanization of forces, of which, except in the guise of religion, he had not the faintest conception" (II, 379). Dreiser sees Clyde's attempt to find solace in religion during these final days as a search for "an easy way out."

Dreiser introduces a last note of irony into the story in the person of the Reverend Duncan McMillan, a nonsectarian minister who visits Clyde daily. Hoping to save the soul before the material body is lost, this man of God encourages Clyde to tell his story. McMillan probes more and more into past events, fascinated by the sheer confusion and complexity of Clyde's life. Eventually he becomes convinced that the condemned man, though perhaps not guilty of actual murder, is guilty in the sight of God for the death of Roberta Alden.[17] McMillan's unselfish desire to help the youth to spiritual peace is frustrated by Clyde's inability to understand the fundamentals of right and wrong. With his courage momentarily strengthened by McMillan's sincerity and piety, Clyde appears to develop religious faith. He even issues a written statement to the youth of America, warning them of his error and challenging them to Christian ideals. To McMillan, these professions of Christian belief are dubious, for he understands that genuine religious belief is beyond Clyde's resources. Perhaps this inability of Clyde's to develop sincere religious convictions constitutes the real tragedy of his life. Dreiser sustains this ironic interplay between McMillan and Clyde until the very end. As Clyde prepares to leave his cell for the electric chair, he speaks a final word to his mother: " 'Mama, you must believe that I die resigned and content. It won't be hard. God has heard my prayers. He

---

17. Warren takes exception to several interpretations of McMillan, rejecting Lehan's view that the minister is a bigot. In a lengthy note cited for page 137 of the text of *Homage to Theodore Dreiser* and appearing on pages 159–66, Warren argues that Dreiser's intention, and thus the meaning of McMillan in the novel, is to show the minister as "a man committed to absolutes but doomed to live in a world of complex definitions and shadowy ambiguities" (163).

The Triumph of Secularism

has given me strength and peace.' But to himself adding: 'Had he?'" (II, 404). This last note of inner doubt is sufficient to convey Dreiser's point that Clyde dies confused, bewildered, and without genuine religious faith. He dies, in fact, much like the cornered animal that he has been from the beginning of the novel.

Any critical analysis of *An American Tragedy* must necessarily offer an interpretation of Clyde's character. The most generally accepted critical evaluation of Clyde holds that he is a weak, amoral, will-less creature whose fate is pathetic rather than tragic because he manifests neither human choice nor human will. Robert Spiller, for example, finds Clyde completely "passive" and therefore concludes that "by removing the only opposition that the individual can supply, the force of his own will for mastery, Dreiser here descends to the lowest possible plane of pure mechanistic determinism."[18] Similarly, F. O. Matthiessen, though more cautious than Spiller, first points out that "a crucial element in our final estimate of this novel is how far he [Dreiser] can enable us to participate in his compassion." Later, after an examination of the novel and of Clyde's role, Matthiessen concludes that "the shallowness of a Clyde prevents his history from ever reaching the transfiguration that Dostoevsky dwells upon in the closing pages of *Crime and Punishment*."[19]

Other critics sympathetic with the basic views of Matthiessen regard the novel as an example of Dreiser's adherence to philosophical naturalism.[20] To some, Dreiser's mechanistic or deterministic assumptions undermine whatever value and meaning he might otherwise have given to the fictional work. Robert Shafer, for one, feels that Dreiser's "difficulty is that his mechanistic naturalism compels him so to select and manipulate facts of experience as to deny, through his narrative, that human life has any meaning or value." Shafer continues, in fact, with the assertion that "precisely for this reason it [the novel] contains no single element of tragedy in any legitimate sense of the word, and it

---

18. Robert E. Spiller, "Theodore Dreiser," in Spiller *et al.* (eds.), *Literary History of the United States* (3rd ed. rev.; New York, 1963), 1203.
19. Matthiessen, *Theodore Dreiser*, 205, 210.
20. It is interesting today to read Stuart P. Sherman's notable attack on Dreiser—"The Barbaric Naturalism of Mr. Dreiser," *Nation*, CI (December, 1915), 648–51—and then to read his very positive later estimation, centered on *An American Tragedy*—"Mr. Dreiser in Tragic Realism," in Sherman, *The Main Stream* (New York, 1927), 134–44.

impresses thoughtful readers as a mere sensational newspaper story long drawn out."[21] This problem of the value and meaning of an artistic work that contains elements of philosophical naturalism has also been considered by Charles Walcutt. Writing about *An American Tragedy*, he states:

> And by what right do we call a naturalistic novel tragic, when its premises strip the protagonist of will and ethical responsibility? The answer lies, surely, in the fact that will is not really absent from the naturalistic novel. It is, rather, taken away from the protagonist and the other characters and transferred to the reader and to society at large. The reader acknowledges his own will and responsibility even as he pities the helpless protagonist. But the protagonist is not an automaton: His fall is a tragic spectacle because the reader participates in it and feels that only by a failure of his will and the will of society could it have taken place.

Walcutt also points out that the naturalistic novelist has some personal views that are an important part of his work: "The naturalistic novelist while he portrays with loathing and bitterness the folly and degradation of man is also affirming his hope and his faith, for his unspoken strictures imply an equally unspoken ideal which stimulates and justifies his pejorative attitude toward the world about him."[22]

Thus, for Walcutt, *An American Tragedy* can have positive meaning, even a moral and ethical message. Although its hero, Clyde, is largely passive and not assertive, the world in which he moves, and the world in which his reader moves, may possess both moral order and ethical values. It is therefore the total world of the novel, not a limited approach to the central character, that finally determines the artistic impact. The significance of Clyde's last days, then, needs to be viewed against the larger implications of the novel. And clearly, the power of the narrative suggests that Dreiser has achieved in *An American Tragedy* a credible if not an absorbing rendition of that world.

That the novel itself is actually concerned with what Walcutt terms "unspoken strictures" and that it implies "an equally unspoken ideal" are all-important aspects of its ultimate significance. Arguing some

---

21. Robert Shafer, "*An American Tragedy:* A Humanistic Demurer," in Alfred Kazin and Charles Shapiro (eds.), *The Stature of Theodore Dreiser* (Bloomington, 1955), 124.
22. Charles E. Walcutt, *American Literary Naturalism: A Divided Stream* (Minneapolis, 1956), 27, 29.

years ago that the work is purposeful and "profoundly moralistic," George F. Whicher comments:

> If such a book as *An American Tragedy* is read as an ordinary novel about an individual hero, it is tedious and practically unreadable. But it is not intended to be so taken. Its subject is not the fortunes of the wretched Clyde Griffiths, but the nature of modern materialism which drives men like sensate particles to their doom. The author of such a work no more looks for special qualities in the individual who illustrates his thesis than a physicist looks for wisdom and self-control in the ions he is observing. Dreiser regards the spectacle of human behavior as the recording angel might view it if he possessed an exceptionally powerful microscope. All distinctions of strong and weak, good and evil, wise and foolish are obliterated by the immensity of the cosmic perspective, and there is no need to focus on a Macbeth or a Lear when any specimen of the race will do as well.[23]

Indeed, Dreiser's fundamental aim in *An American Tragedy* in showing "the nature of modern materialism" is to portray its impact on the typical, if weak, modern individual.

Writing in a similar mood but addressing in particular Book Three of the novel, Karl Heinz Wirzberger, an East German critic, points out that Dreiser's novel is an attack upon the American system.

> We are constantly comparing Mason's fragmentary description with the real facts and come to the realization that not Clyde but the American bourgeoise should stand trial. It is not a unique case of a youthful murderer that is here being tried before the eyes of the law but rather the failure of an established society which has set the dollar as a measure of value, which constantly infects youth with the poison of an unnatural greed for money and power, without feeling guilty when one of these young people becomes a criminal because his implanted ideals bring his miserable existence to an unsurmountable contrast with reality.[24]

Money and money-oriented patterns of behavior, for Wirzberger (and for Dreiser), are the underlying values and goals of modern American society.

The world of money in twentieth century America is of course the world of the secular city. To Whicher's and Wirzberger's evaluations,

---

23. George F. Whicher, "The Twentieth Century," in Arthur Hobson Quinn (ed.), *Literature of the American People* (New York, 1931), 850.
24. Wirzberger, *Die Romane Theodore Dreisers*, 188–89.

Blanche H. Gelfant adds her critical opinion: "In denying responsibility to the individual Dreiser makes it impossible to condemn him as a moral actor. Yet Dreiser's position is profoundly moralistic, for he is indicting a whole society.... His novels carry a mass condemnation for all of modern urban society—for its inequalities that evoke inordinate desires for money; for its spiritual confusion and desolation; for its cultural barrenness and its failure to show man beauty in any form other than that of material things. Thus, his real villain is the city itself. It has created Hurstwoods and Carries, Cowperwoods and Witlas, and weaklings like Clyde."[25]

More recently, in *The Novels of Theodore Dreiser*, Donald Pizer argues that in *An American Tragedy* "Dreiser depicts the falseness and destructiveness of such American illusions as the faith in moral abstractions, the implicit virtue of small-town or rural life, and the association of one's noblest dreams with a wealthy girl." Aware of Dreiser's proclivity toward ideas and positions associated with literary naturalism, Pizer demonstrates that "Dreiser's account of Clyde in the opening chapters of *An American Tragedy* is not a doctrinaire study in hereditary and environmental determinism. It is rather a subtle dramatization of the ways in which a distinctive temperament—eager, sensitive, and emotional, yet weak and directionless—interacts with a distinctive social reality which supplies that temperament with both its specific goals and its operative ethic." Pizer's detailed examination of the novel stresses Dreiser's ability to give his readers a

sense of oneness with a figure who, though weak and ineffectual, desires with a deepening need to be understood. These themes and effects are not coherently related to any single describably tragic theme, either traditional or otherwise. But they and other characteristics of the novel do move us deeply because we sense in them a mature vision of the most poignant strains in the lives of any of us who have ever dreamed.... A work which had its origin in Dreiser's fascination with a distinctively American crime now speaks above all to the "mental, physical, and spiritual suffering" which all men have shared.[26]

Pizer's judgment of Dreiser's vision accurately identifies the author's consistent view of the individual as the wistful, suffering creature who must play the central role in the cosmic scheme of existence.

25. Blanche H. Gelfant, "Theodore Dreiser: The Portrait Novel," in Gelfant, *The American City Novel* (Norman, 1955), 88–89.
26. Pizer, *The Novels of Theodore Dreiser*, 218, 240, 281.

The Triumph of Secularism

Implicit in this view of the individual, particularly in *An American Tragedy*, is Dreiser's conviction that modern man is thoroughly urbanized and secularized. The essential success of this 1925 novel, in fact, is its dramatization of the typical individual in his quest to discover and to sustain himself by secular standards and values that are hostile to him and his true needs. A passage near the end of the novel well illustrates this theme. Waiting to die in the electric chair, Clyde Griffiths thinks of his early years in Kansas City.

> He had longed for so much there in Kansas City and he had had so little. Things—just things—had seemed so very important to him—and he had so resented being taken out on the street as he had been, before all the other boys and girls, many of whom had all the things that he so craved, and when he would have been glad to have been anywhere else in the world than out there—on the street! That mission life that to his mother was so wonderful, yet to him, so dreary! . . . She would never understand his craving for ease and luxury, for beauty, for love—his particular kind of love that went with show, pleasure, wealth, position, his eager and immutable aspirations and desires She would not understand these things. (II, 401)

If we find it difficult to sympathize with Clyde in his moment of self-pity, we cannot fail to appreciate the deep import of his words. They reveal the terms of his true dilemma; namely, "his craving for ease and luxury, for beauty, for love." Thoroughly conditioned and compelled by desire, Clyde is Dreiser's exemplification of what any secular-urban citizen may become.

Writing of Dreiser's characters in general, David Weimer renders a critical judgment especially indicative of Clyde Griffiths' status: "Dreiser's individual is always at bottom adrift in the metropolis. He can only salvage some part of what he is born with, his emotive nature, and hope to give it spasmodic expression. His desire is not to be self-reliant but to be free; not to fulfill himself through adventure, in the manner of the Romantic hero, but to preserve some passional identity."[27] Clyde cannot achieve, much less preserve, a "passional identity," because he required a creative framework in which to develop. He earlier needed, as a child in Kansas City, purposeful traditions and familial security and love. In his quest for that of which he senses he has been deprived, he finds only the illusory promises of the city: the fake standard that ap-

---

27. David R. Weimer, "Heathen Catacombs: Theodore Dreiser," in Weimer, *The City as Metaphor* (New York, 1966), 75–76.

pearance is reality; the proposition that success and money will bring true happiness; and, perhaps quite crucial for Clyde, the compulsive desire to indulge constantly in pleasure. In his analysis of *An American Tragedy*, Robert Penn Warren says of Clyde: "His 'tragedy' is that of namelessness, and this is one aspect of its being an American tragedy, the story of the individual without identity, whose responsible self has been absorbed by the great machine of modern industrial secularized society, and reduced to a cog, a cipher, an abstraction."[28]

Not surprisingly, Clyde ends his life hapless and bewildered, although still possessed by the early desires born in him long ago in Kansas City. He never understands why his pursuit of the golden images of the Green-Davidson Hotel and of the rich Sondra Finchley have failed. He cannot grasp why his life has so soon come to grief, to despair, and to death in the electric chair.

The significance of the story of Clyde Griffiths, however, lies finally in Dreiser's novel as decisive comment on the patterns of America's new commercial-industrial civilization. In unmistakable ways Dreiser shows that twentieth-century attitudes, values, and life-styles result from an urbanized, secularized world view that has displaced an older way of life. Entirely modern in temperament and character, Clyde Griffiths eagerly conforms to urban values and standards, hoping thereby to overcome his deep insecurity and sense of meaninglessness. Empty of beliefs and devoid of the personal means of generating convictions, he is a vessel to be filled by whatever means and for whatever ends the secular-urban world dictates. His life and death suggest conclusively Dreiser's view that modern American civilization is in decline. Expressed another way, Dreiser contends that key American institutions—family, religion, education, government—are not capable of supporting and assisting the average individual in either informing and gratifying his basic needs or providing him with satisfying, creative life roles.

In a broadly defined way, the enduring value of *An American Tragedy* can only be determined against the truth or the falseness of Dreiser's depiction of American civilization in this century. A nineteenth-century realist in artistic approach and conviction, Dreiser has created a novel that represents the way people live and how they confront the

---

28. Warren, *Homage to Theodore Dreiser*, 129.

world in which they live. Dreiser emphasizes neither the rational nor the irrational in his characters, neither the good nor the bad in their behavior. Perhaps unfortunately for Dreiser, as for other realists, this honest, faithful accommodation to perceived conditions does not result from a new vision of man and his world. Still, the portraits and stories of American life captured by Dreiser's realism contain informative, even highly valuable, examples that are meaningful today.

An observation of the American literary critic and comparist Harry Levin suggests an approach to evaluating the continuing importance of realistic novels such as *An American Tragedy*. Although writing about myth, he speaks thoughtfully about the redeeming value of "a fiction": "Now there are two ways of looking at a fiction: we can consider it as a deviation from fact or as an approximation to fact. Fact is always the criterion; and when the facts are under control, we emphasize the degree of deviation; but when we are out of touch with the facts, we utilize fiction to explain the unexplainable by some sort of approximation to it."[29] Dreiser's secular city, with its devastating influence on the individual, is his dominant image of society—a society that had become, for Dreiser, one of those that, in Levin's phrase, is "out of touch with the facts." In using Levin's comment, then, to suggest an approach for evaluation of Dreiser's *An American Tragedy*, the question to ask is simply this: Did Dreiser have the facts under control, and did he give in this novel a proper approximation to them? If the answer is yes, today's readers and critics need to look very carefully at the fabric, condition, and future of civilization in the United States.

29. Harry Levin, "Some Meanings of Myth," *Daedalus*, LXXXVIII (Spring, 1959), 225.

CAROL M. ANDREWS

Faulkner and the Symbolist Novel

Despite the enormous amount of research done each year on the novels of William Faulkner, scholars are only beginning to explore his connections with the modernist movement of the early twentieth century. One of the most important of these connections may well turn out to be the French Symbolist poets, whose influence on the modern novel is so pervasive that Melvin J. Friedman can identify the novels of James, Proust, Joyce, Conrad, Faulkner, and Virginia Woolf as all being "in some sense fictional inheritances from French Symbolist poetry." Friedman coins a term, *Symbolist novel,* to account for the new mingling of prose and poetry in a single work. That Faulkner is working in this tradition can be seen from his conscious or unconscious echo of the Symbolist aim in poetry in describing the feeling evoked in him by *The Sound and the Fury:* an "emotion definite and physical and yet nebulous to describe."[1]

Faulkner's "first mentors," as Hugh Kenner calls them, gave him the title of his first published poem, "L'Apres-Midi d'un Faune," a dreamily erotic and world-weary poem that owes its persona and situation to Mallarmé and that was published in the *New Republic* on August 6,

---

1. Melvin J. Friedman, "The Symbolist Novel: Huysmans to Malraux," in Malcolm Bradbury and James McFarland (eds.), *Modernism, 1890–1930* (New York, 1976), 453; William Faulkner, "An Introduction for *The Sound and the Fury,*" ed. James B. Meriwether, *Southern Review,* n.s., VIII (1972), 709; William Faulkner, "An Introduction to *The Sound and the Fury,*" ed. James B. Meriwether, *Mississippi Quarterly,* XXVI (1973), 414.

1919. Also, Faulkner's translations of four poems by Paul Verlaine appeared in 1920 in the University of Mississippi newspaper, the *Mississippian*. As Martin Kreiswirth has pointed out, all four of these poems—"Fantoches," "Clair de Lune," "Streets," and "A Clymène"—were translated in the appendix to Arthur Symons' *The Symbolist Movement in Literature* (1919), a book Phil Stone probably had in his library. A letter from Stone to James B. Meriwether, dated February 19, 1957, states, "As to the French Symbolist poets, Bill read a good deal of them that I had, some in the original and most in translation, and I think they had some influence on his own verse."[2] But the French Symbolists did much more for Faulkner than influence his early poems. They gave him a form for his novels that would encompass all Yoknapatawpha. As Kenner says, "Faulkner discovered . . . that the Symbolist expansion of incident, provided we imagine the incident in a real world and not in an art world . . . expands it into a kind of unbounded interrelatedness, the kind taletellers count on everyone knowing."[3]

But ironically, Faulkner's affinities with French Symbolism merely reaffirm the Americanness of our greatest modern writer, for these affinities place him firmly within the tradition of American symbolism that Charles Feidelson traces through Hawthorne, Whitman, Melville, and Poe. In fact, Feidelson's definition of the symbolist method seems to

---

2. Martin Kreiswirth, "Faulkner as Translator: His Versions of Verlaine," *Mississippi Quarterly*, XXX (1977), 430; George P. Garrett, "An Examination of the Poetry of William Faulkner," *Princeton University Library Chronicle*, XVIII (1957), 128. The Symbolist influence on Faulkner's poetry has been discussed by Garrett, Kreiswirth, H. Edward Richardson, and Judith L. Sensibar. Richardson, in the first book-length study, points to Faulkner's Symbolist indirection and his use of "devices of synesthesia which tend to merge the amorphous with the concrete, the fluid with the solid, the intangible with the tangible." H. Edward Richardson, *William Faulkner: The Journey to Self-Discovery* (Columbia, Mo., 1969), 77. Sensibar, who presents extensive analyses of *The Marble Faun*, *The Marionettes*, *The Lilacs*, and *Vision in Spring*, focuses on Faulkner's use of the figure of Pierrot, "a mask generated in part by his reading of Arthur Symons' *The Symbolist Movement in Literature* and early Modernist adaptations of the Laforguian Pierrot mask." Judith L. Sensibar, *The Origins of Faulkner's Art* (Austin, 1984), xvii.

3. Hugh Kenner, "The Last Novelist," in Kenner, *A Homemade World: The American Modernist Writers* (New York, 1974), 209. Although Richardson, *Journey to Self-Discovery*, discusses *Sartoris*, Faulkner's third novel, and Sensibar, *Origins of Faulkner's Art*, makes connections between the Pierrot mask and *pierrotique* characters in Faulkner's fiction, Kenner is the only critic to discuss the Symbolist influence on Faulkner in terms of form. Sensibar sees Faulkner's development of multiple points of view as a movement away from the Symbolist influence through the symphonic poem sequences of Conrad Aiken. Aiken had a desire, "not shared by the Symbolists, to create a narrative" (Sensibar, *Origins of Faulkner's Art*, 95). So did Faulkner, but the Symbolists continued to influence his narrative form more than Sensibar allows.

be one of the most apt characterizations available for Faulkner's narrative structures:

> The symbolist . . . redefines the whole process of knowing and the status of reality in the light of the poetic method. He tries to take both poles of perception into account at once, to view the subjective and objective worlds as functions of each other by regarding both as functions of the forms of speech in which they are rendered. Here is the sum of his quarrel with reason. Meaning, for him, as Mrs. Langer puts it, is "a function of a term," not an external relation between word, thought, and thing. "A function is a *pattern* viewed with reference to one special term round which it centers; this pattern emerges when we look at the given term *in its total relation to the other terms around it.*" Once we refuse to contemplate a separate reality "meant by" the word, meaning becomes an activity that generates a pattern.[4]

Viewed in this way, as a culmination of the two symbolist influences on its author, *The Sound and the Fury* becomes an endlessly expanding pattern centered around the lost sister, Caddy. Through her absence (she is equally distant from the subjective and the objective poles of experience), she becomes both an elusive goal and mediator for those, including her author, who would seek her recovery.

As many critics have pointed out, the introduction Faulkner wrote for a proposed 1933 edition of the book gives important insights into its origin: "One day I seemed to shut a door between me and all publisher's addresses and book lists. I said to myself, Now I can write. Now I can make myself a vase like that which the old Roman kept at his bedside and wore the rim away slowly kissing it. So I, who had never had a sister and was fated to lose my daughter in infancy, set out to make myself a beautiful and tragic little girl." André Bleikasten uses this explanation to define the work of art as "a libidinal object or, more precisely, a fetish, an object standing *instead* of something, the mark and mask of an absence." John T. Matthews counters this interpretation with further statements from Faulkner that make the issue more complicated: "When I began it I had no plan at all. I wasn't even writing a book," Faulkner stated in the 1933 introduction. In another, longer version of this introduction, also written in 1933, he said: "I did not realise then that I was trying to manufacture the sister. . . . I just began to write." Matthews comments: "However fine a distinction this may be, the

---

4. Charles Feidelson, *Symbolism and American Literature* (Chicago, 1953), 56.

consequences are considerable. To begin to write, to mark the page, *produces* the mood of bereavement, as if the use of language creates the atmosphere of mourning. Writing does not respond to loss, it initiates it; writing is as much a kind of loss as it is a kind of compensation." His point is significantly close to the idea of language expressed in Jean Moréas' "Manifeste du symbolisme": the poem is to "conjure up, in a specially created penumbra, the negated object, with the help of allusive and always indirect words, which constantly efface themselves in a complementary silence." The nature of language is to negate the world, but also to negate itself as it points toward an even more compelling realm of silence. At one level, *The Sound and the Fury*, born of a kind of silence (the shutting of a door), constantly moves toward the silence at its center, the "beautiful and tragic little girl."[5]

Yet Caddy is also presented as a flesh-and-blood character in a recognizable social setting; she is the little girl who climbs a tree to look in at her grandmother's funeral: " 'Course, we didn't know at that time that one was an idiot, but they were three boys, one was a girl and the girl was the only one that was brave enough to climb that tree to look in the forbidden window to see what was going on". In the various accounts of the genesis of the novel, Faulkner describes his central image differently: in *Lion in the Garden* he says that he began with the children kept away from the funeral, thought of Benjy, and only then arrived at the character of the sister, whereas in *Faulkner in the University* he states that the whole book began with the little girl's muddy drawers. All of these beginnings draw upon an absence, whether the grandmother's death, the idiot's lack of reason, or the girl's loss of innocence, but Faulkner most often in these accounts returns to the image of Caddy. Significantly, he chooses the central image with the most potential for passionate life, and his method of presenting her emphasizes this potential: "Caddy was still too beautiful and too moving to reduce her to

---

5. Faulkner, "Introduction for *The Sound and the Fury*," *Southern Review*, 710; André Bleikasten, *The Most Splendid Failure: Faulkner's "The Sound and the Fury"* (Bloomington, 1976), 46; Faulkner, "Introduction for *The Sound and the Fury*," *Southern Review*, 710; Faulkner, "Introduction to *The Sound and the Fury*," *Mississippi Quarterly*, 413; John T. Matthews, *The Play of Faulkner's Language* (Ithaca, 1982), 19; Jean Moréas, "Manifeste du symbolisme," in supplement to *Le Figaro litteraite*, September 18, 1886, translated and quoted in Clive Scott, "Symbolism, Decadence, and Impressionism," in Malcolm Bradbury and James McFarland (eds.), *Modernism, 1890–1930* (New York, 1976), 209.

telling what was going on, [and I felt] that it would be more passionate to see her through somebody else's eyes."[6]

Caddy is thus a paradox: the most alive of the children, she is transformed by her absence from reality to dream, and like Frank Kermode's romantic image, she offers a "terrible knowledge" to her brothers that they are incapable of sharing. Kermode's romantic image is an emblem for the modern conception of a work of art as it evolved from Symbolist aesthetic—"some sort of complex image, autotelic, liberated from discourse, with coincident form and meaning." This image finds its most perfect embodiment in the Dancer of Yeats's "Among School Children." Ilse DuSoir Lind summarizes the attributes of the romantic image, here represented by Salome, in referring to Marietta of Faulkner's Symbolist dream-play *Marionettes*:

> In this aesthetic tradition, within which Faulkner is clearly working, Salome is the embodiment of motion in the moment of arrest, as before the beginning of her dance. She also represents both life and art—life as experienced directly by the senses (instead of by the intellect) and apprehended as being both beautiful and terrifying; art as a vital force which expresses its influence directly through the senses, exerting a fatal power through the strange beauty it creates. In her own being, Salome is seen also to be the container of eternal contradictions, the emblem of the rhetorical concept of the oxymoron.[7]

Caddy, though a much more humanized figure, represents even more fully than Marietta the woman who is beautiful and terrible in her self-contained power. What Lind does not discuss, however, is the "terrible knowledge" possessed but not directly expressed by the image; it is this knowledge, nondiscursive, nonrational, and nonintelligible, that fascinates the poet.

The germ of *The Sound and the Fury*, the scene of the grandmother's funeral, is entirely contained in Benjy's section. Hugh Kenner attributes the creation of Benjy to the symbolist principle of indirection, according to which we must not be told what the children see. His innocence is in effect an absence, the absence of logic and coherence that diffuses events throughout his section and forces whatever comprehension is possible

---

6. William Faulkner, *Faulkner in the University: Class Conference at the University of Virginia*, ed. Frederick L. Gwynn and Joseph L. Blotner (New York, 1965), 31, 1.

7. Frank Kermode, *Romantic Image* (London, 1957), 110; Ilse Du Soir Lind, "Faulkner's Uses of Poetic Drama" in Evans Harrington and Ann J. Abadie (eds.), *Faulkner, Modernism, and Film: Faulkner and Yoknapatawpha, 1978* (Jackson, Miss., 1978), 72.

to depend on reflexive imagery and associative patterns. But symbolically, this absence becomes a presence; as Kenner points out, "The mind of Benjy Compson is not a process, but a kind of *place* for the elements of the story to exist in." His absence of reason thus functions in both of the ways Gail Mortimer finds typical of Faulkner's use of absence: "(1) a type of causality, being the occasion for other events, and (2) a tangibility that makes of absences places or things within which other things can exist." Benjy's narrative is the first place in which Caddy exists in the novel, and because his evocation of her cannot exactly be called memory, she is more immediately (un-mediatedly) present in this section than the others. And yet from the first, Faulkner calls attention to the symbolic nature of her presentation: "Caddie" literally refers to the golf game rather than Benjy's sister and provokes bellowing only through associations within Benjy's mind. Benjy presents an image, but he cannot comprehend its significance. It is left to the reader to piece together Caddy's meaning for the novel.[8]

What can be put together is an association between Caddy and knowledge; the obvious leader of the children, she climbs the pear tree because she wants to know something that for some reason has been forbidden. She shows several characteristics of the romantic image, not the least of which is the uncommunicableness of what she sees. The children watch the muddy bottom of her drawers until she disappears, but then the dominant image is stillness: "The tree quit thrashing. We looked up into the still branches. 'What you seeing.' Frony whispered"[9]

Even when she returns, she only tells everyone to be quiet and then comments: "They're not doing anything in there. Just sitting in chairs and looking" (54–55). When the children go to bed that night, she still thinks that Damuddy is sick (89). Her knowledge is thus emblematic, not discursive, and the reader must be the one to see in the episode echoes of the edenic fall with its connection of sexuality (the muddy drawers) and death (Damuddy's funeral). Lewis P. Simpson gives one of the clearest summaries of her possible associations: "As she comes to us in Benjy's recreation, Caddy is an avatar of all the women who have borne heirs to the Compson lineage, a Compson princess, a sacred vessel

---

8. Kenner, "The Last Novelist," 200; Gail L. Mortimer, *Faulkner's Rhetoric of Loss: A Study of Perception and Meaning* (Austin, 1983), 82.
9. William Faulkner, *The Sound and the Fury* (New York, 1929), 47. Subsequent references to the novel are to this editon and will appear in the text.

of the family's perpetuation and a symbol of living motherhood. She is also an avatar of Persephone, the goddess of fertility and queen of Hades. She is also an avatar of the Grecian nymphs of the woods and waters. She is also herself, a daring little girl, who is braver than her brothers."[10] Such symbolic resonance is possible precisely because of her nondiscursive presence.

Benjy, of course, sees nothing of these significances; he only knows Caddy as the primary source of love in his life, a substitute for the cold, self-pitying Mrs. Compson. It is difficult to ascertain exactly his understanding of absence and loss. In the Appendix to the novel, written in 1945, Faulkner states that Benjy "loved three things: the pasture which was sold to pay for Candace's wedding and to send Quentin to Harvard, his sister Candace, firelight. Who lost none of them because he could not remember his sister but only the loss of her, and firelight was the same bright shape as going to sleep, and the pasture was even better sold than before" (423). It perhaps does not make logical sense that Benjy recreates with perfect clarity scenes in which Caddy is an active participant and yet bellows when he hears her name, but as Mortimer points out, it is the affective quality of Benjy's experience that Faulkner wishes to convey: "an absence *felt* as an absence, that is to say—in Faulkner's world—a loss."[11] His response may also be a reflection of Mallarmé's dictum that "to name is to destroy"; he is aware of her loss most acutely when he hears her name. Cut off from the world of time and change, Benjy is to some extent a descendant of Faulkner's marble faun; when he says that "Caddy smelled like trees," he creates an image of her innocence that associates her with the nymphs of Mallarmé and Faulkner. But as Matthews points out, he "associates the fragrance of trees contradictorily—both with Caddy's virginal innocence and with the onset of sexual betrayal."[12]

In fact, the imagery of mirrors in this section identifies Benjy as a type of Narcissus who sees in Caddy a reflection of his own needs. Benjy's

---

10. Lewis P. Simpson, "Sex and History: Origins of Faulkner's Apocrypha," in Evans Harrington and Ann J. Abadie (eds.), *The Maker and the Myth* (Jackson, Miss., 1978), 62.

11. Mortimer, Bleikasten, Matthews, and Kreiswirth (see his *The Making of a Novelist* [Athens, Ga., 1983], 144–46) have all dealt with the force of absence in Faulkner's novels; none of them, however, have connected it with the Symbolist aesthetic, in which "the real object, or the absence of a real object, is abandoned for one of pure imagination." Wallace Fowlie, *Mallarmé* (Chicago, 1953), 52.

12. Matthews, *The Play of Faulkner's Language*, 68.

Faulkner and the Symbolist Novel

experience may derive from that of a puzzled farmhand in Faulkner's early prose sketch "Nympholepsy" who has a fleeting, teasingly erotic encounter with a nymphlike figure in a stream.[13] Looking down into the water, he sees "death like a woman shining and drowned and waiting," and as Bleikasten says, "water is thus equated with woman, and the symbolic equation connotes both desire and death—a highly pregnant complex of associations recurring in many of Faulkner's novels, and at the very core of the Quentin section of *The Sound and the Fury*."[14] That Benjy's need for Caddy also has a sexual element can be seen in his attack on the Burgess girl, who seems to be a substitute for Caddy: "I opened the gate and they stopped, turning. I was trying to say, and I caught her, trying to say, and she screamed and I was trying to say and trying and the bright shapes began to stop and I tried to get out" (64). Bleikasten points out that "trying to say" refers to both the writer's creative endeavor and to the character's sexual impulse.[15] But this experience is also a "nympholeptic" episode, for the juxtaposition of the attack and the "bright, whirling shapes" (64) of the anesthesia at his castration links desire and a kind of drowning: "But when I breathed in, I couldn't breathe out again to cry, and I tried to keep from falling off the hill and I fell off the hill into the bright, whirling shapes" (64). In a sense he has achieved reunion with the only person who ever cared what he was "trying to say." But because it is his own projection, the experience leads only to another loss.

Quentin's section continues the revelation of Caddy as a warm, loving, courageous young woman despite Quentin's attempt to twist her sexuality into something horrifying. His degree of success shows him to be to a large extent responsible for her tragedy, and his own tragedy comes from his inability to separate the Caddy he has known from the Caddy he has created. Whereas Benjy's evocation of his sister is tempered by an overwhelming anguish at her loss, Quentin's is charac-

---

13. The sketch "Nympholepsy," written in 1925 but not published until 1973, contains other Symbolist elements. The forest through which the farmhand walks seems to be imbued with some animistic force, perhaps a reference to the god Pan. The "green cathedral of trees" recalls Baudelaire's "Correspondences," and though the protagonist half expects "a priest to step forth," his experience remains sensual rather than spiritual. William Faulkner, "Nympholepsy," ed. James B. Meriwether, *Mississippi Quarterly*, XXVI (1973), 405.
14. Ibid., 407; Bleikasten, *The Most Splendid Failure*, 13.
15. Bleikasten, *The Most Splendid Failure*, 84.

terized by an overriding fear. The beauty and terror of Quentin's image of Caddy is like that of Keats's Moneta or Wilde's Salome; Quentin, in fact, shares several of the characteristics of the Symbolist and Decadent poets—the sensitivity, the aestheticism, and the fascination with death, as well as what Kenner calls the "high finish" on the language of his section of the novel. But Quentin also hearkens back to his American roots: as Faulkner once admitted, "Ishmael is the witness in *Moby Dick*, as I am Quentin in *The Sound and the Fury*."[16] Whereas Melville provides the symbolist vision and its critique in two characters, Ahab and Ishmael, Faulkner incorporates them both in one: close as he is to his creator, Quentin presents a vision he cannot entirely comprehend, and Faulkner uses his monologue to express the possibilities and liabilities of obsession with the image.

If Benjy's interest in Caddy's sexuality reflects a kind of pagan sensuality ("Caddy smelled like trees"), Quentin's is associated with a puritan harshness and repression.[17] The Appendix presents him as one "who loved not his sister's body but some concept of Compson honor" (411). In order to negate his sister's loss of virginity and her subsequent promiscuity, he attempts to transform her behavior into a sin so heinous that it will isolate them forever from the rest of the world: "Roses. Not virgins like dogwood, milkweed. I said I have committed incest, Father I said. Roses. Cunning and serene" (95). Thus, Quentin projects onto Caddy his simultaneous fear of and attraction to sexual experience, and just as she has done at the time of their grandmother's death, she comes between her brother and a fact of existence. As Bleikasten says, she is "a symbolic reminder, perhaps, of the mythic mediating function of woman through whom, for man, passes all knowledge about the origins, all knowledge about the twin enigmas of life and death."[18] This knowledge is as uncommunicable as the truth about Damuddy, and in spite of Quentin's sensitivity, he is as unable as Benjy to comprehend the meaning of Caddy's actions.

What he does is construct an image of his sister that incorporates his

---

16. Kenner, "The Last Novelist," 194–95; Joseph Blotner, *Faulkner: A Biography* (2 vols.; New York, 1974), II, 1522.
17. Cleanth Brooks, *William Faulkner: The Yoknapatawpha Country* (New Haven, 1966), 331–32.
18. Bleikasten, *The Most Splendid Failure*, 54.

deepest desires and fears. Michael Millgate summarizes the aspects of this image.

> In his most agonising recollections of Caddy, [Quentin] sees her at twilight, sitting in the cleansing waters of the branch and surrounded by the scent of honeysuckle, and these three elements of the scene—the twilight, the water, and the honeysuckle—take on an obsessive significance for Quentin himself and operate as recurrent symbols throughout this section of the novel. As water is associated with cleansing, redemption, peace and death, and the honeysuckle with warm Southern nights and Caddy's passionate sexuality, so twilight, "that quality of light as if time really had stopped for a while," becomes inextricably confused in Quentin's mind with the scents of water and of honeysuckle until "the whole thing came to symbolize night and unrest."[19]

These elements recall the visionary experiences of the poetry and "Nympholepsy"; the scent of honeysuckle is simply an addition to the complex imagery uniting death and desire. "Twilight," which is the Symbolist moment of revelation, was the working title of Benjy's section of *The Sound and the Fury*, but Benjy uses the word *twilight* only once, in his description of the attack on the Burgess girl, his own particular union with a nymph (64). The scene of Damuddy's death, which takes place at dusk, is temporally set by indirect clues, such as supper and the lights in the windows. Quentin actually refers to twilight more often than Benjy, and his use of the word always indicates a moment in the past until his last day draws to a close and he approaches his moment of death. At this point appears a passage that Millgate cites as central to Quentin's entire section.

> This was where I saw the river for the last time this morning, about here. I could feel water beyond the twilight, smell. When it bloomed in the spring and it rained the smell was everywhere . . . until I would lie in bed thinking when will it stop when will it stop. The draft in the door smelled of water, a damp steady breath. Sometimes I could put myself to sleep saying that over and over until after the honeysuckle got all mixed up in it the whole thing came to symbolise night and unrest I seemed to be lying neither asleep nor awake looking down a long corridor of grey halflight where all stable things had become shadowy paradoxical all I had done shadows all I had felt suffered taking visible form antic and perverse mocking without relevance inherent themselves with the denial of the significance they should have affirmed thinking I was I was not who was not was not who. (210–211)

---

19. Michael Millgate, *The Achievement of William Faulkner* (New York, 1966), 86. The quotations from the novel in the passage are from pp. 209–11.

Here Faulkner uses twilight to signal a revelation of mocking irony: Quentin finds that his experiences "deny the significance they should have affirmed," and as a result he loses any sense of a stable identity.

The scene that has brought him to this state is the one he relives with uninterrupted intensity while he is fighting Gerald Bland.[20] The remembered scene begins with Caddy's loss of virginity and Quentin's attempted suicide pact with her; in finding his sister at the branch, Quentin describes her in terms that recall the shadowy figure in "Nympholepsy": "she was lying in the water her head on the sand spit the water flowing about her hips there was a little more light in the water her skirt half saturated flopped along her flanks to the waters motion in heavy ripples going nowhere renewed themselves of their own movement" (186). Caddy proves as elusive as the nymph, for she talks to Quentin about her lover Dalton Ames, her thudding heart belying her words as she at first denies that she loves him. She links desire and death as Quentin himself will do: "yes I hate him I would die for I've already died for him I die for him over and over again everytime this goes" (188), but the difference is that Caddy refers to actual experience while Quentin has "never done that" (188). He reveals his impotence when he holds a knife to Caddy's throat but cannot kill her, and again when he calls Dalton Ames to a meeting at the bridge but passes out "like a girl" (201) instead of hitting him. Ironically, Quentin accomplishes something of what he wants, because Caddy sends her lover away, but his presence still remains between them as she responds to the sound of his name: "her blood surged steadily beating and beating against my hand" (203). To Caddy, who lives in actuality, to name is to evoke rather than to destroy, and Quentin finds that union with his sister, either physical or emotional, is impossible. Thus, when we learn that he has committed suicide by drowning himself, we know that he has chosen to go beyond sexuality to a union that promises "peace, nonmemory, stasis, nothingness itself."[21]

Instead of Caddy's passionate sexuality and the changes it heralds in his life as well as hers, Quentin has chosen the safety and stillness of

---

20. Thomas Daniel Young, "Narration as Creative Act: The Role of Quentin Compson in *Absalom, Absalom!*" in Harrington and Abadie (eds.), *Faulkner, Modernism, and Film* 85–87.

21. Gail Moore Morrison, "'Time, Tide, and Twilight': *Mayday* and Faulkner's Quest Toward *The Sound and the Fury*," *Mississippi Quarterly*, XXXI (1978), 352.

"Little Sister Death." This phrase appears in another early work, the allegorical tale *Mayday*, in which a knight on a quest through an enchanted forest is given the choice to relive any past experience of his life or to lose himself in the waters of a flowing stream. In the stream he sees the face of "one all young and white, and with long shining hair like a column of fair sunny water," and after he chooses to join her, St. Francis comments, "Little Sister Death." Quentin's image of Caddy at her wedding is eerily similar: "That quick, her train caught up over her arm she ran out of the mirror like a cloud her veil swirling in long glints" (100). Morrison maintains that Faulkner's source, St. Francis's Sister Bodily Death, does not have the sexual quality Faulkner ascribes to her.[22]

Although some commentators have warned against using the Appendix to interpret the novel, it is interesting that in Quentin's summary Faulkner makes the connection between desire and death even more explicit: "But who loved death above all, who loved only death, loved and lived in a deliberate and almost perverted anticipation of death as a lover loves and deliberately refrains from the waiting willing friendly tender incredible body of his beloved, until he can no longer bear not the refraining but the restraint and so flings, hurls himself, relinquishing, drowning" (411). He gives Quentin the godlike identity bestowed on the poet by the Symbolists:[23] "Who loved not the idea of the incest which he would not commit, but some presbyterian concept of its eternal punishment: he, not God, could by that means cast himself and his sister both into hell, where he could guard her forever and keep her forevermore intact amid the eternal fires" (411). That he has achieved an earthly form of this damnation for his sister can be seen before his death in her telling him she is "sick" and "bad": "*There was something terrible in me sometimes at night I could see it grinning at me I could see it through them grinning at me through their faces*" (138). By 1943 she is the romantic image incarnate: "the woman's face hatless between a rich

---

22. William Faulkner, *Mayday*, ed. Carvel Collins (Notre Dame, 1978), 87.
23. It is a common error to think that all Symbolists had the same idea of the role of the poet. Anna Balakian shows that Symbolist interpretations of the poet as "voyant" ("seer" or "visionary") covered a broad spectrum, from Balzac and Swedenborg's strictly inner visions to Mallarmé's attempt to achieve an Orphic significance in his poetry. The closest to Faulkner's attitude seems to be that of Baudelaire, for whom "the process of the transformation of reality gives the poet a sense of his own divinity, rather than an aspiration toward divinity." Anna Balakian, *The Symbolist Movement: A Critical Appraisal* (New York, 1967), 21.

scarf and a seal coat, ageless and beautiful, cold serene and damned" (415). Fearing her sexuality, Quentin has chosen the chaste serenity of death by water, leaving Caddy her own version of the terrible knowledge possessed by the image. But Faulkner in the Appendix still pictures her as a possible mediator for Quentin: "Knew the brother loved death best of all and was not jealous, would (and perhaps in the calculation and deliberation of her marriage did) have handed him the hypothetical hemlock" (412). Caddy herself becomes Little Sister Death.

In their final remembered conversation, his father says to Quentin "you are not thinking of finitude you are contemplating an apotheosis in which a temporary state of mind will become symmetrical above the flesh and aware both of itself and of the flesh it will not quite discard you will not even be dead" (220). This would be the ultimate ideal of the Symbolist poet, to create himself as separate from the world and yet aware of it, and in a sense the form of Quentin's section suggests this dual existence as Quentin narrates from the moment of death. Yet this illusion is possible only in art; in actuality Quentin simply ceases to be, and no structural device makes this point clearer than the absence in the narrative of his actual death. The figure he has wished union with is his own projected self, and as such it promises only emptiness. Despite the intensity of Quentin's emotion and the significance he attempts to create, Faulkner the novelist untimately separates himself from Quentin the character. As Gary Lee Stonum points out, "However much Quentin's ideals are pure and universal, we are shown that they also proceed directly from his personal, worldly idiosyncrasies."[24] Placing the Symbolist in the real world shows the danger of a purely solipsistic vision.

After Quentin's intensely private and poetic narrative, Jason's comes as something of a relief. At least for the first time in the novel present events and existing people seem to be important, and Jason's villainy has enormous energy and even a darkly comic appeal: "Blood, I says, governors and generals. It's a damn good thing we never had any kings and presidents; we'd all be down there at Jackson chasing butterflies" (286). It is a critical commonplace that as *The Sound and the Fury* progresses it opens out into a more recognizable social world, and although the fol-

---

[24]. Gary Lee Stonum, *Faulkner's Career: An Internal Literary History* (Ithaca, 1979), 83.

lowing comment was made about *As I Lay Dying*, it is equally apparent in Jason's section of this novel "that the basic symbolist form begins to yield to something else." Jason is clearly more social satirist than visionary poet, and yet his affinities with his two brothers and the equally indirect method of his narrative place him also within Faulkner's symbolist aesthetic. The method of his section is to reveal Caddy's doom "refracted through the cheaper doom of her daughter."[25] Just as Quentin has had an important role in provoking Caddy's promiscuity, Jason contributes to that of her daughter; at one point Quentin II tells him pointedly: "Whatever I do, it's your fault. If I'm bad, it's because I had to be. You made me. I wish I was dead. I wish we were all dead" (324). Behind Jason's treatment of Quentin is his bitterness at the loss her mother represents to him—the loss of the job promised to him in her husband's bank. As Bleikasten states, in Jason's section the brother-sister relationship changes "from plus to minus: what Jason feels for Caddy is hatred, hatred as intense and uncontrollable as Benjy's love or Quentin's love-hate."[26]

The inversions of pattern in Jason's section center around Caddy. His is the first section in which she at least communicates with the family in the present, through her monthly checks to her mother and letters to Jason and Quentin. Jason's remembered encounter with Caddy occurs at Mr. Compson's funeral, about which she has not even been told; his reaction is far different from those of her other brothers in parallel episodes: "What are you doing here? I thought you promised her you wouldn't come back here. I thought you had more sense than that" (251). Jason's sense of loss is as deep as Benjy's or Quentin's, and he is equally inarticulate in expressing it: "We stood there, looking at the grave, and then I got to thinking about when we were little and one thing and another and I got to feeling funny again, kind of mad or something" (252). It is impossible, however, to feel sympathy for Jason, because of the means he chooses to get even. He makes a point of informing Caddy of the extent of her exile: "We don't even know your name at that house. Do you know that? We don't even know you with him and Quentin. Do you know that?" (252). He gives her only a momentary glimpse of her daughter for a payment of fifty dollars (253–55), and he tells the story

---

25. Friedman, "The Symbolist Novel," 459; Kenner, "The Last Novelist," 203.
26. Bleikasten, *The Most Splendid Failure*, 150.

with obvious satisfaction: "And so I counted the money again that night and put it away, and I didn't feel so bad. I says I reckon that'll show you. I reckon you'll know now that you cant beat me out of a job and get away with it" (255). But in his efforts to achieve what he considers justice, Jason creates a world as removed from normal reality as those of Benjy and Quentin.

Jason's image of woman is as rigid and life-denying as those of his brothers: "Once a bitch always a bitch, what I say" (223). His section begins with a seemingly trivial absence, the absence of Quentin II from school, but Jason's inability to control her comings and goings as he wishes becomes the central issue of his section. He is not concerned with her personally, but only as symbol: "Then when she sent Quentin home for me to feed too I says I guess that's right too, instead of me having to go way up north for a job they sent the job down here to me" (243). For fifteen years he has been pocketing Caddy's monthly support checks, but as the third-person narrator says in the fourth section of the novel, the money has no value to him in itself: "Of his niece he did not think at all, nor of the arbitrary valuation of the money. Neither of them had had entity of individuality for him for ten years; together they merely symbolized the job in the bank of which he had been deprived before he ever got it" (382). His frustrated attempts to hold on to these two symbols are like Benjy's and Quentin's attempts to hold on to their sister; the irony of his section is that though he has no use for Caddy at all, he will go to almost any lengths to keep what he sees as his due. In doing so, he "fools a man whut so smart he cant even keep up wid hisself" (311–12).

The extent to which he hides the truth from himself can be seen in a typical statement as he prepares the forged check for his mother to burn: "I went back to the desk and fixed the check. Trying to hurry and all, I says to myself it's a good thing her eyes are giving out, with that little whore in the house, a Christian forebearing woman like Mother" (269). Jason's version of Symbolist indirection is a deflection of blame that assures the continuation of the emptiness of the Compson household. In this sense he is like his mother, who, as every section makes clear, is the central absence in the Compson family and yet who takes absolutely no responsibility for its failings. As Cleanth Brooks says, she "is not so much an actively wicked and evil person as a cold weight of negativity which paralyzes the normal family relationships."[27] Jason, the only one of the children who is not considered a reproach by his mother, "a Bascomb, despite your name" (225), is as motherless as the others. Faulkner in the fourth section presents mother and son as mirror images of each other: "When she called the first time Jason laid his knife and fork down and he and his mother appeared to wait across the table from one another, in identical attitudes" (348). In the final section Faulkner presents graphically what has been indirectly apparent all along: Mrs. Compson is the emptiness reflected by the emptiness in the lives of all her children.

Jason's section of the novel ends in a circle, with the emphasis still on getting even: "Like I say once a bitch always a bitch. And just let me have twenty-four hours without any damn New York jew to advise me what it's going to do. I dont want to make a killing; save that to suck in the smart gamblers with. I just want an even chance to get my money back. And once I've done that they can bring all Beale Street and all bedlam in here and two of them can sleep in my bed and another one can have my place at the table too" (329). The futility of Jason's efforts has been obvious all along, but his frustration is brought to a head in the last section of the novel as Quentin II escapes down the pear tree with his savings, almost seven thousand dollars, although he can report only about three thousand, the rest being the remnant of Caddy's money for Quentin. In the Appendix Faulkner enjoys playing with the poetic justice of the robber robbed (424–26). In the fourth section of the novel the emphasis is all upon Jason's outraged pursuit. Critics have pointed out that Jason's obsession with Quentin's promiscuity is as unnatural as his older brother's with Caddy's. It is at least apparent that Faulkner is again presenting a grotesquely distorted "nympholepsy": pursuing his niece around the countryside leaves Jason "drowned" in the blinding headache caused by gasoline fumes. His wild search ends in a futile stasis: "the man sitting quietly behind the wheel of a small car, with his invisible life ravelled out about him like a wornout sock" (391).

But Jason's frustration is not the complete end of the novel. The fourth section also contains a movingly orchestrated vision of wholeness and hope. Faulkner's technique in achieving it is a telling comment upon his

27. Brooks, *Faulkner: The Yoknapatawpha Country*, 334.

failed visionaries throughout the novel. Instead of allowing Caddy to be a mediator between them and certain mysteries of life and death, introducing them by word or example into the motion of life, all of her brothers try to force her into some preconceived notion of what they think woman, especially fallen woman, should be. The beauty and the terror and the uncommunicableness of the image are created by them, but also lost on them. It is part of the great disturbing profundity of the book that Faulkner's "beautiful and tragic little girl" is so absent to her brothers. But in Dilsey's section of the novel the third-person narrator is able to find a medium that makes the mysteries of life and death a presence rather than an absence.

In the Reverend Shegog's sermon the author allows "voice," the oral patterning of the black minister's message, to take complete control over character and scene: "Then a voice said, 'Brethren.' The preacher had not moved. His arm lay yet across the desk, and he still held that pose while the voice died in sonorous echoes between the walls. It was as different as day and dark from his former tone, with a sad, timbrous quality like an alto horn, sinking into their hearts and speaking there again when it had ceased in fading and cumulate echoes" (367). Faulkner is using words as the Symbolists do, words "which constantly efface themselves in a complementary silence." The passage continues: "And the congregation seemed to watch with its own eyes while the voice consumed him, until he was nothing and they were nothing and there was not even a voice but instead their hearts were speaking to one another in chanting measures beyond the need for words" (367).

This experience leaves Dilsey with the calm serenity of faith in something greater than herself. The difference between the frustration of the Compson brothers and the assurance of this sermon points up a danger inherent in the symbolist method, one that Faulkner shows himself very aware of. As Feidelson points out, "Seen rationally, as an object, the world is inaccessible; but, seen as accessible, the world swallows up the visionary."[28] Feeling Caddy's presence to be somehow recoverable, through Benjy's bellowing, Quentin's drowning, and Jason's scheming, her brothers lose themselves in a significance of their own devising. Dilsey maintains her identity through an acceptance of a truth that she

---

28. Feidelson, *Symbolism and American Literature*, 33.

does not try to possess. Her vision is only partial, but as Faulkner expands his novel beyond it, he allows it to take its place in the larger pattern of his narrative. In doing so, he creates a vision of the modern world both beautiful and terrifying.

JULIUS ROWAN RAPER

Once More to the Mirror: Glasgow's Technique in *The Sheltered Life* and Reader-Response Criticism

Following M. H. Abrams' *The Mirror and the Lamp* (1953), critics have grown used to thinking of the literary work as standing in an intermediate position between three elements: the universe, the artist, and the audience. Abrams saw the work competing with the other elements for the critic's attention in a manner that depends on whether the critic's approach is, in Abram's terminology, objective, mimetic, expressive, or pragmatic. In contrast, the technique Ellen Glasgow uses to reveal the characters in her novel *The Sheltered Life* (1932) suggests that the fictional work itself unites the universe, the artist, and the audience, and that it does so through a process that all the elements, in one way or another, share. For Glasgow's novel resembles a pyramid composed of three mirrors with one face turned toward the universe of its characters, another toward the author, and the third toward the reader. The base on which the pyramid rests is the mirroring process that generates the three visible sides. Because the insights thus stated about *The Sheltered Life* include the relationship between the text and the reader, they overlap with the reader-response criticism published by Norman Holland, David Bleich, and Wolfgang Iser. Although my conclusions regarding Glasgow's novel emerged independently of the work of Holland, Bleich, and Iser, they both support and significantly modify the subjective criticism these theorists have succeeded in placing near the center of contemporary critical thought. By using the relationship between characters as a model for the reader's engagement with the text, my approach, in effect, offers a bridge between New Criticism and reader-response critics.[1]

Before turning to the mirroring process in *The Sheltered Life*, a novel from Glasgow's fifth decade as a published writer, it would be useful to recapitulate the development of her method of character delineation. Glasgow came to fiction from the late nineteenth-century realistic and naturalistic traditions in which characters dealt with one another in a novel very much the way the intellectual traditions of the century claimed people do in life—as objects: as users and used, as rivals to be overcome in business or sex, as brides to be bought or won, as lovers to be seduced into husbands, as competitors to be defeated in the struggle for existence. At best, other persons were objects on whom to lavish one's altruism; at worst, they were obstacles to one's compelling self-interests. The representative Glasgow novels of this period carried her protagonists from idealistic illusions about supporting characters to more realistic perceptions: the way, for example, Nicholas Burr, the poor white governor in her first Virginia novel, *The Voice of the People* (1900), moves from his belief in the people of his state to a violent death attempting to break up a lynch mob.

In her late twenties and early thirties, however, Glasgow discovered two contemporary thinkers who stressed a remarkably different relationship between individuals in life and in fiction, one in which people are not objects to one another but mirrors. As early as 1905 she marked the passages in Edward Carpenter's *The Art of Creation* where, in order to explain "the strange psychology of passion," Carpenter employs the Platonic concept of memory: a face is familiar, and fascinating, because it recalls a "God seen long ago, or far down in the mirror of the mind." Love, for example, is a reminiscence, a vision opening up of the celestial world remembered from ages past. In other words, Carpenter used Plato to argue that we continually color the external world with subjective content.[2] In *Wisdom and Destiny*, a book Glasgow read at about the

---

1. M. H. Abrams, *The Mirror and the Lamp: Romantic Theory and the Critical Tradition* (1953; rpr. New York, 1958), 5–7; Norman N. Holland, *5 Readers Reading* (New Haven, 1975); David Bleich, *Readings and Feelings: An Introduction to Subjective Criticism* (Urbana, 1975); Bleich, *Subjective Criticism* (Baltimore, 1978); Wolfgang Iser, *The Act of Reading: A Theory of Aesthetic Response* (Baltimore, 1976).
2. Edward Carpenter, *The Art of Creation: Essays on the Self and Its Powers* (New York, 1904), 129, 164, 239. For more on Glasgow's reading, see Julius Rowan Raper, *From the Sunken Garden* (Baton Rouge, 1980), 12–13.

same period, Maurice Maeterlinck argued for an equally subjective dimension in all relationships between two or more persons: "Let us always remember that nothing befalls us that is not of the nature of ourselves. . . . Whether you journey to the end of the world or merely walk round your house, none but yourself shall you meet on the highway of fate." Judas meets Judas; Socrates, Socrates. Unlike Carpenter, Maeterlinck avoided the questionable theory of Platonic memory. Instead, it is sometimes *ourselves* we find in others (in the simplest sense of the self); other times it is our *potential* that we discover projected upon the world without. Glasgow's marginal markings are unusually heavy for the passages in which Maeterlinck applies this concept to fiction, specifically the discussion of Emily Brontë, in which he notes Cathy's uncanny assertion in *Wuthering Heights:* "I am Heathcliff."[3] If so, then it is theoretically possible to write a novel in which all or many of the supporting characters reveal the protagonist by mirroring the needs and fears, the potential, of the major character—theoretically possible to create a truly psychological novel without the fuzziness of metaphysics or unattached emotion and without the imposition of an arbitrary symbol system. It took Glasgow another twenty years, however—until her book-length portrait of Dorinda Oakley in *Barren Ground* (1925)—to master the technique described by Maeterlinck in 1903.

During those two decades, Glasgow created a number of protagonists, generally heroines—in *The Wheel of Life* (1906), *Life and Gabriella* (1916), *The Builders* (1919), and *One Man in His Time* (1922)—whose stories of personal development begin when the boredom of their ordinary lives creates a longing in them for "something different." This vague but deeply rooted need they inevitably project upon a character of the opposite sex, who arrives from outside their everyday existence. Once Glasgow's protagonists manage to embody their need for "something different" in a potential lover, a period of enchantment ensues, followed usually by disappointment, disenchantment, rejection of the lover, and by introjection or recovery of personal traits previously so unknown to the protagonist that only mirrored in someone else could they become visible. After the reclamation of the projected qualities

---

3. Maurice Maeterlinck, *Wisdom and Destiny,* trans. Alfred Sutro (New York, 1903), 31, 81, 280.

comes a period of relatively realistic adjustment. This pattern of longing, projection, introjection, and insight constitutes the process of psychological growth that, I suggest, forms the base of the pyramid of mirrors Glasgow's best novels place between the universe, the author, and the reader.

Midway through the two decades during which Glasgow was mastering the mirroring technique suggested by Maeterlinck, she wrote a short story, "The Professional Instinct," that underscores the intimate connection between her approach and one of the major movements in twentieth-century psychology. Her protagonist, an "analytical psychologist" named Dr. John Estbridge, finds himself pulled between three women: his bristling, smothering wife; a youthful and yielding professor of philosophy at a college for women; and his true mistress, his science, which he has lavished with passion and which has kept him young. As the narrator tells us: "Like most men, according to the analytical psychologists, he had identified his own dreams with the shape of a woman"—a point underlined when Estbridge's best friend later says to him, "The only thing you ever loved in any woman was your own reflection." *Analytical psychology* is the term Carl Jung chose to distinguish his method of introspective psychology from psychoanalysis after the 1911–1914 break with Freud. The tendency of men to identify their dreams with the shape of a woman reveals one of the key elements of the male psyche as described by Jung, the *anima*, or inner woman of the male personality. As men project their *anima* upon women, so women project their *animus*, or masculine element, upon men. And not only the contrasexual elements, but "all unconscious contents," according to analytical psychology, are "first experienced in *projection*. This means that an unconscious quality of one's own is first recognized and reacted to when it is discovered in an outer object." Only by recognizing and reclaiming such materials is psychological development possible.[4]

This confluence of philosophical, literary, and psychological theories from Carpenter, Maeterlinck, and Jung constitutes the current within which I wish to place Glasgow's technique of characterization in *The Sheltered Life*. Yet this work differs in two ways from the majority of the

---

4. Ellen Glasgow, "The Professional Instinct," in Glasgow, *The Collected Stories of Ellen Glasgow*, ed. Richard K. Meeker (Baton Rouge, 1963), 240, 251; Edward F. Edinger, *An Outline of Analytical Psychology* (Reprinted from Quadrant, I [1968]), 4–5.

novels she had written during the decade and a half before 1932. It is less a story of psychological growth than one of illusions shattered by harsh realities; in this it resembles the books of her earlier naturalistic and critical realist phases. Furthermore, rather than focus on a single character, *The Sheltered Life* looks at the passing world from two points of view, those of General David Archbald and his granddaughter, Jenny Blair Archbald, both of whom receive roughly equal attention as the story unfolds. Jenny Blair, however, is the chief actor in the plot, which revolves around her innocent but destructive crush for the Archbalds' neighbor, George Birdsong, whose wife Eva, the fourth important character, undergoes a maiming operation midway through the story. The domestic tragedy of Jenny Blair, George, and Eva resembles a realistic drama, perhaps an Ibsen play, enacted before the eyes of General Archbald, through whose complex sensibility and historical perspective Glasgow amplifies the meaning of the major events.[5]

Despite its double focus and lack of a psychologically developing protagonist, *The Sheltered Life* makes extensive use of the mirroring technique Glasgow experimented with in the novels of the period between 1916 and 1929 that trace the personality growth of a single character. Because Jenny Blair and the general each have more than one mirroring character, however, and because the latter figures generally reflect unconscious aspects of both protagonists, the minor figures function in more complex ways than do the doubles and foils of traditional literary works. For the same reasons they are also more complex than the comparable figures in most Glasgow novels.

Jenny Blair, for example, when she looks into a mirror, sees herself as Alice in Wonderland.[6] On the far side of that looking glass, however, lies the world of adults, into which she travels half blind to what the various grown-ups actually mean to her half-formed emotions. Although the thought of her Aunt Etta fills her spirit with blackness because Aunt Etta is ugly, invalided, and unwanted by men, Jenny Blair fails to recognize her intimate tie to her aunt: that fear of suffering a fate similar to Etta's contributes to her own longing for affection from a man (66–67, 254). And while she consciously worships Eva (the great beauty of Queenborough who gave up a career in opera to marry George Birdsong)

---

5. See Raper, *Sunken Garden*, 138–39, 147.
6. Ellen Glasgow, *The Sheltered Life* (New York, 1979), 79. Subsequent references to the novel are to this edition and will be given in the text.

as her symbol of order, beauty, and perfection, Jenny Blair could not explain her reasons for blurting out that Eva will be slow about making her will or for responding to Eva's operation with an unmanageable mixture of terror and ecstasy (56–57, 135, 160–61, 266). She cannot acknowledge, even to herself, that Eva is her rival for George.

George similarly mirrors a combination of conscious and unconscious forces working within Jenny. She knows that he has given a focus to her virgin wild desire for mystery and delight, that he excites the winged passion to which she wants to resign her will (206, 212, 222). But she has no conscious inkling that he also fills the vacuum in her emotions left by the death of her father when she was five, that since she was nine, George has added a sexual dimension to a young girl's deepest need, the "lost feeling of security, rightness, fulfillment" that her father might have gratified (39–40, 67, 230, 247).

Three other minor characters play less complex roles in Jenny's psychological drama. Her mother, Cora Archbald, both provides a source for, and amplifies the meaning of, Jenny's evasive idealism. But Cora manages to evade painful realities, not in order to satisfy passions as her daughter does, but for the most high-minded of reasons. Yet both mother and daughter live by telling themselves protective lies (68, 174). Aunt Isabella mirrors Jenny's defiant passion, but she also provides a model of courageous, autonomous, and happy womanhood that her niece ignores by rejecting the independent part of herself in order to yield to George (11, 75, 97–98, 167). The scientific realism of John Welch, Eva Birdsong's adopted cousin, Jenny must also reject because she has suppressed her own critical intelligence. To Jenny's mind, Welch is "perfectly horrid"—chiefly because he calls romantic love a mere "mental fever" at a time when Jenny has sacrificed her own reason to her passion for George (150, 183, 206, 208).

The supporting characters reveal conscious and unconscious elements of General Archbald's personality much as they mirror Jenny Blair. He sees in Jenny Blair herself a repetition of his own youthful rebellion against the strictures of tradition, a perverse freedom to live out his impulses "untrammelled by consideration for others" (131). But his daughter Isabella better expresses these repressed desires, for she has the courage of her appetites. The incident with which she breaks her unwanted engagement to Thomas Lunsford solidly echoes the accident that forced Archbald into a loveless marriage of thirty years to save appearances (11–13, 24–25)—except that by refusing to repeat her father's mistake, Isabella ends up with a third man, the one she wants (97–98). That Archbald doesn't measure his own failure of nerve against Isabella's success indicates that he shares his daughter-in-law Cora's capacity for ignoring unpleasant and painful truths.

Indeed, this evasive tendency in Archbald underscores the major theme of the novel since, in one way or another, all the other characters are his family, his creatures, and the title of the book itself refers ultimately to the manner in which all of them shelter themselves and others from reality.[7] Archbald himself points out that Cora's "higher nature lent itself to deceit" and that "her dissembling became, in some incredible fashion, the servant of goodness" (174). Because he has committed himself to the same benignly protective evasions, he can express no reaction stronger than exasperation when Cora's unthinking dependence blocks him from a second marriage that he well deserves after the thirty years' prison of his first (25–26). Archbald remains as blind as Cora to the pernicious aspects of the evasive idealism they share.

He is more aware of the extent to which his hysterical daughter Etta amplifies by exaggeration the waste of his own life; for he feels that she embodies "all those harsh and thorny realities from which he had tried in vain to escape"—chiefly his ineffectual pity, his impotent desire, and his disappointment (176). He likewise recognizes in George Birdsong an imprudent version of his own generous instincts and of his desire, though for different reasons, to shelter women from reality, especially Eva from the truth of her marriage (143–44, 196). But he never consciously connects his imperfectly faithful neighbor (George) with his own conduct during an affair with a married woman he loved one April sixty years before in England, for she has remained the great love of his life, whereas George's affairs are commonplace philandering (112–18). The general finds John Welch's formulaic realism clean, competent, hard, and alien to his own worldly concern for people. Yet John and the general share the feeling that their knowledge sets them above the others: John, because his science is orderly, nonromantic, antisentimental; Archbald, because his long experience has blessed him with a "gay cynicism" and a "hardened crust of despair" (118, 152). But what the general rejects in distancing himself from Welch returns with sudden

---

7. For a fuller discussion, see Raper, *Sunken Garden*, 138–49.

violence after Jenny Blair's innocence drives Eva to shoot George with his own hunting gun. In their panic, both self-styled men of hard knowledge (Welch and the general) mindlessly conspire to preserve the illusions of the sheltered life by propagating the lie that (because George shot himself accidentally) both Eva and Jenny are innocent (290–91).

The general's regressive behavior in the final scene reminds us of the most important way this book differs from Glasgow's other novels between 1916 and 1932: that neither of its central figures can experience significant psychological growth in a drama in which illusions once shattered are instantly restored. Although there can be no question about the use of mirroring characters to reveal hidden dimensions of the general and his granddaughter, the projections of these two do not give way to the subsequent introjections and insight that made emotional development possible in earlier books. Jenny Blair fails to mature largely because when she was nine, the sense of herself as alive and different "wove a faint pattern of thought" and gradually hardened "into a shell over her mind"(3); almost immediately after this hardening, her conspiracy to keep a secret with George took possession of her hidden self to govern it through the end of the book.

The ending clearly shows the reason the general can no longer develop: he is altogether committed to the make-believe values of the sheltered life, especially as he sees them embodied in Eva Birdsong. But this was not always the case; for Eva herself stands at the end of a long corridor of mirroring figures David Archbald has faced during his extended life. Of these, all who furthered his psychic development belong to a period that ended almost half a century before the present action of the novel begins, in May, 1906. As a child in the decades before the Civil War, he had lived on a plantation dominated by his grandfather, a Virginia Squire Western whose pleasures in life ran to baiting abolitionists, staging cockfights, and hunting deer. From the start, David was different: he wanted to be a poet, he felt pity for living things, the sight of blood sickened him. Even though his poetic sensibility brings out the worst in his grandfather, it is the source of the boy's emotional growth. When young David stares into the eyes of a dying buck pulled down by the hounds, he sees a look that is "to return to him again and again" in the "faces of men, women, children, and animals, all over the world." In their eyes it is his own hunted self, of course, that he sees, and we are reminded of this identification when his grandfather smears the buck's blood over the boy, who in turn vomits on the "anointing hand and the outstretched arm" (102–105).

In his early years Archbald possesses the courage to act on the self-knowledge he finds mirrored in the hunted. As a youth living on the Stillwater plantation, he furnishes food, clothes, and an identifying pass to a fugitive slave and eventually engineers his escape to another county (109–11). As his moral sensibility evolves, it is in part "the old fear and bewilderment of the hunted" that draws him to the "small, shy, pale" English woman he loves in London and intends to liberate from her "sulky, well-set-up sportsman" husband (114). Losing her nerve at the last moment, however, she refuses to give up her children and remains behind to drown herself (116–17). That defeat splits David Archbald in two. The poet, the effective fighter against traditions, the young lover, seemingly his true self, vanishes (118), leaving only the surface man, who returns to Virginia to fight with his people and stays to become a prosperous attorney, an Episcopalian, a passionless husband, a good-enough father, grandfather, and worshiping neighbor of Eva Birdsong: "Except for that one defeated passion in his youth, he had lived entirely upon the shifting surface of facts" (119–20). Or so he thinks.

In fact, the true self that he thought died with his great love has continued to live as his buried life, an unconscious energy that explains his irrational worship of Eva. For, given her immense beauty and the mistreatment by her sportsman husband, Eva is the only woman he knows who mirrors his continuing need for "fulfillment, completeness, perfection" (120). Although he sees her as the symbol of his lost "sense of fulfillment not only in himself but in what men call Divine goodness" (120), the truth is that Archbald must preserve Eva's false role as an ideal because only so will she keep his buried self alive. Rather than relinquish the lost part of himself he has projected on Eva and risk reopening the deep wound of his London defeat, Archbald at the end scurries over to the Birdsongs to lift the shattered Eva to her feet and to shelter his guilt-trapped granddaughter with his pity (291–92). Whatever of himself he has withdrawn from Eva (if anything) he immediately reinvests in Jenny. In doing so, he reclaims nothing and reaches no helpful insight: the protective illusions live on. Consequently, within the present action of the novel, the general no more grows psychologically than does his granddaughter.

To restore to the novel the element of growth found in Glasgow's earlier works, however, we need only bring the author or the reader—the other two faces of our pyramid of mirrors—into focus and make two reasonable assumptions: that we should look to the text itself for clues to reading the text and that the psychological events that transpire when an author or reader gets to know a character probably resemble the psychic processes we have seen occurring when two Glasgow characters know one another well. The relationship of the author, or a reader, to a character, like the tie between characters, may at some point cease to be that of a subject to an object and become instead that of an individual to some element of himself projected onto the character. To describe this identification with a character, I find it helpful to borrow the concept of the *selfobject* created by the influential American psychoanalyst Heinz Kohut. Dr. Kohut developed the *selfobject* concept to describe objects or aspects of the environment that are experienced "as part of the self"; the term thus denotes experiences *bridging* "the inner world of the self and the outer world of the environment."[8] A selfobject is a "psychic reality" unavailable to an *empirical* observer, who would see only an object separated from a subject. This dimension of reality is available, however, to *empathic* observers who combine *introspection* of their own in-depth experiences with the *vicarious* experience of others who report on their involvement with the significant people in their lives. The selfobject is neither all subject (self) nor all object (other); it is a third entity, a psychic reality that comes into being without threatening the empirical existence of either the subject or the object. (I belabor this definition because it may be a difficult one to grasp for thinkers who have been conditioned to accept the Cartesian split between subject and object.

Glasgow's autobiography and her preface to *The Sheltered Life* demonstrate that the selfobject bridge applies to the relationship between herself and her characters. Her first invented character, an imaginary playmate, was the joint creation of the four-year-old girl and her substitute mother, Lizzie Jones, who would spin out bedtime stories together. Glasgow writes: "Out of the dim mists of infancy a hero named

---

8. Heinz Kohut, *The Analysis of the Self: A Systematic Approach to the Psychoanalytic Treatment of Narcissistic Personality Disorders* (New York, 1971), xiv; Ernest S. Wolf, "Psychoanalytic Psychology of the Self and Literature," *New Literary History*, XII (1980), 43–44.

Little Willie had wandered into the strange country of my mind, or, it may be, at the start, into Mammy's. I cannot recall either his earliest background or his first appearance. But, after Little Willie entered our lives, he stayed there, as the closest and dearest of companions, until at last I outgrew him." In her early years Glasgow also projected unconscious elements of herself onto natural objects: "Every tree near our house had a name of its own and a special identity," she recalled. And: "I was born a tree worshiper. I bled within when my father cut down any tree on the road or the lawn."[9] Her description of the origins of *The Sheltered Life* reveals a similar gift, in Coleridge's words, for transferring from her "inward nature a human interest and a semblance of truth sufficient to procure for . . . shadows of imagination that willing suspension of disbelief for the moment, which constitutes poetic faith."[10] Glasgow could recall "no definite beginning or voluntary act of creation" for the novel—only that the background is that of her girlhood and that "the rudiments of the theme must have lain buried somewhere" in her consciousness: "One moment there was a mental landscape without figures; the next moment, as if they had been summoned by a bell, all the characters trooped in together, with every contour, every feature, every attitude, every gesture and expression complete. In their origin, I exerted no control over them. They were too real for dismemberment." But she did, she continues, "select or eliminate" details to preserve "the general scheme of the book" and to recognize and obey the unities (xvi).

The empathic reader may sense in Glasgow's encounter with a figureless mental landscape a reasonably accurate foreshadowing of what happens when a reader confronts the black marks that run across the white landscape of printed pages. One moment there is only the lined whiteness; the next, as if summoned by a bell, voices and people appear moving about inside the reader's head—people who are, at first, someone else—and, finally, only the reader.[11] This is the third face of the pyramid of mirrors with which we began. Aside from the (ultimately arbitrary) black squiggles, everything else that happens when one reads a fiction comes from within the reader. The conversion of words into

---

9. Ellen Glasgow, *The Woman Within* (New York, 1954), 23–24, 27, 51.
10. Ernest S. Wolf points out the connection between the selfobject and Coleridge's poetic faith in "Psychoanalytic Psychology of the Self and Literature," 56.
11. See Raper, *Sunken Garden*, 207, for additional suggestions.

voices, characters, and action arises in part from the reader's education in decoding signs but, in much larger part, from his own conscious and unconscious life of the senses, feelings, and emotions. The characters constitute an undeniable psychic reality of selfobjects composed of hints the author has placed on the page combined with elements of the reader projected onto the author's clues. The words on the page are therefore a mirror in which the reader sees dimensions of himself, some previously well-known, others only half-known, others not known at all. This gift for bridging the chasm between the subject and the character is the first work of both the author and the reader. But it is not their only responsibility; otherwise they would remain where General Archbald ends, still merged with his selfobject, Eva Birdsong. In contrast, the author and the reader must break their tie to the characters.

In "Technique as Discovery," interpreting D. H. Lawrence's declarations that the author in his books "repeats and presents again one's emotions to be master of them"—that "one sheds one's sicknesses in books"—Mark Schorer contends that Lawrence's is "an acceptable theory only with the qualification that technique" enables the author to objectify his emotions, "to discover and to evaluate [his] subject matter, and more than that, to discover the amplifications of meaning of which [his] subject matter is capable."[12] If we combine Schorer's position with Glasgow's statement that she selected or eliminated details from the initial vision of her characters to preserve the general scheme of her book and to obey the unities, we may reconstruct the following speculative account of Glasgow's involvement with her two point-of-view characters, the general and his granddaughter. In her initial state of selfobject oneness with the characters, Glasgow probably projected both conscious and unconscious dimensions of her personality onto them. The general, for example, clearly expresses, as the capacitating character, the opinions of his creator when he reflects on history, the past, and civilization. But one doubts that Glasgow would have acknowledged her own tendency to sacrifice her relatives and friends to the fulfillment of her ideals, although what Archbald does to Eva Birdsong powerfully dramatizes this trait. In addition, Glasgow clearly admired Jenny Blair's vital force and her rebellion. But the author probably would

---

12. Mark Schorer, "Technique as Discovery," in Ray B. West (ed.), *Essays in Modern Literary Criticism*, (New York, 1961), 196, 201–202.

not have accepted the girl's sacrifice of Eva as a mirror of her own selfishness. It is this combination of conscious and unconscious elements from the author that gives the two characters their roundness, the sense that we know them in depth.[13] But as the novel moves toward its catastrophe, Glasgow balances her involvement with Jenny and the general with greater attention to the suffering of Eva by emphasizing Eva's growing sense that she has not been herself for forty years, that for twenty years she has been "somebody else," "somebody's ideal," that she has sacrificed her well-being, not for a great passion, as she thought, but for a shabby marriage to a lawyer capable of seducing his best friend's teenaged granddaughter. As Eva violently awakes from her long self-deception, the author separates herself from the habit Archbald and Jenny have of clothing their self-interest with idealistic and romantic illusions. In short, the tragic scheme of the novel and an increasing empathy for Eva combine to break Glasgow's identification with the point-of-view characters. This increased objectivity represents the author's emotional and critical growth.

To the reader, however, belongs the final insight. To the extent that Jenny and her grandfather come to life, they are also the reader's selfobjects; in him (the reader), they trigger known and unknown fantasies of youthful energy, ancient wisdom, emotional greed, idealistic blindness. But the violence to which they push Eva signals the reader at some point—perhaps when Jenny must *will* her love into being or when Archbald puts his idealism *above* truth—that he (the reader) must break the bond of fantasy that blurs the distinction between himself and the characters. He may share their pity and terror, but he will not pursue his desire or his idealism far enough to become as tragic as they. They may continue to live, and walk about, inside the reader's head until Eva's shot ceases to echo, but he senses the essential limit that separates him from the characters. Thus the reader reclaims that part of himself—the evasive idealism, the selfish passion—called into being through identification with the mirroring characters. Whether he has sufficient insight at the moment to master his fantasies matters less than does his experience that what was once unconscious in him has become conscious, perhaps for the first time.

Fictions continue to exist in part because this coming into con-

---

13. Raper, *Sunken Garden*, 201–205, develops this point.

sciousness of hidden dimensions of the self is beneficial, whether or not insight follows immediately. The mere presence of selfobjects that mirror unknown elements in the reader, of selfobjects in which he merges even temporarily with the characters, brings with it the reassurance that there are others in the world sufficiently like the reader to empathize with him and to understand his secret self: that finally he is not alone. This mirroring or merger itself triggers the psychic transformation that brings greater wholeness of the self.[14] In time and with repetition, insight may follow—but conscious interpretation of what occurs in reading fiction is not nearly as valuable as the experience of identifying with the characters (or, in some works, with the implied author) in order to create selfobjects. For the creative reader, it goes without saying that fiction possesses this power to reveal the reader's inner self as though in a mirror. But critics set on handling literary texts the way natural scientists treat natural objects or the way computers break codes may need reminding that creative reading remains a uniquely human event.

Three recent critics among those who need no reminding of this essential power of fiction are Norman N. Holland, David Bleich, and, to a lesser extent, Wolfgang Iser. I find it significant that though I worked altogether independently of these three, applying a different intellectual tradition, and focusing on the model provided by the characters in the text, my approach to *The Sheltered Life* confirms the main claims of Holland, Bleich, and Iser: that, as Norman Holland puts it, in reading literature, readers "meld with the exterior work so that they no longer perceive a difference between 'in here' and 'out there'" and that the reader experiences "the work as a transformation within himself of unconscious fantasy materials through form and meaning" rather than as "transformations . . . embodied in the literary work."[15] Or as Iser, placing more emphasis on the way the text guides the reader's imagination, phrases it, the text creates an image in the reader's imagination that contains the meaning of the text, something brought into existence through reading "that is to be found neither outside the book nor on its printed pages": "As text and reader thus merge into a single situation,

14. Here I am applying to literature Heinz Kohut's distinctions between the roles empathic mirroring (understanding) and interpretation play in analysis. See Kohut, *The Restoration of the Self* (New York, 1977), 29–32, 87–88, 187–88n.
15. Holland, *5 Readers*, xii, 17–18.

the division between subject and object no longer applies, and it therefore follows that meaning is no longer an object to be defined, but is an effect to be experienced."[16] Holland, Bleich, and Iser deserve the appreciation of readers for putting them back into the literary and critical experience after decades of New Criticism left them out.[17] And yet the approach to *The Sheltered Life* outlined here arrives at the basic reader-response position by focusing closely on the text and by following Glasgow's cues in her novels as to how we are to take her characters—that is, by a simple expansion of the primary New Critical tools; this method uses biographical materials only to add depth of understanding to hints taken from the text.

I stress the independence of my approach because the combination of different method, independence of knowledge, and parallel conclusions may come as near as literary studies ever do to matching the high standard of verification that the double-blind method and replicable results of the experimental sciences strive toward. The congruence of Bleich, Holland, and my own conclusions goes, I think, a long way toward verifying the theory of reader-response that Caroline Shrodes stated with clarity and succinctness almost a quarter of a century ago.

The vicarious experience induced by reading involves identification, including projection and introjection, catharsis, and insight. These manifestations assume a variety of forms precipitated by the reader's "shock of recognition" when he beholds himself or someone close to him. Self recognition may give him a sense of belonging; it may augment his self regard and allay his sense of guilt. The character's troubles may arouse feelings of sympathy and compassion. Or the reader may displace hostility upon the character because he cannot tolerate in himself what he recognizes in the character. A situation in a story may be so compelling that it becomes interchanged in his mind with an episode in his own life and becomes endowed with the affective character of the latter. The change in cognitive and psychic force which may result from vicarious experience may lead to adaptive behavior that is more realistic than the reader's previous adjustment, or the reading may merely reflect the interpreter's existing means of coping, such as repression, rationalization, or projection."[18]

If this is not exactly what Aristotle meant by the cleansing process of catharsis, it is, I suggest, near enough to restore the cycle of the reader's

16. Iser, *Act of Reading*, 9–10.
17. See Holland, *5 Readers*, 12, and Iser, *Act of Reading*, 15–17, for representative comments on New Criticism.
18. Caroline Shrodes, "Bibliotherapy: An Application of Psychoanalytic Theory," *American Imago*, XVII (1960), 314–15.

emotional involvement as a central and useful concern of criticism.[19] So far as I can detect, the only soft spot in the validity of the results that Shrodes, Holland, Bleich, and I arrive at, despite our different approaches, is that all of us share some basic assumptions of the late twentieth-century world view: each of us works, that is, with one modern psychological theory or another. Wolfgang Iser, however, arrives at his parallel position by deliberately avoiding the language and concepts of modern psychology and by employing instead the language of linguistics and the phenomenological tradition growing out of Edmund Husserl and Martin Heidegger.

Yet important distinctions exist between the approach applied here to *The Sheltered Life* and the methods of Holland, Bleich, and Iser. I would like to mention the major ones.

Bleich's suggestion that interpreters of the reader's response start with the basic perception of the work, follow that with an account of somatic and emotional responses and an investigation of associations, and then negotiate a community consensus of interpretation seems a useful contribution. My focus, however, on the interrelationships of characters as a model for the reader's response and my use of the selfobject construct from Kohut place Bleich's commitment to subjectivity, I suggest, in a somewhat larger context and a position less vulnerable to charges of "impressionism and sheer subjectivity."[20]

Holland's insistence that for the reader to respond favorably toward a work, he "must have found something in the work that does what he does to cope with needs or dangers"—that he must have been able to find his "characteristic structure of defense or adaptation" matched by the text—provides a useful partial explanation for the argument here that the reader responds to the ways the text mirrors his needs and fears. Equally helpful are Holland's remarks in passing on the ability of a work to match the reader's defenses by "dividing up reality to deal with it in

---

19. For more on catharsis, see Raper, *Sunken Garden*, xii–xiii, 205–207.
20. Bleich, *Readings and Feelings*, 21–48, 86–93; Murray M. Schwartz and David Willbern, "Literature and Psychology," in Jean-Pierre Barricelli and Joseph Gibaldi (eds.), *Interrelations of Literature* (New York, 1983), 214. A selection of familiar texts that provide even clearer models of the mirroring process than Glasgow's novel could include: Edgar Allan Poe's "William Wilson," Walt Whitman's "Out of the Cradle Endlessly Rocking," Mark Twain's "Facts Concerning the Recent Carnival of Crime in Connecticut," Ernest Hemingway's "A Clean Well-Lighted Place," Lawrence Durrell's *The Alexandria Quartet*, and John Fowles's *The Magus*.

little bits," especially by doubling and splitting the significant figures in an individual's life. Applied to *The Sheltered Life,* Holland's comment suggests that the reader may be able to tolerate the seductive father role played by George Birdsong in part because Glasgow balances George with General Archbald, a benign father, and that readers can accept the weakness of Etta and Eva because the vigor and health of Jenny Blair and Isabella, by offsetting the invalids, gratify the reader's desire for mirroring images of strong assertive women. And yet there is something unnecessarily narrowing and deterministic about Holland's use of the "identity theme," inasmuch as it restricts the range of a reader's response to re-creating from the text "his own characteristic psychological processes"—that is, to matching his personal pattern of defenses and fantasies.[21] For Holland, although "the individual can grow and change infinitely within" his own "style," "once a person's identity theme is established it never changes."[22] This is Jenny Blair's problem because she has allowed "a fragment of personality" to "harden into a shell over her mind"; it is also the general's weakness, inasmuch as he generally finds himself mirrored in the eyes of the hunted and the invalided.

But what of Glasgow's more representative protagonists who long in other novels for "something different," something that comes from beyond their known reality? Holland's difficulty here is that he works with a concept of the psyche according to which for an idea or image to exist in the unconscious mind, it must first have been repressed, and to be repressed, it must first present itself to consciousness. Therefore, even when a reader responds with his unconscious fantasies, he brings to the text only that which previously was presented to consciousness and which remains totally personal; moreover, because they have been repressed, such fantasies must, in some sense, possess a negative quality. The conception of the unconscious that Glasgow appears to be using with the heroines who seek something different (and that my approach employs) is different in that is goes back to Jung, not Freud. In addition to repressed personal elements, this model of the unconscious offers the individual access, in Jung's words, to "unconscious qualities that are not individually acquired but are inherited," including "impulses to carry out actions from necessity, without conscious motivation," and "inborn

---

21. Holland, *5 Readers,* 115, 17, 124, 40.
22. *Ibid.,* 60. See Bleich, *Subjective Criticism,* 121, for his objection to Holland's identity theme on grounds similar to my own.

forms of 'intuition,' namely the *archetypes* of perception and apprehension, which are the necessary *a priori* determinants of all psychic processes." Rather than a predetermined and personal pattern of defenses and fantasies, the Jungian unconscious includes instincts that "compel man to a specifically human mode of existence" and archetypes that "force his ways of perception and apprehension into specifically human patterns."[23] Rather than an identity theme that never changes, this model of the unconscious represents the individual's full *potential* as a man or woman; in its extreme manifestation, this model holds out the possibility of that radical transformation in which the conscious personality turns into its opposite, a "running contrariwise" that Jung (following Heraclitus) calls *enantiodromia*, "the most marvellous of all psychological laws."[24] And it is to this sort of transformation that the reader opens himself when he merges with the characters in the greatest works of literature, texts that mirror not only what he already knows about himself, the way popular forms do, but that also bring forth human dimensions the reader has never known he possessed. This sort of growth goes well beyond the almost predictable responses ("self-duplication" or "reiteration," in Bleich's words) that Holland's identity theory would lead the reader to expect.

Wolfgang Iser's theory of blanks and negations helps account, however, for such extreme changes in the reader inasmuch as the *blanks* in the text (the missing connections the reader must fill) invite the reader's participation in creating the meaning of the text. According to Iser, very complex texts (like Samuel Beckett's) show the reader that his search for meaning is itself a defense and, in doing so, force the reader to transcend himself by opening him to new experiences formerly blocked by projection.[25] Iser's blanks constitute an important contribution, for they help us understand the way the text encourages the reader to project increasingly complex elements onto it. But Iser's approach first mechanizes the text and then anthropomorphizes it. In order to construct his patterns of indeterminacy, he turns the text into a complex word machine, an instrument of self-negation, but then portrays it as a cunning

---

23. Carl G. Jung, "Instinct and the Unconscious" (1919), reprinted in Joseph Campbell (ed.), *The Portable Jung* (New York, 1983), 52. For Freud's concept of the unconscious in relation to Jung's, see C. G. Jung, *Two Essays on Analytical Psychology* (New York, 1936–37).
24. Jung, *Two Essays*, 82.
25. Iser, *Act of Reading*, 167, 184–86, 202–203, 223–25.

intelligence determined to outwit the reader. Part of the problem may be that Iser's linguistic tradition and communications theory seem implicitly to take a machine, the computer with its binary options, as the model for human communications. But the deep reason Iser endows the text with human qualities derives from the French phenomenological tradition in which he works; in deliberately avoiding the concept of the unconscious, that tradition ends up, it seems, foisting off elements of its own humanity upon the objects to which it attends—in Iser's case, upon the text. Compared with Iser's theories, introducing the construct of the unconscious serves, I find, as a valid application of Occam's razor: the unconscious provides a simpler explanation for the phenomena Iser describes than do his mechanical and anthropomorphic views of the text. Restoring the unconscious allows us once more to respond to the characters who emerge from the text, or to the narrator or the implied author—not to machinelike sets of linguistic instructions. No longer mere gaps in a philosophical argument, Iser's blanks become shadows and shadings in rounded characters onto whose dark side we may project our own shadow and unclaimed potential much the way a lover projects himself onto what is sphinxlike, equivocal, elusive, indefinite, and full of promise in women who embody the "anima type" or, if the lover is a woman, upon the fine words, ambiguities, unrealized possibilities, misunderstood and needy qualities of animus-stimulating men.[26] In short, we will respond to the human figures in the text the way Jenny Blair does to George Birdsong's promising words or the general to Eva's fatal expectations. With this personal involvement begins the cycle of projection and introjection that leads the reader, if not the characters, to emotional growth—and often to insight.

My approach to Glasgow's novel differs from the theories of Bleich, Holland, and Iser in these details—it takes the relationships between characters as a model for the reader's response, it expands the concept of the unconscious to allow for significant growth in the reader, and it demechanizes the text and reclaims for the reader human qualities foisted onto it. Even so, focusing on *The Sheltered Life*, or any work of fiction, as a pyramid of mirrors with the process of projection, identification, and merger at its base supports the main arguments of the lead-

---

26. C. G. Jung, *The Development of Personality: Papers on Child Psychology, Education, and Related Subjects* (New York, 1981), 199.

ing reader-response critics. For even though the literary work begins, according to my position, with the author merged with his or her characters, it nonetheless ends in the self-knowledge the reader attains through his own repetition of that vital merger.

JAMES H. JUSTUS

The Power of Filiation in *All the King's Men*

Over the years since 1946 it has become more and more apparent that Robert Penn Warren was less interested in Huey Long as a man than he was in "what Huey did in his world," his gift for "attracting myth," and the "atmosphere of violence" generated by his power. In the most recent of his several accounts of the composition of *All the King's Men*, Warren stresses the Shakespearean links in "the question of power, its various justifications, ethical and otherwise, and its dangers."[1] That issue in Shakespeare's history plays, which Warren taught in his first year at LSU, is "between legitimacy and *de facto* power"; in the American version, for *legitimacy* read *constitutional*. In the dialectical drama of the 1930s, Huey's position, even though constitutional and therefore legitimate, is per se insufficient and inefficient; its success depends upon its potential for expansion—to fill needs, to appropriate functions that seem not to be working, to court the plebes in the best Bolingbroke manner. In this image Willie Stark is created. What Stark achieves on the public level is the remarkable fusion of the Richard factor (the power of legitimacy) and the Bolingbroke factor (de facto power). But Warren's other literary model for his politician is Spenser's Talus, the "iron

1. All quotations from Warren's novel are taken from the first edition of *All the King's Men* (New York, 1946) and will appear in parentheses in the text. Warren's comments on the composition of the novel are drawn from relevant interviews now collected in Floyd C. Watkins and John T. Hiers (eds.), *Robert Penn Warren Talking: Interviews, 1950–1978* (New York, 1980), and Robert Penn Warren, "In the Time of *All the King's Men*," *New York Times Book Review*, May 31, 1981, pp. 9, 39–42.

groom" who remorselessly executes the judgments of his master Artegall in Book V of *The Faerie Queene*; in its southern declension, Talus becomes Willie Talos, who becomes great not from his own strength but from the assorted weaknesses of others. Willie Talos of *Proud Flesh*, the verse play that precedes the novel, in turn becomes Willie Stark of *All the King's Men*. If Shakespeare looms behind the public drama of political power in Warren's novel, Spenser contributes most tellingly to the private, the internal drama of the unfused self: Willie Stark vs. Willie Stark—or, to put it in Jack Burden's terms, Cousin Willie from the Country vs. The Boss.

"The question of power" is of course a grand theme, and we must accept Warren's word that he saw his novel as a working out of that theme in contemporary terms. But I think we cannot confuse the circumstances of composition of this novel with the novel that we read. It may be true that the original *Proud Flesh* was as stylized and inert as most twentieth-century poetic dramas—so much so that the first fictionalized version of the story of Willie Talos was simply waiting for a particularized voice to bring it to life—what Warren has called the narrator's "lingo." But the discovery of Jack Burden did more than add a fillip to a preexisting plot: it changed the plot itself, for by making Jack Burden the narrator of the Willie Stark story, the very "lingo," with its calculated rhetorical efforts, subtly shifted the balance of the characters' weight, and the manner of the telling altered the matter told. What early readers rarely noted was that though Willie Stark is the narrator's explicit subject, the explicit subject of *All the King's Men* is Jack Burden. He is in fact not a subversive narrator. He frankly presents himself as the most complex figure in his account, and he tells us finally more about himself and his difficult moral education than he does about Willie Stark. This impression can be verified quantitatively—by counting the numbers of pages devoted to each—and when we consider the tone, the emphasis, the freighted diction in the segments devoted exclusively to Willie Stark, the qualitative difference makes the imbalance even more striking. Warren's characteristic interest during the long composition of *All the King's Men* was not, in fact, public power and politics but internal division, the divided self whose drama was enacted on external stages. What preoccupied the Warren of "Prime Leaf," *Night Rider*, and *At Heaven's Gate* also preoccupied the Warren of *All the King's Men*. To the unresolved fusion of Cousin Willie and The Boss is added the significant clambering about of competing personas within Jack Burden: Little Jackie, Jackie-Bird, the political fixer, the subversive loyalist, the rebellious son.

Jack Burden is what Anne Stanton calls a smart aleck, and he writes a smart aleck prose: it is by turns rich, resonant, allusive, philosophical, world-weary, and mawkish, drawing alternately on a high modernist literary style and a low gutter vernacular. He can be both touching and exasperating. But Jack Burden does not deceive us. He is his own center of interest, one that he consistently maintains even while involved in the most crucial moments of Willie Stark's life and times. We might wish to know more about the uneasy transition from Willie the Hick to Willie the Boss; we certainly want to know more about the tension between the idealist and the pragmatist in the Willie Stark at the very height of his power—many readers sense an unrendered stage in his internal development during his negotiations with Adam Stanton prior to their mutual deaths. The truth is, however, that Willie Stark has his most useful function not as a protofascist governor with an idealistic vision but as a catalyst in the slow but clarifying spiritual progress of Jack Burden.

Warren says that "the question of power," only partly occasioned by the example of Huey Long, was the generative interest behind the composition of *All the King's Men* as a political work. But what accounts for the larger part of *All the King's Men* that is not political, that heavy impress of the personal, the domestic, the familial? In a curious way, even in this respect the example of Huey Long may have served Warren well, since the trappings of power in the Louisiana of the 1930s were by all accounts of the down-home variety: the raising to a state level of the southern habit of keeping track of boys and pappies and cousins in the extended spectrum of kin; of being accommodating in the exchange of help and favors; of tapping the local and familial needs and identifying them as general; of understanding that the statehouse is the courthouse writ large. Such insights and methods were of course not any less lethal than those that obtained in big city political machines, and they were not less coercive. So here is one source of the pervasive domestic effect of *All the King's Men*. But in addition to the family-oriented Long machine, the effects of which Warren saw all about him in the 1930s, there is also a theory that Warren says he derived from observing Il Duce's Italy in 1939, the extrapolation in political actuality of what he had been reading in Shakespeare, Spenser, William James, Machiavelli, Dante, and Burckhardt: that the natural leader is the one who abhors the vacuum of power, that the great man absorbs the accrued weaknesses of others—their needs, their vacancies. Here is the frame on which the specific Willie Stark story is hung. Though "the question of power" would seem to be primarily a fit subject for public drama, Warren's theory actually italicizes the private drama that makes the political one possible.

The public drama of *All the King's Men*, the narrative rendering of the question of power, is the achieved situation of Stark's relations with Tiny Duffy and the others in his orbit—those demonstrations of a political given inherent in the American version of a royal court. Its constituent reality is articulated by midnight visits to resistant subjects for coercive purposes, choreographed dispatching of emissaries, protocol within and among the entourage, threats, enticements, toleration of infractions if they are minor and the use of predated signed resignations if they are not: all these and more are the textual patterns of relationships already in place, achieved.

But Warren's real interest lies in the more fluid circumstances prior to the demonstrations of achieved power. Here is the area of richer dramatic possibilities, the scene of needs, weaknesses, vacancies. The private drama must untangle the myriad motives behind the acts, causes behind the effects, reasons behind the justifications. It is not surprising that our most vital engagement with Willie Stark is with his internal struggle to do good for the human animal whose condition he has no illusions about; here is the matrix for the clash between idealism and pragmatism, but one that does not cripple his ability to act. This is the aspect of his leadership that interests us, because it first interests Jack Burden, who lurches from one well-considered philosophical position to another. This king's man may not have gone to a Presbyterian Sunday school "when they still had some theology" (358), but his cynical view of his fellow creatures finds common cause with Stark's residual Calvinism. He may keep his ideals under wraps, but he betrays them occasionally in the same spirit as his employer. Jack Burden tacitly acknowledges the self-evident phenomenon that Willie Stark fills up the blankness of others, that his power lies in his readiness to fulfill in himself their potentiality. But he never explicitly acknowledges that he also is being fulfilled by Willie Stark. For most of the narrative that he relates with such compulsion, Jack Burden is never quite sure of the reasons he enlists in Stark's cause, which is to say that, for all his stylish efforts to analyze the motivations of the common followers, he cannot admit to sharing with them the need for Willie Stark. But the looping, periodical syntax; the sweet-and-sour invocation of lonely figures for whom he compulsively supplies imaginary but predictable histories; the tumbling metaphors stimulated not by imagination but by a quiet rage to seize upon the truth of an experience that will lend definition to his need; above all, the temperament that selects the telling moments to relate: all these marks of Jack Burden's technique point inward before they relate outward, to the intricacies of a searching narrator before they validate a searching political hero.

However emphatic the melodrama of the public story and the psychodrama of the private, the real brilliance of *All the King's Men* lies in Warren's connections between the two. Jack Burden is provided generous space for the playing out of all the characteristics that make him a memorable figure—his cynicism, his sentimentality, his pride, his vulnerability, his wit—and Warren allows free exercise of the rhetorical consequences of that playing out in Burden's wide-ranging manipulation of discourse from the pretentious to the vernacular, his pompous philosophical declarations, his pungent witticisms and faux proverbs. Descended from the Hemingway stoic hero, wounded but bearing his emptiness with good-natured fortitude, Jack Burden enfolds himself within the vision that sees Willie Stark as a modern tragic hero and himself a reluctant *eiron*. But most important, the perspective of his own anxiety, the personal and the domestic, makes the public drama possible; it gives immediacy and visceral relevance to the ancient formulaic fall of princes. Given his own anxiety of sonhood, it is inevitable that Burden tends to see Stark at his most vulnerable in the role as father, just as it is that Burden, who is never comfortable with the easy conceptualizing of Stark as redneck tyrant, should domesticate that public role as a kind of Big Daddy, correcting and chastising in his redneck way but also smoothing away problems and embarrassments that all peccant children are heir to.

And Jack Burden is heir to them in a more urgent way than most children. In his narrative he makes it clear enough that his cynicism derives from childhood hurt occasioned by the loss of the father, but within the narrative only Anne Stanton seems to be able to connect his "smart-aleck" manner and the defection of Ellis Burden many years earlier. By rejecting his wife and son and home for a flophouse mission, Ellis Burden becomes a failure in his son's eyes because in the face of a stronger-willed wife he has sacrificed the role of natural authority: what Jack perceives as an unmanning erases the son's natural acquiescence to the father's prerogatives, just as the unmanning also erases the resentful son's natural devotion to the mother. "I could go for the rest of my life and not think about them," Jack tells Anne at one time, but the compulsive recurrence of Ellis Burden in his story contradicts all his denials of concern. In his first visit to the old man, the account is summarized, with not a single exchange recorded. "I had found what I had known I was going to find," Jack glumly records. But what the diction specifies, even in the narrative omissions, is the disagreeable discovery of kinship in a lexicon of downwardness: just as the old man is sketched by such words as *drooped, beneath, sagged down, slack-hanging,* the son appropriates for himself the same language of downwardness: he admits he "had been sinking down in the sleep like a drowning man in water." The price for dismissal of the father as failure is the nagging fear of the son's own failure.

And in the midst of literal failure—after losing his job on the *Chronicle* and before he signs on as Willie Stark's man—Jack Burden visits the man of success, Adam Stanton, the friend of his youth who joins him in recalling childhood days. But even the image of childhood innocence, safety, and love—"Yeah, we did have a good time when we were kids, you and Anne and me" (110)—is recoverable only through reference to its pastness, and even its pleasure is laced with the wry invocation of Edgar Poe. The three of them—"when they were children by the sea"—could resist the kind of death-dealing wind that had killed Annabel Lee; the violent squall from the Gulf "didn't chill us or kill us in the kingdom by the sea, for we were safe inside a white house" (110) presided over by Governor Stanton, Ellis Burden, and Judge Irwin. The image of the children by the sea, safe from the buffetings of fateful nature by virtue of benevolent and loving paternity, is a brief but revealing one whose very summoning up is generated by the knowledge of subsequent loss and felt failure.

Jack Burden's most poignant visit to Ellis Burden's shabby rooms above the Mexican restaurant is in fact the first leg of his journey in pursuing "the Case of the Upright Judge" (169), his investigation of

Judge Irwin for Willie Stark's political blackmail. Burden's vague unease stems not from the political ethics of digging up evidence for potential use against a rival—he has soothed his conscience in that matter by calling himself a historical researcher in pursuit of truth—but from the uncertainty of filial loyalties. In effect Jack Burden, serving one father, goes to seek out damaging information from another father to usurp the authority of still another father. His difficulty here as elsewhere is not public ethics but the violation of domestic piety. And here as elsewhere his attitude toward Ellis Burden becomes a touchstone of his moral growth. The sight of the old man feeding chocolate to what he calls an "unfortunate" revives in Jack a powerful early memory of himself as a child with his circus wagon and crayons listening for his father to say, "Son, here's what Daddy brought tonight." He momentarily feels a lump dissolving in his chest and hears himself murmur, "Father, Father—" (213). The substitution of George, the former aerialist who is now afraid of high places, for Jack, the political aerialist who has acclimated to the heady atmosphere of power, is an achingly appropriate displacement, as Jack himself intuitively perceives. "I had come to this room where Jack Burden leaned against the wall with a cigarette in his mouth. Nobody was leaning over him to give him chocolate" (213). What Jack cannot appreciate at this point in his education is the implication of a larger displacement. Ellis Burden's ministry to George is symptomatic of his larger mission, that of the man who gives up his profession, his social position, and all worldly ambitions to work among the human detritus of society: he becomes the secular saint, the father without habit whose functions are distributed among the family of man rather than concentrated upon the smaller organic family unit.

Jack Burden's story is the agony of filiation; out of the personal search for the father comes the larger story of Willie Stark, whose role as father extends from the domestic and familial to the political and public realms. Burden's task in one sense is to connect his personal drama to that larger one, to see the relevance of his need to the needs of the nameless crowds who support Willie Stark. But that larger drama begins with the personal, not only because it, like all political fictions, remains generalized and abstract until joined by the emotional immediacy of the private, but also because the perspective is that of Jack Burden, son in need.

It is not an accident of narrative sequence that Jack's pivotal visit to

Ellis Burden is immediately followed by a scene on a football Saturday; without formal transition the story moves rawly from what Jack calls "the world of the past" to "the world of the present," and the emblem of the secular saint as father is succeeded by that of the politician as father cheering his athlete son on to victory. Even without obvious narrative linkage, the two episodes glide together on the narrator's emotional undercurrents, specifically those marked by the uncertain chemistry of father-son relationships. For Jack Burden the verbal sign of the past is his own impulsive, almost inadvertent entreaty, "Father, Father—" that is uncomprehended and unreturned; the verbal sign of the present is Willie Stark's "We're all mighty proud of you, boy" (217) that Tom Stark curtly acknowledges and dismisses. From the thin responsiveness of one situation Burden enters the fulsome responsiveness of the other. The wise ass tone cannot conceal envy as Jack writes: "And I said to myself: *If he gets his eyes starry with tears again I am going to puke*" (218).

When near the end of his story Jack Burden can assert that we are all sons of a million fathers, he has moved away from the cynical rhetoric that has been the familiar accompaniment of his private and painful search; the moment articulates the climax in a spiritual journey that for much of the account has seemed to be a matter of meander and drift and happenstance. The generalization is a reminder that from the perspective of this narrator, his real story has been one of fathers and sons. The ethical question of ends and means, goals and methods, idealism and pragmatism, may be the grand scheme, the source of the public political drama that links homegrown fascism with the European variety in a system of echoes and analogies. But the level of story that is compelling is the domestic, the level that validates the emotional vitality in Burden's engagement with his own story. The sequence of that engagement is Burden's loss of a father, his refusal to accept a series of surrogate fathers, the interim solution by which he tacitly embraces Stark as father, the repetition of the initial loss in the deaths of Stark and Irwin, for which he comes to accept a measure of responsibility, and the secular penance he assumes in the care of a nonfather whom he elevates to generic father.

The climax of Jack Burden's spiritual drama comes in the final chapter, but in the very first chapter, when the narrator ostensibly engages the reader with the slick operations of a canny and powerful politician, this sensitive and exasperating man is already laying the groundwork for his own journey toward moral maturity. Chapter 1 not only illustrates the power of a political boss in full ascendancy; it also quietly introduces the major psychological compulsions of the scribe who records the nature of that power. Above all, the chapter provides the most compelling thematic motif that joins the Stark story to the Burden story: the tensions of filiation. That initial chapter is the account of what we assume is a characteristic visit of Governor Stark, a homecoming, undertaken for both filial piety and political exigency. What immediately impresses us, however, is the divided emphasis: we are equally drawn to the substance (the display of Willie Stark at the peak of his power) and the style (the obtrusive manner by which the narrator presents the Boss's techniques with his family, his entourage, and his constituency—and subliminally, perhaps, Burden's aesthetic manipulation as an equivalent of Stark's political manipulation). The description of Mason City, the famous opening that is a virtuoso piece of self-conscious artistry, projects not a populated space so much as it does a sensibility, not a scene for action but a screen for the projection of temperament, a way of seeing. Before we meet Willie Stark, we are introduced to the larger source of his paternity, of his power, his place—the depletion and poverty of his red hills—and to the extended family unit—son, wife, surrogate son (Sugar Boy), and the pervading consciousness of what will clearly become another surrogate son (Jack Burden). Even an overview of the crowd that comes running to pay homage to the Boss precedes a full view of the governor. Indeed, the first description of Stark is not of the man himself but of a poster picture of the governor "about six times life size" (8) hanging above the soda fountain in a Mason City drugstore—an effective device suggesting both the outsize popularity of Willie Stark among ordinary people and the once-removed actuality of the man as legend. The first dramatized instance of Stark as a practical politician is his meeting with a nondescript old man whom the narrating voice calls Old Leather-Face, whose son, he tells the governor, is in jail for killing another man in a knife fight. That vignette of a father-son situation, in which Stark will later intervene, is the first developed instance of the motif that radiates from the narrator's particular sensitivity to such matters.

Jack Burden in that first chapter pays considerable attention to the spatial composition of Willie Stark in relation to others: the crowds that instinctively open up a wedge-shaped space to allow the governor passage, a gesture denoting both awe and adoration; the narrator's repetition of such clauses as "we followed in his wake" (10), "we tailed after him," and "the rest of us in his gang followed behind" (14), to establish the invariable protocol for the physical disposition in leader-follower relationships; the photographer's formal arrangement of family members at the old Stark place for the requisite publicity pictures; and most important, the seemingly impulsive midnight visit to Burden's Landing to see Judge Irwin. Jack Burden is painfully precise in depicting himself spatially centered on the Irwin threshold between the judge and the governor, for he paradoxically loses his centrality, becoming a kind of abstract locus for the two specific, better-limned individuals. For a moment he becomes a tongue-tied child caught between two fathers, as it were, an appropriate physical situation for a person who will be increasingly plagued by uncertainty of his identity (Irwin calls Burden "Son"; Stark calls him "boy"). The moment is only prelude to the more explicit testing of rival paternal loyalties in the library, where Stark strolls uninvited, followed by an angry Irwin. As for Jack Burden: "I followed the pair of them" (47). In the exchange between the two rivals, Burden recedes: literally (to "my spot by the wall") and symbolically, since his barely controlled remoteness, an air of passionless detachment that he tries to project as ennui, is no match for the passion and power expended by the two fathers confronting each other. *"To hell with them, I thought, to hell with both of them"* (49). Regaining his aplomb in the last moments of departure, Burden asserts himself in a verbal show of his own independence, reverting to the characteristic idiom, in his own designation, of "a snot," "a smart guy," competing with adults. Even before arriving at the judge's house, Burden has imagined the "voices" of Burden's Landing remembering "little Jack Burden." Now, upon leaving it, he thinks of himself in terms of a more damaging diminutive—"little Jackie Burden." The scene ends with the Boss reading his regressive thoughts: "Well, Jackie, it looks like you got a job cut out for you" (53).

The episode is set up for maximum dramatic effect, but its power comes from the implicatory clash of two figures who loom large in the narrator's emotional life. The stakes themselves—political influence, delivering the vote to one's own chosen candidate for the Senate—are not finally very important. First, Stark does not see the judge's endorsement of a rival candidate as important enough to alter the outcome of the election; second, the narrator himself deflects interest away from the narrative issue by telling us the outcome (Stark's man, not the judge's, wins the election); and third, Burden diminishes the temporary importance of the issue by leaping ahead three years to the end of the entire story, which finds Adam Stanton dead, Judge Irwin dead, Willie Stark dead. The passage ends—and Chapter 1 ends—with the narrator's musing on *his* relationships, political and personal, and his responsibility in the way these relationships ended. Narrative becomes subordinate to the calculus of filiation: what begins as story ends as theme.

Burden can say at one time that his story and Stark's are in a sense "one story," and he is of course right. As many readers have noted, the deft interweaving of the political plot and the *Bildungsroman* is one of Warren's great achievements. As I have indicated, I would go further and attribute the remarkable unity of the novel to the decisive *imbalance* of its two stories: the political plot functions in effect as a subplot that lends the Burden story, a fictionalized spiritual autobiography, a necessary material edge. What makes Burden run is the same thing that breaks Stark's stride: the heavily charged, momentous assertion of the ordinary, the claim of the mundane in competition with large-scale ambition and the disinterested grappling with grand abstractions. The real source of energy for the novel comes not from the conventional generational tension of Willie Stark and Tom Stark, but from the unresolved, ambiguous, ambivalent father-son relationships that propel Jack Burden forward, the cluster of Burden's Landing fathers.

For much of his narrative Burden's iterated theme is that no father is without flaw. What he sees in Mason City, and ambiguously accepts, is what he more personally experiences at Burden's Landing: being one of the king's men is palatable so long as it can be seen as merely a job, but the fathers of his past are more viscerally intimate, more centrally involved in the cultivation and transmission of his own values; their failures are crucial to his emotional health, not merely to his material well-being. When those watchful and loving men—Judge Irwin, Governor Stanton, and Ellis Burden—stand exposed as men of common clay, the sons rise up to cast them down. There is nothing ideological or intellectual or even emotional in the casual arrogance of Tom Stark's assertion of generational superiority. Indeed, the very casualness of this son's response goes far in neutralizing its youthful cruelty, suggesting even the healthiness of nature insofar as it sets in relief the more-tortured responses of the other two sons to their fathers' weakness: Jack Burden's bitter unease at the saintly behavior of Ellis Burden and his sad disillusion in finding that Judge Irwin had once accepted a bribe, and Adam Stanton's explosive dismissal of his dead father who had protected his friend: "Damn his soul to hell" (269). Out of the swirling entanglements of this drama of filiation come the significant complexities of human conduct, some strands of which eventually touch the ordinary, predictable generational filiation at the governor's mansion. The momentum of the sons' power comes to one climax in Judge Irwin's suicide. The slightly eerie effect of Willie Stark's decline that coincides with Irwin's death—his fumbling and uncertainty, the sapping of his will—is really a matter of the narrator's conscious pacing of these intertwined and parallel narratives. For Burden it is a matter of thematic importance, not narrative necessity, that at the judge's death the Boss begins his "black dog" phase, his dour unpredictability throwing a pall over his associates. Even though he cheers up only when watching his son "uncork his stuff" on the football field, the recovery is limited to the time and place of the game; off the football field lurks the unresolved paternity issue of Tom's affair with a pregnant girl. Because of the actions of the son the father's power is compromised, and with it his resolve to accomplish the good thing without the taint of the usual political chicanery. The paternal power thus begins its gradual unraveling.

Once snagged, the Willie Stark–Tom Stark thread threatens to unravel the entire fabric. Since in its most general sense filiation is the mere fact of the child's relation to a parent, the spectacle of the governor's relation to his constituency is the public version of the crisis dramatized in the personal father-son segment of the plot: the subversion or flouting of paternal authority in the home invites a similar response in the state. In its system of pervasive doublings and reflections, *All the King's Men* establishes the Stark crisis of filiation as crucial to the large public drama, what we might call the matter of the novel. But its significance extends to the ongoing private drama of Jack Burden's more intense crisis of filiation. As narrator, Burden converts most such occasions to his own needs. Even the most recessive segment in the novel, that centering on the Governor Stanton–Adam Stanton relationship, reinforces the dominant problem of filiation at Burden's Landing—the Judge Irwin–Jack Burden–Ellis Burden axis.

At one time Jack feels "peculiarly situated" in having lost two fathers "at the same instant." In gaining his true father in the very act of losing him, he momentarily feels smug at having exchanged the "good, weak father" for the "evil, strong one" (375). But the memory of a half-wit acrobat on the floor being fed chocolate by the selfless father arouses an earlier memory of himself on the floor and hearing, "Here, Son, just one bite before supper." The image of Ellis Burden as paternal nourisher is never quite erased by his perceived weakness. "I had inherited the fruit of the Judge's crime," Jack Burden writes from the Judge's house, "just as some day I would inherit from my mother the fruit of the Scholarly Attorney's weakness" (381). His mother's silver, soprano scream that wakes him when she hears of the judge's death he rather easily interprets as "the true cry of the buried soul which had managed, for one instant after all the years, to utter itself again" (373). But his own true cry of the buried soul comes a bit later, when, again with a telephone call, he learns from the judge's lawyer that he is the sole heir of Irwin's estate. Because the arrangement strikes Burden as "crazy" and "logical," he falls into a near-hysterical fit of laughter that imperceptibly turns into weeping: "It was like the ice breaking up after a long winter. And the winter had been long" (376). In the language of the courts, Jack Burden is both son and heir of Judge Irwin. That familiar doubling phrase *son and heir* is a necessary clarification; as legal scholars tell us, *filius* and *hoeres* are not the same—the first is a term of nature, the second a term of law. The revelation of Jack Burden as *filius* comes with his mother's scream; that of Jack Burden as *hoeres* comes with his laughing and weeping.

Jack Burden stands at the very center of the stage in this drama of filiation, the subsidiary contours of which are drawn by the actors flanking him. As Warren presents it, the crux of that issue is filiation in both its most general and most specific senses. In its thinned-out, nontechnical usage *filiation* signifies the relation of one *thing* to another from which it is derived. But in Burden's case even this generalized filiation is relevant—reflected in his characteristic temperament, a habit of mind that searches out cause and consequence in the nature of things with tenacity even at his most flippant. In its more specific, legalistic usage, *filiation* is the judicial determination of the paternity of a child, especially of a bastard. In this sense Burden, who frets over his supposed legitimacy, not his illegitimacy, performs as his own private eye, poking for clues in "the ash pile, the midden, the sublunary dung heap, which is the human past" (167), but he also functions with split loyalties as both his own prosecuting attorney and defense counsel; he must finally serve as his own judge.

If the fathers are revealed as failures, it is because in the filiation of power the sons arrogate to themselves the privileges of youthful judgment. For Tom Stark, on the most simplistic level, it is the demand for the full satisfaction of appetite; for Adam Stanton, on the most abstract level, it is the demand for the icy consistency and rectitude of idealism. If Tom Stark seems a little unreal, it is because he is capable of no surprise, being a young man with the fullness and predictability of stereotype. If Adam Stanton seems a little unreal, it is because he is stuck in a youthful phase that he has chronologically outgrown, insisting that the world behave according to the configurations he carries about in his head. Of the sons in *All the King's Men* only Jack Burden has been in and passed beyond the purity of youthful appetite (Tom Stark) and the purity of youthful idealism (Adam Stanton). He is capable of change and risk taking. After the judge's death he feels no urgency to remain in "the swim of things," content instead with hammering out the details of the governor's tax bill and preferring the role of valet to that of historical researcher.

With Stark's death Jack Burden has in effect lost three fathers, and in the agony of his long and painful search it is as if only then can he accept the privations of the past and accept the risks of the future. Although he quotes with approval the Machiavellian adage that men may forget the death of the father but never the loss of the patrimony, his own story counters such materialistic reductiveness. Jack Burden assumes the care of Ellis Burden, enfolding him literally back into Burden's Landing in the very house where he had once played chess with Judge Irwin. Burden will reject his double patrimony—the judge's house and Ellis Burden's weakness. What he had once observed of Tom Stark—that "the son was merely an extension of the father" (388)—is the grim truth of all dramas of filiation. What rescues the grimness of Jack Burden's case is his willing acceptance, beyond idealism and disillusion, of the common frailty of all sons and fathers.

BLYDEN JACKSON

Richard Wright in a Moment of Truth

Many people, if not most, perhaps never associate Richard Wright with the state of Mississippi, which is another way of saying that they do not associate him with the South. He was, however, a Mississippian, a southerner, and to call him that is not merely to demand due recognition for the statistics of his birth and residence during his plastic years, but also to recognize a fact of the utmost importance in understanding the growth and peculiarities of his artistic imagination. Richard Wright still remains best-known as the author of the novel *Native Son*. Four years before *Native Son*, however, he had published a novella which he called "Big Boy Leaves Home." It is of this earlier and relatively unnoticed novella that I wish to evangelize.

"Big Boy Leaves Home" is a story which proceeds from beginning to end as a simple, straight-line narrative. Mechanically, at least, it is assembled like a play, detachable into five episodes, each as clearly discrete as a scene in a formal drama, and each, along the time scheme of the novella, placed somewhat later than its immediate predecessor, until the action, at the point which in a theater would ring down the final curtain, conveys Big Boy, the story's titular protagonist, northward toward Chicago, secreted in the covered back of a truck.

The first episode breathes something of the atmosphere of a rural Eden. On a clear, warm day in Mississippi four self-indulgent Negro boys

Reprinted from the *Southern Literary Journal* with permission of the author.

are discovered in a wood on the outskirts of the little town in which they and their families reside. The boys are Big Boy and his constant companions Lester, Buck, and Bobo. It becomes quickly obvious that Big Boy is the natural leader of the four and the constant recipient of hero worship from the other three. It becomes equally obvious that the four should not be where they are, for it is a school day and they are decidedly of school age. They are, then, young rebels giving full vent to some of their rebellious tendencies. And yet it does not appear that they are criminally inclined. They are, rather, healthy and high-spirited cousins-german of Huck Finn, with a proper ambivalence of attitude toward the queer world of adults and a proper interest in enjoying their youth while they still have it to enjoy. They are not, it must be confessed, altogether nice by the standards of a Little Lord Fauntleroy. Their language, for example, runs to words not used in polite child-rearing circles. Their sense of fun expresses itself too often in the sadistic exploitation of some defenseless victim's physical discomfiture. They know, too, about sex, and not through programs of sex education. Even so, they cannot be classed as juvenile delinquents. Nothing about them stamps them as young practitioners of vice and violence. But just as undeniably they cannot be classed as adults. To recognize this fact is of the utmost importance in a reading of their story. They like to try to act like grown-ups. What normal adolescents do not? Nevertheless, as adults, they are actually only innocents, actually only ingenues uninitiated into most of what are often called the facts of life. To be classed as adults, they have still seen far too little of the scattered and extensive middens of corruption which tend to separate in a most decisive manner prototypical adulthood from even the latest phase of nonadulthood. Their innocence does not make them as pure as the driven snow. But it does permit them still to think and act like irresponsible children. And it is as irresponsible children, out for a children's lark, that they suddenly, and capriciously, decide to quit their wood—one is strongly tempted to say their enchanted forest—and go swimming, trespassing on the land and the pond of Ol Man Harvey, a white man noted for his lack of love for Negroes and, not incidentally, noted especially to them for his aversion to their swimming in his pond.

The second episode takes them, consequently, from their open wood to Ol Man Harvey's pond. For a golden moment it is as if they had not left the wood, as if they are still, as it were, in the innocent world of their enchanted youth. They swim, appropriately for innocents, in the nude. They have, at least temporarily, abandoned swimming and are sunning themselves, still in the nude, on the beach of Ol Man Harvey's pond when they look up and find, fixedly regarding them from a spot on the pond's opposite bank, a white woman whom they do not know and who does not know them. Abruptly their story has changed worlds. It has crossed a line. The woman watching them clearly is already virtually on the verge of hysteria. They try to prevent an apparently all-too-impending disaster, to assure the strange white woman, who looms between them and their clothes, that all they want is to get those clothes and depart the pond in peace. But this woman is not part of the world of the beginning of their story. She belongs to the world controlled and interpreted by adults. In that world, at least when "Big Boy Leaves Home" was written, all Negro males, even young and with their clothes on, were potential rapists. And so this woman screams, and screams again, for someone named Jim, and Jim himself, a white man from her world, comes apace, with a rifle in his hands. He asks no questions and pauses not at all to profit from a single bit of rational analysis. Instead, he fires and kills two of the potential rapists, Buck and Lester, instantly. But Bobo and Big Boy, in a manner of speaking, have better luck. They survive the white man's initial barrage. Swiftly a moment of violent confusion ensues, and then ends, with the white man's rifle somehow in Big Boy's hands. Unable, as he sees it, under the circumstances to resort to any other method of deterrence, Big Boy shoots to death the white man, and he and Bobo, with their clothes and the now expendable garments of Buck and Lester, vanish in the direction of the town.

The third episode changes the setting from a white adult world to a black. Big Boy has managed to make his way home to his own house. Presumably, so has Bobo. At Big Boy's house his parents and his sister now are told about the terrible thing which has happened at the pond. Hastily they summon, for advice and counsel, a handful of the respected elders of their local black community. The elders summoned decide that Big Boy perforce must hide himself for the evening and the night in one of a set of pits dug for kilns on the side of a hill overlooking a main highway known as Bullard's Road. Word is to be sent to Bobo to join Big Boy in hiding there. At six in the morning Will Sanders, a son of one of the counseling elders, will pick the two boys up. By a fortuitous coincidence Will is already scheduled, just after the approaching dawn, to drive a load of goods to Chicago for his employers, a trucking company.

In the fourth episode Big Boy does reach the prescribed hill safely and does conceal himself deep within a chosen pit. He is waiting now for Bobo. Darkness comes, but no Bobo. What does, however, arrive at last, direfully impinging itself upon Big Boy's consciousness, is a mob that gathers on a hill directly across the road from the one in which he is concealed and from which he can hardly fail to see, as from a seat within the mezzanine of a theater or concert hall, virtually any atrocity that the mob may intend to perpetrate. And the mob does perpetrate a major atrocity. It has captured Bobo and it brings him to its hill. As Big Boy watches, helpless to intervene or withdraw, it proceeds there, on its hill, to tar and feather Bobo and to burn him at the stake. Then, as a rain begins to fall, the mob, its baser appetites assuaged, melts away in small groups into the night.

The fifth and final episode is muted and brief. Morning comes, and with it, unobtrusively parked on Bullard's Road, Will Sanders' truck, into which, collected from his night-long perch, Big Boy is safely stowed and thus spirited away to Chicago, famished and thirsty, and bereft forever of the kind of innocence which had still been largely his before the incident at Ol Man Harvey's pond.

"Big Boy Leaves Home" was accepted for publication in the spring of 1936. It seems actually to have been written down in the summer and fall of 1935. It seems also to have a discernible prehistory to which I wish now to allude, for reasons that I trust will appear as I proceed.

Richard Wright fled the South in 1927, two months after his nineteenth birthday. He went directly to Chicago, where, by 1932, led by his enthusiastic attachment to a John Reed Club, he had become a Communist. His Communist affiliation brought him eventually into association with a fellow Communist who, like himself, was a Negro born and bred at a considerable distance below the Mason and Dixon Line. Wright speaks of this black fellow Communist, under the almost certain alias of Ben Ross, in Wright's version of his own experience of communism, which he originally contributed, under the title, "I Tried to Be a Communist," to the *Atlantic Monthly* in 1944. This so-called Ross, who had a Jewish wife, the mother, by him, of a young son, interested Wright deeply. Wright saw Ross as "a man struggling blindly between two societies," and felt that if he "could get . . . Ross's story . . . he could make known some of the difficulties in the adjustment of a folk people to an urban environment."¹ Therefore, he persuaded Ross, in effect, to sit for a pen portrait. On occasion he interviewed Ross for hours in Ross's home. Meanwhile, however, the Communist command in Chicago had become cognizant of Wright's interest in Ross and had begun to view this interest with mounting concern. Once aware of the Party's apprehensions, Ross ceased to speak freely to Wright either of his life or himself. This inhibition of Ross's responsiveness sabotaged Wright's original hopes. Through Ross, moreover, Wright had met some of Ross's friends and, expanding on his original plan, had conceived the notion now of doing, with Ross and Ross's friends all in mind, a series of biographical sketches. Now, however, not only Ross but all of Ross's friends as well had become afraid to talk to Wright, as Wright had once had ample reason to suppose they might. Wright consequently altered his intentions. In virtually Wright's own words, after he saw that he could do nothing to counteract the effect of the Party's powerful influence, he merely sat and listened to Ross and his friends tell tales of southern Negro experience, noting them down in his mind and no longer daring to ask questions for fear his informants would become alarmed. In spite of his informants' reticence, he became drenched in the details of their lives. He gave up the idea of writing biographical sketches and settled finally upon writing a series of short stories, using the material he had got from Ross and his friends, building upon it and inventing from it. Thus he wove a tale of a group of black boys trespassing upon the property of a white man and the lynching that followed. The story was published eventually under the title of "Big Boy Leaves Home."²

Corroboration of Wright's direct testimony in "I Tried to Be a Communist," and some further suggestions concerning the genesis of "Big Boy Leaves Home," are supplied in Constance Webb's biography of Wright.³ This biography, it is of some significance here to note, bears the character of an official life. Indeed, in the book's introduction Miss Webb so defines the nature of what she has done in no uncertain terms. In this introduction, that is to say, she first makes specific allusion to her personal friendship with Wright and his family, which began, she tells us, when Wright was at work on *Black Boy* in the earlier 1940s and

1. "Richard Wright," in Richard Crossman (ed.), *The God That Failed* (New York, 1949), 115.
2. *Ibid.*, 119–20.
3. Constance Webb, *Richard Wright* (New York, 1968).

lasted until his death. She cites the many materials, such as notes, letters, telegrams, manuscripts, and ideas for new books which, from the time of her decision in 1945 to compose a study of him and his work, in full knowledge of her plans, Wright delivered to her over a period of fifteen years. She also refers to her many long hours of conversations with Wright in New York City, on Long Island, and in Paris; to her continuing relations with Wright's wife after Wright's untimely death; to the assistance provided her by Wright's brother, Alan, Wright's close boyhood friend Joe C. Brown, and Wright's literary agent, Paul R. Reynolds, Jr.; to the aid given her by an impressive number of Wright's fellow authors and others of Wright's acquaintances who were in a position to speak of Wright with some authority; and, finally in this present context, to the access granted by Wright and his family to hundreds of letters from Wright to Wright's editor, Edward C. Aswell.

With these credentials, which are not to be summarily dismissed, Miss Webb positively identifies the pseudonymous Ben Ross as one David Poindexter, a black member of the Communist party, who had been born in southwest Tennessee in 1903 and had come North when he was seventeen. The family attributed by Miss Webb to Poindexter is the same as that attributed by Wright to Ross. In all the other details which she stipulates, moreover, including Poindexter's status as the original of Big Boy, Miss Webb assimilates Poindexter to the person whom Wright, conceivably in order not to expose a friend and benefactor to possible jeopardy, named as Ross in "I Tried to Be a Communist." But when she reports directly on the genesis of "Big Boy Leaves Home,"[4] Miss Webb does not parrot what Wright had once said about his determination, if he could, to use Poindexter, or Ross, as an instrument by means of which he could make known some of the difficulties attendant upon the adjustment of a folk people to an urban environment. In this context, as a matter of fact, she makes a statement which would seem to contradict Wright's own about the folk. She says, instead and unequivocally, that in his first series of short stories, *Uncle Tom's Children* (the series of which "Big Boy Leaves Home" became a part), Wright set himself a conscious problem, the explication of the quality of will the Negro must possess to live and die in a country which denies him his humanity. Furthermore, applying her statement to "Big Boy Leaves Home" specifi-

4. *Ibid.*, 125.

cally, she asserts, within her analysis of that story, that "Big Boy Leaves Home" represents this quality of will as being "only that of the most elemental level—the ability to endure," for, she finally adds, the lesson to be extracted from Big Boy's experience is the dependence of his survival "upon the communal nature of the black community which planned, aided, and organized an escape."[5]

When she says that Wright, in creating "Big Boy Leaves Home" and the other stories in *Uncle Tom's Children*, "set himself a conscious problem," the significant word is *conscious*. She has left no doubt, as already indicated here earlier, of her conception of her relationship with Wright. He made of her, according to her implication it is clear, an alter ego privy to virtually all of himself that he could communicate to her or anyone. Furthermore, although the word *conscious* does not appear in her declaration that Big Boy's story was planned to demonstrate how his community rallied round him to ensure the preservation of his life, it seems unmistakably clear that here she speaks, too, as a medium who is reporting not only what was in Wright's mind, but also what she would contend he knew was there. Here, then, is testimony, much of it of a hearsay nature indeed, but nevertheless purporting, in its general trend, to have the value of evidence which Wright himself could not have failed to give had he ever had to speak about the intended function of "Big Boy" under solemn oath in a court of law. It reveals, to repeat for emphasis, that Wright had chosen a definite thing to do when he wrote "Big Boy Leaves Home" and that he was not confused as to the nature of that thing. It seems to argue also Wright's own belief that he had substantially achieved his conscious intent.

Writers, however, sometimes belie their own intentions. Sometimes, moreover, what they do actually may well seem better than what they thought they had intended. No one, I think, would argue seriously for a reading of "Big Boy Leaves Home" as an account of an adjustment by an agrarian folk to an urban setting, deeply though Wright once indicated that he was interested in Ross-Poindexter and drenched though he once was in Ross-Poindexter's life and history. If then, however, "Big Boy Leaves Home" is to be read primarily as a parable about the quality of will necessary for the Negro to solve the major problem which he faces in his American environment, and if the message of such a parable

---

5. *Ibid.*, 157, 159.

centers in an account of the manner in which one Negro community expressed the quality of its will through its capacity to save some of its own, then neither the form nor the content of the parable is aesthetically impressive. "Big Boy Leaves Home" becomes then only an exercise in the depiction of a failure. Its focal point, if not its climax, must then be found to be in its third episode, for in this episode the representatives of the Negro community do gather, in Big Boy's home. The preacher, Elder Peters, is there, and Brother Jenkins and Brother Sanders, with Big Boy's parents and his sister. They commune with each other. But with what results? Big Boy's father can only berate Big Boy on the folly of his disobedience to his mother's injunction to go to school. The women in the house can only watch the men gathered there in virtually unbroken silence. No one can respond affirmatively to the distressed father's plea for financial aid. The sister has done some service in bringing to the house the three outside counsellors. The mother gives Big Boy simple food to take with him when he leaves. Still, it is chance alone and Big Boy's own animal excellences which pave the way for his escape from certain death. No effective aid reaches Bobo. No account is taken of provisions to safeguard Big Boy's family, who, as Big Boy later overhears in his kiln, are burned out of their modest dwelling. The most that can be said when all is done is that Big Boy did elude his would-be slayers and that a fellow Negro, who happened to be going in that direction anyhow, drove him North.

But to read "Big Boy Leaves Home," whatever Wright's original conscious aims, in accord with the form dictated for it by its own development, and to sense its content shaping itself to match that form, and its function emerging as the strong, inevitable concomitant of both, is to witness what well may be one of the three or four finest moments in Negro fiction. Of this inherent form and content it is now high time to speak.

It will be remembered that Big Boy's story is shaped into five episodes, five scenes conducting a flow of action and related meaning from a point of attack to a conclusion which should round out and justify the whole. This form, at least in its handling here, is flexible as well as fluid. It permits variations of pitch and tone and atmosphere which all contribute to the story's total impact. At the beginning the pitch is moderate. The tone and atmosphere are genial, almost sweet. The function of the content is expository. The identity of the protagonist is established and the condition of all four of the boys made known. And beyond all this a theme is adumbrated. For these boys are scholars out of school. They have interrupted their vocation for a holiday of their own making. Still, the fact is clear. They are young, much untaught, and at an impressionable age. To learn, to grow, in other words, in one way or another, is their métier. It is hard to see how they should live through any single day without acquiring some new knowledge. In what they are reside the germs of what this tale must be. Then comes the first progression, bringing with itself a proper set of changes. At the swimming hole the white world intrudes. The mood of the first episode is shattered by the killings. In a swirl of strident sound and emotions at high pitch and harshly tuned, with corresponding action that is equally cacophonous, a motif of pain and mystery, the ugliness of racist custom is introduced. Then comes an interlude with a reduction in pitch and a moderation of tone, but without a return to the relative serenity of the introduction, as Big Boy spends a moment with his own kind in his father's house. But this interlude is also prelude, and a fitting one, to the big scene of the story. This big scene, as the logic of the story would demand, is the lynching on the hill, the spectacle of Bobo coated with hot tar and white feathers, burning in the night. This, as we shall see in terms of content, is the moment of truth in the story. It is also the very peak of the wave of form, when pitch and tone and atmosphere all coalesce at their highest points. The story cannot end at such a level of crescendo and fortissimo. It does not; it declines to the low key of its final episode when Big Boy, all passion spent, drifts off to slumber on the bed of the truck that bears him away to the North. But let us return to the lynching on the hill.

I have said that for this story it is the moment of truth. And it is. It is the moment when Wright, whether wittingly or not, gathers up the essence of that which he is struggling to express and stores it all into one symbol and its attendant setting. For the spectacle of Bobo aflame at the stake does constitute a symbol. It is a symbol, moreover, the phallic connotations of which cannot be denied. Indeed, the particularity of its detail—the shape of its mass, its coating of tar, the whiteness of the feathers attached to its surface or floating out into the surrounding air—are almost all too grossly and gruesomely verisimilar for genteel contemplation. Whether Wright so intended it or not, the lynching of Bobo is symbolically a rite of castration. It is the ultimate indignity that can be inflicted upon an individual. Such an indignity strips from a man his manhood, removes from him the last vestige of his power and the last resort of his self-respect. In the lynching of Bobo, thus, all lynchings are explained, and all race prejudice. Both are truly in essence acts of castration. It is not for nothing that the grinning darky, hat in hand and bowing low, his backside exposed as if for a kick in the buttocks, seems so much a eunuch. He has accepted in his heart the final abasement, the complete surrender of his will, and so of his citadel of self, to anyone with a white skin. He has capitulated to the most arrogant demand which one human creature can make upon another. This, then, is the true anatomy of racism. It makes no difference where or how it prefers its claims, whether in an apology for its own being so adroitly composed as the novel *So Red the Rose* or in the blatant conduct of the old-style sheeted Ku Klux Klan. What racism demands is that every white man should be permitted to reserve the right to visit, with impunity, upon any Negro whatever, any outrage of that Negro's personality the white man chooses to impose. This, then, is the symbolism of Bobo's burning body on the hill. But around that symbolism clusters another set of facts put into another pregnant image. For, as Bobo burning illustrates the essence of one indispensable aspect of racism, the mob illustrates another. It is an efficient mob, a homogeneous grouping. Yet no one has really organized it. It has no officers and no carefully compiled manual of behavior. Still, it operates like a watchmaker universe. Its members know what they are supposed to do, and they do it, as if they were performing the steps of a ritual dance—which of course they are. For that is the real secret of the people gathered around Bobo on his Golgotha. They are responding not only to xenophobia and to an obscene lust for power. They are responding also to an urge equally as neanderthal in its origins. They are acting tribally, even as every lodge brother, black or white or yellow or red, who ever gave a secret handshake and every Babbitt who ever applauded a toastmaster's feeble attempts at jollity at the luncheon of his service club.

To belong, to conform, and thus to avoid the existentialist nightmare of exercising the prerogative of individual freedom of choice; to be able to contribute all of one's own release of foible and malice to custom that must be followed for the good of the community; to accept the myth that at some time in the misty past a voice, as it were, from some local Sinai spoke to the elders of the tribe and told them how certain things must be done and what prescribed rites must be followed to avert the anger of the gods; thus to be exempted from a sense of guilt at one's own evil; thus to hallow the meanest of the herd instincts; thus to institutionalize mediocrity's hatred of the indomitable spirit and its envy of strength and beauty; this is the pathos, and yet an important part of the explanation, of the capacity to endure of the tribe. This is also as much a part of racism as its lust for power. The castration and the tribalism complement each other. Without either, racism would not be at all exactly what it is. To perceive them, to really take them in, is, as Henry James might say, to see and know what is *there*. And it is part of the excellence of form in this story that Big Boy does see them, that by the story's own handling of its arrangements he is put in such a position that he cannot do otherwise. For, as this story so manages the sense of form which shapes its episodes to place its big scene right, it regulates concurrently another element of form, its control of its own point of view, to the end that at the proper point in the narrative's development the impression it conveys of who is doing the seeing will be as right as the prominence and the substance of what is to be seen.

Thus, at the beginning of the story we are aware of, and share, to some extent, in the consciousness of all the boys. But this is Big Boy's story. It is really he whose loss of innocence, as it were, and compulsory education under special circumstances embody all that this story has to say. And so, increasingly, as the story moves from the open country to the lynching on the hill, Big Boy's consciousness becomes the sole point of view. Yet this constriction and this concentration are really the ultimate outgrowth of a rather delicate continuous maneuver of adjustment. Throughout the bulk of his story Wright's handling of his point of view is as dramatic as his separation of his matter into scenes. We watch the characters perform. We hear them talk. From outside their consciousnesses we infer their thoughts and feelings. Yet we identify increasingly with Big Boy, if for no other reason than that we see nothing which he cannot see and hear nothing which he cannot hear. But after Big Boy bids adieu to his parents and their friends and, successfully negotiating his sprint through hostile territory to Bullard's Road, comes to bay at last crouched deep within his kiln, we become more and more intensely one with him. We wonder with him why Bobo has not come, share with him his reverie as he relives the events of his day, mourn with him for Buck and Lester, regret with him that he did not bring with him his father's shotgun, and finally, in fantasy, imagine with him that he is blasting away with that shotgun as he withstands a mob. As white men searching for the Negro "bastards" drift down *his* hill, we share, too, his fear, and finally, as the lynch mob gathers, our senses become, like his, preternaturally acute, to watch with him in anguish and extreme distress the torture and destruction of the last of his close boyhood friends. Thus the heightening and the concentration of the point of view join with the elevation of the episode and the power of the symbolism and the imagery to speak in blended voices acting in mighty concert of the inner nature of racism and to trace its roots deep down into the past of human psychology and custom.

It is not a quality of the Negro will which this story explicates, nor is it anything to do with folk adjustment in a city. Far from either. It is, rather, the psychology, and the anthropology, of American racism. It is a lesson given to Big Boy and through him to the world at large. It is a lesson, moreover, which rounds off beautifully both the form and substance of "Big Boy Leaves Home." For the plot of this story represents a progress, not a conflict. Its succession of vignettes combines to form a curious kind of sentimental journey in which Big Boy does leave home; does lose, that is, his relative state of innocence; and does experience an illumination, an exercise in education, that provides him with a terrible, but richly freighted, insight into the adult world.

It has been rather customary not to think of Richard Wright as a southern writer, except, of course, by the accident of birth. I cannot share that view. A writer belongs, I would argue, in the final analysis, to the country where his artistic imagination is most at home. Wright clearly supposed that this country, for him, was not the South, just as he supposed that in "Big Boy Leaves Home," in spite of the resemblances between Ol Man Harvey's pond and the pond in Jackson, Mississippi, around which Wright had played in his own youth, he was writing about Ross-Poindexter and, in a philosophic vein, either about a folk people seeking a new adjustment in a setting alien to their past or struggling for self-gratifying survival against a powerful outer world hostile to their hopes. Indeed, in one of the major episodes of *Black Boy*, his own account of his youth and early manhood, Wright tells of his last encounter with his father, an encounter that occurred after twenty-five years of absolute separation between the two, as well as, also, after Wright had published *Native Son*. He meets his father on a Mississippi hillside. He tries to talk to him, and then he says, "I realized that, though ties of blood made us kin, though I could see a shadow of my face in his face, though there was an echo of my voice in his voice, we were forever strangers, speaking a different language, living on vastly different planes of reality." On one level of interpretation Wright here does speak true. Between him and his father time and experience had fixed an impenetrable gulf. But the possibly implied symbolism of the confrontation is false. Deep at the core of his own being, whether as a person or as an artist, Wright always remained his own Big Boy who never did leave home, and it was always true that the closer he could get to the homeland of his youth, which was also the homeland of his creative skill, the happier he was in the fiction he was able to produce.

Wright's last considerable essay into fiction was his final novel, *The Long Dream*. In startling ways it reproduces all the significant elements of "Big Boy Leaves Home." Its setting is a Mississippi town and, incidentally, one which, for all of his obvious intentions to have it otherwise, he does not update from the Mississippi which he quitted as a youth. Its protagonist is a Negro boy as exceptional among his peers as Big Boy is among his. Moreover, this boy too is in the process of growing up, for *The Long Dream*, like "Big Boy Leaves Home," is an initiation story. Fire figures prominently in the drama of *The Long Dream*. Indeed, fire repeatedly plays a mythopoeic role in Wright's important fiction, as in the furnace of *Native Son* or the collision of electrically driven monsters in the subway wreck of *The Outsider*. The Negro elders of "Big Boy Leaves Home" reappear in the protagonist's father, the doctor, the madam, the mistress, and the father's helper of *The Long Dream*. They are no more potent in the latter work than in the former. They have neither the grace nor the glory of the father in "Fire and Cloud" or the mother in "Bright and Morning Star." The strange white woman who precipitates catastrophe for the protagonist of "Big Boy Leaves Home" precipitates catastrophe also for the protagonist in *The Long Dream*. And as at the end of "Big Boy Leaves Home," Big Boy is headed for another life in another world, so at the end of *The Long Dream* its protagonist is on a plane en route to Paris. The real difference, indeed, between "Big Boy Leaves Home" and *The Long Dream* is in the relative quality of the art of each. James Baldwin, whose attitudes toward Richard Wright are much too complex for quick definition, once referred, with complimentary intent, to Wright as a "Mississippi pickaninny." In so doing Baldwin directly was comparing Wright with the Existentialists amongst whom Wright, in his later life, found himself consorting in Paris, and was thus paying genuine respect to a capacity in Wright to see life as it actually is and not according to some evanescent theory, which Baldwin thought he could divine in Wright, but not in Sartre and his disciples—and which, additionally, Baldwin, in pensive mood, attributed to the lessons Wright had learned during Wright's rough-and-tumble existence as a boy and precocious adolescent in the Delta South. I think the phrase is apt, especially since it is clear that through it Baldwin intended no racial slur. For Wright was a child of his own youth. Out of that youth he derived not only his practical sense of hard reality but also the home country for his artistic imagination. Thus in much more than the mere statistics of his place of birth is he a southern writer. When he follows his home country north, as he does in the first two books of *Native Son*, he is still on his native ground. When he tries to return to it, as in *The Long Dream*, seeing it through other eyes than truly his own, he has deserted the one source of his greatest strength. He has become, that is, in all too sad a consequence, his own Big Boy away from home.

PEGGY WHITMAN PRENSHAW

The Harmonies of *Losing Battles*

Of the works of modern American fiction that form the subject of this collection, Eudora Welty's *Losing Battles*, a product of the 1960s, is the most recent. Welty wrote the novel while living in Mississippi during troubled times, a period of pain and confusion for the state as well as for the country at large. For her it was also a time of personal pain that saw the deaths of her mother and two brothers, which left her the sole survivor of her immediate family.

In several interviews she has discussed the composition of the novel. It came in "spurts," she says, over a period of six or eight years, during which time she had many responsibilities at home. She told Walter Clemons that originally she saw the work as "a long story, the family telling a newcomer, while they waited for his homecoming, the tale of how Jack Renfro got sent to prison," and that she expected to conclude it when he turned up on the front porch. "I might not have had the courage to start," she said, "if I'd known what I was getting into. It started out to be short and farcical, but as people became dearer to me—it changed. When I got Jack home to the reunion, I realized I'd just begun."[1]

What Welty has given us in the character of Jack Renfro is an extraordinary modern hero, a Jack quite unlike Burden and Gatsby and Barnes, a man whose affirmation of life is one of the surest and deepest such

---

1. Walter Clemons, "Meeting Miss Welty," in Peggy Whitman Prenshaw (ed.), *Conversations with Eudora Welty* (Jackson, Miss., 1984), 31.

affirmations we have in American literature, especially in modern fiction. Written in hard times about even harder times—the depression-poor red clay hill country of northeast Mississippi in the 1930s—*Losing Battles* celebrates the joy and energy and exuberance that coexist with wounds and death in this life's battles. The glory of the novel, Seymour Gross has written, is that it allows you to feel what it would be like *really* to believe in life."[2]

When the novel was published in 1970, the first major fiction by Welty in fifteen years, reviewers unanimously took account of the robust, celebratory presence of the novel, with its large cast of characters and its infinitely rich presentation of scene. The reviews were numerous and lengthy, for the most part leading features in the Sunday, April 12, review sections of the major newspapers. Giving evidence of the literary world's recognition of the novel as an addition to the canon of major American fiction, many reviewers pronounced *Losing Battles* the book that would absolutely and finally dispel anyone's lingering inclination to regard Welty's work as "regional," insofar as the word may be taken to mean "minor."

In the *New York Times Book Review* James Boatwright proclaimed the novel a "gift to cause general rejoicing," presented on the occasion of Welty's sixty-first birthday, and a "major work of the imagination." For him, the book's liveliness and inventiveness gave evidence that "Eudora Welty possesses the surest comic sense of any American writer alive." Then he added, as if to forestall any inference that comedy is some lesser literary form, "It is a comedy that takes no easy liberties, that presents character without fake compassion or amused condescension, a comedy that releases, illuminates, renews our own seeing, that moves in full knowledge of loss, bondage, panic and death."[3]

The truth is, however, that Welty's ebullient, talk-filled social comedy, which opens with a rooster's crow and closes with a resounding chorus of "Bringing in the Sheaves," struck many reviewers as sharply at odds with its times. A comedy not absurd or black or macabre, *Losing Battles* differed strikingly from most of the fiction of the postmodern era. To a fellow writer like Reynolds Price, the variance was reason for

---

2. Seymour Gross, "A Long Day's Living: The Angelic Ingenuities of *Losing Battles*," in Peggy Whitman Prenshaw (ed.), *Eudora Welty: Critical Essays* (Jackson, Miss., 1979), 340.
3. James Boatwright, "I Call This a Reunion to Remember, All!" *New York Times Book Review*, April 12, 1970, p. 1.

celebration. Writing in the Washington *Post*, Price begins by comparing the new novel and Welty's work generally with a mainstream dominated by an urban, experimental fiction. Welty's "plenitude and serene mastery" expose the "thinness" of the diet readers have been surviving on, Price writes, fiction that he describes as "little dry knots of fashion, self-laceration; windy flights from 'plot and character' into bone-crushingly dull (and ancient and easy) 'experiment' and, throughout, a growing and maiming attachment to the modern city as the only scene for fiction."[4] By contrast, *Losing Battles* is rich in pleasure and laughter—pastoral and comic, wonderfully imagined. He finds it "perhaps the funniest novel since *Huckleberry Finn*," suggesting through the comparison not only a quality of tone and style linking the two works but the serious regard due the breadth of vision and understanding embodied by *Losing Battles*.

In most respects this novel came on the literary scene in 1970 with nearly unanimous praise, but in the reviews one frequently confronts the comment that the book is an anomaly, that perhaps it even belongs to another, different time. The mainstream to which *Losing Battles* belongs, rightly discerned by the contemporaneous reviewers, is that of Austen, Tolstoy, Mark Twain, Hardy, and Mann. These are the novelists of works profoundly social, fiction that not only reflects the individual's lonely separateness, but—rarer, much rarer in this century—portrays the family's and community's intricate connectedness. Indeed, to writer Joyce Carol Oates, Welty's portrait of the Beecham-Renfro clan of Boone County, Mississippi, for all its vitality and fullness, produces the rather dispiriting effect of reminding the reader how utterly remote such lived life is from the present condition.

Unlike Reynolds Price, Oates sees the Weltian civilization as extinct, unreachable except through books. "In 1970 the concerns of *Losing Battles* are extinct. The large happy family and its outdoor feast are extinct; the loyalty to a postage-stamp corner of the world is extinct; the unquestioning Christian faith, the complex and yet very simple web of relationships that give these people their identities, binding them to a particular past and promising for them a particular, inescapable future: all extinct." Oates admires the novel, one might even say reveres it, and

---

4. Reynolds Price, "Frightening Gift," Washington *Post*, April 17, 1970, p. C-1. Reprinted in Price, *Things Themselves: Essays and Scenes* (New York, 1972), 139–42.

yet for her it belongs to an irremediably distant past. She suggests that the pleasure and value of the novel lie not in the illusion of verisimilitude so much as in the reminder of what has been lost. The novel offers something like a palliative for modern estrangement. "To know our own origins, or to know alternate possibilities for our own lives, we must study Miss Welty's fiction, for we will not get this kind of knowledge from life. Its time is past; it is extinct."[5]

Reading the novel produces the same kind of wry, elegiac mood in Jack Kroll, who in *Newsweek* spoke of the effect as exhilarating and saddening. "Exhilarating because you are in the hands of a master, and saddening because that kind of mastery is rapidly disappearing from the world, from culture, from consciousness itself." Even so, he concludes that *Losing Battles* is not nostalgic; rather, "It is tough, insistent, secure in its sense that everything delightful and profitable in human affairs is an act of love staving off dissolution, the losing battle that is the fate of the most sentient of species."[6]

Assurances that, for all its comedy and feeling, the novel does not partake of sentimentality or nostalgia recur throughout the reviews. Howard Moss in the *New Yorker* notes that Welty's portrayal is neither "ingratiating nor sentimental. In its large design, human meanness and failure are given their just due." Linda Kuehl writes that to mistake Welty's "shared jubilation for sentimentality . . . would be to misread the book entirely." Indeed, reviewers in 1970, as well as academic critics in later, more detailed essays, have all attempted to convey a sense of the novel's subtleties and enormous breadth. Kuehl writes, for example, of a fiction that "bursts at the seams with life while secret reaches of the soul reverberate darkly."[7]

At the center of Welty's vision in this and much of her other work is the resolution of opposites, the balancing or harmonizing of dualities. Kuehl, among many others, has observed this pattern, noting that Welty juxtaposes "darkness and light, death and life, pathos and joy, ignorance and wonder, and nowhere more abundantly than in . . . *Losing Battles*." In *Anatomy of Criticism*, Northrop Frye comments that "the theme of

---

5. Joyce Carol Oates, "Eudora's Web," *Atlantic*, CCXXV (April, 1970), 120.
6. Jack Kroll, "The Lesson of the Master," *Newsweek*, April 13, 1970, p. 90.
7. Howard Moss, "The Lonesomeness and Hilarity of Survival," *New Yorker*, July 4, 1970, p. 74; Linda Kuehl, "Back to Backwoods Mississippi for Granny's 90th Birthday," *Commonweal*, September 18, 1970, p. 465.

the comic is the integration of society," and his observation succinctly explains why Welty has so frequently turned to comedy as the fictional mode most congenial to her vision of life.[8]

In theme and form what is most central to *Losing Battles* is just such a pattern of reconciliation and balance—what I have chosen to call here its harmonies. In every sense of the word the book embodies reunion. Jack comes home from Parchman penitentiary to redheaded Gloria and daughter Lady May, home for Granny Vaughn's ninetieth birthday and the annual August reunion of the Renfro-Beecham clan. In the wake of his return come Judge and Mrs. Moody, the voice of the law and citizenry of the larger world, who are nonetheless pulled irresistably into the family circle, guest prisoners for a time in Beecham territory. During the day and a half of the book's present action, the family recovers its past, holding it suspended in the present through the telling and retelling of its stories. Even Miss Julia Mortimer, who for years was the bane of existence for every child in Banner, Mississippi, is redeemed from loneliness and death through the family's shared recollection of her life and the community's attendance at her funeral.

The past is brought living into the present, as the judge's Buick is held perilously but safely aloft Banner Top Hill by Uncle Nathan's homemade sign proclaiming "DESTRUCTION IS AT HAND." The parched earth yields to rain; the blazing sun resolves into the full moon—all these patterns and more suggest the deep doubleness that marks life. The Weltian dualities of love and separateness are everywhere manifest in this book—the comedy does not ameliorate them. The darker human impulses and threatening turns of fate are held at bay only by the family's sturdy refusal to acknowledge them.

The family, busily protesting and protecting one another, seems one great clump of noisy life; nonetheless their solidarity and invulnerability are ever fragile. Grandpa Vaughn has died while Jack was in prison, and this may very likely be Granny's last reunion. Twelve-year-old Vaughn is a dreamer, already captive to the lure of books and ideas that lead to a separate, introspective life. Uncle Nathan is a lonely wanderer, maimed in body and spirit by the guilt he suffered from murdering another. Even the steadfast Beulah faces the night harboring a

---

8. Kuehl, "Back to Backwoods Mississippi," 465; Northrop Frye, *Anatomy of Criticism* (1957; rpr. New York, 1966), 43.

painful memory: " 'My son in the pen.' Miss Beulah's voice said, travelling up the passage from the dark bedroom. 'My son had to go to the pen.' "[9] Deprived of Jack, the family has lost truck, horse, and very nearly its sustenance. When Jack asks the whereabouts of his beloved horse Dan, Aunt Beck explains, "We had to shoot him." He persists, "Lead me to his grave," only to be told by Etoyle, "He was drug off to the renderers." The ensuing exchange between Jack and his mother fully dramatizes the desperate circumstances of the family and the comic revelation of their plight.

> "I always said my horse was going to be buried under trees," Jack gasped out.
> "We have to have coal and matches and starch," Miss Beulah listed for him. "And flour and sugar and vinegar and salt and sweet-soap. And seed and feed. And we had to keep us alive. Son, we parted first with a nanny goat, then a fat little trotter. Then the cow calved—"
> "Mama, I ain't going to make you tell me any more of the tale," said Jack. "Not in front of all of 'em." (90)

Hanging on to old Bet the mule, displaying a new tin roof on their old house, their pride intact, they seem no less a miracle than the beautiful night-blooming cereus that opens suddenly on the evening of the reunion. "Not a drop of precious water did I ever spare it," says Beulah. "I reckon it must have thrived on going famished" (349).

Of course, it is precisely their refusal to admit to the desperateness of their circumstances, their refusal to see themselves as poor and ignorant and isolated, that empowers them and allows them to prevail against adversity. Carol A. Moore and Larry J. Reynolds have both observed that the family members make a strength of their weakness by willfully maintaining their illusions about themselves in stories that ritualize and exalt their lives.[10] This analysis of the family's willfulness and strength is exactly that of Julia Mortimer, who says in her letter to Judge Moody: "All my life I've fought a hard war with ignorance. Except in those cases that you can count off on your fingers, I lost every battle. . . . A teacher teaches and a pupil learns or fights against learning with the same force behind him. It's the survival instinct   It's the desperation

---

9. Eudora Welty, *Losing Battles* (New York, 1970), 359. Subsequent references to the novel are to this edition and will appear in the text.
10. Carol A. Moore, "The Insulation of Illusion and *Losing Battles*," *Mississippi Quarterly*, XXVI (Fall, 1973), 651; Larry J. Reynolds, "Enlightening Darkness: Theme and Structure in Eudora Welty's *Losing Battles*," *Journal of Narrative Technique*, VIII (Spring, 1978), 134.

of staying alive against all odds that keeps both sides encouraged. But the side that gets licked gets to the truth first" (298).

Since its publication *Losing Battles* has been the subject of extensive critical attention, much of which has been focused upon themes and techniques that define the opposing "sides," the mighty adversaries in the novel. These opposites, represented by the family and their nemesis, Miss Julia, have been discussed in diverse but often related approaches. Michael Kreyling discusses the opposition of the mythical consciousness, expressed through family ritual and the circle motif, and the historical consciousness, exemplified by the individual, Julia Mortimer, who is dedicated to progressive change.[11] M. E. Bradford and Thomas Landess see the family combatants as representing the ancient communal bond of human beings tested against Julia's modernist abstraction and rationalism.[12] Mary Anne Ferguson places the heroic opposition of the Renfro-Beecham family and Julia Mortimer in the context of a comic epic.[13] In more than two dozen substantive articles on *Losing Battles* to date, Welty critics have focused upon these and other patterns of contrast and union in the novel. Less often have scholars grappled to take account of what is perhaps the most radical counterpointing in the novel—the ceaseless stream of talk, talk, talk, the luxuriant spillage of things in this world held fixed by black type on a white page.

In an essay entitled "Speech and Silence in *Losing Battles*," James Boatwright develops some particularly helpful insights into the complementarity of the two sides in the novel, whose "weapons" he identifies as speech and silence. "By speaking we honor the whole world of duty, of love, of our community with others, our need for them.... In silence we assert our separateness, our joy in the soul's integrity; we pay homage to the perdurable and dangerous truth about our condition—its final solitude." Recalling the description of Jack's listening to Uncle Homer ("he leaned forward with his clear eyes fixed on the speaker as though what was now being said would never be said again or repeated by

11. Michael Kreyling, "Myth and History: The Foes of *Losing Battles*," *Mississippi Quarterly*, XXVI (Fall, 1973), 639–49.
12. M. E. Bradford, "Looking Down from a High Place: The Serenity of Miss Welty's *Losing Battles*," in John F. Desmond (ed.), *A Still Moment: Essays on the Art of Eudora Welty* (Metuchen, N.J.: 1978), 103–109. See also Thomas H. Landess, "More Trouble in Mississippi: Family vs. Antifamily in Miss Welty's *Losing Battles*," *Sewanee Review*, LXXIX (1971), 626–34.
13. Mary Anne Ferguson, "*Losing Battles* as a Comic Epic in Prose," in Prenshaw (ed.), *Eudora Welty: Critical Essays*, 305–24.

anybody else" [79]), Boatwright describes Jack as "a great *listener.*" By contrast, Miss Julia, the exponent of the written word, the tireless reader of books, is preeminently the silent one. "The written word is a form of silence in *Losing Battles.* It is radically discontinous from the spoken word: it proceeds from solitude, from a furious need to say the truth."[14]

In his discussion of speech and silence in the novel, Boatwright approaches what I regard as the most extraordinary harmony wrought by Welty in *Losing Battles,* the fusion of two ways of knowing—the way of listening, *hearing* the reunionists speak, and the way of seeing, taking in the image of the words on the page, interpreting, analyzing their meanings. This is a book of voices, a written story of spoken words, a book that trusts for 436 pages a technique that Hemingway used best in his shortest stories—an effaced narrator, indeed at times a nearly invisible narrator, with dramatized voice and gesture carrying the full weight of the novel. It is a technique Welty has used earlier in "Petrified Man" and, in the special, limited way of the monologue, in "Why I Live at the P.O.," "Shower of Gold," and *The Ponder Heart.* She has said that with *Losing Battles* she set out to write a "pure talk story," and even though the story began slowly to turn into a novel, she stayed with her presentational technique. "I wanted it all to be shown forth," she told Charles Bunting in 1972, "the way things are in a play, have it become a novel in the mind of the reader . . . understood in the mind of the reader. The thought, the feeling that is *internal* is *shown* as external. That was why it was a comedy. Because anything that's done in action and talk is a comedy."[15]

Earlier, she had spoken to Linda Kuehl of the difficulty and delight she found in writing the dialogue that composes the novel. "Sometimes I needed to make a speech do three or four or five things at once—reveal what the character said but also what he thought he said, what he hid, what others were going to think he meant, and what they misunderstood and so forth—all in his single speech. And the speech would have to keep the essence of this one character, his whole particular outlook in concentrated form. This isn't to say I succeeded. But I guess it explains why dialogue gives me my greatest pleasure in writing."[16]

---

14. James Boatwright, "Speech and Silence in *Losing Battles,*" *Shenandoah,* XXV (Spring, 1974), 12.

15. Charles T. Bunting, "'The Interior World': An Interview with Eudora Welty," in Prenshaw (ed.), *Conversations with Eudora Welty,* 46.

16. Linda Kuehl, "The Art of Fiction XLVII: Eudora Welty," in Prenshaw (ed.), *Conversations with Eudora Welty,* 77.

The blend of voices and motifs, a harmony that has been compared with that of Mozart, came slowly and deliberately, as we can see from Suzanne Marrs's annotated bibliography of the *Losing Battles* papers, housed in the Mississippi Department of Archives. Long conversations and whole scenes were rewritten many times, sometimes discarded. Welty has said she cut out at least as much as she kept in. What she kept in, as many critics have observed, is a novel that is all surface, or so it seems, brilliantly reflecting the world and the reader, who peers into its pages as onlooker and collaborator. Louis D. Rubin, Jr., wrote in an early review essay that "everything is out on the surface, but the art *is* the surface, and every inch of the surface must be inspected." Indeed, reading the novel is such strenuous activity because we have really to pay attention, to listen to and see everything.[17]

In one of the most detailed of the studies of Welty's technique in *Losing Battles*, Robert Heilman has shown in what respects the surface impression of haste and casualness belies the highly ordered design of the book.[18] Without question, the novel does bear intricate design; like Miss Julia, it has "designs" on everyone. There are tropes and symbols that interconnect every element of the novel, from the cock's crow in the opening line to Jack's raised voice at the conclusion:

> Bringing in the sheaves,
> Bringing in the sheaves!
> we shall come rejoicing,
> Bringing in the sheaves!
> (436)

But getting at one design, isolating one thread, is finally elusive. The concentrated essence of the novel ultimately does not lie in analysis but, more insistently than in any other novel I know, in the process of one's hearing and holding in the imagination the world it presents. The access to the hearing and imagining of this wholly literary world, however, is the seeing eye and the symbol-decoding intelligence.

Welty's form is tantalizingly playful and serious—the written drama

---

17. Suzanne Marrs, "An Annotated Bibliography of the *Losing Battles* Papers," *Southern Quarterly*, XXIII (Winter, 1985), 116–21; Bunting, "'The Interior World,'" in Prenshaw (ed.), *Conversations with Eudora Welty*, 47; Louis D. Rubin, Jr., "Everything Brought Out in the Open: Eudora Welty's *Losing Battles*," *Hollins Critic*, VII (June, 1970), 3.

18. Robert B. Heilman, "*Losing Battles* and Winning the War," in Prenshaw (ed.), *Eudora Welty: Critical Essays*, 269–304.

that implicitly (and explicitly) debates the superiority of orality versus literacy, of talk versus books. This is, of course, one of the most ancient of battles, the argument over the utility and value of writing. The Renfros and Beechams have no less a defender than Plato, who likewise used the written dialogue to question the wisdom that can be got from writing. In the *Phaedrus*, Socrates says of writing that it has a "strange quality about it, which makes it really like painting: the painter's products stand before us quite as though they were alive; but if you question them, they maintain a solemn silence. So, too, with written words: you might think they spoke as though they made sense, but if you ask them anything about what they are saying, if you wish an explanation, they go on telling you the same thing, over and over forever."[19]

Just such static impotence of the written word is the argument the family impatiently makes to Judge Moody, who stubbornly insists that nothing but "written proof"—birth certificates, deeds, tax receipts, poll books—can prove one's existence and identity. In the scene in which everyone is engaged in trying to ascertain the parentage of Gloria, Judge Moody charges that the reunionists have told "a patched-together family story and succeeded in bringing out no more evidence than if their declared intention had been to conceal it." In the effort to establish Sam Dale Beecham and Rachel Sojourner as Gloria's parents, the family brings forth a postcard from Sam Dale signed, "Your loving husband." To the judge, "a postcard isn't the same evidence as a license to marry, or a marriage certificate." To the family, the direct evidence from one of its own, supported by direct testimony, is superior proof. " 'There's a whole lot more of Sam Dale in that postcard, if you know how to read it!' Miss Beulah cried. 'And Granny saved it from destruction, kept it in her Bible, showed it to you! Granny's word is as good as gold, don't you believe it? She's better than any courthouse, anywhere on earth' " (322–23).

Even Gloria, the prize pupil and chosen successor of Julia Mortimer, eventually joins the proponents of the spoken word, despite the fact that earlier she had sought to express her wifely support and affection for her husband in letters. She had regularly written to him in prison, up until the day before he returned to Banner, although a visit to the penitentiary would have proved far more beneficial to Jack than her letters had. As he explained to Gloria, other inmates had the advantage of having their

19. Plato, *Phaedrus*, trans. W. C. Helmbold and W. G. Rabinowitz (New York, 1956), 69.

family come to plead for their early release: "The smartest they had, the pick of their family. That's who'd be elected to come to Parchman and beg. Or else how would the poor lonesome fools ever get out of there? Renfros and Beechams and Comforts relied a hundred percent on me and Aycock's own behavior to turn the trick. Now that's the slow way" (110).

Unlike Gloria, Miss Julia herself never underrated the power of the spoken word; in fact, it was just that power that she recognized as the chief obstacle in the contest between her and the loving young suitor for the allegiance of Gloria. "The very last time I was over the bridge," Gloria tells Jack, "she tried to talk me out of listening to you" (170). Later, however, when Gloria wanted to have her choice of wifehood over schoolteaching vindicated, she thought to visit Miss Julia to prove "How wrong she was. How right I was." To make her case conclusively, she intended to present her baby, Lady May—"I was only waiting till she could talk," she explains to Judge Moody (322).

Perhaps nowhere is the tension between the spoken and written word more richly elaborated than in the long middle section of the novel, in which the family members recall the tenure of Miss Julia, the one person who, as Miss Beulah says, "wanted us to quit worshipping ourselves quite so wholehearted!" (236). The lengthy passage is a tour de force, a simulation of spontaneity so persuasive that one nearly forgets to look beneath the surface. The topic of conversation is Julia Mortimer, but in the course of the exchange the reunionists obliquely reveal as much of themselves as of their former teacher. What is revealed is not only their ironic castigation of books, but their delight in having vigorously contested the issue with their heroic teacher.

> "You'd never forget the name of Miss Julia Mortimer," Aunt Beck said. . . .
> "She taught us every one. I can see her this minute while I tell it, thumping horseback to school, wrapped up in that red sweater," cried Aunt Birdie. "Red as a railroad lantern, of her own knitting. Ready to throw open school and light straight into us. . . ."
> "She had designs on everybody. She wanted a doctor and a lawyer and all else we might have to holler for some day, to come right out of Banner. So she'd get behind some barefooted boy and push," said Uncle Percy. "She put an end to good fishing." (234–35)

With great subtlety Welty suggests in this long, unmediated passage of dialogue the ineffable mystery of human beings, men and women who cling to the present moment, fiercely resisting introspection, and yet who claim our sympathy because their passionate engagement of life proves a match for Julia Mortimer's high-minded rationalism.

"She was ready to teach herself to death for you, you couldn't get away from that. Whether you wanted her to or not didn't make any difference. But my suspicion was she did want you to *deserve* it," Uncle Curtis stated.

"How did she last as long as she did?" marvelled Aunt Beck.

"She thought if she told people what they ought to know, and told 'em enough times, and finally beat it into their hides, they wouldn't forget it. Well, some of us still had her licked," said Uncle Dophus.

" 'A state calling for improvement as loudly as ours? Mississippi standing at the foot of the ladder gives me that much more to work for,' she'd say. I don't dream it was so much palaver, either," said Miss Beulah. "She meant it entirely." (240)

The family very well understands the different resources they and their schoolteacher drew upon: they had themselves, kin and clan, support and entertainment for one another in the red clay hills of northeast Mississippi. Julia Mortimer had the printed word, "letters and parcel post travelling all over Mississippi." She had her books.

"Full of books is what she was," said Aunt Beck.

"Oh, books! The woman read more books than you could shake a stick at," said Miss Beulah. . . .

"She'd give out prizes for reading, at the end of school, but what would be the prizes? More books," said Aunt Birdie. "I dreaded to win. . . ."

"Yes'm, she taught the generations. She was our cross to bear," said Uncle Dolphus as the laughter died away. (240)

In *Losing Battles* Welty dramatizes a struggle between two evenly matched adversaries—foes, to be sure, who travel divergent roads to get to their truths. These opposites depend upon and complement one another, however, in ways that seem vital and necessary for the flourishing of life. Indeed, the complementarity of family and teacher, spoken word and written word, love and separateness, forms the central structure of Welty's psychic landscape, as we see clearly in the recent autobiographical lectures, *One Writer's Beginnings*. Her earliest and primary memories are those of listening to the sounds of home and family—clocks, songs sung by her parents, and stories, endless beloved stories, that were tied to her first discoveries of love and dependence, sex and death. When Welty reaches most directly for the essential emotions of human experience, she does so in words that can be heard. "Ever since I was first read to, then started reading to myself," she writes in the first lecture, entitled "Listening," "there has never been a line read that I didn't *hear*."[20]

Growing up, getting one's distance from the family, is viewed as an act of seeing. It is also the act that enables the writer Welty to transmute human experience into print. "Getting my distance, a prerequisite of my understanding of human events, is the way I begin work.... Frame, proportion, perspective, the values of light and shade, all are determined by the distance of the observing eye."[21] In *Losing Battles* Julia Mortimer is forever trying to make her Banner pupils *see*, but it is not her pupil but rather one of the younger generation, twelve-year-old Vaughn—whose clear-sightedness comes from his own searching curiosity—who sees the vast secret world beneath the surface of Banner.

In the only section of the novel not dominated by dialogue, Vaughn Renfro struggles to separate himself from the voices of the reunion. Wakeful and alert after everyone else has gone to sleep, he moves through "moonlight the thickness of china," in wonderment at the secret night. "Even after people gave up each other's company, said goodbye and went home, if there was only one left, Vaughn Renfro, the world around him was still one huge, soul-defying reunion" (363). But his capacity for wondering and seeing do defy the reunion, and the unmistakable evidence of the defiance is his possession of a book—"the new geography that he'd traded out of Curly Stovall. He dragged it to his cheek, where he could smell its print, sharper, blacker, dearer than the smell of new shoes" (365).

The second and third parts of *One Writer's Beginnings* are entitled "Learning to See" and "Finding a Voice." For Welty, one of the most visual of writers, the destination of the developing artist lies ultimately beyond seeing, in the discovery (or recovery) of one's separate human voice. And for her the essential act of reading is the *hearing* of what is seen in type. Through such hearing, one collaborates with the writer in celebrating life and, Welty implies, comes as near as one may to seeing its hidden secrets. Louise Gossett has observed that Welty approaches life's ultimate questions always with narrative, never with metaphysics, and perhaps no other work so fully evinces this observation as does

---

20. Eudora Welty, *One Writer's Beginnings* (Cambridge, Mass., 1984), 11.
21. Ibid., 21.

The Harmonies of *Losing Battles*

Losing Battles.[22] This prose drama, performed in the imagination of the reader, is as elusive and various and vital as a moment seized and held.

At the end of her life, when Julia Mortimer, the magnificent seer in this novel, speaks her final words, she does so to old Willy Trimble, who finds her alone and dying, her nurse, Lexie Renfro, having left her to attend the reunion. "What was the trip for?" Willy recalls that Julia asked. The chorus of family immediately attacks the question. "But she hadn't been anywhere, had she?" Aunt Beck says. Willy replies, "I didn't come with any answer. . . . She picked the wrong one to ask. It's the chance you are always taking as you journey through life" (241).

Julia Mortimer's question is put only slightly differently by the baby, Lady May, speaking her first sentence to "what sounded like great treads going over her head," the pelting of rain on the tin roof after the long day's reunion. "What you huntin' for, man?" she says. No answer for either old woman or baby. For Eudora Welty's Banner Mississippians, there are only the saying of the question and, in reply, the telling, over and over, of remembered stories. The human voice asking and remembering, trying to see and trying to love. Welty gives us in this bountiful novel, in form and theme that continuously imitate and recapitulate each other, this full range of an earthly harmony.

22. Louise Y. Gossett, "Eudora Welty's New Novel: The Comedy of Loss," *Southern Literary Journal*, III (Fall, 1970), 134.

MARTHA E. COOK

Flannery O'Connor's *Wise Blood:* Forms of Entrapment

On May 18, 1952, the Sunday New York *Times* had the following as its predominant headline: "20,000 PARADE ON FIFTH AVENUE TO HAIL ARMED FORCES DAY." The major sports headlines proclaimed, "GIANT RALLY TOPS CUBS, 9–8; DODGERS ROUT PIRATES, 12–7." And the cover story for the *Book Review* was a large article on George Orwell's *Homage to Catalonia* by Granville Hicks entitled "GEORGE ORWELL'S PRELUDE IN SPAIN"; it carried the heading, "THE STORY OF AN IDEALIST WHO FOUGHT A LOST CAUSE, BUT WHO NEVER LOST FAITH IN MANKIND." In such a context of patriotism and tradition, one is surprised that Flannery O'Connor's *Wise Blood* was even reviewed in this and other major papers and magazines when it appeared in the late spring of 1952. But this unorthodox first novel was thoroughly reviewed, by reviewers who ranged from the well-meaning to the vituperative, from some who tried to understand what O'Connor was doing to one who commented in *Time* that "all too often it reads as if Kafka had been set to writing the continuity for L'il Abner."[1]

Wise Blood is an artistic creation of considerable sophistication, undeserving of such a flippant attack as that of the anonymous reviewer for *Time*. It is tightly unified by patterns of images, by parallel events, and by doubling of characters, all of which function together to develop a convincing theme. Reading carefully, following O'Connor's clues

1. "Southern Dissonance," *Time*, June 9, 1952, p. 110.

(which are more obvious than subtle), the reader moves with Hazel Motes through a series of events that reveal his acceptance of his role as a believer. O'Connor's theme is not what Hazel believes or how he or anyone else practices belief; it is rather the necessity of acknowledging one's spiritual heritage, whatever it happens to be. The careful reader, understanding this theme, will see Hazel at the end of the novel as a positive character because he is finally able to accept the faith that has been his since birth and to practice it in his own way.

One of O'Connor's recent critics maintains that in her fiction in general O'Connor "was manifestly hesitant to 'tell' enough to make textual meanings unambiguous to the nonreligious."[2] I would not think of arguing that O'Connor's fiction, particularly *Wise Blood*, is easy reading. There is ambiguity, but it is an ambiguity that challenges, and not merely confuses, her reader. The text of *Wise Blood* contains all that any reader, religious or nonreligious, needs in order to discover O'Connor's theme. Whether Hazel's faith (or O'Connor's, of which I will say more later) is the reader's is not the point; what affects the reader is finally the power of O'Connor's words as she unfolds the story of this strange, troubled, lonely young man.

The form of the novel is circular: Hazel moves around, but he continues to come back to the same place, either literally or symbolically. On the one hand, he is seeking the security of a place, a home, which he has lost through the passage of time; on the other, he is trying to stay on the move to escape what he sees as the entrapment of the religious faith that is his heritage. Through blindness, the loss of his physical sense of sight, Hazel is able to see, to understand, to believe again; within the positive limits imposed by belief, he finds the ultimate freedom that religious faith offers and thus finds his true identity and his true spiritual home.

Wise Blood opens with Hazel Motes on a train going, the reader quickly learns, away from his rural childhood home toward the city of Taulkinham. This scene introduces the major patterns of imagery that recur as O'Connor moves Hazel around in circles through the course of the novel until he stops at the place where he began, not literally, but symbolically. Instead of feeling the freedom of movement that the train

---

2. Carol Shloss, *Flannery O'Connor's Dark Comedies: The Limits of Inference* (Baton Rouge, 1980), 126.

might represent, Hazel seems to feel trapped in the train car, afraid of being unable to escape, as the opening sentence reveals: "Hazel Motes sat at a forward angle on the green plush train seat, looking one minute at the window as if he might want to jump out of it, and the next down the aisle at the other end of the car."[3] Though Hazel professes to be eager to get to the city, where, he says, "I'm going to do some things I never have done before" (13), his actions indicate that he is not looking forward to where he is going, but rather backward to where he has been.

Hazel's physical appearance likewise serves an important function. In this scene he is dressed in new clothes, and he has "a stiff black broad-brimmed hat on his lap, a hat that an elderly country preacher would wear" (10). Shortly the reader learns of Hazel's grandfather, whose "own face was repeated almost exactly in the child's" (22), and Hazel's desire to survive his army experiences "uncorrupted" so he can return home, even though all of the members of his family have already died, "to be a preacher like his grandfather" (21). Before he goes away, Hazel is sharply aware that his faith is his heritage. "He had a strong confidence in his power to resist evil; it was something he had inherited, like his face, from his grandfather," he thinks (23). Having suffered a serious physical wound and severe loneliness and alienation, he returns with a desire to reject his heritage. But his appearance indicates how difficult such a rejection will be.

In these first pages of the novel O'Connor begins to develop one of her most effective patterns of imagery, using place and places after the fashion of the best southern fiction, as well as with deeper significance because of the religious dimension of this work. In the train scene O'Connor uses place to represent not only home but also status and position in society. Mrs. Wally Bee Hitchcock is able to place Hazel by the $11.98 price tag on his coat sleeve (10). Hazel in turn is able to place the porter as "a Parrum nigger from Eastrod" (12). He is angry at the man for refusing to accept his identity with his home, yet he rejects his own homeplace in talking with Mrs. Hitchcock. When he went into the army, Hazel had determined to tell anyone who tempted him "that he was from Eastrod, Tennessee, and that he meant to get back there and stay back there" (23). But Eastrod as a place has disappeared; his home is

---

3. Flannery O'Connor, *Wise Blood* (New York, 1962), 9. Subsequent references to the novel are to this edition and will be given in the text.

only "the skeleton of a house" (26). When Mrs. Hitchcock asks the natural question, "Are you going home?" Hazel replies, "No, I ain't" (13). But O'Connor foreshadows the circular movement to the concluding scene of the novel in this first scene, for Mrs. Hitchcock's pronouncement, "Well, there's no place like home" (11), will be echoed by Hazel's landlady in the final scene.[4] Home turns out to be exactly where Hazel is headed, though in a spiritual rather than an earthly sense.

Hazel goes to the city of Taulkinham to escape his faith; yet ironically it is in that place rather than in Eastrod, the place of his ancestors, that he finally acknowledges the power of his religious belief. But first he again rejects his homeplace in a conversation with Enoch Emery, a strange, lonely young man who has more in common with Hazel than Hazel wants to recognize. Enoch is struggling to place Hazel, to find some connection with him; he mentions the town of Melsy, near Eastrod, where Hazel has in fact caught the train. But Hazel disclaims any knowledge of the place. Later Hazel openly admits his own feeling of placelessness, of not belonging, when he buys a car which can also serve as a "house." "I ain't got any place to be," he explains (73). By emphasizing Hazel's homelessness, O'Connor is emphasizing that he does not belong in the world of Mrs. Hitchcock and Enoch. He is aware of his homeless state not only in a literal but in a metaphorical way, yet at this point he is unable to accept the belief that would provide him with his true spiritual home.

A car more traditionally functions as a symbol of mobility than of security, as an instrument of motion instead of a place, and Hazel sees his car in this way as well. To the mechanic who is honestly telling him how worthless the car is, he says, "I told you this car would get me anywhere I wanted to go." The mechanic replies prophetically, "Some things . . . 'll get some folks somewheres" (127). Hazel persists in believing that he needs to move to find his place, his home. Yet the reader senses that Hazel does not need to move; he needs only to accept the heritage of faith passed on from his mother and grandfather. By the end of *Wise Blood*, the significance of earthly place has been subsumed in the larger significance of spiritual place. Hazel Motes is then seen as

---

4. John R. May makes this connection in "Flannery O'Connor," in Jeffrey Helterman and Richard Layman (eds.), *American Novelists Since World War II* (Detroit, 1978), 382–83 Vol. II of *Dictionary of Literary Biography*, 40 vols. to date.

having found his real place, his true home, when he acknowledges the faith that he has inherited and accepts his true identity; in other words, he has come back where he started.

The notion of place associated with belief appears a number of times in *Wise Blood*, often when Hazel is attempting to convey his new unbelief. When he is told that he should have a church to preach in, he explains, "My church is the Church Without Christ. . . . If there's no Christ, there's no reason to have a set place to do it in" (106). Hazel seems to have forgotten his grandfather, who was controlled by an overpowering belief in Christ but who used his car as a church: "His grandfather had traveled three counties in a Ford automobile. Every fourth Sunday he had driven into Eastrod as if he were just in time to save them all from Hell, and he was shouting before he had the car door open. People gathered around his Ford because he seemed to dare them to. He would climb up on the nose of it and preach from there and sometimes he would climb onto the top of it and shout down at them" (21). As Hazel's grandfather illustrates, Hazel's desire to escape Christ by avoiding a place will not work. When Hazel discovers the hypocrisy of the supposedly blind preacher Hawks, he preaches his first real sermon—"from the nose of the car," just like his grandfather. And the theme of his sermon is place: "Where is there a place for you to be? No place. . . . Nothing outside you can give you any place. . . . If there was a place where Jesus had redeemed you that would be the place for you to be, but which of you can find it?" (165–66). Hazel will find the place for him to be, but first he must destroy the falseness of Solace Layfield and Hoover Shoats's Church of Christ Without Christ.

The central pattern of imagery that functions to show Hazel's attempts to deny his faith is coffin imagery. Through real coffins, coffinlike objects or places, and imagined or dreamed coffins, Flannery O'Connor reinforces the reader's growing sense of the inescapability of the faith that Hazel first encounters through his preacher grandfather, whose identity Hazel eventually assumes. The first mention of a coffin in the novel is Hazel's memory of the first coffin he ever saw, his grandfather's; Hazel is disillusioned that his seemingly all-powerful grandfather allows the coffin—or "box," in the country idiom Hazel often employs—to be shut. Immediately following this remembered scene is the account of the deaths of two of Hazel's brothers; at the death of the second one, he is upset at the thought of himself in the coffin in place of his brother: "what if he had been in it and they had shut it on him" (20). Then comes the bizarre description of his father's burial; Hazel sees his father, like his grandfather, as powerless to prevent being shut up in his coffin.

The opening chapter of the novel ends with Hazel's dream of his mother's burial. During the dream, his berth on the train becomes like a coffin to him. Significantly, it is the porter from home, from the place associated with his grandfather, who refuses to respond to Hazel's cry, "I can't be closed up in this thing" (27). Of course Hazel is not only closed up in the sleeping berth; he is symbolically trapped by his close identification with his grandfather, even to the point of reflecting the old man's appearance. In time he will accept that identification and with it the belief that he accepted without question when he was a child. But he will also find his own individuality. Although he resembles his grandfather, he is not his grandfather; he is an individual who must come to terms with his own spirituality.

O'Connor reminds the reader of this crucial scene in a grimly comic way through the stories of Sabbath Lily Hawks, another lonely character who seeks out Hazel's company as Enoch Emery does. Her stories involve unwanted children, such as she is, and entrapment or enclosure in coffinlike or prisonlike structures. The first portrays a beautiful mother who rejects her unattractive child, finally strangling it and hanging it in the chimney. It haunts the woman, "staring through the chimney at her," the girl emphasizes (52). The second depicts an evil grandmother who rejects her grandchild because of its goodness. She locks it in a chicken crate where it prophesies her death and damnation: "It seen its granny in hell-fire, swoll and burning, and it told her everything it seen and she got so swoll until finally she went to the well and wrapped the well rope around her neck and let down the bucket and broke her neck" (122–23). Surely Hazel must be affected by these tales; regardless, they function for the reader to reinforce the feeling that Hazel is trapped by his past and his own sense of mortality.

The scene in which Hazel imagines himself instead of his brother in the coffin prefigures a crucial scene in which Hazel dreams that he is "not dead but only buried. He was not waiting on the Judgment because there was no Judgment, he was waiting on nothing." Most tellingly, he expects his release to come through Asa Hawks, the fake blind preacher: "He kept expecting Hawks to appear at the oval window with a wrench, but the blind man didn't come" (160–61). Earlier, Hazel had chastised Hawks for not trying to save him. When Hazel awakes from this dream, he goes to Hawks, picks the lock of his room, and strikes a match before his seeing eyes.

Reflection, mirroring, and doubling serve many functions in *Wise Blood*. The most obvious is to identify Hazel's heritage of faith to the reader through repeated references to his resemblance to his grandfather. Hazel is first seen with his preacherlike hat, which turns out to be so important to him that he misses the train after a stop because he is running to retrieve his hat, which has been blown off by the wind. With the hat goes the identity of being a preacher like his grandfather, which he at first denies. The taxi driver who takes Hazel to Mrs. Leora Watts, the prostitute, says, "You look like a preacher." He adds: "It ain't only the hat. It's a look in your face somewheres" (31). And of course Mrs. Watts torments him: "Momma don't mind if you ain't a preacher" (34). Early on Hazel identifies himself as a preacher, and of course he continues to wear the hat. When Mrs. Watts mutilates what she has referred to as his "Jesus-seeing hat" (60), he buys a completely different one that in his hands turns out to look "just as fierce as the other one had" (111). This is the hat that Sabbath Lily Hawks throws across the room as she seduces him. From the first scene the hat and other images function as links between Hazel and his grandfather, to reinforce his sense of being trapped by his spiritual heritage. Eventually he will discover his own way of acknowledging his belief and find his identity as an individual rather than a reflection of the old man.

Characters such as Enoch Emery, Onnie Jay Holy, Solace Layfield, and, most important, Asa Hawks also mirror Hazel, but they ultimately serve to move him around to the greater freedom that his heritage ultimately represents. Emery, for example, not only supplies the "new jesus" for Hazel's Church Without Christ, a mummy found in a "coffin-like" case (97), but he also takes on a new identity himself as the godlike Gonga the gorilla. This transformation may well be a comic foreshadowing of Hazel's eventual assumption of the role of the only true prophet in the novel.

The character of Onnie Jay Holy tries to pervert the teachings of Hazel by creating a mirror image of Hazel's "church," called the Holy Church of Christ Without Christ, for purely materialistic purposes. Holy, actually a fraud with the equally wonderful name of Hoover Shoats, turns up with an imitation Hazel in the person of Solace Layfield. The ironically labeled "True Prophet" even drives a "rat-colored car" like Hazel's, which itself reminds Hazel of the Ford from which his grandfather delivered his sermons. When asked by a woman on the street if he and Layfield are twins, Hazel responds ambiguously: "If you don't hunt it down and kill it, it'll hunt you down and kill you" (168). Hazel is of course thinking of his attempts to destroy the religious faith of his grandfather, which haunts him. This image of killing is clearly related to the pattern of coffin imagery in the novel. In fact, death proves to be the ultimate confinement for Hazel—but it is not a negative confinement. It is within the security of belief that Hazel moves through death to his true spiritual home.

O'Connor skillfully uses the false prophet to illustrate to Hazel the falseness of what he is doing in preaching of the Church Without Christ. Hazel looks at Solace Layfield and sees not just someone who resembles himself, but himself. "He was so struck with how gaunt and thin he looked in the illusion," the narrator says, "that he stopped preaching. He had never pictured himself that way before. The man he saw was hollow-chested and carried his neck thrust forward and his arms down by his side; he stood there as if he were waiting for some signal he was afraid he might not catch" (167). Hazel is reminded by the image of Layfield of what he is trying to escape, but he also seems to get the proper signal, for he realizes that he must destroy this fake prophet. He does so by the heavily symbolic act of destroying the imitation car, then repeatedly running over Layfield with the true car, the Essex. Because of the fraud and hypocrisy involved in Shoats's and Layfield's operation, the reader must accept the validity of Hazel's acts of violence, which are seen in the context of the novel to be carried out in the name of true religion, regardless of Hazel's pretense that he is preaching the doctrines of a church with no Savior. The instrument of violence is the car, which symbolically carries the faith of Hazel's grandfather from the past into the present, as well as carrying Hazel toward a state of acceptance of that faith.

Reflection is used even more significantly through the character of Asa Hawks, the fake blind preacher. Hawks has attempted to blind himself as an act of faith, but he failed. Hazel's literal destruction of the fake prophet Solace Layfield is foreshadowed in the novel by his symbolic destruction of Hawks through the exposure of his hypocrisy.

Sneaking into the supposedly blind preacher's room, Motes strikes a match in the sleeping Hawks's face: "The two sets of eyes looked at each other as long as the match lasted; Haze's expression seemed to open onto a deeper blankness and reflect something and then close again" (162). The reader subsequently learns that the reflection here is of the greatest significance when later in the novel Hazel attempts to blind himself as an act of faith—and succeeds.

Before making that commitment, though, Hazel must destroy Layfield and then experience the destruction of his own car. Frustrated by the attempts of Hoover Shoats and Sabbath Lily Hawks to control him, he determines to leave Taulkinham. The real meaning of having a car has, he believes, become clear to him as he makes his plans: "The entire possibility of this came from the advantage of having a car—of having something that moved fast, in privacy, to the place you wanted to be" (186). After killing Layfield, Hazel spends the night in the car, then heads out of the city. In a truly comic scene a stereotyped southern highway patrolman learns that Hazel does not possess a driver's license, so he pushes the Essex over an embankment, just as Hazel had pushed Layfield's car into a ditch. The policeman drawls, "Them that don't have a car, don't need a license" (209). In destroying Hazel's car, the policeman has destroyed what Hazel originally saw as his instrument for freedom, the means of moving away from his past, and also as his security, his home. The car actually represented further entrapment, further repetition of the role of his grandfather. O'Connor does not allow Hazel a simple resolution of his conflict, however. Rather than freeing Hazel from that role as a prophet, the loss of the car paradoxically allows Hazel greater mobility, freeing him instead to find his own belief, to be himself instead of being his grandfather. In a symbolic circular movement, he goes directly from the place where the car is destroyed back into the city and blinds himself, using lime, as Asa Hawks had tried to do, succeeding where Hawks had failed. Hazel thus accepts his role as a believer, but shows that he must practice that belief in his own way.

Imagery and symbolism of eyes, of seeing and blindness, are central to the novel, functioning to connect parallel events and to link characters, as well as to convey a central theme of seeing or understanding. O'Connor begins with Mrs. Hitchcock's seeing into Hazel's eyes in life and ends with Mrs. Flood's seeing into Hazel's eyes in death. Isaac Rosenfeld, reviewing the novel in the *New Republic*, said of Hazel's act of blinding himself: "Hazel Motes' mutilation is the inevitable consequence of his religious position; there is no escaping Christ. But the author's style ... is inconsistent with this statement. Everything she says through image and metaphor has the meaning only of degeneration."[5] Yet one does not have to be a biblical or classical scholar to be aware of the rich positive symbolism associated with blindness. Throughout *Wise Blood,* in fact, the eye imagery is a source of contrast to the imagery of entrapment. From the beginning, Hazel's eyes are seen by Mrs. Wally Bee Hitchcock as a clue to his true self: "Their settings were so deep that they seemed, to her, almost like passages leading somewhere" (10). Sensing the depth of Hazel's character, she tries to see into his eyes, to understand him. But his eyes lead to the self he is attempting to deny.

Even the unperceptive Sabbath Lily realizes that Hazel's eyes are unusual: "They don't look like they see what he's looking at but they keep on looking" (109). He is of course looking for a way out, a release from what he perceives as entrapment. Mrs. Flood asks, "Why had he destroyed his eyes and saved himself unless he had some plan, unless he saw something that he couldn't get without being blind to everything else?" (216). She is of course precisely correct here. When Hazel realizes that nothing else matters but belief, he cuts himself off from everything else. When the novel ends, Mrs. Flood looks into Hazel's eyes until "he was the pin point of light" that even she could see (231). The eye imagery and other images of reflection function not to convey degeneration, as Rosenfeld suggests, but to indicate the inevitability of Hazel's acknowledgment of belief—a positive rather than a negative theme for O'Connor.

From the point of Hazel's blinding himself until the conclusion of the novel, O'Connor focuses on this inevitability of Hazel's role as a believer. He puts rocks in his shoes, as he had done as a youth to punish himself for his first awareness of his own sexuality; this awareness is symbolically connected to the experience of seeing a naked woman in a coffinlike "box" at a carnival sideshow (62). He even puts strands of barbed wire around his chest. Mrs. Flood, who seems to need the spiritual cleansing her name suggests, has not acknowledged her own spirituality. So she attacks Hazel for these practices, for doing "something that people have quit doing," but his reply is simple: "They ain't quit

---

5. Isaac Rosenfeld, "To Win by Default," *New Republic,* July 7, 1952, p. 19.

doing it as long as I'm doing it" (224). His self-punishment, like his blinding himself, serves ironically as a source of liberation for his true self.

Though Mrs. Flood in her limited view tries to convince Hazel that he has no place in the world except his place in her house, the reader sees that Hazel's blindness not only gives him identity but moves him into another world. In the words of an old Protestant hymn, this world is not his home, and he pleads with the policemen at the close of the novel to let him "go on where I'm going" (230). When in death he returns to Mrs. Flood's house, she says more wisely than she knows, "I see you've come home!" Images of seeing and of motion dominate the concluding passage of *Wise Blood:* Mrs. Flood "shut her eyes and saw the pin point of light but so far away that she could not hold it steady in her mind. She felt as if she were blocked at the entrance of something. She sat staring with her eyes shut, into his eyes, and felt as if she had finally got to the beginning of something she couldn't begin, and she saw him moving farther and farther away, farther and farther into the darkness until he was the pin point of light" (231–32). With the powerful conclusion, the reader realizes that not only has Hazel Motes gone home to the spiritual place where he has been headed since the days of his childhood, but he has possibly drawn Mrs. Flood along with him.

In an early review that is more perceptive than most, Carl Hartman makes the point that "in the process of denying the validity of all martyrdom and its accompanying mysticism and perversions, Haze has ended up placing himself in a position which is susceptible of a similar interpretation; the only forms he can find for his denial are those traditional ones which, because of the very nature of their place in society, can only serve to trap rather than free him."[6] If I read Hartman correctly, all he needs to do is to take this line of reasoning one step further, to see that what appears to be negative entrapment—Hazel Motes's inability to escape the faith of his grandfather and his own practice of his belief—is rather freedom from the confinement of the earthly world. Thus, O'Connor's character Hazel is seen to be truly free only when he appears to be restricted by his bizarre ways of practicing his faith, above all, by blinding himself. About the midpoint of the novel Hazel says ironically that he is peaceful because "my blood has set me free" (141). At that

---

6. Carl Hartman, "Jesus Without Christ," *Western Review* XVII (1952), 79.

point he is neither peaceful nor free, but he is both at the conclusion of the novel.

The power of Flannery O'Connor's novel *Wise Blood* as a work of art is seen as she draws her reader, like Mrs. Flood, not necessarily into a particular state of belief, but into an acceptance of Hazel Motes's state of total commitment to belief. For Hazel, entrapment by faith becomes the greatest freedom of all. In *Wise Blood*, as in some of O'Connor's later works, one is tempted to see images and symbols of entrapment—coffins and other tomblike enclosures—as related to the author's growing feelings of being confined by physical illness. She worked to revise this novel extensively after she became ill and was forced to return home to Georgia. She did not know at first how severe her illness was or that she would never be able to live independently again, but she must have suspected both. Since her father had died with lupus, she knew precisely how serious a disease it can be. Here and elsewhere, however, these images and symbols must also be seen as womblike, reflecting feelings of another kind of confinement, not at all negative, represented by the definite beliefs of her Catholic faith. One can easily see that Hazel's life is simplified once he turns from fighting the idea of Christian belief back to accepting that belief and expressing it, albeit in extreme ways.

However, the early reviews of *Wise Blood* indicate that many readers in addition to Isaac Rosenfeld and Carl Hartman missed O'Connor's point; they were either unable or unwilling to see the positive dimension of Hazel's character. Martha Smith, writing in the Sunday Atlanta *Journal and Constitution*, summed up Hazel in the following manner: "Molded into his fearful character by an environment and heritage of horror, he moves undeviatingly on to his personal disaster, helped on his way by as unsavory a bunch of helpmates as you'd find under any stone." This failure to see Hazel's final experience as positive is not simply provincial narrowness. William Goyen, himself a master of the grotesque, said in the *New York Times Book Review*: "The story of this novel, darting through rapid, brute, bare episodes told with power and keenness, develops the disintegration and final destruction of Hazel." Goyen appreciates O'Connor's art but misses her theme, seeing Hazel as falling apart rather than finding the spiritual wholeness that O'Connor intends. Oliver LaFarge missed both the theme and the art, saying sarcastically in the *Saturday Review* that "Perhaps Miss Flannery's aim was a savage and bitter study of the nethermost depths of a small town, with special reference to the viciousness of itinerant preachers."[7] O'Connor's careful artistry deserves a closer reading than most reviewers seem to have given, and one is tempted to see not only her youth but her sex and her region as responsible for the kind of condescension LaFarge, the anonymous reviewer in *Time*, and others displayed.

Given the continued popularity of *Wise Blood*, such reviews might be simply amusing now. But they were no doubt responsible for O'Connor's feeling the necessity of adding a preface to the novel on the occasion of the tenth anniversary of its publication. Since 1962 the novel has carried its author's statement of the theme. Acknowledging that the novel "was written by an author congenitally innocent of theory, but one with certain preoccupations," O'Connor continues: "That belief in Christ is to some a matter of life and death has been a stumbling block for readers who would prefer to think it a matter of no great consequence. For them Hazel Motes' integrity lies in his trying with such vigor to get rid of the ragged figure who moves from tree to tree in the back of his mind. For the author Hazel's integrity lies in his not being able to" (5). In other words, she wants to be sure that her reader understands her "certain preoccupations"—the primacy of the religious faith that is operating both in her characterization of Hazel and in her own life.

Perhaps the preface, more than the novel itself, has been responsible for the antagonism some critics have expressed concerning O'Connor's attitude toward her reader. I think particularly of Carol Shloss's recent study and Martha Stephens' earlier one. Both express the view that O'Connor's work on the whole is aimed at the religious, perhaps even the Catholic, reader and is not intended by the author to be appreciated by the lay reader.[8] Much of the most positive criticism of O'Connor's work comes indeed from critics who openly profess a sympathy with O'Connor's own religious views, and attempts to look at her work from a purely literary perspective have been few. Thus Shloss notes that "the publication of her first Christian essay . . . dramatically changed the tenor of critical response" to O'Connor's fiction.[9] This point is true in

---

7. Martha Smith, "Georgian Pens 'Wise Blood,' a First Novel," Atlanta *Journal and Constitution*, May 18, 1952, p. 7; William Goyen, "Unending Vengeance," *New York Times Book Review*, May 18, 1952, Sec. F, p. 7; Oliver LaFarge, "Manic Gloom," *Saturday Review*, May 24, 1952, p. 22.
8. Martha Stephens, *The Question of Flannery O'Connor* (Baton Rouge, 1973).
9. Shloss, *O'Connor's Dark Comedies*, 13.

that the essay seems to have given Christian readers an approach to her work and thus resulted in more positive responses than the early reviews. Yet this essay and others like it may have inhibited the kind of artistic analysis that is, as I have shown here, so rewarding.

Wise Blood, Flannery O'Connor's first novel, has been subjected to many readings and misreadings since its publication in 1952. Though it has received more positive criticism since O'Connor added an explanatory note in 1962, critics still have difficulty in viewing Hazel Motes's acceptance of belief in the way O'Connor intended. For example, in a recent volume aimed at the general reader, the student of O'Connor's fiction and nonfiction, the author maintains that in *Wise Blood* "the movement of the story is towards Haze's conversion; the tension develops through Haze's inner conflict."[10] A careful study of the symbolism and imagery reveals that O'Connor is not portraying a traditional conversion, in which one goes from a state of disbelief to belief or from a lack of faith to true faith. Hazel Motes is presented in the novel as struggling against the acceptance, the acknowledgment of the belief that has been his since childhood but that he has tried to reject. Rather than a conversion, O'Connor presents a circular movement back to an original state of belief.

One should not have to resort to studying O'Connor's essays and speeches reproduced in the volume *Mystery and Manners* or the letters in *The Habit of Being* or elsewhere in order to understand the theme of *Wise Blood*. However, looking at these sources reveals support for the interpretation I have developed and may help the reader who has difficulty with the nature of belief as O'Connor presents it. Understanding how she views dogma in another context may help the reader who sees any particular set of beliefs as confining. O'Connor makes it plain in speeches and essays and letters that she is very comfortable with the dogma of the Catholic church, for she saw it not as a restricting, but as a liberating element of her religion. Although she states in a letter to a friend with whom she had many discussions of religion, "If you're a Catholic you believe what the church teaches," she also explains, "For me a dogma is only a gateway to contemplation and is an instrument of

---

10. James A. Grimshaw, Jr., *The Flannery O'Connor Companion* (Westport, Conn., 1981), 66.

freedom and not of restriction."[11] As O'Connor spells out in her 1962 preface to the novel, this kind of freedom is a difficult concept: "Freedom cannot be conceived simply. It is a mystery and one which a novel, even a comic novel, can only be asked to deepen" (5). Characterizing the role of a Christian novelist in the 1957 essay "The Fiction Writer and His Country," O'Connor emphasizes the same idea of freedom: "I have heard it said that belief in Christian dogma is a hindrance to the writer, but I myself have found nothing further from the truth. Actually, it frees the storyteller to observe. It is not a set of rules which fixes what he sees in the world. It affects his writing primarily by guaranteeing his respect for mystery."[12]

Interesting and valuable as such sources are, all one need do is give *Wise Blood* a close, careful, sophisticated reading. The text of the novel includes all the evidence one needs to follow Hazel Motes's inexorable path to the acceptance of his own kind of belief. Whether the reader shares this belief is not essential to experience the power of Flannery O'Connor's words in *Wise Blood*, to appreciate the ambiguities and richness of style that mark her literary achievement. *The Violent Bear It Away* likewise gives O'Connor an opportunity to develop a rich pattern of imagery and symbolism that is simply not possible in the confines of the short stories for which she is better known.

11. O'Connor to "A," in Flannery O'Connor, *The Habit of Being: Letters*, ed. Sally Fitzgerald (New York, 1979), 103, 92.
12. Flannery O'Connor, *Mystery and Manners: Occasional Prose*, ed. Sally and Robert Fitzgerald (New York, 1970), 31.

KIERAN QUINLAN

The Moviegoer: The Dilemma of Walker Percy's Scholastic Existentialism

There can be little doubt that Walker Percy is among the two or three most important philosophical novelists writing in America today. His early training as a medical doctor and his apparently dramatic switch to a serious study of philosophy after several bouts of illness in the forties are well known. Less familiar, perhaps, is his upbringing in the home of his cousin and foster parent, the poet William Alexander Percy, from whom he learned not only the requirements and joys of a practical stoicism but also the tradition of that austere Catholicism from which the elder Percy had conscientiously and painfully turned away in his youth. Indeed, Walker Percy has said of his cousin that "even when I did not follow him [in intellectual commitments], it was usually in *relation* to him, whether with him or against him, that I defined myself and my own direction."[1]

Ten years were to elapse, however, between Percy's emergence from the sanitorium in 1944 and his first significant publication. It was to be still another seven years before the appearance of his first novel, *The Moviegoer,* in 1961.[2] His preparation, therefore, was long, very personal, and, above all, highly intellectual. And it is these same traits that tend to characterize his several novels also, both in their form and in their

---

1. Walker Percy, introduction to William Alexander Percy, *Lanterns on the Levee: Recollections of a Planter's Son* (Baton Rouge, 1973), xi.
2. Walker Percy, *The Moviegoer* (New York, 1961). References to the novel are to this edition and will be given in the text.

function. In short, Walker Percy has always seen himself as a writer with the definite mission of passing on his own hard-won insights so as to alter the lives of his readers.

Percy's convalescent studies covered a very broad range of works in at least three distinct areas: existentialist philosophy and literature, Catholic theology, and contemporary semiotics. All of these concerns were to reappear in one form or another in his novels. To begin with his existentialist interests, then, it is clear that these were always more in the religious tradition of Kierkegaard and Marcel than in the atheistic alternatives of Heidegger and Sartre. Indeed, Kierkegaard appears to have had by far the greatest influence on him and even to have led him directly to embrace Roman Catholicism.[3] Referring on one occasion to his previous training as a medical doctor, Percy made clear how this thinker caused him first of all to change to philosophy: "After 12 years of scientific education, I felt somewhat like the Danish philosopher Soren Kierkegaard when he finished reading Hegel. Hegel, said Kierkegaard, explained everything under the sun, except one small detail: what it means to be a man living in the world who must die."[4] His own experience of illness had strained not only his belief in the eventual success of the scientific enterprise but also his faith in the efficacy of his cousin's impersonal and detached stoicism. In consequence, the protagonists of Percy's stories at least begin as existential searchers conscious of their abandonment in an absurd universe that treats them as mere objects. Where they end up, of course, is an entirely different matter. Furthermore, Percy has never quite managed to shed his scientific training or to resolve the problems posed by the philosophical implications of such procedures.

Thomas Aquinas, Jacques Maritain, Romano Guardini, and Christopher Dawson were prominent in his reading of Catholic authors. Maritain and Guardini are usually associated with an interim phase in Catholic intellectual life between the old Cartesian scholasticism of the early and mid twentieth-century church and the newer, secular-influenced theologies of Karl Rahner, Bernard Haring, and others that flourished in the sixties and seventies. In other words, Percy's theological understanding tends to be that of a well-informed lay Catholic

3. Percy is quoted on Kierkegaard in Thomas LeClair's "Walker Percy's Devil," *Southern Literary Journal*, X (Fall, 1977), 3.
4. Walker Percy, "From Facts to Fiction," *Book Week*, December 25, 1966, p. 6.

of the postwar years, at once sensitive to certain modern scientific developments and yet determined to resist any secularizing interpretation of the religious phenomenon. More interestingly, Percy seems to have avoided—or not to have known—those very theologians who were most influenced by the existentialist philosophers: Rahner, for example, was trained by Heidegger himself and wrote his first major work in light of this training.[5] Just as another Catholic thinker, the French Jesuit Teilhard de Chardin, was in the forefront of contemporary research in the field of anthropology but out of step with recent shifts in theological understanding, so, too, has Percy persisted in a commitment to a dynamic view of philosophy while holding to a rather static religious position. This dichotomy causes serious problems for the plot and narrative of *The Moviegoer*. The efficacy of the Eucharist, for example, on which an important part of the plot turns, requires a Thomistic justification and could not easily be supported by an appeal to an existentialist theology. Here again, Percy's novels seem to begin with an existential situation only to conclude with a resolution as definite—though unfounded—as that of any scholastic syllogism.

Finally, Percy's acquaintance with the writings of the semioticians and linguistic philosophers includes the works of Charles Morris, Susanne Langer, Charles Peirce, Noam Chomsky, and Ludwig Wittgenstein. Several factors have recommended this particular study to him. One is that the major philosophical concerns of the present century, both in Europe and America, have centered around the phenomenon of language to such an extent that belief and unbelief tend to be explained in terms of understanding or misunderstanding the function of linguistic reference in human communication rather than in a discussion of so-called metaphysical reality. Another, and related, factor—and one that has already been mentioned—is that Percy has always retained a strong commitment to the procedures of the empirical sciences and that the examination of linguistic behavior is in accordance with this orientation. Though this interest is not prominent in *The Moviegoer*, it is partly present in some of the dialogue between Binx and Lonnie in which the latter expresses traditional religious clichés with all the wonder of first discovery.

5. I have traced the conflict between empiricism and transcendentalism in Rahner's theology in "Is Love of Man the *Only* Way to God?" *Catholic Mind*, LXXVI (February, 1978), 29–37.

Between 1954 and 1961, then, Walker Percy published at least ten philosophical essays in well-regarded journals in the field, though it should be added that these were not essays that provoked subsequent discussion among serious philosophers. He also attempted a book about the philosophy of language, the manuscript of "which the publisher didn't even bother to return and I didn't bother to ask for." Though only two of these essays, "The Man on the Train" and "The Loss of the Creature," directly suggest the kinds of themes that were to appear in his earliest fiction, the other eight—all of them more or less highly professional attempts at bridging the gap between the quasi-scientific methods of the linguistic semioticians and the more intuitive ponderings of the existentialists—do so indirectly.[6] In fact, in all of his philosophical writings Percy tends to unite the methodologies learned during his scientific training with those he has more recently acquired from the writings of Catholic Thomistic philosophers and the existentialists. The problem is that his frequent assertions of faith in these essays— "The Message in the Bottle," in which Percy attempts to argue that religion belongs to a special category of knowledge called "news" and is therefore not subject to verification in the usual empirical fashion, being perhaps the most notorious example—do not flow logically from his initial premises.

My argument is that the same problem is present, though in a somewhat different way, in his novels. Thus, I am taking a position rather at odds with that recently presented by Patricia Lewis Poteat in her important study *Walker Percy and the Old Modern Age*. There she states that she "assumes that the brilliant success of the novelist, together with the *systematic* and therefore philosophically revealing confusion of the essayist, discloses the profound differences between the novel and the philosophical essay as instruments of reflection."[7] I believe that the same confusion or dilemma is to be found in both.

It is my contention, then, that the *form* of *The Moviegoer* can be seen to resemble that of Percy's philosophical essays. This is not at all to say that the novel contains material that is excessively didactic in nature— what Reynolds Price has referred to in regard to Percy's other novels as

---

6. Percy, "From Facts to Fiction," 9; Walker Percy, *The Message in the Bottle* (New York, 1975).
7. Patricia Lewis Poteat, *Walker Percy and the Old Modern Age: Reflections on Language, Argument, and the Telling of Stories* (Baton Rouge, 1985), 8.

"occasional lumps of unprocessed Franco-American metaphysics"—but that the overall *framework* is similar.[8] Thus, in the essays, Percy generally combines insights from modern, scientifically oriented semiotics with elements of a rather outdated Catholic Thomism and with existentialist philosophy, all in the service of some kind of affirmation of faith, usually quite unsupported and of very dubious philosophical merit.[9] The essays begin with a genuinely existentialist dilemma but then proceed by a kind of scholastic examination of several possible solutions, only to end in the Aquinian resolution characteristic of that thinker's *Summa Theologia*. Likewise, in the novels, a character finds himself in a situation for which existentialist philosophy has provided a descriptive vocabulary of words such as *alienation, everydayness, malaise*, and so on; he must then work out his salvation between the poles of a scientific analysis of the human condition and some other form of belief—usually several varieties of stoicism and Christianity; finally, he comes to an acceptance of the Christian message in a way that, as Percy himself has admitted, all too often takes the reader by surprise and strains his credulity.[10] In Kierkegaardian terminology, it is a journey from an aesthetic, through an ethical, to a religious mode of existence. Or as Martin Luschei noted of *The Moviegoer*, the movement is dialectical: from thesis, to antithesis, to synthesis.[11] Although there are, of course, many nuances and subtleties in the description of this progression, the general pattern nevertheless remains.

Percy himself, it must be admitted, does not always see his novels in quite this way. For instance, in 1966, five years after its first publication, he described what he conceived of as the *form* of *The Moviegoer*.

> When I sat down to write *The Moviegoer*, I was very much aware of discarding the conventional notions of a plot and a set of characters, discarded because the traditional concept of plot-and-character itself reflects a view of reality which has been called into question. Rather would I begin with a *man* who finds himself in a *world*, a very concrete man who is located in a very concrete place and time. Such a man might be represented as *coming to himself* in somewhat

---

8. Reynolds Price, Review of Walker Percy's *Lancelot*, in *Washington Post Book World*, February 27, 1977, p. E7.

9. Martin Luschei, *The Sovereign Wayfarer: Walker Percy's Diagnosis of the Malaise* (Baton Rouge, 1972), 65–66.

10. See John Carr, "An Interview with Walker Percy," *Georgia Review*, XXV (Fall, 1971), 329–30.

11. Luschei, *The Sovereign Wayfarer*, 65–66.

the same sense as Robinson Crusoe came to himself on his island after his shipwreck, with the same wonder and curiosity.[12]

The theme of beginning "from the subjective"—which, according to Sartre, both Christian and atheist existentialists have in common—is quite evident in this quotation. But with Percy, the openness of simply seeing what will happen generally ends all too soon. And indeed when the manuscript of Percy's novel arrived at the offices of Alfred A. Knopf, its first editor found it to consist of "only forty good pages and a rather evangelical Catholic ending."[13] Though Percy may have thought himself to be among those novelists who were rejecting Victorian forms and plots and characters, with their fixed identities and contrived endings, it is difficult to place him more than tangentially in such company. Instead, one might argue that the "evangelical Catholic ending" is the hallmark of a Walker Percy novel every bit as much as a happy ending typifies a Victorian narrative. Again and again the rigidities of Thomistic scholasticism seem to have triumphed over the openness that characterizes European existentialism in all of its varied forms.

It is in confrontation with a contemporary novelist such as William Gass that Percy's traditionalism, his desire above all to tell a story and make a point, becomes strikingly apparent. His comments in a 1976 symposium with Gass on the works of Robbe-Grillet cast an interesting reflection on his 1966 statement about *The Moviegoer*: "I think Robbe-Grillet, like so many of the French, tends to fall victim to theories. He develops theories for fiction, which can be fatal. His theory was to get rid of all the appurtenances of fiction, namely plot, characters, narrative, theme and so on, and reduce it to geometry. As someone said, the only good novel he ever wrote was a novel called *Jealousy* and that was because he was jealous of his wife at the time."[14] The *form* of a Percy novel, I want to suggest, is itself less open, less plotless, less genuinely existential and probing, and has more of a hidden agenda, than Percy has implied; this is so because, just as Robbe-Grillet wrote well out of his passion of jealousy, Percy writes well out of his Catholic convictions. The form is used to lead to a definite conclusion every bit as much as in a philosophical essay.

---

12. Percy, "From Facts to Fiction," 9.
13. Alfred Kazin, "The Pilgrimage of Walker Percy," *Harper's*, June, 1971, p. 81.
14. Donald Barthelme, William Gass, Grace Paley, and Walker Percy, "A Symposium on Fiction," *Shenandoah*, XXVII (Winter, 1976), 9.

The *function* served by this *form* is never in doubt in Percy's conception of it, though it may be so among his nonconverted readers. During the symposium with William Gass, Percy also said: "It's hard for me to imagine any novelist not being motivated by some desire to approach some kind of truth or what he thinks to be the truth. If I didn't think that I don't think I'd bother to set pen to paper." And in an essay of 1971 entitled "Notes for a Novel About the End of the World," he stated: "Since the true prophets, i.e. men called by God to communicate something urgent to other men, are currently in short supply, the novelist may perform a quasi-prophetic function ... the novelist can make vicarious use of catastrophe in order that he and his reader may come to themselves."[15] *The Moviegoer*, then, is designed not only to tell about a Robinson Crusoe figure, but to make the reader become aware of being such a castaway: its purpose is to provoke an existential commitment.

Binx Bolling, the protagonist of *The Moviegoer*, is a successful stockbroker living in a nondescript suburb of New Orleans. He feels himself submerged, however, in the "everydayness" of the world around him and suffering from the presence of what he calls the "malaise." Prior to his experience of the malaise, he had tried to find meaning in life by reading only "fundamental" books such as *War and Peace, A Study of History,* and *What Is Life?* "During those years," Binx says, "I stood outside the universe and sought to understand it" (69). But when he had completed *The Chemistry of Life* and understood that the main goals of his search had been reached or were in principle reachable, he found *himself* left over: "There I lay in my hotel room with my search over yet still obliged to draw one breath and then the next" (70). As a result of this experience—which echoes, of course, Kierkegaard's response to Hegel—Binx now approaches the problem from an altogether different angle. "What takes place in my room is less important," he observes. "What is important is what I shall find when I leave my room and wander in the neighborhood. Before, I wandered as a diversion. Now I wander seriously and read as a diversion" (70).

The *existentialist* solution to Binx's problem is to attempt to overcome the malaise of "everydayness" by immersing himself in the concrete reality of his surroundings. Thus, to escape being an "anyone

---

15. Ibid., 6; Percy, *The Message in the Bottle*, 10.

anywhere," Binx becomes friendly with the owners and box-office ladies of the movie houses he attends. He also tries to escape from everydayness and anonymity by successfully achieving Kierkegaardian "repetitions" and "rotations." *Repetition* results when one revisits a scene after years of absence or rereads a book: the experience is of a heightened sense of awareness of the intervening time. *Rotation* likewise leads one to a heightened awareness of reality. Binx defines it as "the awareness of the new beyond the expectation of the experience of the new. For example, taking one's first trip to Taxco would not be a rotation; but getting lost on the way and discovering a hidden valley would be" (144). Binx's more usual kind of rotation, however, is achieved by attending the movies or by engaging in amorous affairs with a succession of his secretaries.

The action of the novel takes place during the pre-Lenten Mardi Gras just before Binx's thirtieth birthday. He is becoming uneasily aware that even rotatory and repetitional experiences get used up and fail to guard against the impingement of everydayness. Unfortunately, he cannot have recourse either to the romantic stoicism of his father's family or to the stolid Catholicism of his mother, because neither of these beliefs is intelligible to him. Surprisingly, however, he reports their respective convictions with great clarity, a clarity that draws attention to the author's philosophical agenda perhaps more than to Binx's actual dilemma.

The attitude on his father's side is represented by his Aunt Emily, who explains her philosophy to him in the following way: "I don't quite know what we're doing on this insignificant cinder spinning away in a dark corner of the universe. This is a secret which the high gods have not confided to me. Yet one thing I believe and I believe it with every fibre of my being. A man must live by his lights and do what little he can and do it as best he can. In this world goodness is destined to be defeated. But a man must go down fighting. That is the victory. To do anything less is to be less than a man" (54). Binx's response to this is to say that she is right "even though I do not really know what she is talking about."

The same is true of his attitude toward his mother's Catholicism: "My mother's family think I have lost my faith and they pray for me to recover it. I don't know what they're talking about. Other people, so I have read, are pious as children and later become skeptical. . . . Not I. My unbelief was invincible from the beginning. I could never make head or tail of God" (145). The only thing that Binx "understands" is that a search must be undertaken if he is to escape from the grip of everydayness and that while "it no longer avails to start with creatures and prove God," neither is it possible "to rule God out."

Binx perceives the inadequacy of his Aunt Emily's stoicism in the way in which she handles both himself and her neurotic stepdaughter, Kate: her appeal is to principles that are no longer readily apparent to the younger generation. When he returns from a trip to Chicago on which he had taken Kate without her stepmother's knowledge, Aunt Emily chastises him with a long reassertion of stoic principles, concluding with:

> I did my best for you, son. I gave you all I had. More than anything I wanted to pass on to you the one heritage of the men of our family, a certain quality of spirit, a gaiety, a sense of duty, a nobility worn lightly, a sweetness, a gentleness with women—the only good things the South ever had and the only things that really matter in this life. Ah well. Still you can tell me one thing. I know you're not a bad boy—I wish you were. But how did it happen that none of this ever meant anything to you? Clearly it did not. Would you please tell me? I am genuinely curious. (224)

Binx is unable to offer a satisfactory explanation for his behavior.

The other embodiments of philosophical stoicism with which he has to deal are his dead father and Sam Yerger, a family friend. Binx comes to see the hollowness of the narcissistic romanticism that led his father to find an escape in going to war and being killed above the wine dark sea of Crete: it is a solution that fails to come to terms with the actual world of the here and now. Sam Yerger's brand of stoicism, on the other hand, is initially attractive. He has lived an interesting life with great enthusiasm and has written several successful books, including *The Honored and Dishonored*, which "dealt with the problem of evil and the essential loneliness of man" (168). But it is clear from the way in which Binx describes Sam's life and the somewhat trendy solution that Yerger has proposed for the cure of Kate's neurosis that his is not considered to be a desirable form of existence.

The Catholics in the novel include Binx's stolid mother, her children, Uncle Jules (Aunt Emily's husband), and Harold Graebner, the man who saved Binx's life when they were soldiers in Korea. On a visit to Chicago, Binx finds that Harold is equally suffering from the malaise and trying to relive his past achievement—and hence his Catholicism is of little comfort. Uncle Jules is an "exemplary Catholic," but Binx wonders why he takes the trouble, for "the world he lives in, the City of Man, is so pleasant that the City of God must hold little in store for him" (31).

Lonnie, Binx's crippled half-brother, is the only Catholic in the novel who inspires the protagonist to undertake a religious search or at least to keep such an option open. For Lonnie, words are not worn out, and so it is possible to tell him that he is loved without any necessity for circumlocution. In spite of his maladies, Lonnie remains a devout believer, especially in the rather pious consolations of popular Catholicism, which he somehow manages to make partially striking and novel. He is by no means perfect, however: he confesses to Binx that he was envious of the academic success of his dead brother, and he listens to his transistor radio with a kind of frenzied need for stimulation that seems to undercut the adequacy of his religious convictions. Though there is reason to believe that the Eucharist he offers up for Binx is instrumental in the latter's subsequent conversion, there is nothing in the encounter between the two that adequately suggests such a possibility.

Less prominent in this novel than in Percy's subsequent fiction is the promise of scientific humanism. Such a possibility, however, is never very real for Binx. When he notices a businessman from St. Louis on the train to Chicago clipping out a newspaper article in which "the gradual convergence of physical science and social science" is predicted, he muses wryly: "As late as a week ago such a phrase . . . would have provoked no more than an ironic tingle or two at the back of my neck. Now it howls through the Ponchatoula Swamp, the very sound and soul of despair" (191).

The greater portion of the novel is devoted to portraying the various philosophies from which Binx must make his choice. It is only toward the very end of the story that he can be seen to advance from Kierkegaard's stage of aestheticism (in which he is mainly interested in experiencing the concreteness of the world) to that of morality. The neurotic Kate can be said to be the "disaster" that awakens him to a sense of moral responsibility, which he exercises in choosing to marry and take care of her. In Marcel's terms, his is a progression from self-consciousness to its opposite, intersubjectivity.

The development thus far is very natural and convincing. The real problem arises in interpreting the last few pages of the novel, in which Binx supposedly, and with Lonnie's example, makes a leap of faith to Kierkegaard's religious stage. On Ash Wednesday a year before Lonnie dies, Binx can look at a prosperous Negro who has just emerged from church and wonder whether or not the indistinct mark on his forehead represents the action of God's grace. When the boy dies, however, the ever truthful Binx tells his young half-siblings that their dead brother will rise again on the last day, a statement intended by Percy to be an affirmation of faith even if the text itself remains unclear on the issue. As Percy explained in a 1971 interview: "The implication is that . . . you see, in *The Brothers Karamazov*, Alyosha does the same thing with those kids. One of the kids says, 'Is it true we're all going to rise up on the last day and be together?' A little boy named Kolya had just died. And so Alyosha said, 'Yeah, that's true. We're really going to be there.' And the kids say, 'Hurrah for Karamazov!' And so this was a salute to Dostoevsky."[16] Indeed, when John Carr suggested that *"The Moviegoer's* two main characters escaped alienation by confirming each other's alienation," Percy replied that "in the end Binx jumps from the esthetic clear across the ethical to the religious." But that it should require this extratextual explanation to convince even as sympathetic a critic as Thomas Daniel Young of Binx's final leap, suggests that to a degree an ending consistent with Percy's own philosophical and theological views has been imposed upon the narrative rather than allowed to arise naturally from it. And, indeed again, when Carr protested, "This guy is now a Christian! I didn't see this coming," Percy admitted: "Most people didn't see it at all. In fact, most people will deny it's in there."[17] Precisely.

The Moviegoer, then, survives as an interesting novel in spite of the fact that its *form*—whether considered as Kierkegaardian or as paralleling the philosophical essays—does not achieve the *function* that Percy intended for it. Binx is a highly engaging character whose descriptions of his search—and of the bayous in particular—are immensely appealing, though his final conversion is relatively unconvincing. To convey the supernatural in terms of the natural is, of course, by definition impossible. But Binx's change of heart, or at least his progress to a more ardent faith, is not adequately prepared for. This is what I mean by characterizing the outcome as an exercise in scholastic existentialism.

16. Carr, "An Interview with Walker Percy," 328.
17. Carr, "An Interview with Walker Percy," 328, 327, 329–30; Thomas Daniel Young, *The Past in the Present: A Thematic Study of Modern Southern Fiction* (Baton Rouge, 1981), 164–65.

Percy has explained his alternations between writing philosophical essays and novels as "the fruit of twenty years" off-and-on thinking about the subject [of man], of coming at it from one direction, followed by failure and depression and giving up, followed by making up novels to raise my spirits, followed by a new try from a different direction or from an old direction but at a different level, followed by failure, followed by making up another novel, and so on."[18] Perhaps it was only with the appearance of *Lost in the Cosmos* in 1983 that Percy finally succeeded in making his form serve his function, for there the reader is compelled to come into that awareness of himself that, in my opinion, this wonderful narrative, *The Moviegoer*, does not achieve. In his novels, as in his philosophical essays, Percy fails to prove the truth of his religious convictions. That he should even want to do so, that his convictions should persist in spite of opposing philosophical arguments of his own making, is an indication of his—and perhaps our—peculiar dilemma at the end of the twentieth century.

18. Percy, *The Message in the Bottle*, 10.

MARK WINCHELL

Beyond Existentialism; or, The American Novel at the End of the Road

There seems to be widespread agreement that the hegemony enjoyed by narrative realism from the time of Mark Twain and William Dean Howells until just after the Second World War is now a thing of the past. Although such distinguished novelists as Saul Bellow and John Updike continue to labor in the old tradition, a younger generation of writers (or "fictionists," as they prefer to call themselves) are finding their models in the neo-fabulism of Beckett, Pinter, Kafka, Hesse, and Borges. Persons unsympathetic to this trend attribute it to the fact that almost all "serious" writers of the postwar era are university educated. Divorced from the broad range of experience outside the academy, the younger novelists base their writing not on life but on books. The "fictions" thus produced hold a mirror not to nature but to themselves. "[T]he introduction of realism into literature," writes Tom Wolfe, "was like the introduction of electricity into machine technology. It was *not* just another device. It raised the state of the art to a new magnitude."[1] If Wolfe is correct, then what we have witnessed in recent American fiction is nothing less than a power shortage.

Over the past quarter century few if any writers have had a more profound influence on the American novel than has John Barth. The six books that he has published during this time are, in his own words,

---

1. Tom Wolfe, introduction to Tom Wolfe and E. W. Johnson (eds.), *The New Journalism* (New York, 1973), 34.

"novels which imitate the form of the Novel, by an author who imitates the role of Author."[2] Accordingly, *The Sot-Weed Factor* (1960) is a parody of the historical novel; *Giles Goat-Boy* (1967) a travesty of science fiction; *Lost in the Funhouse* (1968) a spoof of the multimedia craze; *Chimera* (1972) a metamythic metafiction; *Letters* (1979) what Leslie Fiedler calls a "death-of-the-death-of-the-art-novel-art novel"[3]; and *Sabbatical* (1982) a neo-fabulist blend of nightly news and academic whimsy. It is not with these books that I propose to deal, however, but with Barth's first two novels—*The Floating Opera* (1956; revised edition, 1967) and *The End of the Road* (1958; revised edition, 1967). Given the philosophy of life and art implicit in these two early works, one can see why Barth's more recent and more famous books are conceived as imitations of imitations. By the time he came to the end of *The End of the Road* (and some would argue much earlier), Barth had exhausted the possibilities of representing life directly.

The Floating Opera and *The End of the Road* can be read as companion pieces because they were originally conceived as installments in a series of novels that Barth had planned to write on the subject of nihilism: "The plot of one would not be continued exactly into the plot of another, he explained in a letter to the *Library Journal*, nor would they have any specific characters in common. But they would . . . all have one *similar* character, 'some sort of bachelor, more or less irresponsible, who either rejects absolute values or encounters their rejection.' The flagship of the series, *The Floating Opera*, he said, was his 'nihilistic comedy.' "[4] Although it is not clear what Barth meant in using this oxymoron, it is probable that he did not intend some ultimate affirmation. Properly speaking, *The Floating Opera* is not a nihilistic *comedy*, but a satire on the philosophical concept of nothingness.

It would be wrong to say that Barth challenges the notion that there is an objective moral order grounded in a reality commonly experienced by all men. That challenge was mounted by the modernist fiction of the two or three generations prior to Barth. When we get to what has been termed the postmodernist era, the absurdity of an objective moral order is so taken for granted that the defiant individualism of modernism

---

2. John Barth, "The Literature of Exhaustion," *Atlantic*, August, 1967, p. 33.
3. Leslie Fiedler, *What Was Literature?* (New York, 1982), 74.
4. David Morrell, *John Barth: An Introduction* (University Park, Pa., 1976), 1, 3.

itself seems passé. To appreciate this salient distinction, one need only compare Barth's vision with a classic modernist treatment of nothingness—Ernest Hemingway's "A Clean Well-Lighted Place." According to Carlos Baker, Hemingway's greatest achievement in this story lies in his "development through the most carefully controlled understatement, of the young waiter's mere *nothing* into the old waiter's Something—a Something called Nothing which is so huge, terrible, overbearing, inevitable, and omniscient that, once experienced, it can never be forgotten."[5] It is perhaps Barth's greatest achievement to make us regard such romantic existentialism as old hat, really a concealed "yes" posing as a "no" in thunder.

In *The Floating Opera* Barth's protagonist, Todd Andrews, arrives at his distinctively postmodernist nihilism by passing through three preliminary stages—those of the rake, the saint, and the cynic. The first of these begins when, as an adolescent, he is initiated into the absurdity of sex by a more experienced schoolmate—the slatternly Betty June Gunter. His account of youthful lust proceeds in a fairly conventional way until the actual coupling with Betty June. Unfortunately, at this point, Todd catches a glimpse of himself and his *inamorata* in his dresser mirror: "Betty June's face buried in the pillow, her scrawny little buttocks thrust skywards; me gangly as a whippet and braying like an ass."[6] In response to this scene, Todd explodes with laughter. It puts a damper on the copulation but gives him an ironic perspective on life that sustains him until his infected prostrate and the wrath of Betty June (who has since been driven to prostitution by Todd's mirth and the accumulated woes of life) nearly unman him in a grotesque encounter during his riotous college days at Johns Hopkins. In an oblique allusion to *Hamlet*, Barth has entitled the chapter that describes the initial amours of Todd and Betty June "A mirror up to life."[7]

In the first published version of *The Floating Opera*, a chapter that precedes by a few pages the narration of Todd's loss of innocence de-

---

5. Carlos Baker, *Hemingway: The Writer as Artist* (Princeton, 1952), 124.
6. John Barth, *The Floating Opera* (Rev. ed.; Garden City, N.Y., 1967), 123. Subsequent references to this work are to this edition and will be given in the text.
7. Although Stephen L. Tanner discusses *The Floating Opera* as "John Barth's Hamlet," the value of his essay is seriously undermined by his use of the first published version of the novel. See Stephen L. Tanner, "John Barth's Hamlet," *Southwest Review* LVI (1971), 347–54. The revised (or restored) version could be more aptly described as Barth's anti-Hamlet.

scribes a group of pallbearers pausing in their labors to nudge a pregnant cat out of the way. "I smiled and walked on," Todd tells us. "Nature, coincidence, can be a heavyhanded symbolizer." This same observation appears in the revised edition of the novel (which is largely the restoration of a text that Barth previously had been unable to publish in its original form); however, here it comes as a reaction not to the docile presence of a mama cat but to the randy assignation of a pair of dogs. In the restored novel, Todd describes an aged Chesapeake Bay retriever bitch coming out from behind a hydrangea bush and onto an undertaker's porch. She is followed by a "prancing, sniffing young mongrel setter" who "clambered upon her at once, his long tongue lolling."

> Just then the door opened and the pallbearers came out with a casket. Their path was blocked by the dogs. Some of the bearers smiled guiltily; an employee caught the setter on his haunches with an unfuneral kick. The bitch trundled off the porch, her lover still half on her, and took up a position in the middle of the sidewalk, near the hearse. The pair then resumed their amours in the glaring sun, to the embarrassment of the company, who pretended not to notice them while the hearse's door was opened and the casket gently loaded aboard. (109)

Not only do the dogs in the restored novel give this scene of "life-in-the-face-of-death" a much stronger satiric bite, but they also provide a better catalyst to Todd's memory of Betty June, whom he was preparing to enter in the classic canine posture.

The other great love of Todd's life is Jane Mack, the beautiful and sexually liberated wife of his best friend, Harrison Mack. His affair with Jane seems to have only marginally greater significance for Todd than do his more fleeting trysts with Betty June and others. It appears to be in the novel primarily to allow Barth to poke fun at the sentimental pieties of open marriage. The fatuously broad-minded Harrison has contrived the dalliance as a way of simultaneously flouting convention and showing affection for a buddy. (Although a similar situation will result in catastrophe in *The End of the Road*, it is played essentially for laughs in *The Floating Opera*.) Whether or not Stanley Edgar Hyman is correct in viewing this arrangement as less a triangle than an inchoate *menage-a-trois*, Barth's women exist largely to give his men something to talk about and, occasionally, to share in the sublimated homoeroticism of the whorehouse.[8] In what is perhaps the only truly generous impulse

---

8. Stanley Edgar Hyman, "John Barth's First Novel," in Joseph J. Waldmeir (ed.), *Critical Essays on John Barth* (Boston, 1980), 78. Hyman calls this "'the Albertine Strategy,' an

that he has in the entire novel, Todd urges Jane to disrobe for the saturnalian delight of an aged oyster-boat captain.

For reasons that are never made entirely clear, Todd decides to become a saint when the vengeful Betty June pours a bottle of rubbing alcohol on his crotch several years after the thrusting skywards of her "scrawny little buttocks" had turned him into an hysterically jolly rake. This period of religious contemplation ends when his father's suicide brings Todd face to face with what Camus regarded as the only truly serious philosophical problem—judging whether life is or is not worth living. Actually, he manages to avoid confronting that issue directly by adopting the mask of the cynic, a persona that causes him to give his inheritance of five thousand dollars to the richest man in town and to become an unusually diligent lawyer. What Barth had in mind with this three-stage philosophical evolution is anyone's guess; however, it is conceivable that he intended a parody of Kierkegaard. As a rake Todd begins at the aesthetic (for him the hedonistic) phase of existence; as a saint he proceeds to a religious phase; and as a cynic he arrives at the plateau of an ethical (or philosophical) life. By placing the religious vision in the middle of the process, Barth suggests that the Heavenly City is not man's final destination but an outpost on the way to somewhere else. Also, by equating the aesthetic life with a kind of slapstick hedonism and the ethical life with a sardonic fatalism, he devalues more secular ports in the storm.

Having passed through rough approximations of the three primary realms of human value, Todd goes through two additional transitions, neither of which seems more convincingly motivated than his earlier conversions. The first of these two final stages begins when Jane asks an apparently innocuous question about his clubbed fingers. Because this malformation is indisputable proof of Todd's heart disease (itself a kind of existentialist synedoche for life lived on the edge of death), Jane's question causes him to confront the fact that all of his personae have been only masks "to hide my enigmatic heart" (223). At this point "the impulse to raise my arms and eyes to heaven was overpowering—but there was no one to raise them to" (226). Consequently, he decides to commit suicide.

---

affair with a man variously disguised as an affair with a woman." He goes on to note that this motif is "obsessive in the work of James Joyce, in which two male friends attain symbolic union by sharing the body of a woman."

Because Todd is around some years later to tell us of the crucial decision, we realize that he did not carry it out. The suspense, then, lies in learning why. On the day that Todd had planned to kill himself but did not (June 21 or 22, 1937—he cannot remember which), he had witnessed an evening's worth of cornball entertainment on the floating opera that gives the novel its title, slipped backstage to turn on the gas vents, and then reemerged to wait for the explosion that would have sent himself and 699 other people out of this veil of tears. In the first published version of the novel Todd interrupts his suicide to come to the aid of little Jeanine Mack (daughter of Jane and possibly of Todd himself), who has gone into convulsions. His concentration broken, he decides that he might as well live. When the novel was restored to its original form, however, this maudlin deus ex machina had been scrapped. Todd's plan is now foiled either by hidden ventilation on the boat or by the officiousness of a wandering crew member. With his life spared by a fluke, Todd forswears further attempts at self-destruction. "I began to realize," he tells us, "a subtle corner had been turned. I asked myself, knowing that there was no ultimate answer, 'Why not step into the river?' as I had asked myself in the afternoon, 'Why not blow up the Floating Opera?' But now, at once, a new voice replied casually, 'On the other hand, why bother?'" (246–47).[9]

Among the many literary allusions in this novel the most frequent and explicit ones are to Shakespeare's plays, particularly *Hamlet*. In the key scene on the floating opera these allusions are filtered through the tradition of southwest humor. When the showboat's major attraction (Miss Clara Mulloy—"the Mary Pickford of the Chesapeake") comes down with laryngitis, the captain drags out a young trouper named T. Wallace Whittaker to emote a few choice lines from the Bard. The reaction of the crowd is predictably derisive as it throws pennies at this "broad-beamed, Sunday-schooly young man" (234).[10] Because all three of the speeches that Whittaker delivers (the seven ages of man from *As*

---

9. A similar realization is attained by Maria Wyeth at the end of Joan Didion's *Play It as It Lays* (New York, 1970). At the end Maria compares her stance with that of a more conventionally nihilistic friend who had committed suicide. She tells us: "*I know what 'nothing' means, and keep on playing. / Why, BZ would say. / Why not, I say*" (214).

10. This description hardly sounds like something that the sophisticated Todd Andrews would say, but it would be perfectly in character coming from the mouth of, say, Huck Finn.

You Like It,[11] the funeral oration from *Julius Caesar*, and the "To be or not to be" soliloquy from *Hamlet*) focus on the meaning of life and death (from sensuous, ethical, and religious standpoints respectively), they have an obvious thematic importance at this presumably climactic point in the novel. By joining the rubes in their reaction to high art, Todd may be suggesting that he already has begun to question the ultimate significance of the issues to which Shakespeare is addressing himself. In any event he and the rest of the audience find an old-time darky minstrel routine and a simulated steamboat race more enjoyable than Whittaker's histrionics. The evening concludes not with the explosion that Todd had planned, but with a mock explosion that is all part of the show.

The boat as a microcosm of society is a trope that probably goes back as far as Noah's ark. By making his microcosm a tawdry showboat, however, Barth seems to be offering a further comment on life. Just so that we will not miss the point, he has Todd make the relevant connection in the opening chapter of the novel.

The boat wouldn't be moored, but would drift up and down the river on the tide, and the audience would sit along both banks. They could catch whatever part of the plot happened to unfold as the boat floated past, and then they'd have to wait until the tide ran back again to catch another snatch of it, if they still happened to be sitting there. To fill in the gaps they'd have to use their imaginations, or ask more attentive neighbors, or hear the word passed along from upriver or downriver. Most times they wouldn't understand what was going on at all, or they'd think they knew, when actually they didn't. Lots of times they'd be able to see the actors, but not hear them. I needn't explain that that's how much of life works. (7)

If life is a stage, it is one that is built not on a firm foundation but on a Heraclitian flux.

When Jerome Kern and Oscar Hammerstein viewed the human predicament from the perspective of a showboat, they wrote "Ol' Man River," a song in which an old black man named Joe is "tired of living and scared of dying" ("thus conscience does make cowards of us all"). Because Todd

---

11. See Thomas J. Richardson, "Is Shakespeare Dead?: Mark Twain's Irreverent Question," in Philip C. Kolin (ed.), *Shakespeare and Southern Writers: A Study in Influence* (Jackson, Miss., 1985). Richardson notes that in one instance, the southwest humorist Sol Smith "records a member of his company reciting the 'seven ages of man' from *As You Like It* while he is bumped and jostled by a waiter coming and going through a kitchen door" (75).

Andrews appears to be bored with *both* living and dying, simple inertia keeps him afloat. (It is interesting, if not particularly crucial, to note that the showboat on which Edna Ferber based the novel that was transformed into the Kern-Hammerstein musical was the same "floating opera" that inspired Barth's novel.) Summing up his final philosophy (or perhaps antiphilosophy), Todd writes in his journal: *"There's no final reason for living (or for suicide)"* (250); later he reflects: "To realize that nothing makes any final difference is overwhelming; but if one goes no farther and becomes a saint, a cynic, or a suicide on principle, one hasn't reasoned completely. The truth is that nothing makes any difference, including that truth. Hamlet's question is, absolutely, meaningless" (251). If this view is where *The Floating Opera* ends, it is where *The End of the Road* begins.

Although not as generic a parody as Barth's later books, *The End of the Road* is rife with parodic overtones. Originally labeled by *Time* magazine as "a novel of ideas," it actually satirizes the novel of ideas. All of the sententious dialogues between its primary antagonists, Joe Morgan and Jake Horner, simply prove that if ideas have consequences, they are liable to be different from those intended. As just about everyone who has commented on *The End of the Road* agrees, Joe and Jake represent competing philosophies of life. Even when called different names by different critics, both philosophies absolutize the presumed relativity of human values (which is the liberating insight that takes Todd Andrews beyond the abyss and into the void). Because Jake harbors fewer illusions and holds to fewer principles, he seems marginally closer to the truth that there is no truth. The fruit of this realization, however, is a life that fluctuates between emotional paralysis and amoebalike docility. Joe, on the other hand, midwifes disaster by adhering doggedly to the ideals of honesty and reason. In the process he gives honesty a bad name and seems living proof of Santayana's quip that the madman is not one who has lost the ability to reason, but one who has lost everything but the ability to reason. Finally, somewhat off center stage, is Jake's doctor—a dusky mountebank who is the novel's most thoroughgoing pragmatist and most obvious charlatan.

The battlefield on which Joe and Jake wage their philosophical combat is Joe's wife Rennie. In thus positing a sexual triangle, Barth calls to mind not only *The Floating Opera* but also certain hoary conventions of love literature, none of which are treated any more reverently than are the pretensions of the novel of ideas. As suggested by Jake's surname and his involvement with Rennie, *The End of the Road* is meant to be a tale of cuckoldry. Although Barth did not read William Wycherley's *The Country Wife* until after he had written his novel and was asked by a student whether Wycherley's Horner was the model for his own, Jake is clearly at the end of a tradition of literary rakes. However, the romantic values that redeemed the older tales of cuckoldry have long since vanished.

From the time of Chaucer and Boccaccio through to the late Renaissance, the cuckold was usually an impotent old fool who had forced a healthy young girl into an unnatural union. For a worthy younger lover to violate this union was not so much adultery as poetic justice. By the Restoration, however, the romance of young love has been relegated to a subplot, and the horn giver is no longer a dashing matinee idol but a cynical character actor who is motivated less by love or lust than by the sheer thrill of conquest. Still, the cuckold remains a buffoon who gets no more than his just comeuppance and is frequently tricked into abetting his own humiliation. What we see in Barth's novel is an even further degeneration of the prototype. Joe and Rennie appear to be domestically happy and sexually compatible; Jake possesses no obvious charm; his seduction of Rennie occurs without ostensible motivation; and the affair continues not because Joe is duped, but because his perverted logic insists that it not end until it can be rationally explained.

If the situation of the novel traduces the values of cuckoldry and courtly love, then the characters of Jake and Joe play havoc with the venerable paradigms of the Dionysian and Apollonian lovers. Although Jake is a man of impulse, that impulse is usually to lethargy, and Joe's commitment to reason causes him to knock his wife cold when she disingenuously apologizes for the absence of furniture that neither she nor Joe desires. It is a case of Dionysus as wimp and Apollo as wife beater.

About a third of the way through the novel Rennie compares Joe and Jake with supernatural figures a bit more familiar than Dionysus and Apollo. "I think of Joe as I'd think of God," she says; a bit later she adds: "I thought Joe had invited the Devil to test me. . . . But this Devil scared me, because I wasn't that strong yet, and what was a game for Joe was a terrible fight for me. . . . Then when Joe saw how it was, he told me that the Devil wasn't real, and that he had conjured up the Devil out of his own strength, just as God might do."[12] But of course Joe and Jake are not God and the Devil, not even in a symbolic sense. They are merely men playing those roles rather ineptly in an Eden suspiciously like the Eastern Shore of Maryland. If Rennie is Joe's creation, then—like God—he has forced her to confront the implications of her own freedom and has tested her virtue by exposing her to temptation. What were conditions for high tragedy in the age of Milton simply set the stage for farce in a world that our social scientists, as well as our philosophical nihilists, tell us is beyond freedom and dignity. As deity Joe Morgan is less the omnipotent God of the Old Testament than the fraudulent Wizard of Oz. The turning point of the novel occurs when Jake, camping the role of Satan, invites Rennie to peek through the windows of Heaven as her God sits in his living room picking his nose and stroking the fount of his power.[13]

Just exactly what kind of God Joe thinks he is is not entirely clear. Early in the novel he tells Jake: "When you say good-by to objective values, you really have to flex your muscles and keep your eyes open, because you're on your own. It takes *energy;* not just personal energy, but cultural energy, or you're lost. Energy's what makes the difference between American pragmatism and French existentialism—where the hell else but in America could you have a cheerful nihilism, for God's sake?" (44).[14] Joe is clearly a man of energy, but his philosophy fails the primary test of pragmatism—it does not work. Having dispensed with the objective values of traditional morality, he adheres to subjective ideals with the foolish consistency that Emerson considered the hobgoblin of little minds. As the creation of a conservative novelist, Joe would have been a case study in the perils of private mania. However, when Barth rejects Joe's example, it is not because he wants to take us

---

12. John Barth, *The End of the Road* (Rev. ed., Garden City, N.Y., 1967), 58, 63. Subsequent references to this work are to this edition and will be given in the text.

13. Although Rennie's illusions do not survive her act of voyeurism, Jac Tharpe maintains that "so long as Joe does appear sufficiently invincible even to support a caricature of himself, he sustains an order sufficient for any being that is nothingness, until nothingness reveals that being *is* nothingness." Jac Tharpe, *John Barth: The Comic Sublimity of Paradox* (Carbondale, 1974), 32.

14. Despite the distinction that Joe makes here, some critics have persisted in reading *The End of the Road* as an existentialist novel. Jean Kennard, for example, sees Jake, Joe, and the doctor all as representatives of different varieties of existentialism. See Jean E. Kennard, "John Barth: Imitations of Imitations," *Mosaic* III (1970), 116–31. But to the extent that Barth invokes existentialism at all, it is to debunk it as a disingenuous attempt to give substance to the void.

back to the old verities but because he has already gone beyond existentialism—to a nihilism cheerful enough to reject the urge to wave imaginary crucifixes at real vampires. What we have is, in Jake's apt phrase, a world "without weather." In such a world Joe plays the fool by tenaciously clinging to the role of meteorologist.

If Joe Morgan is a pragmatist *manqué,* then Jake's doctor is the genuine article. Rather than adhering slavishly to a given treatment, he is willing to try any quack nostrum until he finds one that works. He recommends homosexual liaisons for his older patients and puts Jake on a therapy that involves the study of everything from almanac trivia to prescriptive grammar. "If the alternatives are side by side," he says, "choose the one on the left; if they're consecutive in time, choose the earlier. If neither of these applies, choose the alternative whose name begins with the earlier letter of the alphabet. These are the principles of Sinistrality, Antecedence, and Alphabetical Priority" (79–80). Unfortunately, the doctor fails to realize that arbitrary principles can have unexpected consequences. Partly as a result of of the doctor's counsel of passivity, Jake has allowed himself to be manipulated into the grand morality play that Joe is orchestrating. This leads to his affair with Rennie, who subsequently becomes pregnant and threatens suicide. In order to save her from killing herself, the doctor performs an abortion, during which Rennie becomes fatally asphyxiated on her own vomit.

Judged by purely pragmatic standards, the doctor proves no more successful than Joe. He fails to cure Jake, who is narrating his story from the doctor's convalescent farm, and he even botches the abortion. Rather than saving Rennie from self-destruction, he ironically creates the conditions that lead precisely to that fate (she chokes on her own vomit, after all). Had he been competent enough to warn her not to eat a large meal, he might have saved her, even if he had successfully performed the one surgical procedure whose object is the termination of human life. Surveying the carnage he has wrought, the doctor observes: "This thing was everybody's fault. . . . Let it be everybody's lesson" (183). This is the principle of equivocation.

By the end of the novel Jake has once again regressed to immobility and is preparing to return to the railroad terminal where his story had begun. (Appropriately enough, the last word of *The End of the Road* is *terminal.*) Joe is now calling *him* for advice, and Jake can only reply, "God, Joe I don't know where to start or what to do" (188). A bit earlier he had told us: "The terrific incompleteness made me volatile; my muscles screamed to act; but my limbs were bound like Laocoon's—by the serpents Knowledge and Imagination, which, grown great in the fullness of time, no longer tempt but annihilate" (187). In a world where knowledge and imagination are seen as destructive forces, the novel as a representation—much less an idealization—of life must necessarily be dead.

As Thomas Daniel Young has noted, *The End of the Road* is the culmination of a philosophical development (or degeneration) that had its seeds in early modernism. Although Young confines his focus to southern writers (a category to which Maryland's John Barth arguably belongs), the process that he describes is not exclusively regional. The loss of traditional religious and cultural values in the early years of this century (as Virginia Woolf observed, "On or about December, 1910, human nature changed") inspired a variety of improvisational responses. The programmatic conservatism of many southern modernists was an attempt to maintain the forms of an ordered life even after its substance had vanished—what John Crowe Ransom called ritual without dogma. (Ironically, the "progressives" of the New South were more old-fashioned in maintaining an implacable faith in the upward spiral of history.)

The tenuousness of this solution has led other writers—ones as diverse as Allen Tate, Walker Percy, and Flannery O'Connor—to seek a return to the old dogmas. Barth, who is more of a Sunbelt nihilist than a southern modernist, has gone in the opposite direction and given us what Young describes as "a world devoid of *both* dogma and ritual."[15] Or to put the matter in a more broadly American context: Deprived of the light of common day in which the nineteenth-century realists worked, Barth's immediate predecessors suffered through a dark night of the soul, wrestling with Camus' one truly serious philosophical problem. In their wake John Barth has taken us a crucial step farther; for, at the end of the road, we find neither light nor dark and fewer things than are dreamt of in Camus' philosophy.

15. Thomas Daniel Young, *The Past in the Present: A Thematic Study of Modern Southern Fiction* (Baton Rouge, 1981), 189.

Contributors

CAROL M. ANDREWS received the Ph.D. from Vanderbilt University in 1984. She is currently Assistant Professor of English at Armstrong State College in Savannah. She is completing a manuscript on William Faulkner's *The Sound and the Fury.*

JOHN C. CONDER, Professor of English at Vanderbilt, has published two books—*A Formula of His Own: Henry Adams's Literary Experiment* and *Naturalism in American Fiction*—and essays on various American writers.

MARTHA E. COOK, Associate Professor of English at Longwood College and Co-editor of *Resources for American Literary Study,* has published a number of articles, primarily in the field of southern literature; most recent are a bibliographical essay on Flannery O'Connor and a section in *The History of Southern Literature* (1985). She is currently completing a study of the portrayal of women in American fiction of the 1920s.

DONALD A. DAIKER is Professor of English and Director of the Center for the Study of Writing at Miami University in Oxford, Ohio. He is co-author of *The Writer's Options: Combining to Composing* and *Literature: Options for Reading and Writing,* and he is co-editor of *Sentence Combining and the Teaching of Writing* and *Sentence Combining: A Rhetorical Perspective.* His articles and reviews on literature and composition appear in many journals, including the *Hemingway Review,* the *Fitzgerald-Hemingway Annual, Studies in Short Fiction, Research in the Teaching of English, College Composition and Communication,* and *Language and Style.*

JOSEPH K. DAVIS is Professor of American Literature at Memphis State University. He has served as Senior Fulbright Lecturer in Poland (1964–1965) and West Germany (1971–1972), and in 1972–1973 under a grant from *Die Deutsche*

Forschungsgemeinschaft of Bonn, West Germany, he worked to develop a chair of American Studies at the University of Stuttgart. In addition to two college texts, he has published various articles on Henry James, R. P. Warren, Tennessee Williams, John Cheever, John Updike, Flannery O'Connor, William Faulkner, and other American writers.

A. E. ELMORE holds the B.A. from Millsaps, the J.D. from the University of Mississippi and the Ph.D. from Vanderbilt. He wrote his dissertation on F. Scott Fitzgerald. He has won NEH grants for postdoctoral study at Berkeley and Chicago. Other publications are on Thoreau, Faulkner, the poet Robert Herrick, and criminal law. He taught English and American literature for several years at Hampden-Sydney College. He was formerly a public defender in Las Vegas and a staff attorney for legal services in Tuscaloosa, where he also teaches as an adjunct professor at the University of Alabama Law School. He is now Professor of English and Drama at Athens State College in Alabama.

BLYDEN JACKSON is Professor of English Emeritus at the University of North Carolina at Chapel Hill, author of *The Waiting Years*, and co-editor (with Louis D. Rubin, Jr.) of *Black Poetry in America*. He is a senior editor of, and a contributor to, *The History of Southern Literature*.

JAMES H. JUSTUS is the author of *The Achievement of Robert Penn Warren* (1981) and numerous essays on writers of the Southern Renaissance. He is presently writing a study of the literature of the Old Southwest and preparing an edition of Joseph G. Baldwin's *Flush Times of Alabama and Mississippi* for the LSU Press. His "Poe's Comic Vision and Southwestern Humour" recently appeared in Robert A. Lee (ed.), *Edgar Allan Poe: The Design of Order*.

DOUGLAS PASCHALL teaches English and comparative literature at the University of the South. He is editor of a collection of works by living Tennessee writers entitled *Homewords* and was founding editor of *Touchstone*, the magazine of the Tennessee Humanities Council. His most recent essays have been on aspects of critical theory, Shakespeare, and Andrew Lytle.

PEGGY WHITMAN PRENSHAW is editor of the *Southern Quarterly* and Dean of the Honors College at the University of Southern Mississippi. She has edited *Eudora Welty: Critical Essays* (1979), *Conversations with Eudora Welty* (1984), and *Women Writers of the Contemporary South* (1985). She is author of *Elizabeth Spencer* (1985).

KIERAN QUINLAN obtained a B.A. in philosophy at Oxford and a Ph.D. in English at Vanderbilt. He has recently completed *John Crowe Ransom: Defining a Secular Faith* for the LSU Press and is working on a philosophical critique of Walker Percy's essays and novels. He has written on contemporary American, British, and Irish authors for *World Literature Today, Southern Review*, and a variety of other publications. He is currently Assistant Professor of English at the University of Alabama at Birmingham.

Contributors

JULIUS ROWAN RAPER is the author or editor of three books on Ellen Glasgow published by LSU Press: *Without Shelter: The Early Career of Ellen Glasgow; From the Sunken Garden: The Fiction of Ellen Glasgow, 1916–1945;* and *Ellen Glasgow's Reasonable Doubts: A Collection of Her Writings.* He has also written a variety of articles, poems, and fictions. Currently he is writing a book on Durrell, Fowles, Barth, Pynchon, and other contemporary writers, with the working title "Narcissus and the Creatures of Stone." He taught American literature at Greek universities for four years as a Fulbright Visiting Professor and is Associate Professor of English and American Literature at the University of North Carolina, Chapel Hill.

MARK WINCHELL received his Ph.D. from Vanderbilt and is now Associate Professor of English at Clemson University. A prolific writer, he has written many essays on modern American writers. He has written books on Joan Didion, William Buckley, Leslie Fiedler, and Herman Talmadge.

THOMAS DANIEL YOUNG is Gertrude Conaway Vanderbilt Professor Emeritus at Vanderbilt University. He has written more than two hundred essays on modern American and southern writers. Among his twenty-five books are *Gentleman in a Dustcoat: A Biography of John Crowe Ransom* and *The Past in the Present: A Thematic Study of Modern Southern Fiction,* both published by LSU Press.

Index

Abrams, M. H., 9, 136
Aristotle, 150
Arlen, Michael, 68, 73–74
Aswell, Edward C., 175
Austen, Jane, 186

Baker, Carlos, 227
Balakian, Anna, 129n
Baldwin, James, 182–83
Balzac, Honoré de, 129n
Barth, John: novels of, 225–26
—*End of the Road, The*: parodic overtones in, 12, 232; nihilism in, 226, 235–36; affair in, 228, 232–33, 235; competing philosophies in, 232–35; existentialism in, 234n; ending of, 235–36
—*Floating Opera, The*: nihilism of, 12, 226, 227; Todd Andrews as saint and cynic, 227, 229; Todd Andrews' reaction to Betty June Gunter, 227–28, 229; Todd Andrews' relationship with Jane Mack, 228–29; Todd Andrews' planned suicide, 229–30; floating opera scene in, 230–32; literary allusions in, 230–32
—other works: *Chimera*, 226; *Giles Goat-Boy*, 226; *Letters*, 226; *Lost in the Funhouse*, 226; *Sabbatical*, 226; *The Sot-Weed Factor*, 226
Baudelaire, Charles, 125n, 129n
Beckett, Samuel, 153, 225
Beethoven, Ludwig van, 89

Bellow, Saul, 61, 225
Bergson, Henri, 28, 29n
Berofsky, Bernard, 32
Bishop, John Peale, 88
Bleich, David, 136, 149–51, 153
Bleikasten, André, 9, 120, 125, 126, 131
Boatwright, James, 185, 190–91
Boccaccio, Giovanni, 233
Booth, Wayne, 2, 4, 6
Borges, Jorge Luis, 225
Bowers, Fredson, 37
Bradbury, Nicola, 13
Bradford, M. E., 190
Brill, Abraham, 95
Brontë, Emily, 138
Brown, Joe C., 175
Browning, Robert, 60
Bruccoli, Matthew, 62, 88
Bunting, Charles, 191
Burckhardt, Jacob Christoph, 10, 159
Burke, Kenneth, 87, 88

Camus, Albert, 98, 229, 236
Carpenter, Edward, 137, 139
Carr, John, 223
Carroll, Lewis, 79
Caws, Mary Ann, 26
Chaucer, Geoffrey, 233
Chomsky, Noam, 215
Clark, Donald Henderson, 84
Clemens, Samuel. *See* Twain, Mark
Clemons, Walter, 184
Coleridge, Samuel Taylor, 146

Index

Conrad, Joseph, 2, 59, 60, 62, 67, 84, 118
Cox, Harvey, 94n
Cox, Kenyon, 66
Crane, Stephen
—*Red Badge of Courage, The*: characterization in, 5–6, 28–29, 30–31; Henry Fleming as psychological and social type, 28–29; irony in, 29–31; narrative vision in, 29–30; images of the sun in, 31–32, 34, 68; determinism in, 32–33, 35, 37–38; Henry Fleming's responses to battle, 33–36; ending of, 35, 37; Henry Fleming's illusions, 36–37, 38; free-will reading of, 37; Wells's view of, 57–58
—other works: "The Open Boat," 5–6, 28, 32; *Maggie*, 28–30; "The Blue Hotel," 28–30

De Man, Henry, 87, 88, 89
Dante Alighieri, 10, 68, 81, 85, 159
Darrow, Clarence, 99
Darwin, Charles, 95
Dawson, Christopher, 214
Determinism, 32–33, 35, 37–38, 111
Dickens, Charles, 66, 84
Dostoevsky, Feodor, 98, 111, 223
Dreiser, Theodore: views of American civilization, 94–98, 94n, 96n; interest in crimes of violence and passion, 98, 98n
—*American Tragedy, An*: theme of, 7–8; naturalism of, 8, 111–12, 114; as critique of American civilization, 93–94, 98–99, 113–17; pursuit of money and pleasure in, 94, 97, 102–106, 113, 115–16; religious fundamentalism in, 94, 97, 101–102; secularism in, 94, 94n, 97–98, 113–17; basis in the Gillette-Brown case, 99; Clyde's childhood, 100–102; commercial success of, 100; nature of tragedy of, 100, 101n, 111–12, 116; structure of, 100; Clyde's young adulthood, 102–105; women in, 103; Clyde's relationship with Roberta Alden, 106–108; Clyde's relationship with Sondra Finchley, 107; Clyde's trial and death, 108–11, 115; drowning of Roberta Alden, 108, 108n; Clyde's religious atonement, 109–11; role of Duncan McMillan, 110–11, 110n; determinism in, 111; interpretation of Clyde's character, 111–13

—other works: *Sister Carrie*, 93, 94; *Jennie Gerhardt*, 94; *The "Genius,"* 94; *The Titan*, 95; *A Hoosier Holiday*, 96; *Hey Rub-A-Dub-Dub*, 96–97

Eastman, Max, 95
El Greco, 87, 91
Eliot, George, 67
Eliot, T. S.: "Portrait of a Lady," 20; "The Love Song of J. Alfred Prufrock," 20, 60; literary allusions in, 60–61, 66, 68; *The Waste Land*, 60–64, 73, 78–81, 85–86; view of Fitzgerald, 61, 81; "The Hollow Men," 67
Ellis, Havelock, 87
Emerson, Ralph Waldo, 234
Existentialism, 182–83, 214–15, 217, 219–20, 223, 234n

Faulkner, William: influence of French Symbolist poets, 118–21, 119n; poetry of, 118–19, 119n
—*Sound and the Fury, The*: point of view in, 8; four parts of, 58–59, 86; influenced by Fitzgerald and Hemingway, 58; first-person narrator of, 60; Eliot's *Waste Land* and, 61; feeling evoked in Faulkner by, 118; absence in, 120–21, 123, 124, 124n; Caddy as central image, 120, 121–22, 134; origin of, 120–21; Benjy's section, 122–25, 127; Caddy as romantic image, 122, 123–24, 129–30; Benjy's view of Caddy, 123–25, 126; Quentin's section, 125–30; Quentin's view of Caddy, 125–30, 131; Caddy's sexuality, 126–30; influence of French Symbolist poets on, 9, 122, 124, 124n, 129, 129n, 130, 134; Jason's section, 130–33; Jason's relationship with Caddy, 131–32; Mrs. Compson's role in, 132–33; Dilsey's section, 133–35
—other works: *Light in August*, 8; *As I Lay Dying*, 58, 60, 131; *Sanctuary*, 61; *Faulkner in the University*, 121; *Lion in the Garden*, 121; *Marionettes*, 122; "Nympholepsy," 125, 125n, 127–28; *Mayday*, 129
Feidelson, Charles, 119–20, 134
Ferber, Edna, 232
Ferguson, Mary Anne, 190
Fiedler, Leslie, 226
Fielding, Henry, 2–3

Index

Fitzgerald, F. Scott: influences on other authors, 58–59; admiration of T. S. Eliot, 61; intelligence of, 64–66
—*Great Gatsby, The*: allusions to contemporary novels, 68, 73–75; Conrad's influences on, 84; critical reactions to, 6–7, 59; impressionistic method of, 7; visual images in, 7, 62–63; Fitzgerald's view of, 57, 92; length of, 57, 58, 59; sales of, 58; lyrical intensity of, 59–60; compared with *The Waste Land*, 60–61, 63–64, 73, 78, 79–80, 85–86; first-person narrator of, 60; author's editing of, 61–62; Eliot's view of, 61; Conrad's influences on, 62; image of the nightingale in, 63–64; literary allusions in, 64, 66, 68; sources of title, 66–69; compared with Kipling, 67–73; sun images in, 68; Gatsby's association with colors of yellow and gold, 69, 75–76; Frazer's influence on, 70, 76–80, 83, 89; images of bird and egg in, 70; Gatsby's relationship with Daisy, 71–72; biblical allusions in, 72–73, 80, 83; significance of "the great" in title, 75–79; Lewis Carroll's influences on, 79; vegetation symbols in, 79–80; Christianity in, 80, 86; Milton's influences on, 80–81, 84; Dante's influences on, 81; Goethe's influences on, 82–83; four settings of, 85–86; Spengler's influence on, 86–92
—other works: *Tender Is the Night*, 59; "Absolution," 62; *This Side of Paradise*, 65, 75; *The Beautiful and the Damned*, 74

Fitzgerald, Zelda Sayre, 65, 71
Flaubert, Gustave, 4
Ford, Ford Madox, 3
Frazer, Sir James George, 61, 70, 73, 76–80, 83, 89
French Symbolist movement, 118–20, 119n, 122, 124, 124n, 129, 129n, 130, 134
Freud, Sigmund, 89, 95, 139, 152
Friedman, Melvin J., 118
Frye, Northrop, 187–88

Garnett, Edward, 58
Gass, William, 218–19
Gauss, Dean Christian, 88
Gelfant, Blanche H., 114
Giorgone, 87

Glasgow, Ellen: influences on, 137–39; concept of the unconscious, 152–54
—*Sheltered Life, The*: mirroring technique in, 9–10, 136, 140–45, 147, 149, 154–55; reader-response criticism and, 136–37, 149–55; character delineation in, 137–40; Eva Birdsong's role in, 140–41, 142, 143, 144, 147–48; Jenny Blair's psychological drama, 140–41, 143, 147–48, 152; General Archbald's psychological drama, 141–44, 147, 152; George Birdsong's psychological drama, 141, 142–43; John Welch's role in, 141, 142, 143; evasive idealism in, 142–44, 148; author's relationship with characters in, 145–48, 155; selfobject concept and, 145–49, 151; origins of, 146; reader's relationship with characters in, 146–55
—other works: *The Voice of the People*, 137; *Barren Ground*, 138; *Life and Gabriella*, 138; *One Man in His Time*, 138; *The Builders*, 138; *The Wheel of Life*, 138; "The Professional Instinct," 139

Goethe, Johann Wolfgang von, 82–83, 85
Gossett, Louise, 196
Goyen, William, 209
Graham, Kenneth, 13
Graham, Sheilah, 64, 65, 83
Grebstein, Sheldon Norman, 39n
Gross, Barry, 87, 88
Gross, Seymour, 11, 185
Guardini, Romano, 214

Hardy, Thomas, 186
Haring, Bernard, 214
Hartman, Carl, 208, 209
Hawthorne, Nathaniel, 119
Hegel, Georg Wilhelm Friedrich, 214, 219
Heidegger, Martin, 151, 214, 215
Heilman, Robert, 192
Hemingway, Ernest: view of morality and immorality, 40, 40n; view of Fitzgerald, 64, 71; stoic hero in, 160; narrator in, 191
—*Sun Also Rises, The*: grace under pressure in, 6, 40; circular movement of, 39, 39n; importance of Book Three, 39–40, 40n; nihilism of, 39, 39n; images of washing and cleansing in, 40–41, 44–46; Jake as developing character, 39, 39–40n, 40–41; morality

and immorality in, 40; Count Mippipopolous' role in, 41–43, 51; Jake's relationship with Brett, 41, 45–47; bicycle race in, 43–44; metaphor of bullfight in, 43–44, 47, 48–50, 54; Romero's role in, 43–44, 50–51, 54; Cohn's role in, 44–45; final encounter of Jake and Brett, 47–55; taxi rides in, 52–53, 52n; Jake's manhood, 53–56; author's editing of, 58; Eliot's *Waste Land* and, 61
—other works: *Death in the Afternoon*, 40n; *The Old Man and the Sea*, 59, 60; "A Clean Well-Lighted Place," 227
Heraclitus, 153
Hesse, Herman, 225
Hicks, Granville, 198
Holland, Norman N., 136, 149–53
Homer, 68
Howells, William Dean, 225
Husserl, Edmund, 151
Hyman, Stanley Edgar, 228

Inglis, Tony, 13
Iser, Wolfgang, 136, 149–50, 153–54

James, Henry: authorial voice in, 1–2; narrative techniques of, 1–2, 180; role of reader, 5; Eliot's view of, 61; influence of French Symbolist poets on, 118
—*Wings of the Dove, The*: plot of, 5; difficulties of, 13–14; complicit manoeuvres in, 14–17, 25–26; duplicity in, 16; Milly as dove, 17, 22–23, 25n; Milly's betrayal, 17; pressures on Kate Croy, 17–18; Densher's character in, 18–20; Densher's complicity with Milly, 20–21; Milly's complicit manoeuvres, 21–23; narrator's complicity with reader, 21; Kate's relationship with Densher, 23–25; Milly's peril, 23–24; melodrama of, 25–26; Milly's bequest, 25, 26–27; critical responses to, 26
—other works: *The Art of the Novel*, 1; *The Awkward Age*, 1; *The Ambassadors*, 13; *The Golden Bowl*, 13
James, William, 10, 34–35, 159
Joyce, James, 1, 118, 229n
Jung, Carl, 139, 152–53

Kafka, Franz, 98, 198, 225
Kazin, Alfred, 64–65, 66
Keats, John, 86, 126
Kennard, Jean, 234n
Kenner, Hugh, 118, 119, 122–23, 126
Kermode, Frank, 122
Kierkegaard, Soren, 214, 217, 219, 222, 223, 229
Kipling, Rudyard, 67–73
Kohut, Heinz, 149n, 151
Kreiswirth, Martin, 119
Kreyling, Michael, 190
Kroll, Jack, 187
Kruse, Horst, 66
Kuehl, Linda, 187, 191

LaFarge, Oliver, 209–10
LaFrance, Marston, 35
Landess, Thomas, 190
Langer, Susanne, 215
Lawrence, D. H., 73, 147
Levin, Harry, 117
Le Vot, A. E., 84
Levy, Leo, 26
Lind, Ilse DuSoir, 122
Loeb, Jacques, 95
Long, Huey, 156, 158
Long, Robert, 84
Lubbock, Percy, 1–3, 5
Luschei, Martin, 217

Machiavelli, Niccolò, 10, 159, 169
Mackenzie, Compton, 68
Maeterlinck, Maurice, 138, 139
Makurath, Paul, 67
Mallarmé, Stéphane, 118, 124, 129n
Mann, Thomas, 186
Marcel, Gabriel, 214, 222
Maritain, Jacques, 214
Marrs, Suzanne, 192
Marx, Karl, 74, 89
Matthews, John T., 120–21, 124
Matthiessen, F. O., 25n, 111
Melville, Herman, 119, 126
Mencken, H. L., 59, 83, 88
Meriwether, James B., 119
Millgate, Michael, 127
Milton, John, 80–81, 84, 85, 234
Mizener, Arthur, 64
Moore, Carol A., 189
Moreás, Jean, 121
Morrell, Lady Ottoline, 13
Morris, Charles, 215

Index

Morrison, Gail Moore, 129
Mortimer, Gail, 123, 124
Moss, Howard, 187

Naturalism, 8, 111–12, 114
Nietzsche, Friedrich Wilhelm, 89, 95
Nihilism, 39, 39n, 226, 227, 235–36

Oates, Joyce Carol, 186–87
O'Connor, Flannery: illness of, 209; religious faith of, 210–12; traditionalism of, 236
—*Wise Blood*: gothic grotesquerie and, 11–12; reviews of, 198, 208, 209–11; circular form of, 199, 201; critical responses to, 199; Hazel Motes as believer, 199, 201, 207–12; opening of, 199–200; Hazel Motes's appearance, 200; significance of place in, 200–202; coffin imagery in, 202–203, 209; Asa Hawks's role in, 203–204; stories of Sabbath Lily Hawks, 203; mirroring technique in, 204–206; Onnie Jay Holy's role in, 204–205; reflection in, 204, 205–206; imagery of eyes, seeing, and blindness, 206–208; preface to, 210, 212
—other works: *Mystery and Manners*, 211; *The Habit of Being*, 211; "The Fiction Writer and His Country," 212; *The Violent Bear It Away*, 212
Orwell, George, 198
Osborn, Scott, 68

Pease, Donald, 33–34, 35–36
Peirce, Charles, 215
Percy, Walker: illness of, 213, 214; study of philosophy, 213–16; training as a medical doctor, 213, 214; existentialism and, 214–15, 217; semiotics and, 215–16; philosophical writings of, 216–17; Catholicism of, 217, 218; traditionalism of, 236
—*Moviegoer, The*: philosophical viewpoint in, 12; Catholicism of, 213, 214–15; publication of, 213; form of, 216–18, 223–24; editor's view of, 218; existentialism in, 219–20, 223; romantic stoicism in, 219, 221; Catholicism in, 220–22; ending of, 222–23
—other works: "The Loss of the Creature," 216; "The Man on the Train," 216; "The Message in the Bottle," 216; "Notes for a Novel About the End of the World," 219; *Lost in the Cosmos*, 224
Percy, William Alexander, 213
Perkins, Maxwell, 7, 57, 58, 62, 86, 87, 92
Pinter, Harold, 225
Pizer, Donald, 114
Plato, 137, 193
Poe, Edgar Allan, 119
Poindexter, David, 175, 176, 181
Porter, Katherine Anne, 11
Poteat, Patricia Lewis, 216
Pound, Ezra, 61
Price, Reynolds, 185–86, 216–17
Proust, Marcel, 118

Rahner, Karl, 214, 215
Ransom, John Crowe, 236
Reader-response criticism, 136–37, 149, 55
Reed, John, 95
Rembrandt, 87, 89
Reynolds, Larry J., 189
Reynolds, Paul R., Jr., 175
Robbe-Grillet, Alain, 218
Rosenfeld, Isaac, 206–207, 209
Ross, Ben, 173–75, 176, 181
Rothstein, Arnold, 84
Rubin, Louis D., Jr., 192

Salinger, J. D., 59
Sartre, Jean-Paul, 183, 214, 218
Sayre, Zelda. *See* Fitzgerald, Zelda Sayre
Schloss, Carol, 210
Schorer, Mark, 147
Secularism, 94, 94n, 97–98, 113–17
Seldes, Gilbert, 88
Shafer, Robert, 111–12
Shakespeare, William, 10, 68, 156, 157, 159, 230–31
Shelley, Percy Bysshe, 70, 84, 86
Shrodes, Caroline, 150, 151
Simpson, Lewis P., 123–24
Sklar, Robert, 86–87, 88
Smith, Martha, 209
Socrates, 193
Spengler, Oswald, 74, 79, 86–92
Spenser, Edmund, 10, 156–57, 159
Spilka, Mark, 53
Spiller, Robert, 111

Stallman, Robert W., 47, 86
Stephens, Martha, 210
Stewart, W. K., 88
Stoddard, Lothrop, 74–75
Stone, Phil, 119
Stonum, Gary Lee, 130
Swedenborg, Emanuel, 129n
Symbolist movement, 118–20, 119n, 122, 124, 124n, 129, 129n, 130, 134
Symons, Arthur, 119

Tamke, Alexander, 66
Tate, Allen, 236
Teilhard de Chardin, Pierre, 215
Thackeray, William Makepeace, 84
Tharpe, Jac, 234n
Thomas Aquinas, 214
Thoreau, Henry David, 8
Tolstoy, Leo, 3, 186
Trask, David, 66
Turlish, Lewis A., 74
Twain, Mark, 66, 68, 186, 225

Updike, John, 225

Venable, Ben, 65
Verlaine, Paul, 119
Virgil, 68

Walcutt, Charles, 112
Waldhorn, Arthur, 39–40n
Warren, Robert Penn: view of Dreiser, 116
—*All the King's Men*: influences on, 10, 156–57, 159; power in, 156–59; Jack Burden's role in, 157–58; Willie Stark's role in, 157, 159–60; father-son relationships in, 160–69; Jack Burden's relationship with his father, 160–63, 166–69; Jack Burden's relationship with Willie Stark, 160, 162–66, 167; Judge Irwin's role in, 167–69
—other works: *Proud Flesh*, 10, 157; *At Heaven's Gate*, 157; *Night Rider*, 157; "Prime Leaf," 157
Wasserstrom, William, 33, 34–35
Webb, Constance, 174–76
Weimer, David, 115
Wells, H. G., 57–58, 77
Welty, Eudora: earliest memories of, 195–96; hearing of what is seen in type, 196; as visual writer, 196
—*Losing Battles*: Jack Renfro as hero, 10–11, 184–85; narrative technique of, 11, 191; affirmation of life in, 184–85; composition of, 184; as comedy, 185–86, 188, 190, 191; reviews of, 185–88; role of family in, 186–87, 188–90; harmonizing of dualities in, 187–88, 195; love and separateness in, 188; Julia Mortimer's role in, 189–90, 192, 194–97; speech and silence in, 190–91; dialogue in, 191–92; written versus spoken words in, 192–94, 195; Vaughn Renfro's role in, 196
—other works: "Petrified Man," 191; "Shower of Gold," 191; *The Ponder Heart*, 191; "Why I Live at the P.O.," 191; *One Writer's Beginnings*, 195–96
Weston, Jessie, 78
Wharton, Edith, 85
Whicher, George F., 113
Whitman, Walt, 119
Wilde, Oscar, 126
Wilson, Edmund, 61, 88
Wirzberger, Karl Heinz, 113
Wittgenstein, Ludwig, 215
Wolfe, Thomas, 58, 225
Woolf, Virginia, 13, 118, 236
Wright, Alan, 175
Wright, Richard: as southerner, 170, 181, 183; Communist affiliation of, 173–74; death of, 175; last encounter with father, 181–82; Baldwin's attitudes toward, 182–83; existentialism and, 182–83
—"Big Boy Leaves Home": theme of, 10; plot of, 170–73; structure of, 170, 177–78; lynching in, 173, 178–79; mob in, 173, 179–80; publication of, 173, 174; genesis of, 174, 175; quality of will for survival in, 176–77; racism in, 180–81
—other works: *Black Boy*, 10, 174, 181; *Native Son*, 10, 170, 181, 182, 183; "I Tried to Be a Communist," 173–75; *Uncle Tom's Children*, 175, 176; "Bright and Morning Star," 182; "Fire and Cloud," 182; *The Long Dream*, 182; *The Outsider*, 182
Wycherley, William, 233

Yeats, William Butler, 74, 88, 122
Young, Philip, 39, 39n
Young, Thomas Daniel, 223, 236